Lady Loring's Dilemma

Dilemma

A Regency Novel

CATHERINE KULLMANN

Willow
Books

Cover images antique miniature and engraving from the author's private collection.
Cover design by BookGoSocial

ISBN: 978-1-913545-96-3

First published 2022 by
Willow Books
D04 H397, Ireland

Regency Novels by Catherine Kullmann

The Duchess of Gracechurch Trilogy *The Malvins*

The Murmur of Masks

Perception & Illusion → The Potential for Love

The Duke's Regret

The Lorings

A Suggestion of Scandal

Lady Loring's Dilemma

Stand Alone

A Comfortable Alliance

Novella

The Zombi of Caisteal Dun

To Anne and Douglas, Carmel and Peter, Christine and Noel, Clare and Ted, Dearbhaill (also remembering Klaus), and Margaret and Nicolas, with love and gratitude for many decades of much-cherished friendship. Long may it continue!

Author's Note

Lady Loring's Dilemma is a sequel to A Suggestion of Scandal and written in response to readers' requests, and my own curiosity about what happened next. The action takes place from June 1814 to May 1816.

In some of my previous novels, I have discussed the unequal marriage laws in Regency England but have avoided the question of marital breakdown. What price would a wife have to pay if she sought happiness elsewhere? Should she continue to obey a vindictive husband who will neither forgive her or set her free? If not, what choices has she?

List of Characters

Delia, Lady Loring, née Eubank	Estranged wife of Sir Edward Loring Bt.
Mrs Eubank	Delia's mother
Mrs Robertson	Makes friends with Delia in Harrogate
Elspeth and Kirsty Robertson	Her daughters
Hughes	Delia's maid
Lord Stephen FitzCharles	Delia's first love
Lady Mary Arkell, *Contessa Della Torre*	Stephen's maternal aunt
Lady Qualter and Mrs Lyndall	Lady Mary's married daughters
Susan Lyndall and Anna Qualter	Lady Mary's granddaughters
The Duke of Gracechurch	Stephen's nephew

Piero	Stephen's major-domo
Gianluca	Piero's brother
Luca	Piero's and Gianluca's father, and Lady Mary's steward
Chloe Loring	Delia's and Edward's daughter
Sir Julian Swann-Loring, né Loring	Edward's son by his first wife
Rosa, Lady Swann-Loring, née Fancourt	Julian's wife; Chloe's former governess
The dowager Lady Loring	Edward's mother
Lord Swanmere	Julian's maternal grandfather (Julian is his heir through his mother)
Amelia and Jonathan Glazebrook	Amelia is Julian's and Chloe's 2nd cousin
Martin and Cynthia Glazebrook	Their son and daughter

Miscellaneous

Sir Jethro Boyce	Old crony of Sir Edward Loring
Venerable Archdeacon Barnaby Boyce	Sir Jethro's cousin
George Crosbie	The archdeacon's wife's nephew; an adventurer
Lydia Crosbie	His wife

Residences

Loring Place	Sir Edward Loring
Swanmere Castle	Julian, Rosa, Chloe, Lord Swanmere The dowager Lady Loring
Arkell House	Lady Mary's home, near Ripley, Yorkshire
Villa Della Torre	Lady Mary's home, near Nice
Gracechurch House	London
Stanton Priory	Duke of Gracechurch's Seat

Book 1

Delia

Chapter One

Harrogate, Yorkshire, June 1814

Delia's pencil skimmed over the page, capturing the mysterious, shimmering rocks above the deep pool, the sun-dappled river flowing peacefully only yards away, the steep slope on its opposite side and the castle commanding the heights above. *Impossible to do it all at once; better make several quick sketches to form the basis for a larger painting.* Immersed in her work, she scribbled reminders of summer greens, dappled shades, and the play of light on leaves and clear water.

The Robertson ladies, her companions on this outing, had discovered a stall where various petrifications—objects that had been so long exposed to the calciferous water of the Dropping Well that they had turned to stone—were laid out to tempt the visitor. While they debated the merits of a curled wig over a bird's nest, another party descended the steps to the pool. Delia glanced up casually as they passed, among them a gentleman of middling height, broad-shouldered and well-proportioned... it couldn't be...

"Stephen."

She must have spoken aloud because he looked back, paused, then swept off his hat to reveal silver-streaked, nut-brown curls framing his forehead. *He's cut his hair*, she thought. And then, *Ninny! It must be twenty years since gentlemen cut their hair in protest at Pitt's powder tax and twenty-five years since you last met.* Stephen's long, unpowdered hair had then been combed back and tied neatly at his nape, a style that today would be regarded as antediluvian.

Even as these thoughts flitted through her reeling mind, she heard him say, "Delia?"

"Yes."

His voice was a little deeper, but had the same timbre. She had removed her gloves when she started sketching, and his outstretched right hand was also bare. She suppressed a shiver at the first touch of skin on skin, then his hand clasped hers in a real hand-shake—neither the slight touch of fingers nor the abbreviated bow suggesting a hand kiss that was the current fashion.

"It really is you," he said with a pleased smile, then called to his companions, who waited some yards ahead. "Go on. I'll catch up with you later."

"Yes," she said, drawing her hand away. "I'm sorry—I was so surprised—I spoke your name without thinking…"

"I would know your voice anywhere."

"Oh." She felt herself flush

"Do you live here?"

"Not permanently, no. I am staying with my mother in Harrogate. What brings you here?"

"I am visiting my aunt. She lives near Ripley."

Delia saw the Robertsons glance over. "Your friends are waiting, as are mine."

"Yes. May I call on you?"

The last thing Delia needed was Lord Stephen FitzCharles presenting himself at Ivy Lodge. Their friendship had caused her mother to leave Brighton all those years ago. "It were better not. My mother leads a very quiet life. She is something of an invalid." "I see. It is good to see you again, Delia." She turned her left hand so that her wedding ring glinted in the sun. "I am Lady Loring now." "Lady Loring." The boyish smile faded. He bowed. "I shall take my leave of you, then." "Goodbye, Lord Stephen."

They hadn't been able to say goodbye that last time, she thought as she watched him walk away. He had the same brisk stride and still tilted his head slightly to the left as if he regarded the world through a quizzing glass.

When she looked back, theirs had been an innocent affair, boy and girl really—she barely seventeen and he three years older, just down from Oxford. She had first seen him at the Post Office in Brighton, beside Miss Widgett's Circulating Library, where she had been sent to obtain a new volume of sermons for her mother. Two days later, at Monday's Ball at the Castle Inn, he had been presented to her as a dance partner by the master of ceremonies. She had gone with her brother and his bride. Belinda had been gratified to make the acquaintance of a duke's younger brother and had readily agreed when he asked if he might call.

One encounter led to another. Lord Stephen was frequently to be found on The Steyne just at the time Delia was running her mother's daily errands and he soon got into the habit of falling into step with her. Before long, they took an extra turn on The Steyne before he saw her home. There was an ease between them from the beginning, a sense of companionship that, although definitely not fraternal, was also not flirtatious, or at least not obviously so. She could talk to him in a way she had not been able

17

to talk to anyone else since her father died, at times laughing over some absurdity, at others dissecting more serious matters.

But it was not long before unkind comments reached her mother's ears and she was called to account. Her mother had refused to listen to her professions of innocence.

"Don't be a greater fool than I think you are," Mrs Eubank had said contemptuously. "Friends indeed! Who are you to look to a duke's son? If he has shown an interest in you, it can only be a left-hand one. I blame Belinda for encouraging him. If I had known, he would not have been admitted to this house."

The repetition of these sentiments to her daughter-in-law resulted in an altercation of epic proportions, culminating in the younger woman flinging at the elder that she was now the mistress of the house and would decide who was to be received and who not.

Responsible as she was for her young daughter, she could no longer remain in a house where every rake-hell might seek entrance, Delia's mother retorted. She would avail herself of the farsighted provision in her dear husband's will that allowed her an increased jointure should she choose to set up her own establishment rather than remain under her son's roof. She would remove somewhere more salubrious than Brighton where the moral tone had deteriorated since it became a favourite haunt of the Prince of Wales, not to mention his cronies like Lord Stephen. She and Delia would leave within the week and Delia was to remain at home until then.

Delia still shuddered when she remembered that week. Her brother was furious, for an increase in his mother's jointure meant a matching reduction in his own income and he was overheard informing his wife that some of it must come from her pin money. Belinda said it was worth it to be rid of the old cat, and she was only sorry for her sister-in-law, who now would have no respite. Delia was cast down at the thought of living in Harrogate, of all places, and miserably angry at all three adults who between them had contrived to remove her from the only home she had ever known, and from all her friends.

Her clothes and few fripperies folded and packed away in a large trunk, she had wandered from room to room, gathering together her other possessions; her work-basket from the parlour where they sat in the evening, and the books that were her own from the family bookcase there; her music from the fortepiano where she had struggled with tedious sonatas; her prayerbook from the drawer in the hall table. Finally, she went upstairs to the big room that took up the whole top floor and had been her father's studio. Even before she could hold a pencil or brush, he had drawn and painted little pictures for her in a special sketchbook. Here it was. She put it to one side and then looked for her own portfolios and sketchbooks—memories of happy hours spent together. Finally, she assembled an assortment of paints, brushes, pencils and all the other tools she could fit into the satchel he used when going on a sketching expedition. At the last, she retrieved a clever portrait her father had dashed off of the two of them in the studio some years previously. In it, she stood at her easel and he leaned forward to demonstrate something to her. *The Little Artist* he had called it and while many visitors had admired it, he refused to sell it or have a plate engraved from it. It was hers now.

Had Belinda done this before her wedding, collected the remnants of her past life to take with her? But she would have had her bride-clothes and wedding gifts too, and her bridegroom at her side. Delia's mother had not been happy that Simeon had married at only twenty-three; she had expected to be mistress of the house for some years to come. Perhaps she had been glad of the excuse to leave and not cared what the parting meant to her daughter.

And only two weeks ago, Delia had again collected her most precious belongings to take to Harrogate. Banished in disgrace by an outraged husband, she had had trunks piled on the roof and bags in the boot of the carriage. Who knew when or if she would be allowed return home to Loring Place?

She quailed inwardly at the echo of her husband's icy tones. 'I shall not inform your mother of your disgrace, but you are not to take this as meaning that I in any way condone your adultery. I have yet to consider whether or under which conditions I might permit you to return to Suffolk.' And worse: 'Chloe is no longer your concern. My mother has taken her to visit my sister. They will not return until after your departure.'

He had forbidden her to write to Chloe as well. He couldn't stop her writing, she thought suddenly, even if there was no point sending the letter as the postbag went first to her husband. She would purchase a special notebook for the letters. Please God, one day she could give it to her daughter. The new finishing governess would be arriving soon. She hoped Chloe would find her sympathetic. Enough! There is no point in repining, she told herself fiercely. You cannot change what happened; you must live with it.

Deliberately, she put the memories aside and concentrated on her surroundings. Opposite her, a massive rock loomed high over a deep, limpid pool into which water fell from above. Rather than gushing forth in a single stream, the water flowed slowly over the rock, spreading out to form a translucid veil that dripped tinkling, plinking into the crystalline depths. Mosses and ferns clung to the wet stone and here and there a straggly shrub found a tenuous footing in a deeper crevice. Tall trees arched above, creating a shadowy, mysterious world where ancient nameless creatures might lurk.

"Be careful!" Mrs Robertson called as Elspeth and Kirsty circled the pool, stripping off their gloves to trail their fingers through the clear water or lean over to catch a glittering droplet.

Delia turned a page. What a charming scene. Her pencil flew again.

"Lady Loring. Lady Loring?"

Delia blinked and looked up into Elspeth Robertson's smiling face.

"I beg your pardon, Miss Robertson. I was too engrossed in my task."

"Mamma says would you like to take a nuncheon at the inn before we walk back?"

"Certainly."

"May I see?" Miss Kirsty asked as Delia closed her sketchbook. "Oh, these are wonderful. To be able to do it so quickly. How clever you are! Would you do a little portrait for me? I should love to send it to my father. It is five years since he was home, Lady Loring. I imagine he would pass me on the street and not know me."

"I doubt that," Delia said. "You are very like your mother. But I should be happy to take your likeness if you wish."

"It is wonderful to see Kirsty so well," Mrs Robertson said as they strolled to the inn. "We quite despaired of her at Hogmanay—New Year's Eve, I mean. Whether it is the waters or the excitement of several balls a week I cannot say, but one cannot deny that the regular, gentle exercise required to walk from one well to another and the stimulation of agreeable society are in themselves a tonic."

"Very true."

No doubt Harrogate was most enjoyable when one had the pleasure of putting up at the Granby or the Queen's Head where the company dined, breakfasted and drank tea together as well as attending the balls hosted in turn by the fashionable inns. Delia, however, must stay with her mother, a devout valetudinarian who lived year-round in Harrogate and despised what she described as seasonal invalids using their supposed ailments as an excuse for dissipation. "Spa Swallows," she called them. "Summering here and wintering in Bath."

Almost as if she read her thoughts, Mrs Robertson said, "I was wondering, Lady Loring, if you would like to join us some evening for a dish of tea in our parlour? I have my own equipage and confess I weary of a public table."

"I should be delighted to. Thank you."

Delia was pleased to accept, but wondered how she could best return the compliment. Perhaps on one of the evenings when her mother played Quadrille elsewhere. Each member of the long-established group of four ladies had her 'day'—Mrs Eubank's was Tuesday—when she entertained the others, offering a simple supper of tea, sandwiches and cake, each lady priding herself on her special recipes.

Revived by toasted tea cakes and cups of frothy chocolate, the ladies were about to leave when another group entered the inn, calling to the landlord for the trout they had ordered earlier. It was Lord Stephen and his party. Delia could not bring herself to cut him, and, at her smiling nod, he came over with a vivacious elderly lady who had the same characteristic tilt of the head. A flurry of introductions followed. The lady was his aunt, Lady Mary Arkell, *Contessa Della Torre*. Delia vaguely remembered her romantic story—married to a Piemontese nobleman who, together with their only son, lost his life fighting Napoleon's invading army, she had managed to get herself and her daughters to Villafranca and from thence, on her yacht, to England. She had been much fêted at the time, but had then sunk into obscurity.

Or merely not cared to be in the public eye, Delia thought, as she greeted the lady's two daughters, sons-in-law and two granddaughters who were of an age with the Robertson girls. Before she knew what was happening, addresses were exchanged and Mrs Robertson promised to bring her girls to a *déjeuner al fresco* at Lady Mary's in three days' time.

"And you, too, of course, Lady Loring," her ladyship said. "I'll send proper notes in the morning."

"Is your carriage here?" Delia asked Mrs Robertson as they began to walk back to Harrogate.

"No. I keep a small town-carriage with just one horse, but it would be too uncomfortable for such a journey. By post chaise was wearisome enough, with all the changes."

"I can imagine. May I take you and your daughters up on Thursday? It will be too far to walk, even if we wished to arrive hot and dishevelled."

"That is very kind of you, Lady Loring. Thank you."

Chapter Two

To my dearest Daughter Chloe, from her ever-loving Mother. Tears filled Delia's eyes as she read the words she had just inscribed on the first page of the new sketchbook, a handsome, oblong article bound in red Morocco leather with a gold trim. It was expensive, but only the best was good enough for Chloe. When would she see her daughter again? She had not been permitted to say goodbye to her—the girl had been whisked away without her knowledge or, indeed, consent. But, when all was said and done, a mother had very few rights, and a wife even fewer.

She closed her eyes, trying to see again that dear face, and shuddered at the image of Chloe lying on the floor of that cursed cottage, red blood seeping down her neck. No, she would not let that be her lasting memory of her daughter. She took a sheet of paper and began to sketch a picture of Chloe in her first ball gown. After several false attempts, she had a likeness that satisfied her. Tomorrow, she would use her paints to copy it into the book. And she would paint one of herself, she resolved. If she never saw her daughter again, she could leave her this remembrance. But today she would compose a special, separate letter that she would leave sealed and locked away from any inquisitive eyes.

Harrogate, 21 June 1814

Miss Chloe Loring

My dearest Chloe,

I cannot know if you will ever see these lines. I have been forbidden to write to you and, even were I to disobey and risk posting this letter, I doubt that it would ever reach you. I have therefore resolved to write frankly to you, and to keep this letter safe until a happier and more opportune time permits me to put it into your hands. But it may also be that you receive it only after my death. I cannot bear the thought that your last memories of me should be tied to those final, dreadful days at Loring Place. Please, I beg you, look beyond them to the happy times we spent together....

The tears fell faster now, splashing onto the page. She carefully blotted them away and sanded the paper, then gently shook it until she was certain the ink was dry before deftly folding the sheet, addressing it to Miss Chloe Loring, Strictly Private, and sealing it by pressing her thumb into the hot wax. Delia bore the little pain stoically—it was nothing compared to the pain in her heart.

~~~

Arkell House, Lady Mary's home, stood at the end of a tree-lined avenue; an old, single-storied building with six diamond-paned casements on each side of a front door set in a Gothic archway. The grey stone was softened by the pink of climbing roses and the centre door stood hospitably open when Delia's carriage drew up at two o'clock on Thursday. Lady Mary came out to meet them.

"Welcome, welcome! Are you happy to sit outside? There are canopies and shade enough to protect our complexions while we may still enjoy the sun. Winter here is dark and dreary enough."

As she spoke, she led them through a tiled hall to another door that opened directly onto a square—Delia wasn't sure was it more courtyard or garden. The part nearest the house was paved some five or six yards wide, providing a smooth floor on which stood several groups of tables and chairs, while at one end a long table was pushed against the house wall. This whole area was framed by a wooden pergola-like structure wreathed in climbing plants and furnished with cream linen canopies that could be extended to provide shade as desired. Flower beds planted with rosemary and lavender interspersed with the most magnificent carnations she had ever seen lined the two side walls, filling the air with an intoxicating scent. Between them, formal parterres hedged with box were laid out between gravel paths; at a central fountain, a classically draped nymph gracefully poured water from a raised ewer. The fourth side of the quadrangle opened onto a lush, green lawn that led the eye to a rustic park that invited further wanderings. Delia's charmed gaze looked from one felicity to another.

Lady Mary's daughters, Lady Qualter and Mrs Lyndall, and the two granddaughters rose from cushioned chairs, one of the granddaughters brandishing four bats. "There you are! Shall we play Battledore and Shuttlecock?"

The Robertsons readily agreed. As the four young women headed towards the lawn in a flurry of sprigged muslin and long ribbons, they could be heard agreeing to abandon formal address. "I am Anna," Miss Qualter said, "and my cousin is Susan."

Miss Robertson admitted to Elsbeth while Kirsty said cheerfully, "You already know my name."

"It is pretty, and quite unusual," Susan said.

"I was baptised Christiana, after my grandmother, but everyone says Kirsty."

"They are so happy to have company of their own age," Lady Qualter said. "We love to come here each summer—it reminds us of happy times with dear Papa and our poor brother, but the girls get bored after a couple of weeks."

"Do you not attend any of the balls in Harrogate?" Mrs Robertson asked. "It is only an hour's drive, and it is bright until quite late now."

Mrs Lyndall looked at her, surprised. "We never have. Susan is not out yet."

"Neither is Kirsty, but surely here it must be permitted? The balls are quite sedate affairs, I assure you. There is a full moon next Friday when the ball will be at the *Granby Hotel.*"

"Let us go," Lady Mary said. "If we all go, the girls will be well chaperoned."

"And in the meantime, they will be occupied checking their gowns and practising their dance steps," Lady Qualter added.

If only Chloe were here, Delia thought, remembering how her daughter had blossomed during the house party in May. At least I was able to give her first ball. But to mention the girl now might give rise to questions she preferred not to answer. How to explain Chloe's absence from Harrogate, for one. If asked whether she had children, she would not lie, but she would not proffer the information. She strolled over to the flower-bed. "What magnificent carnations. I have never seen such splendid ones."

"They are a speciality of Nice," Lady Mary said. "There they bloom in the winter and are sent to Paris and Turin, previously even to London, tightly packed in wooden boxes."

"But that would take weeks. How could they possibly survive?" Mrs Robertson asked.

"You cut off a little of the stalk, and steep them for two hours in vinegar and water before putting them in fresh water. They will bloom for the best part of a month."

"Did you bring the plants with you?"

"Yes. We bought this property after our marriage—my husband felt the southern summer would be too hot for me. We always had a yacht, so it was easy to bring the things we missed or favoured from one place to another."

"What did you take back to Italy?"

"Some good Yorkshire hams and cheeses," Lady Mary said.

"Books," Mrs Lyndall added, "and we always had our riding boots and habits made here."

Lady Qualter began to laugh. "One year we brought back hens—Mamma thought our local variety here would be more robust than the ones at home. The captain had no objection to a daily supply of fresh eggs, but it took all his self-control not to wring the cock's neck. And we would have applauded him, for you cannot imagine how loud a cock-a-doodle-doo is until you have heard it below deck."

"Then, when the French invaded, my husband sent me and the girls back. We took as much as we could, for who knew whether our home would be destroyed or looted." Lady Mary sighed. "We never thought it would take so long, or that we would never see one another again." She sighed again. "But that is long ago. Should you like to stroll a little? It is a pleasant walk up to the temple, and a wonderful prospect from there."

The path curved up a small rise to a pretty, round gazebo that was no more than a base and a roof separated by graceful columns. From it, Delia could see how the park sloped gently to the bank of a small stream crossed by a small bridge, and rose more steeply on the other side to a craggy rock on which perched a dramatic ruin—two stone walls at right angles to one another and, separately, a graceful arch that framed a solitary tree. It was so perfectly placed that she wondered whether her hostess had also had it constructed.

Before she could ask, Mrs Robertson exclaimed, "How picturesque. What is it?"

"An old chapel, built, I believe, where a saintly hermit once lived. There is a path that goes past it and over the hill into the next valley. And there, if I am not mistaken, come our gentlemen."

Three riders emerged from the trees, having skirted the ruin, and now headed down towards the stream.

"Shall we meet them at the bridge?" Mrs Lyndall led the way down.

Lord Stephen was the first to clatter across the wooden structure. He doffed his hat, saying, "Ladies. What a charming welcome." Then his eyes found Delia's and a familiar smile curved his lips. "Lady Loring. Good day, ma'am."

"Good day, Lord Stephen, gentlemen."

"If you'll excuse us, ladies," Sir John Qualter said, "we shall ride ahead and change our clothes so that we don't join you reeking of the stables."

"It is fortunate that none of them could be considered dandies," Lady Qualter said after they had waved the men on. "Otherwise, we must wait at least an hour for our dinner."

When they were bidden to table, Delia could only stare at the bright array of salads and other cold dishes laid out to tempt the appetite on a hot day. Here were not only lettuces and cucumbers, but tomatoes with fresh basil, slim green beans, small tender peas, and other vegetables that she did not recognise. A whole salmon gleamed appetisingly on a bed of dill, surrounded by half-moons of lemon. Breast of veal had been filled with a green-flecked forcemeat, in the centre of which gleamed the white and yellow of hard-boiled eggs. Ham had been shaved into thin, curling slices and piled beside crisp rolls and a dish of butter curls on ice. Stone jugs of ale and lemonade glistened with moisture while bottles of white wine and soda water also waited, chilled, to revive dry palates.

It was not easy to balance a table of nine ladies and three gentlemen. Delia was surprised that Lady Mary had not declared this to be a ladies-only affair and provided a separate table elsewhere for the gentlemen. That would have been her husband's preference, had she presumed to arrange such an event. Lady Mary took the centre of one long side of the table and placed Lord Stephen opposite her, with Delia on his right. Her sons-in-law took head and foot of the table and she contrived to distribute the other ladies so that none was sitting beside a spouse, sister, or parent.

"This is so much more civilised than sitting on a blanket, trying to protect your plate from the ants and looking for somewhere even enough to set down your glass so that you can use a knife and fork," Lord Stephen said to Delia as she tasted the veal. "My aunt has really combined the best of both her worlds."

"Have you visited her other home? You always spoke of doing the Grand Tour."

"Yes. I was fortunate that I was able to travel abroad before the revolution in France and everything that followed. I spent several months with her, then I made my way home across the Gotthard Pass and down to Basel, where I took a boat down the Rhine to Rotterdam, and from there a packet boat from Hellevoetsluis to Harwich."

"It sounds wonderful."

"It was. Travel stimulates all the senses, provided one is open to new thoughts and ideas. There are too many Britons who find fault with everything because it is not like home. Then they should stay at home and not inflict their company on their unfortunate fellow-countrymen. They seek you out only to complain, as if they must assert their own superiority."

She laughed. "I can see how dreary that must be. How long were you away?"

"Almost two years."

"How did you manage over the mountains? Did you take your valet?"

He began to laugh. "I did, but not the one who came with me from England. Simmons was a fussy little man who had been with me since I went to Oxford. He turned out to be a good sailor and was quite happy in Nice where he looked down his nose at everything foreign, learnt the minimum of foreign phrases to get by, and was convinced that if he only spoke English slowly enough and loud enough, everyone would understand him. Fortunately, he mutinied when he heard of my proposed route home and downright refused to accompany me, begging my aunt to permit him to remain with her until she next returned to England. She agreed to take him as far as the first English port, so I gave him a good character and paid him what I owed him, and a bit more so that he would get home safely."

"Many young men would not have been as generous."

He seemed embarrassed by her quiet praise. "It suited me, I suppose. I can dress myself. I hired a stout fellow recommended by my uncle and had Simmons give him some hints about the care of my traps. Piero was much more useful, especially once we had acquired the mules."

"Mules?"

"Two to ride, and one for the baggage. By far, the best way to manage the mountain pass."

"What did you do with them when you reached the Rhine?"

"I sold the mules. I would have given them to Piero if he had wished to return home, but he decided to continue the journey. He is still with me. He calls himself my major-domo, but will turn his hand to anything."

Delia would have liked to learn more about his present life, but it would not do to appear to monopolise his attention. It would be disastrous if even a breath of scandal attached itself to her name now. It's too easy to talk to him she thought, as she turned to listen to Lady Qualter.

In a lull in the conversation, Susan Lyndall said to Stephen, "I thought you would have stayed in London as long as the Allied Sovereigns remained, Cousin."

"Not I. I have had enough of them and their antics. Town is usually bad enough in June, but their visit made it impossible to move at times."

"I believe there is to be a grand masquerade in honour of Wellington at Burlington House," Sir John Qualter said, "but only after the Sovereigns have left."

"Yes; tickets are not to be had for love nor money," Stephen answered.

"Did you try for one?" Mr Lyndall asked. "I should have thought it was your sort of thing."

"When I was younger, perhaps, but every year I get more out of patience with the *beau monde*."

"The Turks have a saying, 'the fish stinks first at the head'," Sir John said. "The poor King is not at fault, for he cannot help himself, and Her Majesty still adheres to the standards of her youth, but anyone who looks to the Regent or his family for guidance or moral values is sadly at a loss."

"That is true," Delia said. "But the King and Queen are not completely without blame. They were not always old, and nobody could argue that they had the best interests of their children at heart when it came to their marriages. Take the Prince and Princess of Wales, who never met before their wedding; the marriage was doomed from the beginning."

"I remember the talk at the time," Stephen said. "It was the price of having his debts paid."

"So few of the surviving royal princes and princesses have married," Lady Qualter said. "Only three of the twelve. I agree with you, Lady Loring. That can hardly be coincidence."

"My mother said that the King will only consider dynastic marriages for his children," Stephen said. "He was thwarted in his own first love for Lady Sarah Lennox—"

"And afterwards begrudged his children such happiness?" Mrs Lyndall asked. "That is so mean-spirited."

"Although I don't think everyone should be allowed marry their first love," her sister said. "Frequently, it is a wild infatuation. That is where a parent must carefully guide their child away from a poor choice."

"Do you agree, Lady Loring? What is your prescription for a happy marriage?" Stephen asked.

Delia felt herself grow hot, then cold. He had been her first love. Was she to deny it now? But what right had she to preach about marriage? She and Stephen had always spoken honestly to each other, she remembered. Summoning all her courage, she said, "Couples must deal fairly with one another and keep their promises, especially the ones made during courtship and the wedding ceremony."

"A simple solution," Mr Lyndall said.

"Do you think so?" Lady Mary asked. "How many couples can you think of whom it can be truly said that they deal fairly with one another?"

He grinned. "Present company excepted, I hope, Mamma-in-law."

"The law gives husbands an unfair advantage," Miss Robertson pointed out.

"They may choose not to exercise it," Delia said quietly. "Not abuse their position or lord it over their wives. Remember, if she is to obey and serve him, he is to comfort her. They are both to love and honour the other."

"You are right, Lady Loring," Mrs Robertson said. "It behoves us as parents to encourage our children to be particular in their choice of spouse, and also to be fully aware of what marriage entails."

Elsbeth and Kirsty looked embarrassed, Delia thought. She was relieved when Lady Qualter changed the subject, saying, "Girls, Mrs Robertson thought we might enjoy a ball at the *Granby Hotel*. What say you?"

~~~

"How do you come to know Lady Loring?" Lady Mary asked her nephew that evening as he accompanied her on her usual inspection of the greenhouses and orangery. "The two of you seemed very... comfortable together today. Indeed, your question about marriage encroached on the personal. I expected her to fob you off with a light remark, yet she answered seriously. Is she one of your *chères amies*?"

"No," he said shortly, then continued. "We knew one another more than twenty years ago, in Brighton. She lived there then, with her family."

"Brighton?" She bent to inspect some ripe eggplants. "You were very young then."

"I had just come down from Oxford."

"And what happened?"

"Nothing. We met a few times, danced together, walked together, talked. I called on her family. And then, suddenly, she was not at home and was not to be seen about town either."

"Were your affections engaged?"

"Of course they were. I was twenty, full of the joys of spring. But it was very much a boy and girl affair—quite innocent—and nipped in the bud before it could become anything more."

His aunt stared at him. "That is why you were so blue-devilled that year when you came to stay. I thought it was just that you were at loose ends after leaving Oxford. It is a big change for a young man, having lived in a mostly masculine environment for so many years, suddenly to be without his particular coterie."

"That's true, although I didn't see it so at the time. Is there anyone more puffed up in his own esteem than a cockerel just released from tutelage?"

"Mr Brummel, for one," her ladyship said, "or the Prince Regent if it comes to that. In a young man it is natural, and quite harmless. Did your brother not take you in hand? He was your guardian, after all."

"Only until I was twenty-one, but he paid very little heed to me generally. A room was kept for me at Stanton, but nobody cared whether I was there or not. And my mother had her position at Court." Stephen put his arm around the older woman. "You were the one who offered me a home, who cared about me. I've never thanked you, have I?"

"Nor should you. What I did, I did out of love. You have been a son to me, especially since..." She faltered and fished for her handkerchief. "Perhaps now, with that Monster safely on Elba, I shall be able to go and find their graves."

"Once the Continent has calmed a little, I am sure you can. But not at once. Bonaparte spread himself like a blight over so many countries, supplanting rulers with his family and supporters. What took more than a decade to create will not be undone in a few months. Just think of all those armies trying to return to their own countries, and the French presumably released to their homes."

"I had not thought of that. Still," she brightened, "I may plan, may I not?"

He hugged her. "Of course you may, my dear. You were always good at that."

"It is better to look ahead than to look back. What about you, Stephen?"

"About me? What do you mean?"

"While we were talking, I thought, 'What does he look ahead to?' and I could not answer. We are the best of friends, or so I thought, and I have no idea what your innermost concerns are; whether you have any passions or interests that go beyond the every-day. You have never married, never settled, but were content to lead a bachelor life, satisfied with your London rooms and country visits outside the Season. Now that does not seem to be enough for you."

"Of course it is." The answer was automatic, instinctive. Why should it not be enough?

"Come, sit with me." She led him to a leafy arbour where she patted the cushioned bench.

"Why this sudden interest, Aunt?" he asked as he sat beside her.

"Earlier, you seemed quite jaded; then, with Lady Loring, you were different—more alive, somehow."

"She was always easy to talk to."

"What did you talk about today, later, I mean, when you went apart after we had eaten? I have rarely seen you so animated."

"The West Indies."

"The West Indies? In what context?"

"You may not have been aware that your father owned property there; it came to me when I was twenty-one as part of my mother's marriage settlement. Delia and I had discussed it in

Brighton. She knew that I was very uneasy about owning people, even at a distance."

"I knew nothing about it. What happened?"

"I came of age while I was with you in Villafranca, remember? You gave a wonderful party to celebrate."

"That was a splendid night."

"When I finally returned home, I had to endure a long session with my brother and his man of business, who handed me all the deeds and records relating to my inheritance." Stephen smiled faintly. "Neither was happy. Apparently, the entailed property was heavily mortgaged, but my inheritance was secured through the settlement. To be fair, Gracechurch accounted for everything scrupulously, but he seemed to feel that my mother and I were a drain on his estate. His father had made a bad bargain, he said."

"Hmph. His father was determined to marry a girl forty-five years his junior," Lady Mary snapped. "The least he could do was provide properly for her and her children."

"Be that as it may, I decided to see for myself what things were like in the West Indies. I still had no establishment of my own, so it was easy to repack my trunks and set off. Piero and I sailed from Bristol. The voyage took a good month. The company on board ship was pleasant enough, and I kept my eyes and ears open. I had not written that I was coming—the letter and I would have arrived more or less together, and I also wanted to take them by surprise." He shivered suddenly. "I had read of the horrors of slavery, of course, but nothing you read can prepare you for the reality. To see human beings treated like beasts in every way, worse frequently than we would treat any animal we owned and, adding insult to injury, this treatment not only taken for granted but justified by virtue of our assumed superiority. The hypocrisy of degrading people and then using their degradation as proof of their inferiority made me sick.

"I had my first lessons on the ship. The other passengers welcomed me as one of them, and were very free with their advice. I must show from the first day that I was master." He smiled wryly. "I did, but not as they expected it."

"How do you mean?"

"To cut a long and wearisome story short, thanks to the advice and assistance of a gentleman on board who was on a similar but better-planned mission, I was able to free the enslaved on my estate and take them to Philadelphia where a *Society for Improving the Condition of Free Negroes* helped them settle and find work."

"Was that not very expensive?"

He shrugged. "The costs were covered by the proceeds from selling the property itself. It fetched less than if I had sold it fully manned, as it were, but I could not continue to profit from such an enterprise. Indeed, when I returned home, I sought out Mr Wilberforce and continue to work with him and the other abolitionists."

"I had no idea. You never said anything here."

"I knew we were of one mind there; I did not have to convince you of the evils of the trade. And here I need not be always on the alert for an opportunity to voice my opinions."

"The trade has been stopped. Do you continue to work for the abolition of slavery itself?"

"Behind the scenes, yes. It is a question of subtly changing minds and hearts and will take longer. Too many fortunes remain founded on it and, when it comes to the abuses, out of sight is out of mind."

"That is frequently the case." His aunt got up. "It is getting dark; we should go in. I am sorry if I misjudged you, Stephen."

Stephen rose with her. "There is no need to apologise, Aunt. You go ahead. I'll come later."

The last light of day gilded the western sky. Somewhere a blackbird piped a final challenge and a light breeze rippled through the flowers, releasing the heady scents of summer. Stephen sat down again and inhaled deeply, letting his breath flow out slowly, taking with it the tensions and excitements of the day.

Delia. They had resumed their customary conversation as if the intervening years had never existed. How was it possible that you only realised how much you had missed somebody when you met them again?

Then, in Brighton, he had wondered for days if he had offended her, although she had never given any hint of it. Or, worse, had she suddenly been taken ill? Then he had encountered her brother on The Steyne. In response to Stephen's tentative enquiry, he had informed him that his mother and sister had gone to Harrogate.

"To take the waters?"

"No. They have removed there permanently."

Stung by the thought that she had not mentioned a word of this imminent departure, all Stephen could do was mutter, "Thank you."

All joy had vanished with her. And, fool that he was, he once again experienced that immeasurable lightness of heart when he was with her—that sense of rightness and happy anticipation of an illimitable future with her at his side. He had experienced it with no other woman—those amicable liaisons had been for mutual physical pleasure, but no more.

Today's fashions did not suit her as well as the pre-revolution styles that had shown off her trim waist. He approved of the much less voluminous locks and the neat little bonnet that caressed her head and framed her face. Her chin was a little rounder and her cheeks fuller, but her nose still had that little tilt that reminded him of a kitten. She was still beautiful; her arched, dark eyebrows hadn't changed, nor had her expressive eyes whose fluctuating mixture of browns with hints of gold and green had fascinated him from the start. But those eyes were warier now. Although they had lit up when she saw him, she had immediately schooled her features to display no more than a polite interest. She had spoken very little of herself, too, either to him or to others; content to listen and throw in the occasional remark, but deflecting any more personal interest. But, as his aunt had pointed out, she had answered his question honestly. What did her answer reveal of her own marriage, he wondered?

What did she think of him? He was no longer the slim youth she had met in Brighton, and his hair was more salt-and-pepper than russet brown, but at least he was no baldpate.

What was he thinking? She was married. If he had any sense, he'd make some excuse and leave in the morning. And go where? What explanation could he give his aunt? He was tired of London, tired of the *ton*. For two pins, he'd bolt to the Continent. Talking to Delia had reminded him of the pleasures of foreign travel, pleasures that had been impossible for over a decade. Perhaps he should offer to go ahead of his aunt as a sort of scout, to see what state her properties were in. Piero would be more than happy to return to his native country.

Chapter Three

Apart from attendance at her mother's dinner table, Delia's day was her own. Her maid brought up her breakfast at nine o'clock and afterwards she dressed for the day. The weather was clement and by half-past ten, she had commenced her daily round. On arriving in Harrogate, she had taken out Season subscriptions at Hargrove's in High Harrogate and the Promenade Rooms in Low Harrogate. She started her day by looking in at the former, sipping at a glass of water at The Old Spa, and then walking along The Stray to the Tewit Well for a second glass, idly observing the comings and goings, and exchanging pleasantries with other visitors. From the Tewit, she continued on to the Promenade Rooms. At some stage each morning she met the Robertsons, and they went on together, indulging in a little shopping or a cup of chocolate or an ice before they parted. After dinner, she painted, wrote in her journal or Chloe's book, or read the books she had borrowed from the library.

She was forbidden to correspond with her daughter and had no reason to assume that a letter to her husband would be well received. With the passing days, she had found herself sinking into a sort of stupor in which only today mattered. The outings to the Dropping Well, and Lady Mary's had shattered this passivity, as had the reunion with Lord Stephen. What would he, what would her new acquaintances say if they knew that she had been banished to Harrogate, and why?

Why, oh why, had she yielded to Simon Purdue's blandishments?

She had been content enough with her humdrum life in a country backwater as the second wife of a much older man until her husband decided to celebrate both his sixtieth birthday and the defeat of Napoleon Bonaparte with a week's festivities to be held between the first and second Spring Meetings at Newmarket, two occasions that Sir Edward never missed. She didn't know what maggot had got into him, but neither effort nor expense were to be spared—there would be a house party of relatives and friends, a cricket match and an ox roast to which tenants and neighbours were also to be invited, and a ball at which their sixteen-year-old daughter would make her first appearance in society.

Sir Edward had returned from the races bringing Sir Jethro Boyce, an old crony for whom suitable accommodation had to be found in the already packed house. He had made no apology for this disruption, nor had he commented on his wife's arrangements for the week ahead, except to forbid anything other than quiet entertainments on the Sunday, vetoing cards, dancing, and boisterous games such as forfeits.

Despite twenty years of managing her husband's household, this was the first time Delia had been tasked with arranging such a large and complex event. By the day of the cricket match, she was nauseous from the pervasive smell of the roasting ox and completely exhausted from the strain of the preceding days. She had had to summon all her reserves to welcome Mr Purdue, a slim, dark man of about forty who had recently inherited the Old Hall from his uncle and on this occasion was making the acquaintance of his new neighbours. It had fallen to her to introduce him to the other guests; as a result, they spent considerable time together. He had gracefully expressed his appreciation of the invitation. He was an entertaining companion, and she was conscious of envious glances from other matrons. In his company, she became less tense and found herself enjoying the festivities.

He had sought her out at the ball quite early on, and they had danced a long set together. When the finishing dance was called, he happened to be near her and had immediately requested her hand. Flown with the success of the ball, she was reluctant to refuse him, although she knew she risked a rebuke from her husband for granting him a second dance. In the event, Sir Edward said nothing; indeed, when Purdue made his farewells, he had invited him to come and eat his mutton with them on Saturday when most of the guests would have left.

The remaining guests departed early on Monday morning. Sir Edward and Sir Julian, his son from his first marriage, were among those returning to the Newmarket. Julian had gone out of his way the previous evening to compliment her on the success of the festivities, 'Which seemed to happen effortlessly but required a great deal of coordination behind the scenes, ma'am'. Her husband had grunted a reminder that he expected to see her at breakfast to bid farewell to their guests.

He had left her the next morning with a dry peck on her cheek, a salute that owed more to the presence of others than to any husbandly sentiment. It had taken all her self-control not to turn her cheek away from him, not to cry, "Is that all you have to say to me, sir? Have you no word of appreciation to add to those of your guests?" Indeed, he had accepted the guests' thanks and compliments as his due, going so far as to say jovially, "Perhaps we should make an annual event of it."

"An annual event? God forbid," his mother said as the last carriage rumbled down the avenue. "I am exhausted, and you must be too, Delia. We should be grateful we are rid of the men for a week and can recover in peace. I am going back to bed."

"What would you like to do today?" Delia asked Chloe. Her daughter was out now; she would not send her back to the schoolroom. "Shall we drive into Bury, look at the shops?"

Chloe's face fell. "Miss Fancourt and I thought to walk over to see Mrs Crewe. I promised to come and tell her all about the ball. We can't go tomorrow because it's Tuesday, and I have my music and art lessons. But I'll come to Bury with you, if you wish, Mamma."

Stung that the girl preferred a visit to her old nurse to an outing with her mother, Delia snapped, "No, you must do as you like." She would go alone.

She encountered him at the entrance to Rackham's Library.

"Good morning, Lady Loring. An unexpected pleasure."

"Good morning, Mr Purdue."

"You are just the person to advise me. Is there a good guidebook to the area?"

"Mr Gillingwater's book is said to be excellent, but it is best that you talk to Mr Rackham himself."

"Indeed? After you, ma'am." Delia found herself ushered into the building before she could even think of protesting. If she were honest, his attentions had soothed her hurt feelings and roused instincts long lulled into dormancy.

He cleverly left much unspoken. Had he requested her to meet him privately, she would most likely have said no, but he had a way of assuming that what he wished, she wished too, saying 'Let us' or 'Shall we?' rather than 'May I?' or 'Will you?' Captivated by his skilful attentions and convinced that his interest was genuine, she consented to show him the garden and succession houses so that he might see what grew here and did not refuse to accompany him when he wished to see exactly where their estates marched. Then she agreed to inspect the secluded gamekeeper's cottage with him. That was when he had first kissed her. And that was the moment when she should have said, 'No'.

But by then she was besotted with him, sighing for him like a green girl. What was the harm in a couple of kisses, even some more daring caresses? It could lead to nothing permanent, she knew, but she would have this week at least to remind her that she was still attractive, desirable even. Once her husband returned, their meetings must stop. Purdue became more persuasive, and two days later she found herself on her knees in front of him in the spruced-up cottage.

And then the door had opened; her daughter and her governess had rushed in, seeking shelter from the rain.

Delia shuddered and closed her eyes. She could hardly remember what had happened next. Chloe had fallen and hit her head. Miss Fancourt went to her and Delia had shooed her away, tending to the girl herself. Purdue had taken her and the unconscious Chloe home but would not take the governess, too. The doctor was sent for. Chloe came round, thank God. Delia was beside herself by his time and her maid had made up a soothing draught for her.

She was asleep when her husband and stepson arrived home from Newmarket and it was the next morning before she spoke to Sir Edward. Miss Fancourt had not returned and Julian had called on Purdue and his version of events was already being whispered about at Loring Place.

Would it have helped if she had made a clean breast of things then? She would never know. For two weeks she had lived in dread of being found out. In the end, she had brought about her own downfall, which, she thought bleakly, served her right. While moralists would condemn her dalliance with Purdue, she was more ashamed of her letter to the owner of the Bath Academy, where Miss Fancourt had been educated, blackening the governess's character. Delia was grateful that in the end it had harmed no one but herself.

And then had come word of Purdue's betrayal, proof that she had been nothing but an amusement to him while he was obliged to remain in the neighbourhood. Finally, the whole house of cards had collapsed, and she was forced to confess her fault to her husband. She shuddered as she remembered his wrath, which had culminated in her banishment to Harrogate.

She was to remain here until September at least, he had said. And what then? If it were not for Chloe, she would not care if she never saw Loring Place again. Having failed in her duty to present her husband with another son, to him she was at best a convenience, a sort of superior housekeeper who relieved his aged mother of any duties and kept him company at table when he decided to dine at home. He, too, had deceived her from the beginning. No man was to be trusted.

She squared her shoulders. She must make the best of Harrogate and hope that things would take a turn for the better.

This evening she would drink tea with the Robertsons and perhaps her mother would like to accompany her to the concert of sacred music in the Promenade Rooms on Sunday. And if she were to go to the Granby ball with the Robertsons on Friday, she must see if the Pomona ball gown had to be taken in—all her clothes felt looser.

Chapter Four

"What troubles you, Delia?"

Delia looked up at Lord Stephen FitzCharles. "What do you mean?"

He gently lifted the sketchbook from her lap. "You have been sitting here for at least twenty minutes, facing one of the most romantic, ivy-entwined, Gothic ruins in the country and you have not drawn even one line. Usually, your pencil flies over the pages."

"I had not thought you so observant, my lord."

"Where you are concerned, I am." He sat beside her on the big block of stone. "Come, tell me what is the matter."

She hesitated. In recent weeks, the party from Arkell House and the Robertsons had made several outings together, in which Delia was always included. Whether this was out of courtesy or because the Robertsons did not have their own carriage, she was not sure. Together they had admired Ripon Cathedral, were astounded by the wild disorder of rocks at Brimham Crags, and today they roamed the magnificent ruins of Fountains Abbey.

It was more than a month since she had left Loring Place and she had not heard from her husband since. On her departure from Suffolk, he had coldly handed her the reduced pin money due to her on the June quarter day together with the quarter's wages for

Hughes, her maid. No provision had been made for John Coachman, and she had been obliged to provide his six guineas from her own funds.

The Harrogate Season ended in November when those businesses dependent on the visitors for their livelihood shut their doors until the next May. She remembered all too well the harsh winters, unrelieved by any form of entertainment. And if she were to remain so long, there would be bound to be talk, both here and in Suffolk. She would also have to explain to her mother why she was not allowed return to her own home.

The other members of their party were scattered among the ruins—it would be some time before any of them drew near. Stephen would not judge her harshly; at least she didn't think he would.

She met his eyes and said baldly, "My husband sent me here in disgrace. I'm an adulteress."

He put his hand on hers. "I am sure there is more to the story than that. Do you want to tell me about it?"

It was a relief to unburden herself. He listened quietly and shook his head at the end of her tale. "Poor Delia. And he is not inclined to be generous, or merciful?"

"No. I do not think he cares enough about me to forgive the affront to his self-esteem."

"Will he not miss you?"

"I doubt it. The servants will manage and, for the rest—he has had his first wife's maid in keeping these twenty years and more. He has a house in Ipswich where they are known as Mr and Mrs Edwards."

"He told you this?" Lord Stephen asked incredulously.

She snorted. "Of course not. I overheard the housekeeper talking to the land steward years ago. When I challenged him, he said it was no concern of mine, and my position remained unaltered by it."

"Good God! And he has the effrontery to sit in judgement on you."

"Unlike her husband, a wife is expected to take her marriage vows seriously," Delia said savagely. "He observed none of his."

"How did you come to marry?"

She stared unseeing into the distance. "I don't know; it… just happened. My mother and I came here directly from Brighton. Harrogate was even smaller then, especially outside the Season. As year-round inhabitants, we did not generally attend the balls and other entertainments, so my life was very quiet. But sometimes a visitor came who had an introduction to someone in my mother's small circle. So it was that year with old Mr Philbert—his cousin is one of my mother's bosom-friends. He was a merry old gentleman, interested in everyone and everything, but had a good heart and such an innate kindness that he never tried one's nerves, as some overly enthusiastic persons do. We first met him at church and then we, or at least my mother, met him frequently at the various wells or when she was visiting his cousin.

"When his great-nephew, Sir Edward Loring, came to visit, my company was requested to help divert him. He was a widower, not long out of mourning, they said, but it was two years since his wife died. I learnt later that Mr Philbert thought I was a pretty-behaved girl and would make a suitable new wife for him. Be that as it may, Mr Philbert convinced my mother to allow me to attend a ball at the *Granby*. He and Sir Edward were staying there, and he introduced me to Mrs Greene, a fellow guest who agreed to chaperon me. I was terrified—I had not danced since we left Brighton, but Mrs Greene showed me the steps.

"It was like a rainbow when the sky clears at the end of a dull, rainy day. Sir Edward danced twice with me and invited me to drive to Knaresborough with him the next day. He hired a phaeton. Another day, we came here. When Miss Philbert invited her cousins and friends to an evening party, he stood by the fortepiano when I played.

"There was another ball, and Mr Philbert gave a dinner before it in his private parlour. Even my mother came. I sat at Sir Edward's right hand, and he was most attentive. Afterwards, he led me out for the first dance and the master of ceremonies had us go to the top of the first set. I was nervous, but he led well and I managed without any difficulty. The next day, he called and made me an offer."

She shook her head. "I was very willing to love him, perhaps too willing. And when he suggested we call the banns the next Sunday, for we were in my parish, and could marry after the third calling, there seemed no reason to object. His great-uncle approved and my mother had consented. This way, he would not have to make the long journey north again from Suffolk.

"Those three weeks were full of gaiety. They passed in a whirl, for I also had to have my bride-clothes made. Mr Philbert gave me a pair of diamond bracelets that had belonged to his wife. He said I reminded him of her, and of their daughter who died when she was young. They had no other children and when he died some years later, Edward was his heir. I think that expectancy was what brought him, Edward, I mean, to Harrogate. And so we married and left for Suffolk. That was our wedding journey. We were to go to London the next year for the Season, but then his father died and that was that."

"His father was still alive?"

"Both his parents were. His mother still is."

"How did they take the news of his wedding? Were they forewarned at least?"

"Yes. He wrote to tell them he was bringing his bride home."

Stephen frowned. "Would his father not have had to sign the marriage settlements?"

"I don't know anything about that. He was forty, after all."

"How did his parents receive you?"

"They were not unwelcoming—they said everything that was proper—but it was clear that I was a poor match compared with his first wife, who was Lord Swanmere's only child and heiress. They thought he had fallen for a pretty face. Perhaps he had, or he had been overly persuaded by his great-uncle. Who can say? But his real reason for marrying again was to sire another son."

"Another? He already had one?"

"Yes, Julian. He was fifteen then. That was also a problem."

"Did he resent his father's marriage?"

"I think so. He never said it directly, and was always scrupulously polite to me—"

"The sort of politeness that is like a blow in the face?"

"A bit, but that's not what I meant. Had she lived, Julian's mother would have succeeded her father as baroness in her own right. Edward would have been content to be the power behind the throne, but he could not bear to see himself supplanted by his own son, who was now the heir presumptive. He planned to break the Loring entail and leave everything to his second son. He could not leave the baronetcy, of course, but the whole estate would bypass Julian."

"Would Julian not have had to agree to this?"

"Yes, when he was twenty-one, but Edward was sure he could convince him that it was the right and fair thing to do." She shrugged. "But there was no second son, just one daughter. That did not endear me to him."

"From what you say, his first wife also bore him only one child. It is as likely that the fault, if it may be called so, lies with him."

"These matters are always laid at the wife's door, Stephen," Delia said wearily. "Really, it is not so much that we grew apart as that we never grew together. I had not realised the extent to which the pleasant tenor of our days in Harrogate was due to his uncle's influence. But I don't think any woman has clear expectations of what her married life will be. A man may assume that everything will go on as before, except that it will be more comfortable because he will have his wife at his beck and call, while a woman knows nothing will be the same again. I don't mean just the intimate side of marriage, although most girls are not at all prepared for it, and it can be quite a shock to them. But she must leave all that is familiar. She may not be mistress of her new home but must make a place for herself in that of her husband's parents. His mother, on the other hand, knows that her tenure as mistress of the house will last only as long as her husband lives."

"I know," he said quietly. "My mother was a much younger second wife. I was fifteen when my father died; my elder brother who succeeded him was forty-six, four years older than my mother—his wife was only two years younger than she was."

"What happened?"

"She had to yield the ducal suite to her stepson and daughter-in-law, of course, and move to the dower house. When her year of mourning was up, the Queen offered her a place at Court and she was quite happy there, I believe. I was away at school, but my brother allowed me to regard Stanton as my home until after I came down from Oxford. I have a set in Albany now. My nephew is now the duke. I go to Stanton occasionally but, although it was never formally agreed between us, my country home is with my aunt. But you were telling me about your marriage."

"Edward turned out to be quite strait-laced, with very little generosity of spirit. His mother might have been more conciliating, but her husband was taken ill quite suddenly and died within six months of my arrival at Loring Place. It took her some time to recover from the shock, and by then Edward was established as master and I as mistress. There is no dower house, just a widow's suite that in other times is used for important guests, so she continued to live with us but, apart from dining with us, kept herself quite apart.

"I was happiest when Chloe was small, before she had a governess. I could spend as much time as I liked with her, playing and reading to her, or going for walks. Then her nurse wanted to marry, and I knew it was time she had a governess. I wanted to give her everything I had not had. I will say this for Edward; he never quibbled at paying for her drawing, music, and dancing masters, or for Madame le Brun's French lessons. I hope that he continues to do so. Her new finishing governess was to start at midsummer. I hope she proves satisfactory. Oh, Stephen, I worry so about my daughter. But she is no longer any concern of mine, Edward says."

Delia's voice broke and, to Stephen's horror, tears filled her eyes and spilled down her cheeks. She batted furiously at them, but they would not be stilled. He turned so as to shield her as much as possible from inquisitive gazes and pressed his handkerchief into her hand.

"Shush, now. There, Delia, there, there. Surely if you were to seek his forgiveness, he would relent?"

She shook her head. "I doubt it. As a magistrate, he exacts the full penalty of the law no matter how heart-rending the circumstances. I have seen mothers on their knees pleading for their sons who were caught poaching, more youthful mischief than anything else, but he would not relent and the boys were transported. I fear he would be as severe with me. He was quick to remind me that the law gives him more power over me than any gaoler has over his prisoners. Is that really true, Stephen? Can he dispose of me as he wishes? Have I no rights under the law?"

"I don't know, Delia. Would you like me to find out for you? I could consult a solicitor on behalf of a lady of my acquaintance. There would be no need to mention your name."

"Would you, Stephen? I feel so helpless."

He tried to put himself in her place and could not. Even in his miserable first weeks at school, he had known that matters could only improve. But to have no rights, no hope… "What should I ask him? Is it your desire to return home to your daughter and husband?"

She sniffed. "I don't care about my husband, but I'll endure anything if I can live freely with my daughter. Can he really keep her from me?"

"I'll find out," he promised. "Do you come to my aunt's birthday celebrations next week? I shall try and have an answer for you by then."

She smiled through her tears. "Thank you, Stephen. You are a true friend indeed."

~~~

I wonder how many hundreds of people lived and worked and prayed here over the centuries, Delia wrote the next day in Chloe's book. *They must have thought their Abbey would stand for ever, but it only took the unrestrained power of one man to destroy it. Now the magnificent buildings are roofless and bare, their stalwart tower and arches exposed to the elements, grey stone silhouetted against the sky. And yet something remains of their former purpose, something undefeated, something divine.*

On the page opposite, the greys and greens of Stephen's 'ivy-clad, Gothic ruin' rose ragged against an overcast sky. The little group of visitors below provided a sense of scale and lent additional colour to the monochrome image. A gentleman in a maroon coat, buff breeches, and top boots stood to one side, his head slightly tilted as he surveyed the scene. Delia touched the figure very gently so as not to smudge the paint. Dear Stephen. She could not remember when last someone had seen her need and spontaneously offered their help.

The portraits of Chloe and her self-portrait had turned out well. Could she capture a gentleman as accurately? Not for Chloe this time, but for herself. Eyes closed, she began to call up his face—oblong, with high cheekbones and a square chin, straight eyebrows, a crooked nose—relic of a schoolboy mishap, neat, small-lobed ears. She began to draw the individual features on a scrap of paper. Deep-set, dark eyes. Beautiful lips, with a pronounced cupid's bow. What would it be like to trace that sculpted mouth with her finger instead of sketching it with her pencil?

Once she had captured that little tilt of the head and the way he narrowed his eyes, she took a new sheet and began to draw in earnest. She took her time, first sketching lightly, a piece of stale bread to hand to erase any errors. When she was satisfied, she deepened the lines, then used the lightest touch of her watercolours to bring her friend to life so that he gazed at her with the same smiling concern that had brought her to the brink of tears the previous day. Friends—that was all they could be to one another now, but even such a connection was precious. She would treasure the memory of these weeks, whatever happened.

Chapter Five

Lady Mary held an open day on her birthday. Neighbours, tenants, and their families called to wish her well and join in the games and pastimes set up in the park.

"No ox roast, thank heavens," Delia said to Stephen as they watched a game of bowls. "Edward insisted on having one for his birthday celebrations in May and the Place still stank of it a week later. We had to take down all the curtains on that side of the house and wash them as well as airing the rooms."

"No fear of that here. As you know, my aunt prefers lighter fare. Speaking of which, would you care for a glass of *ponch à la Romaine*? My man is a dab hand at it and always makes some to mark my aunt's birthday. It is not generally put out on the refreshment tables, for it would be a case of caviar to the general, you know; besides, it must be kept cool."

"What is it?"

"It can best be described as a lemon sherbet refined with old cognac and rum."

"It sounds delicious. I'm surprised your aunt's cook allows his kitchen to be invaded."

Stephen laughed. "It is a special concession, due in part to the fact that the recipe starts with pounding the finely pared peel of three dozen lemons with two pounds of sugar for at least half an hour so as to extract the essential oils."

"A strong arm is needed?"

"Definitely. This way."

They slipped unnoticed into the rose garden and made their way along the gravel paths to the shaded garden hall. Stephen ushered her into a small parlour. "We'll be undisturbed here," he said as he tugged the bell-pull.

Once they were supplied with glasses of the aromatic, deliciously cool punch, he closed the door and looked gravely at her. "I went into York and spoke to Henderson; he is a well-respected solicitor who advises many of the landed gentry hereabouts."

"What did he say?"

"To start, I asked if a husband could keep her daughter from her mother? He said, yes, pointing out that the Regent is doing exactly that at present."

She closed her eyes briefly and sank onto a sofa, but waved him away when he started towards her. "No, no. Go on."

Better to get it over with, he thought, and continued. "I then asked if your husband could prevent you from returning to the marital home. Here, his reply was not as definite. He had not come across this before—more usually, a husband is trying to retrieve his errant wife."

"How could he do that?"

"By suing in the Ecclesiastical Courts for restitution of conjugal rights, including cohabitation."

"How can the courts compel a wife to return to her husband?"

Stephen made a face. "Previously, she could be required to do so on pain of excommunication, but apparently fear for their immortal souls is no longer enough to compel some wives to return to the marital home. Last year, a law was passed, providing that they could be imprisoned for up to six months if they refused to obey the court's decree."

"Only last year?" Delia was shocked. "It sounds like something from the dark ages."

"In many ways, the so-called dark ages were more enlightened than we are now," Stephen said grimly. "I asked Henderson whether a wife could also appeal to the courts to have her rights restored. This is where he began to hem and haw and mutter about coverture and chattel. Finally, he said he was not aware of a case where a wife fought against being denied her conjugal rights, but that was not to say it might not be essayed, although it was something no woman of delicacy could well do."

He raised his hand and let it fall. "And there you have it, Delia. You would be ruined either way, and especially if he were to challenge your suit on the grounds of your indiscretion."

"He said he had not decided what he would do, and that I was not to assume that he condoned my adultery."

"Forgive me if I am too blunt, but from what you told me, it cannot be shown that you committed adultery. You were foolish and indiscreet, but it was not adultery."

"Not...?"

"No. There must be proof of full congress—with penetration. Henderson confirmed this," he added when she stared at him. "There must be witnesses."

"Oh!" She put her hands to her flushed cheeks. "We never— but I would admit anything before I let Chloe be called to give evidence."

"I am sure you would. That is another reason why you would not want to bring a case in the courts." He came and sat beside her. "Henderson said that if his sister were in such straits and determined to return to her husband, he would make very clear to her that she would be delivering herself up to him in every possible way. If she persisted, he would advise her to write to her husband, throwing herself on his mercy. But men's promises to women are easily made and as easily broken, and she would have no guarantee that she would be allowed see her daughter again. Why, the man could have married the girl off in the meantime, he said, and his wife would be none the wiser."

Delia turned white at this and he put his arm around her. "Do you think that is likely?"

She thought for a moment. "I do not think he would go out of his way to pursue it, but if an eligible offer came his way, he might not refuse it."

"What manner of man is he? Warm-hearted? Hot-tempered?"

"I don't think he has a heart," she said bitterly. "He likes to rule the roost. He is very set in his ways, will not tolerate change. I would not call him covetous, but he is possessive, proprietorial if you like. He will not let go; he saw no reason why he should not retain his mistress when he remarried and can apparently reconcile his keeping her with an otherwise puritanical conscience. What is his, is his and let no man take it away—look how resentful he is of his son's ousting him at Swanmere. That is why he might eventually let me return, although I doubt that he would ever properly forgive or forget. I would always be there on sufferance."

"And his temper?"

"He is—irascible; quick to fire up if something does not suit him and will not brook contradiction or interference, as he puts it, especially from his wife. I very soon learnt not to question him. He likes to remind me that the law permits him to correct me as he thinks fit. He has more power over me than any gaoler has over his prisoners, he says."

"Dear God! What a way to live."

"I had no choice," she said simply. "Where else could I go? Even now, my mother does not know why I am here. I would have to confess all if I wished to remain with her indefinitely; throw myself on her mercy. I don't know how she would react." She suddenly laughed shrilly.

"Delia? Delia! What is it?"

She pressed her fingers to her lips as if trying to hold back her laughter. "I just remembered that we came to Harrogate because someone tattled that you and I were spending time together."

"What?"

"Yes, she said the intentions of a duke's son towards me could not be honourable."

"They were, I assure you, in so far as I had any at that stage. I was definitely not planning to set you up as my mistress."

"I never thought you were. I no more thought of the future then than you did." She sighed. "We were so innocent. It was a special time, and she stole it from us."

He nodded. "I was distraught when you disappeared. I called at the house but was told you were not at home. I was angry for months that you had not seen fit to tell me you were leaving."

"I couldn't, Stephen. I was not allowed leave the house once she found out about us."

"Poor Delia." He pressed a kiss to the side of her forehead and rested his head on hers. They sat in silence until the tall clock in the corner struck the hour.

She straightened up. "We should not tarry too long. Did this Henderson say anything else?"

"Just that your husband is obliged to support you in the manner to which you are accustomed, whether you live together or apart, and even in the case of divorce."

"He has reduced my pin money to the strict terms of our marriage settlement," she said dully. "It is thirty pounds per quarter, but when Chloe was born, he increased it to fifty, and added another twenty for Chloe."

"That is for your personal use, not to put a roof over your head and supply you with the necessities of life. He would have paid all the household bills as well."

"Yes."

"Apart from being reconciled with your daughter, what do you want from life, Delia? Really want, in your heart of hearts?"

"I want to be loved," she blurted out. "I want someone who cares about me, Delia Elizabeth. Someone who will sit with me and laugh with me and comfort me, and I will comfort him and together we will face everything life throws at us. Someone who is interested in the things that interest me or is prepared to learn about them. And I will learn about what interests him so that he can discuss it with me. And I will not be alone." She dashed her hand across her eyes. "Oh, listen to me, babbling like a silly girl who has read too many fairy-tales. I know I can't have that."

Stephen's heart leapt as he listened. Was that not what he sought, too? Someone to share his life, to build a new life with? And she was the right woman—he felt it in his core. Her husband had relinquished all moral right to her. But then there was her daughter. How could he encourage her to abandon her?

He leaned forward and kissed her gently, the innocent first kiss he should have given her when she was seventeen. "If only we could turn the clock back; if we could meet again before you were wed…"

Her lips trembled. "But we can't. What's done is done, and there is no going back. Thank you, Stephen, for everything." She drew away from him and stood. "We should join the others."

She went to the overmantel mirror and tidied her hair before donning the bonnet she had discarded when they came into the parlour. The deep brim shaded her face and her eyes. No one would notice her distress.

He forced himself to smile at her. "You go on ahead—there is no point in creating talk by coming out together. I'll follow in a few minutes."

~~~

Stephen watched Delia walk down the path. Her shoulders were slumped. When she reached the gate, she straightened into her usual graceful posture, and stepped through, disappearing out of his sight. One day soon, he would lose sight of her forever. Even if she remained with her mother and he with his aunt, once the seasonal guests had left Harrogate, it would be impossible for them to meet regularly without causing talk.

Sighing, he dropped onto the sofa. What sort of life would she have if she returned to her husband? And what would her life be like if her banishment continued? One heard appalling stories of wives more or less imprisoned in their own homes, or sent to live in remote places.

Henderson had looked him in the eye. "The law is not kind to women, Lord Stephen. If it were my sister, I would make very clear to her that in returning to her husband, she would be delivering herself up to him, body and soul. Much depends on the man's disposition. If he is kindly, and his wife contrite, he will take her back and try to put the whole business behind them. But if he is the vengeful sort, or is inclined to hold a grudge, she will be on sufferance for the rest of their life together, never allowed to forget her fault and subject to all sorts of petty tyranny as a result. Does the lady have any brother or other male relatives who might intervene on her behalf?"

"She has a brother, but I doubt that he would do anything," Stephen had replied. "And I fear her husband is more the latter sort."

The little solicitor shook his head. "If she had the means, she would be best advised to remove to a remote part of the country, change her name if possible, and live quietly until he dies. He is considerably older, you said."

"Then she loses all hope of a connection with her daughter," Stephen pointed out.

"Very true. Then she must try to weigh the likelihood of her being allowed to see the girl against the treatment she can expect from her husband."

If she came to him, it would mean living abroad for several years, Stephen thought. Would she agree? Did he want that? And how might he ensure that she would never be in want? He must think it through before talking to Henderson again.

~~~

Lady Mary's birthday marked the end of her house party. Her daughters and their families departed a couple of days later, leaving Stephen alone with his aunt. He rode to Harrogate most mornings to join Delia on her daily rounds, but as they generally met the Robertsons along the way, this went uncommented by the gossips and quizzes.

"Shall we go to the ball tonight?" Mrs Robertson asked the next Monday as they left St. John's Well. "This is our last week— we have taken our rooms until the thirty-first, which is Sunday."

"Do let's, Mamma," Miss Kirsty pleaded. "I hope you will come too, Lord Stephen. Then we may be assured of at least one partner. And we can see who the newcomers at the other hotels and lodging houses are."

"Pay no attention to her, Lord Stephen," Mrs Robertson said. "You should not feel obliged to come all the way from Knaresborough just to dance with Miss Impertinence."

"I assure you it will be a pleasure," he said. "If this is to be your last week, then we must make the most of it, must we not, Lady Loring?"

"Yes, indeed," Delia said, although her spirits had plummeted. Without the Robertsons to sit bodkin, it would be less easy for them to meet unremarked.

"How long do you intend to remain in these parts?" she asked him.

"I have not decided yet."

He was interrupted by a cry of 'Papa' and turned to see the usually sedate Miss Robertson pick up her skirts and run into the arms of a sun-burnt, kilted officer, quickly followed by her mother and sister so that the four were fused in one fierce embrace.

"Let us walk on," Delia said. "It will be some time before they come to themselves and then they will wish to be alone. It is over four years since the major was at home, Mrs Robertson told me."

Stephen nodded and offered her his arm. "Have you given any further thought to our previous discussion?" he asked quietly.

"I have thought about little else; my mind is in a maze—but at the end of the day, I really have no choice. For Chloe's sake, I must attempt to reconcile with my husband before it is too late."

"I understand."

"I am determined to write to him this week, if only I knew what to say."

"Should I ask Henderson for some suggestions that you may incorporate into your letter? You do not want to sound too business-like, or imply that you have taken legal advice."

"I cannot imagine anything more likely to annoy him. He would like me to grovel, I daresay, but even Christ forgave the woman taken in adultery."

"Perhaps you should remind him of that."

"Perhaps." They walked on in silence. After some minutes, she said, "I wish I could hope to make such congenial acquaintances as the Robertsons again. I shall miss them. We formed such an agreeable group with your cousins, whether it was to go to the balls or the theatre or undertake our little excursions."

"I hope you will still call on my aunt. I know she will be very happy to see you."

"I should be delighted to. Does she stay here all winter?"

"More or less. Sometimes she visits friends for a week or two, but this is her home. I imagine that once it is safe to travel, she will resume her habit of spending the winters abroad. I hope she does while she is still able to travel."

"How old is she?"

"Sixty-five."

"Only five years younger than my mother? I had thought it more. It is probably because your aunt is so lively and is interested in everything."

"She has an adventurous disposition," he said dryly.

"She also has not become embittered, although life has dealt her a bad hand. There is a lesson there, is there not?"

"An important one," he agreed.

"Lady Loring, Lord Stephen." The Robertsons had caught up with them. "May I present my husband, Major Robertson?"

After a flurry of greetings, the reunited family took their leave. "We shall forgo the ball tonight," Mrs Robertson said.

"Of course," Delia said. "You will have much to talk about."

"I shall not go either," Delia said to Stephen when they were on their own. "I do not think it would be wise, without another lady in the party."

"I suppose not. A pity—I was looking forward to dancing again with you."

~~~

As it turned out, the Robertsons decided to cut short their stay and leave for Scotland on Wednesday. On Tuesday, the major rode beside Delia's carriage when his ladies paid a farewell call on Lady Mary. Delia would have gladly lent them the carriage, but Mrs Robertson wouldn't hear of it. "We have become firm friends these past weeks. I hope, dear Lady Loring, that we shall remain in contact after our departure."

"Yes, of course," Delia replied but could not help wondering whether the lady would be so anxious to maintain the acquaintance if she knew the real reason for her new friend's stay in Harrogate.

Was she always to carry this burden of guilt; live in apprehension that the truth would out? Supposing she met Purdue again? Or Miss Fancourt or that man, Chidlow? They could ruin her with a word. And what had the servants suspected at the Place? What rumours had circulated in Bury? *Oh, what a tangled web we weave*, she thought. And why are women judged so harshly?

"You seem to have recovered your spirits, Delia," Mrs Eubank said at dinner that afternoon. "Do you still intend to remain here until September, as Sir Edward originally requested?"

"Yes, ma'am, if it does not inconvenience you," Delia replied, startled.

"I am happy to do my duty, as you know, but I must arrange for a new companion to replace poor Eliza. You will not wish to remain over the winter, I am sure, and I should prefer not to be alone. There are always some weeks when I do not leave the house."

"Yes, of course." Her mother had said nothing up to now about finding a replacement for the cousin who had died in April and it had not occurred to Delia that her bedroom might be required for a new incumbent. She really must write to Edward, she resolved. Or would it be wiser to say nothing and simply leave for home in September, saying that her mother could no longer put her up?

Chapter Six

"There you are, Stephen." Lady Mary smiled at her nephew. "I hope you were able to conclude your business successfully."

"More or less." He stooped to kiss her cheek. "How did you spend your day?"

"Very pleasantly. Lady Loring called. Only look what she brought me. Isn't it clever? I had not realised she is so talented."

"Nor I," he said, admiring the large watercolour of Anna, Susan, and the Robertson sisters playing Battledore and Shuttlecock on the lawn, as they had so often in recent weeks, while their parents, Lady Mary, and Stephen looked on. Delia had even included herself, seated to one side, sketching busily. "She has captured the essence of those days. They are not portraits precisely, but you could not mistake one of the girls for the other."

"I shall have it framed and hang it here to remind me of such a happy visit. She left this for you. She said it was some information you had requested."

"Thank you." Stephen slid the letter into his pocket. He would read it when he was alone.

Monday, 31st July

Dear Stephen,

I received this with this morning's post. I am distraught. I shall be at St. John's Well at eleven tomorrow morning. Please be there.

Delia

Frowning, he opened the enclosed letter.

Loring Place, 29 July 1814

To Lady Loring,

Madam,

I write to express my disappointment and disapproval at your failure to return the carriage and John Coachman to their rightful place. You can have no need of the first and it is not right for the second to be idle. I expect to see him returned here with the carriage within a se'ennight of your receipt of this letter.

I trust you are comporting yourself meekly and continue to reflect on the error of your ways. You will remain where you are for the winter, after which, depending on the accounts I receive of your behaviour, I shall judge whether and on what terms you may be permitted to resume your marital duties.

I leave you to the sting of your own conscience, advising you to use this time wisely so that you achieve a true repentance of your sins.

Your injured spouse.
Sir E. L.

Stephen shook his head in disbelief. The writer of the lines had two concerns—that his coachman not be idle and his wife enjoy neither comfort, nor amusement, nor entertainment. What sort of mean-spirited vindictiveness was this? In another age, he would have had her immured in a convent.

Stephen had resigned himself to the fact that Delia would put her daughter first and his sense of honour prevented him from trying to persuade her to change her mind. But now? Could he honestly encourage her to return to such a man? Surely, she had a right to consider her own happiness? He looked again at her husband's letter. Perhaps Sir E. had overplayed his hand. She should have a choice, at least, he resolved; should know that there was an alternative to abject surrender to an implacable tyrant.

If she wished to comply with her husband's instructions, she must send the carriage back within a week. She must decide before then. He was conscious of the enormity of the step he was about to ask her to take. While he would do his utmost to ensure that she never regretted it, she must choose to come to him.

Torn between dread and hope, Stephen opened his writing slope and took out the draft paragraphs Henderson had handed him earlier. He could not see her sending them in reply to this letter. He drew a sheet of paper to him. Better start jotting things down, he thought—if she comes, there will be much to be done and not much time to do it. A little bubble of excitement, of anticipation, rose within him. It was strange to be in the throes of love at this time of life. No other woman had felt so right to him;

she completed him in so many ways. All he wanted was her at his side.

~~~

She was already at the spring the next morning, standing outside the small octagonal building and sipping distastefully at her glass of chalybeate water. Stephen had the attendant fill his own glass and forced himself to slow down as he went over to her.

"I wonder why we persist in drinking this stuff," he said as he gulped it down.

"I tell myself I feel better for it, but I am not entirely convinced."

He looked across The Stray where riders, carriages, and grazing sheep vied for space. "It is a beautiful morning. I borrowed my aunt's phaeton—it is at The Queen's Head. Will you drive out to Plumpton with me?"

"That would be delightful."

They turned as one, continuing to speak lightly of nothing in particular until they reached the inn. The phaeton and pair were drawn up outside, a groom in attendance. Stephen handed her up into the seat and took his place beside her.

She unfolded the rug and spread it over her knees while he gathered the reins and picked up his whip. "Let them go," he called to the groom, who scrambled up into the seat behind.

"The hood will prevent him from hearing anything," Stephen assured Delia as they drove away. "We can talk freely."

"This is an excellent idea; I wondered how we would manage. All I could think of when I wrote that note was that I had to talk to you."

"I'm sorry I was not there when you called. My aunt is delighted with your painting, by the way."

"I'm glad."

"You are very talented."

"My father was an artist, and I spent as much time as I could in his studio. I learnt a lot from him."

She fell silent as he laboriously made his way past a laden cart, then stopped to let three ladies cross the road in front of him. Once they were on the turnpike and he had paid the toll, she said abruptly, "I spent all Sunday trying to compose a letter to my husband, but now I think it pointless."

"I agree. I have never read a colder, more heartless missive. Even if you could bring yourself to grovel, I think you would only feed his desire to chasten you."

"To make matters worse, my mother assumes I shall leave her in September and wishes to engage a companion for the winter. I could confess all to her, throw myself on her mercy, but what if she does not permit me to remain with her? It has not really suited her to have me here for the summer as I occupy the room a companion would have. She will be most disapproving of my behaviour, too. What then? Am I to return home on the stagecoach and beg for admission? Everything in me rebels at the thought. And what are these reports he speaks of? Will he sink to quizzing John Coachman about my comings and goings? If so, he will be up in arms about my new friends and our outings, not to mention the balls and concerts I attended."

"He is playing cat and mouse with you. Who is to say what further expiation he may require when winter is over?"

"By then, it will be almost a year since I saw Chloe. He will have turned her against me, I am sure of it."

She sounded so desolate that he longed to take her in his arms, but all he could do was touch her hand fleetingly. "Tell me about her."

He listened, smiling, as first haltingly and then more fluently, her memories unfolded. "You seem to have been fortunate in your governess."

"Yes. I treated her badly at the end. I did write a letter of apology, but—she is the only person I have ever knowingly attempted to harm. After Chloe's injury, and that was unintentional, that is what I regret most."

He couldn't stop himself asking, "You don't regret Purdue?"

"I am angry that I let myself be taken in by his attentions and, yes, I regret it, but he means nothing to me." She turned to look at Stephen. "He was the only one. I did not make a habit of it, you know. Everything was so different, with all the excitement of the house party, and I was so relieved that all went well, and then, suddenly, they all had left…" She shook her head. "I am not trying to excuse myself, but I still have not completely understood what happened and why."

She relapsed into silence. Arrived at Plumpton, he helped her down from the phaeton and they strolled along the paths, the only sign of her distress being the way her hand gripped the fabric of his sleeve. At last, they came to a secluded seat sheltered by yew hedges, from where they could admire the rocks and the lake.

"Here we can talk undisturbed," he said. "How can I help you, Delia?"

"I don't know, Stephen—perhaps just listen to me. I am at my wit's end. Today is Tuesday. If I obey this command, I must send the carriage back on Saturday at the latest. In doing so, and remaining here, I accept his, his dominion and authority over me, do I not? I am complicit in my own subjugation. The church and the law say I consented to it when I married him."

"Do you not agree?"

"We both made promises. If I vowed to obey and serve him, he swore he would love and cherish me, comfort me and honour me. I intended to keep my vows, and I did my best even after he had broken all of his, was persistently unfaithful to me. Did he not also break our marriage? If it were not for Chloe, I would send his precious carriage back to him and vanish."

"Leave him? Where would you go?"

"I don't know. Scotland, perhaps. I don't think he would look for me there. I have never spent all of my allowance and I brought my savings with me." She smiled faintly. "I don't know whether I had a foreboding that it might come to this, or was afraid he would—did you know that if a wife does not spend all of her pin money, the husband may take it back?"

"What?"

"He explained it all to me when we were first married. The purpose of pin money was to enable me to dress suitably and otherwise carry out my duties as his wife. I pointed out that it would be prudent to put some aside each quarter because from time to time I would need more expensive garments—a ball gown, perhaps, or a fur-trimmed cloak. He couldn't really argue with me because he had also said that I had to manage with what he gave me and not come looking for my mantua-maker's bills to be paid. I also have my jewellery. I could sell that and earn a little by teaching drawing and watercolours, or painting miniatures. It would be a simple life, but I could manage, I think. But if I do that, I have lost Chloe. Perhaps I have lost her anyway."

"If you want my honest opinion, while he might continue to dangle the prospect of a reunion with her, I think it is unlikely that he will permit it. But remember she will not always be so young, and in some years' time, you will be able to approach her directly. She may not be so unforgiving."

"I hope you are right."

"But you have another choice; I have hesitated to mention it as long as it seemed likely that you could be reconciled with Chloe. But if you are considering leaving him, would you trust yourself to me, come to the Continent with me?"

"The Continent?" she repeated faintly.

"Yes. My aunt is anxious to return to Nice, discover what remains of her home there. I thought to go ahead of her in the autumn and ensure there are no unpleasant surprises. You could come with me."

She stared at him. "Stephen, are you asking me to be your mistress?"

"I would rather say my beloved companion, my wife in everything but name. I do not mean a temporary liaison, Delia, but a permanent one."

"Oh." Her eyes filled with tears. "If only we could. But what it would mean for you? Whatever about on the Continent, I could not live with you in England. And even abroad—you can dress it up as 'beloved companion' Stephen, but I would be your mistress; you would not be able to present me to your acquaintances. No decent woman would agree to it. You would be cut off from your friends."

"Then we shall make new ones."

She shook her head. "You would be shut out from the society that is your birthright."

"And of which I am heartily sick. I don't see why we shouldn't make a new life for ourselves. There are ways of managing these things."

"Are there? I am very ignorant of such matters."

"Yes. But, if you cannot see your way to it, I'll do my best to help you settle elsewhere, although I fear it will be a lonely, difficult life for you. What do you want, Delia? If you had a free choice?"

"A free choice?" She sat for several minutes, gazing at the lake. Then she turned to him. "Were I completely free, I would go with you. My heart ached at the thought that you would soon leave and I would never see you again."

"Delia!" He caught her hand. "Does that mean you care for me?"

She nodded, her lips curving into the most beautiful smile. "So much."

"Then live with me and be my love."

She took a deep breath. "Yes."

He touched her cheek gently. "I want more than anything to take you in my arms, but dare not risk it here. I swear I will do my utmost to ensure you will never regret your decision."

Her hand turned to grip his. "I'm sure I won't. Oh, Stephen!" She shook her head, smiling at him so tenderly that he could only smile back, as lost for words as she was.

At last, he stirred. "We must make plans. But first I must tell you that I consulted Henderson yesterday. He tells me I can set up a trust for your sole and separate use so that your husband would have no claim on it. You will always have a sufficient income for your needs. Should I die, the trust will also provide you with a cottage at a place of your choice—either in England or elsewhere."

She stared at him. "You will provide me with an independence for the rest of my life? Why would you do that?"

She looked so puzzled that he didn't know whether to shake her or kiss her. She wasn't used to anyone caring about her, he realised. "I care about you. No, damn it, I love you, Delia. This is what a man does for the woman he wants to spend his life with. We cannot marry, but I can make you secure, at least. As for the rest, we do not have the time to work everything out now but, if you entrust yourself to me, we shall do it together."

"And will you entrust yourself to me, Stephen?"

"Yes. I'll give my heart into your keeping. Promise you that there will be no other woman for me. I will deal with you honestly and honourably, not put my happiness before yours, and care for you in sickness and in health. This I do swear."

Her hand turned to grip his and solemnly, word for word, she made the same pledge to him. Tears sparkled on her eyelashes as she finished, "this I do swear."

He raised her hand and kissed it. "My love."

"My love," she repeated softly, lingering over the words. "Nobody has ever called me that before, nor I have I ever said it to anyone."

He kissed her hand again. "My only love."

They sat quietly hand in hand, in a dream of happiness. It couldn't last, Stephen knew. There had been several violent storms while he was in the West Indies and, once or twice, he had experienced that peculiar hiatus the locals called 'the eye of the storm' when all suddenly calmed only for the battering and buffeting to start again with renewed vigour some hours later.

That was where they were now, he thought. But all would not be plain sailing from now on and he must work out how to navigate the shoals ahead as easily and safely as possible.

Chapter Seven

Harrogate, 7 August 1814

Miss Chloe Loring

My dearest Chloe,

I *am sure you are asking yourself how can I call you my dearest when I am about to leave you, perhaps forever. I know the Law—and Society—will consider my conscious decision to abandon my marriage unjustifiable. Very likely you will, too. I want to try and explain nonetheless and hope that when you are older, you might understand a little.*

It is hard to know where to start and I will not force on your notice or weary you with details of the twenty years I spent as your father's wife. Suffice it to say that not even for the dubious security provided by matrimony can I continue to remain subject to him, as much a bondwoman as any unfortunate in the colonies. When, unexpectedly, the doors to my cage were opened and a new world appeared, I chose freedom.

In placing my trust in Lord Stephen, I may be disappointed, but he will never be able to remind me, as Sir Edward did, that the law gives a husband more power over his wife than any gaoler has over his prisoners. If Lord Stephen and I remain together, it will be of our free will, because we have a kindness for each other and take pleasure in one another's company. My only regret is that the price I must pay for this new happiness is my continued separation from you.

But you should know that I cannot be sure that Sir Edward will permit me to see you again, even if I crawl to him and beg him on my knees. 'Chloe is no longer your concern', he told me coldly. His last words to me were that I may not write to you, but I have chosen to disregard this prohibition.

Chloe, please do not think too harshly of me. Remember me, especially when the time comes for you to choose a husband. Do not permit yourself to be hurried into marriage without doing your best to satisfy yourself that your husband will truly love, comfort, and honour you until the end of your life—that he will consider these vows as binding on him as they are on you. Sadly, in our world, only a wife pays a price for breaking them. Her husband's broken vows do not diminish in any way his power over her.

My darling girl, I beg your forgiveness for everything. Think kindly of your mother. Perhaps, one day, Heaven will grant that we meet again. Never doubt that I love you and always will.

Mamma

Delia folded the paper, addressed and sealed it, pressing her thumb into the hot wax. She touched her lips to it before putting it to one side and drawing a half sheet of paper to her.

Catherine Kullmann

Harrogate, 7 August 1814

To Sir E. Loring.

Sir,

Your carriage and coachman are returned to you herewith. Please be advised that, finding myself unable to comply with your further directions, I will, by the time you receive this, have left for the Continent.

I commit our daughter to you as a sacred charge whose wishes and well-being must always be placed above your own. May you be more faithful and considerate to her than you ever were to me.

Lady L.

She read the lines again. They would serve. She looked around her bed-chamber. The trunks were full; her carriage dress lay ready. It would only take Hughes ten minutes tomorrow morning to pack the last things into the valise. She had written an excellent character for the maid; it and a purse were tucked into the satchel that held her sketchbook, pencils, and paintbox. She now added the letters to her daughter and her husband, closed her writing box, and set it on top of the trunk.

Her mother, Hughes, and John Coachman took for granted that she was travelling to Suffolk. Stephen would meet them tomorrow. He knew just the spot to wait; he would wave down her carriage and have her belongings transferred to his. It would only take a few minutes, then they would be on their way.

Dear Stephen. She could hardly believe that he loved her. It seemed like a miracle. She had abandoned all hope of love so

84

many years ago when she realised she was nothing more than a convenience to her husband. And then to meet Stephen again. And he loved her! Dreamily, she got into bed. The last time she would sleep here. She could only be glad, she thought as she snuffed the candle.

What would their life together be like? Far removed from that of the wife of a country gentleman, she was sure. She would have to take her cues from him. But he was easy to talk to—she would not find it difficult to ask his advice or explain any hesitations or reservations she might have. He would be patient with her, and she would be patient with him. We are probably both quite set in our ways, she thought. We shall have to make room for each other in our inmost lives. It is good that we are going abroad—it will be a new experience for both of us. I will need a new maid. Thank goodness I kept up my French, speaking it one day a week when Madame Lebrun came. Even old Lady Loring joined us. But we never practised giving instructions to a lady's maid. Trying to work out the French for 'wavy, not curly', Delia fell asleep.

~~~

At last, the carriage slowed. Delia peered out of the window. He was there, as promised.

"I leave you here, Hughes," she said to the maid, who perched primly opposite her. "I am sorry to part with you, but I am going to the Continent and think you would not be comfortable there. Here you have what is owing to you at quarter day, and another quarter's wages on top of that as well as some money for John Coachman's and your expenses. One of these letters is your character and the other two are for Loring Place. You may continue there with John or, if you prefer, have him set you down where you please. In that case, give him the letters for Miss Chloe and Sir Edward."

Hughes stared at her, chalk-white. She took the letters and the purse of money, but it was some moments before she stammered, "May I not come with you, my lady?"

"Thank you, Hughes," Delia said gently, "but it is wiser not. I doubt that you would wish to leave England for a longer period. And you do not speak any other language, so you would find it difficult to manage in France and Italy. I have given you an excellent character, and I am sure you will have no trouble in finding another place."

The carriage door opened. "My lady."

She took Stephen's hand and stepped down. He waved two footmen forward. One took the satchel and writing box from Hughes and placed them in Stephen's carriage before going to assist the other in removing her other belongings.

"I leave you here, John," she said to the coachman, who looked on impassively. "Hughes has money to cover your expenses until you reach the Place."

"Very good, my lady."

She nodded to him and passed on to the other carriage. Once inside, she collapsed onto the seat, shaking. Stephen pressed her hand. "I'll just be a moment."

She watched as he spoke to the coachman and the postillion who would return the horses to the *Granby* at the end of the stage.

"Just two trunks and a valise?" he asked her when he returned.

"That's all."

"Excellent." He nodded to the footman, who closed the door and climbed up behind. As they drove away, Stephen leaned over and drew up the blinds on the windows. Then he took her in his arms, holding her comfortingly until the shaking ceased.

"Better?" he asked when she sat up.

She nodded before remembering that he probably could not see her in the dim light. "I'm sorry. I had not thought it would affect me so."

"My darling Delia, you are not made of stone. You need not apologise or think you must hide your feelings from me. From now on, we face everything together, good times and bad. This is the first step on our new road." He kissed her gently, waiting for her response before his lips and tongue demanded more. She froze for a moment, and then opened for him, welcoming him. At last, he raised his head. "And now I must confess that our plans have already changed."

Delia felt the blood drain from her face. Had she made another grievous error in judgement in trusting him? She had to moisten her lips before she could whisper, "How?"

"Last night, I told my aunt all. Although I tipped the postillion enough that he should not blab, there is always the risk that word gets out, creating a scandal here in Harrogate. It could reach her ears or your mother might seek her out, looking for her daughter. It is highly unlikely, but your husband might come here, too."

Delia gasped. "I never thought of that. It was good that you thought to warn her. Was she very disapproving?"

"On the contrary, she said that in the course of a long life, she had learnt not to judge and that if we both felt in our heart of hearts that this was the right thing to do, and were prepared to face any consequences, she would support us."

"In what way?"

"By coming with us; that is, as far as the world is concerned, you will accompany her and I shall escort you both. It will confuse the quizzes, she said."

"I should think it will; it confuses me. Having left home as a mistress *in spe*, am I now advanced or relegated to being a lady-in-waiting?"

"You are annoyed." Stephen seemed surprised.

"Yes," she replied crossly. "I thought the days of having others determine my life for me were over."

"Oh, Delia! I'm sorry. Perhaps I have not explained it very well. According to her, it would make it easier for you to take your place in English society again, should you wish to. You will not have burnt your boats completely. But if you really do not like it, we shall travel alone."

"I suppose you must return to Arkell House first."

"I'm afraid so. She would not be ready to leave until tomorrow, so my baggage is still there."

"Did you tell her the whole story, about Purdue as well?"

"No, I said you had been indiscreet, and your husband was being exceedingly stiff-rumped about it, banishing you here and not permitting you to see your daughter, but I did not go into any details."

"That is something, at least." She took a deep breath. "I hadn't thought I would have to face anyone today. And I've no maid. It's all very awkward. It's like when Edward told me we would be living with his parents."

"Not as bad as that, I hope. We'll take two carriages, for one. A travelling chariot is really only comfortable for two. I have no wish to spend a long journey sitting bodkin or with my back to the horses, and as a gentleman, I could do no less. And I think you will find my aunt very sensible of the awkwardness of your situation. She will make you welcome; I am sure of it. And should she not, we shall not remain with her, I promise you."

So it proved. Lady Mary threw her arms around Delia. "Welcome, my dear. Now, I am sure you are ready for some breakfast, for I imagine you were not able to choke down a thing earlier. Stephen will take you up while they make the tea and coffee, or do you prefer chocolate?"

Delia was about to murmur politely that she really didn't mind, when she stopped. "A cup of chocolate would be just the thing," she said frankly. "Thank you, ma'am."

Stephen led Delia up the broad oak stairs and down to the end of a wide corridor where he ushered her into an airy bedroom. "You are here. I am through there," he added, pointing at a second door. "The key is here, on your side. Another time, she said, she would give us a suite with our own sitting-room, but it was not worth moving my traps just for the one night."

"I suppose not."

"Tell me when you are ready to go down." He kissed her quickly and vanished into the next room.

A tap on the door heralded the arrival of a neat maid. "I'm Ruth, my lady," she said as she curtsied. "I'm to wait on you while you are here." She stood aside to let footmen carry in the first trunk. "What do you wish me to unpack?"

"Just the valise now." Delia took off her dark red velvet hat and let the matching Cossack mantle slip from her shoulders. "I need the spencer that matches this—there is a chill wind today."

A glance in the mirror satisfied her that her hair was still tidy, but it was not really dressed for company. "And there is a lace cap trimmed with carnations in the top tray of one of the trunks," she added.

There was no doubt that Hughes had had a knack for trimming hats and caps; she had created the pretty flowers from scraps of velvet and the leaves from green ribbon, placing the little nosegay coquettishly over the left ear—just enough to brighten the lace but not too elaborate for a morning cap. Delia was touched and surprised by the maid's request to accompany her, but it would not have done. She would need someone who knew how things were done in France. It was a pity she could not have warned Hughes in advance, but she could not risk word of her plans escaping.

"This one, my lady?"

"Yes." Delia carefully positioned the cap on her hair and tied the ribbons, then slipped her arms into the spencer. Time to take the first step into her new life. Leaving Ruth to her work, she went across the room and tapped gently on the connecting door to Stephen's room.

He opened it immediately. "All set? Let us go down."

Delia felt dazed. Going by their interconnecting rooms, she was apparently to be *maîtresse-en-titre,* with no pretence or other obfuscation. And yet, Lady Mary seemed to feel she could or should shroud this association in a veil of respectability. Unsure whether to be pleased or annoyed, Delia said very little until she had fortified herself with chocolate and fresh breakfast cakes. She dabbed her lips with her napkin and said, "Thank you for your hospitality, ma'am."

"My dear Lady Loring, it is nothing. I daresay you are wishing me to the devil, or at the least asking yourself why should I meddle in your and Stephen's affairs?"

Delia had to smile. "I should not put it so impolitely, I hope, but I cannot help wondering why you would support such scandalous behaviour."

Her ladyship's lips firmed. "I abhor bullies. I will be frank, Lady Loring. I could understand your husband's anger when he learnt of your indiscretion, even that he sent you away for a period of reflection. But I cannot abide this cat-and-mouse business, keeping you on tenterhooks without knowing if and when you may return home; he even rubs salt in the wound by requiring you to explain your need to prolong your stay with your mother. And to forbid any contact with your daughter is simply cruel, both to you and to her. I do not wish to pry," Lady Mary continued, "but I imagine your husband did not suddenly become petty and controlling."

"No." Delia blinked away tears. She had not known how much she needed to hear Edward's behaviour condemned so roundly. "Thank you for your understanding."

"I have seen the attachment grow between you and Stephen, and he has told me of your previous acquaintance. It is your choice to make your life together, but you should see if you can mitigate any adverse consequences. By travelling with me, you will avoid any initial scandal, as well as doing me a favour."

"In what way?"

"I do not know if my home in Nice, the *Villa Della Torre* still stands, but I must go there. Yours and Stephen's company would make the journey so much easier."

The older woman looked so desolate that Delia instinctively laid her hand on hers. "Of course we'll go with you."

Lady Mary's hand turned to grip Delia's. "We shall go via Paris where I shall pay my respects to the King. He was long enough in exile, poor man, not to mention all he and his family endured before. But it will not be the Paris I remember."

"We cannot turn the clock back," Stephen said. "But remember, Aunt, you will still have your home and your daughters and granddaughters here. It is not a question of one or the other. All that you have built here will remain."

"That is true." Lady Mary rose. "If we are to leave tomorrow, I have much to do today."

"Is there any way I can help?" Stephen asked.

"No, I thank you, but I must leave you to your own devices for now."

~~~

"Good night, Milord."

"Good night, Piero."

As the door closed behind the major-domo, Stephen eyed the other door that led to the adjoining room. Under his aunt's roof was not how he had anticipated beginning this new liaison. Delia was skittish, her initial responses always tentative, and he had relied on the enforced intimacy of a long carriage drive, followed by the closer quarters of the yacht and the novelty of being at sea, to engender a greater familiarity.

Would it be wiser not to go to her tonight, or would she view this as a rejection? Or, worse, would she see his visit as an obligation? *If you are like this*, he thought, *Heaven alone knows* what is going through her mind. She has burnt her boats; dismissed her maid and sent a letter to her husband with the coachman. Better to talk it out with her. He tightened the belt of his banyan and tapped on the door.

It opened immediately. She was ready for bed, her dark hair hanging in a mass of curls about her shoulders over a ruby red dressing-gown tied down the front in a succession of bows. White frills peeped out at the collar and wrists, and from beneath the hem.

She smiled when she saw him and stood back to let him enter. "I wasn't sure—"

"If I would come?" He held out his hand. "Drink a glass of Madeira with me while we talk about the day and other things."

She let him lead her to the chaise longue. He poured two glasses from the decanter that stood on the nearby table and peered dubiously at the brown liquid. "This doesn't look like Madeira."

She sniffed at her glass, then took a sip. "Orange wine. Many ladies prefer it, and pride themselves on their recipes."

"Good God! How is it made?"

"Seville and sweet oranges, lemons, sugar, and water are left to ferment. Afterwards, the liquor is refined with brandy and matured in casks for several months. This is very good. You should try it."

He tasted it gingerly. "I suppose if you don't think of it as wine, it's not too bad. Used you make it?"

"Mrs Walton, the housekeeper at Loring Place, made it every year. I believe old Lady Loring, the dowager, brought the recipe with her."

He set his glass down and put his arm around her. For a moment she stiffened, then rested against him. He brushed her hair back and kissed her forehead. "This is not where you expected to be tonight."

"No. At least, I expected to be with you, but not in your aunt's home. It is a little strange."

"Tomorrow night, we'll be on board the yacht. Are you a good sailor?"

"I have no idea. I don't get carriage-sick."

"That's good."

She had finished her wine, and he took her glass and put it on the table. "Delia, there is one thing I must say to you."

"What is that? You are very solemn."

"I long to take you to bed, but there must be no sense of obligation between us. This is not a marriage-bed, and you owe me no marital duty. Do you understand? There will be days when you are tired, or unwell, or perhaps we have been arguing. Then you can say, 'No, Stephen, not tonight', without fear of any repercussions. I will not be angry and I will never force you."

She turned in his arm to look up at him, then slowly reached up and drew his head down so that her lips met his. It was a soft, gentle kiss, and he returned it slowly, teasing her until she opened to him. He lifted her onto his lap, holding her against him as he felt her hand slide round to his nape. He tugged open the first bow of her dressing-gown and spread the collar wide, so that he could trace kisses down her neck to the top of her breast.

"Make me yours," she whispered.

He lifted her and carried her to the bed, then followed her down to take her fully in his arms.

"The candles."

He lifted his head. "Do you want them out?"

She drew a breath, then said, "No, leave them burning so I can see you."

Chapter Eight

Dearest Chloe,

*Y*esterday, *we made our bows and curtsies to the restored King of France at the Tuileries Palace. Lady Mary was particularly anxious to pay her respects to Louis XVIII as she knew him from the old French court and had visited him in Buckinghamshire. First, we had to be fitted out with the correct costume de présentation. Although he retains many of the older fashions—his hair, for example, is elaborately styled, powdered, and tied back in a queue, the King has not forced ladies back into their unwieldy panniers but has retained the style adopted by the Empress Josephine, where a train is fitted to a normal satin evening gown. Most ladies also wear feathers. Waists are very short here and petticoats are full. It is not a style that suits me, but when in Rome….*

The fashion is for white, as a compliment to the Duchesse d'Angoulème, *Queen Marie Antoinette's unfortunate daughter, who was held in solitary confinement during the Terror. Do you remember discussing her sad fate with Madame Lebrun? I never thought then that I would be presented to her in Paris, but Lady Mary and I have also called on her. Although she is happy at the ousting of Bonaparte, her return to Paris has also revived old, unhappy memories. They say she swooned when she first arrived at the Tuileries, the last place she had lived with her family before their attempt to flee France. However, she wore/wears white satin to Court, with lappets, and all follow suit, although it is not a colour that is flattering to older ladies, in my opinion.*

To return to the King; that day we were escorted by Lord Stephen. Having passed through the grand entrance of the Tuileries and up the staircase, we progressed through a series of ante-rooms. Lady Mary, as an English lady known to the King, was received first; Lord Stephen and I with her. We were led into an inner room where the King sat, surrounded by his attendants. He rose and welcomed her in English. Curtseying, she replied how happy she was to be able to greet His Majesty here. After she had presented Lord Stephen and me, she and the King chatted for some minutes. He cuts a strange figure, very corpulent and suffering badly from the gout so that when he goes abroad, he sometimes uses a wheeled chair. He wears a blue coat of the style he wore in England, Lady Mary tells me, but with the addition of epaulettes and a pale blue sash slanted across his body. Indeed, we were amused to learn that many of the returning nobility requested that they be awarded the appropriate military rank so that they could also wear epaulettes, as otherwise, they risked being mistaken for ushers of the chamber.

Opposite, you see my attempt to reproduce the scene. Here am I curtseying. I have done it from this aspect so that you can see the effect of the train. It is more elegant, you will agree, than the English hoops.

Delia put down her pen and carefully sanded the page. She enjoyed writing these little reminiscences for Chloe; they helped fix the wonders of Paris in her mind. The *Louvre* was still full of plundered works of art that Bonaparte had had conveyed here from all over Europe. No doubt France would not be allowed to retain this loot, but at present they could all be admired here. Stephen had managed to get permission to visit the *Louvre* outside its regular opening hours and several mornings had taken her there early so that she could wander through the great rooms admiring the antique statues and magnificent paintings that were exhibited in the galleries of the ancient palace. She did not try to copy the splendours of a Correggio, a Rembrandt, or a Dürer but took the time to absorb their genius, afterwards making notes of what had impressed her most.

With Lady Mary, she had explored the shops on the Boulevards, while Stephen had escorted them to the little shops beneath the arcades of the *Palais Royale*, explaining that ladies should not venture beyond these into that den of dissipation and vice. "I have heard of an officer spending all his leave here, saying that all his needs might be met under this roof."

Prices were very favourable compared with England but, apart from the court ensemble, Delia did not buy much. They would not remain long in Paris, and she did not know what she would need in the south. From what Lady Mary said, she led a much less formal life there. Her one indulgence had been a supply of canvases, paints, brushes, and other supplies from *Belot* in the *Rue de l'Arbre Sec*. They had passed this premises coming from the *Louvre* and Stephen had waited patiently while she consulted the colour merchant. He had only intervened when she started looking at easels, and then just to ask if it would be possible for bulkier items to be sent to Nice at a later date, so as not to arrive before them. On being assured this could be arranged, he had accepted the offer of a chair and watched attentively as she made her choice.

If she had not loved him before, she would have loved him then. She was constantly amazed by his desire to be with her, by his interest in her activities and pursuits. There was nothing controlling in this; on the contrary, he encouraged her to spread her wings, asking only to fly with her. She had never known such harmony with another person, not even with her father, for with Stephen there was the added spice of gratified desire. She could not write about this in Chloe's book, of course. Almost as if he had sensed her thoughts, the door opened, and he came in.

"Are you finished? May I see?"

Smiling, she turned the book.

"You have a gift for capturing a likeness," he said after a couple of minutes. "That's the King and his attendants to the life. And my aunt, too. When we are established in the south, you must paint a portrait of her."

"I shall have to practise with oils first. I haven't used them since I left Brighton and my father's studio."

He put his arm around her. "We must see that you have a studio at the Villa where you can leave everything undisturbed."

"That would be wonderful! Somewhere with north light, Stephen."

"North light? Why?"

"There is no direct sun, so the light is more constant—it's better for your colours."

"North light it shall be, then."

She turned and put her arms around his neck. To give and receive affection openly was still deliciously new. Of all the changes she had experienced since leaving Harrogate, it was the most surprising, and the one that had taken most getting used to. Stephen had been understanding of her initial shyness and was attuned to her reactions and responses. It had been like dancing the minuet, that intense focus on your partner, eyes meeting and hands touching, with delicious delays and secret smiles, while all the time, the underlying rhythm of the music bound them together even when separated by the dance.

She had met the challenges posed by the voyage to Calais, the debarkation in France, the journey to Paris, and the rigours of French inns with a combination of interest and equanimity, but she was still wary of the happiness she had found with Stephen. Sometimes she woke in the night and gently rested her hand on the warm back beside her, feeling how it rose and fell, unable to believe that he was there. Now she returned his kisses eagerly. This, too, was new; to be an active participant rather than the passive recipient of her husband's attentions.

His embrace tightened. "Come." Before she knew it, he was sprawled on the day-bed, opening the fall of his pantaloons.

"The maid," she protested when he wanted to draw her to him. "She will be in soon."

"Then you had best lock the door and come here quickly."

Enticed by the wicked glint in his eye, she hurried to comply. This was no stately minuet but a fast and furious bolero that left them gasping for breath and smiling.

Delia had always enjoyed Lady Mary's company, but a deeper friendship had developed between the two women in recent weeks, the older woman treating the younger as a niece. She had slipped into calling her Delia, as Stephen did, and the servants, led by Piero who tended to ignore the niceties of English etiquette, referred to the two ladies as la Lady Mary and la Lady Delia.

Delia was entranced by the location of the apartment Lady Mary had taken, the whole first floor of one of the former great houses—or *hôtels* as they were called here—on the *Île Saint-Louis*, an island in the middle of the Seine. It was not very large, roughly 600 by 250 yards, and she loved to stroll along the quays and little streets, dashing off impressions from every angle and perspective—the tall houses huddled together; the river flowing beneath their windows, the inner streets made more narrow by the buildings rising on either side and, best of all, the view of *Notre Dame,* looking across to the *Île de la Cité* from the end of the island. It was like being on the prow of a boat, she told Stephen, with the wind tugging at your bonnet. Back at her window, she tried to capture the ever-changing light and colours with her brush.

And outside was Paris itself, with the older palaces and beautifully laid out gardens all within walking distance, while a short drive took them to Versailles and Saint-Cloud, where one might view the deposed Emperor's apartments as well as Marie Antoinette's *Trianon.*

"It's no different to going to Hampton Court, I suppose," Lady Mary remarked, "just the…the history is much more recent."

"At times, one feels like an intruder," Delia agreed.

The sojourn in Paris had not been easy for Lady Mary. The return of the King had seen an influx of royalists to Paris and while she had rejoiced to find several old friends among them, she had also been saddened by news of the fate of many others during the Terror. "Even if it all happened many years ago, I only learnt about it today," she said one evening to Stephen and Delia. "I am so glad that you are with me—I do not think I could have borne it by myself."

They moved chiefly in French circles, although some English visitors were also to be met there. Delia found she was accepted without question and, to her great relief, had not encountered anyone she knew.

~~~

"Is London like this?" Delia asked one evening as they returned from a performance of *La Jerusaleme Délivrée* at the *Opéra*.

"Like what?" Stephen asked idly.

"Exciting. Paris is like a firework—it seems to fizz and sparkle. The days are too short—there is so much to do and see. Everything is just that bit more. I have never seen an opera, but here I could sit forever listening to the singers or watching the ballet—the unity, the precision, the grace—and they have so many scene changes, and all managed so adeptly, that all doubt is suspended and you believe what you are seeing—the entry of Godfroy into Jerusalem, for example, and the illuminated heavens."

"The opera here is far superior to London," Stephen said. "The performers take pride in their work, not only the serious operas like we saw tonight, but also the lighter ones at the *Opéra Comique*. And the audience does so too—there is none of the ill-mannered behaviour one sees in London where, for many, what happens on the stage is merely the backdrop to the more important matter of seeing and being seen."

"I find London boring compared with Paris," Lady Mary agreed. "Perhaps it is the people—the English are so insular, convinced of their superiority. To hear them talk, they defeated Bonaparte single-handed—they ignore the Russians and the Prussians, although it was their taking Paris that caused him to abdicate. I do not want to detract from Wellington's victories in the Peninsula, but that was only one front. There are also all those who gave their lives fighting Bonaparte all along the way, but they are forgotten now."

Delia rested her hand on Lady Mary's. "Their sacrifice was not in vain," she said quietly.

"I hope not, my dear."

Interlude—Sir Edward Loring at Home

16 September 1814

Dear Ned,

I see from The Morning Chronicle *that your lady is disporting herself in Paris, though why she feels it necessary to be presented at Louis's court, I do not know. But that is the ladies for you, I suppose. You are a wise man, to have encouraged her to travel with Lady Mary Arkell, and so avoid the necessity of going yourself.*

If you tire of the bachelor life, do come and stay with me. Bring your guns and dogs—the partridge are plentiful this year.

Yours, etc.
Jethro

Sir Edward Loring tossed the letter from his oldest friend onto his desk and looked at the stack of unopened newspapers on the library table. He was not long returned from Swanmere Castle, where he had attended the wedding of his son and heir, and taken his leave of his daughter, who would in future live with her brother. Shrugging, he leafed through the pile until he found *The Morning Chronicle* of the sixteenth.

Report from Paris: Among recent visitors to the French capital we met Lady Mary Arkell, Contessa Della Torre, *accompanied by Lady Loring and escorted by her nephew, Lord Stephen FitzCharles, who have broken their journey in Paris to pay their respects to the restored monarch at the* Tuileries. *Lady Mary is the widow of that gallant* Piemontese *who, together with their only son, gave his life fighting the Corsican Monster. Now that the Monster has been defeated, her ladyship proposes to spend the winter at her marital home in the County of Nice.*

What the devil? How dare Delia flaunt her absence to the world? And damn Jethro's impertinence, assuming that Edward had condoned and permitted this jaunt. He had done nothing of the kind. Still, he thought as he poured himself a glass of brandy, better to have their acquaintances believe that than make it known that his wife had fled there with her latest lover. But she would not get away with it. There must be something he could do, some way he could make her pay.

Chapter Nine

Delia was shocked to read the little article in *The Morning Chronicle*. She had not expected her presence in Paris to be so remarked upon. She handed Stephen the newssheet, open at the offending paragraph. "That is unfortunate, don't you agree?"

He shook his head. "On the contrary, it is all part of my aunt's grand plan."

"In what way?"

"It makes your being here quite normal, unscandalous, if that is a word. Nothing anyone could raise an eyebrow over." He came and kissed her. "And what we do in the privacy of our own four walls is nobody's business but our own. Now, what would you like to do today?"

When she eyed him cautiously, he laughed and said, "Out with it!"

"I should like to go to *Ste. Geneviève*."

"The church the revolutionaries made into their *Panthéon*, and Bonaparte had reconsecrated, which is rather odd when you come to think of it? We shall if you like, but why do you find it so interesting?"

"Not the building itself, but I am told there is a marvellous prospect of the whole city and surroundings from the outside of the cupola. I should like to make some sketches."

"Of course." By now, he was used to her passion for sketching. "Let us go now, before it gets too hot. And I have a box at the *Opéra Comique* for this evening."

"Wonderful!" She gave him a quick kiss. "I must change into a walking dress and collect my things. I won't be long."

Piero was tidying the bedroom when Stephen came in. "Milord. May I have a word?"

Stephen toed off his slippers and sat to pull on his boots. "What is it?"

"Do you remember my brother, Gianluca?"

"About twelve when we left? A bright lad?"

"Yes."

"What about him?"

"I ran into him yesterday." Piero took a soft cloth and rubbed the finger marks from Stephen's boots. "There is a tavern, *Le Tarasque,* where men from the south meet. It is not *Niçoise* but still a little like home. He was sitting in a corner with a glass of wine, smoking his pipe. I didn't recognise him—grey-haired, thin, his face drawn and a scar down one cheek. But he knew me—he said it was because I resemble our father.

"'*Piero, c'est toi?*' he said, as if he couldn't believe his eyes. And then, when I just stared at him, '*C'est moi, Gianluca.*'

"'Gianluca? My brother? Impossible,' I said, but then he pushed his tobacco pouch across the table. 'Perhaps you'll recognise this. Our grandfather gave it to me the day I was marched away, so that I would not forget home.' It is a singular piece, made out of leather and decorated with a fringe and coloured beads. *Grandpère* was very proud of it—he bought it from a sailor who had it from an indigenous American. It was very faded now and worn very soft, but I knew it still.

"I was shaking. 'Brother,' I said, and then he came into my embrace. It was...." Piero shook his head. "I cannot describe it. We talked for hours. He had been conscripted into the usurper's army, in the *levée en masse* of '97. He fought everywhere, even into Russia—he was a sergeant by then. He finally made it back last year. He's lame; it doesn't hinder him much, but he can no longer march for hours at a time, and he was invalided out. When he heard we were going home next week, he asked if there might be a seat for him on the box or up behind. He offered to work in exchange—help with the horses, the baggage, keep an eye out for brigands and marauders, do whatever is needed. I said I could not promise anything, but would ask you."

He looked pleadingly at Stephen. "The *diligence* is so expensive and, with his injury, it would take him many months to walk to Nice, if he was not taken up for vagrancy along the way. I don't know if my mother still lives, but I do not think I could face her, Milord, and say I had left him behind."

"No," Stephen agreed. "Bring him to see me tomorrow, about this time, and we'll see what can be done. I'm going out now with Lady Delia."

The interior of *Ste Geneviève* was imposing, Delia supposed, as she looked at the rows of columns and the succession of vaulted ceilings that led to the magnificent space under the cupola, but she could not like it as a church. It was too bombastic, too loud— every sound from the tap of Stephen's boot heels to the murmurings of the priest officiating at the far altar, reverberated, creating a constant susurration that rose and fell, almost as if the building was a living being. There was nowhere that offered escape or invited to prayer or quiet contemplation. She and Stephen waited near the entrance until the priest had turned to face his small congregation and raised his hand in a blessing, then preceded by his acolytes, left the altar.

"I wonder how one gets to the cupola," Delia said.

An elderly gentleman who had attended the service stopped at her words. "May I be of assistance, Madame?" His English was fluent but accented.

"Is it possible to go up to the outside of the cupola?" Stephen said. "Madame wishes to sketch the panorama from above."

"Possible certainly, but the ascent is arduous. There are more than two hundred steps."

Stephen cocked an eyebrow at Delia. "It is your decision."

"I should like to try," she said.

"Ah, the English ladies are indefatigable," the gentleman said. "If you permit, I shall escort you."

Indefatigable indeed, Stephen thought as they wound their way up the dusty stone steps, climbing ever higher. Ahead of him, Delia did not falter. She had donned comfortable half-boots and shorter skirts for this outing, so that the ascent was enlivened by glimpses of her ankles beneath the rhythmically swaying fabric. Her neat, English bonnet, completely out of fashion here where tall, high crowned confections were all the rage, was also perfectly suited to the narrow space. At last, they reached the top step and emerged onto the exterior colonnade that surrounded the massive dome.

Beyond the rooftops, the silver Seine could be glimpsed as it flowed tranquilly around the two islands of the medieval city and on past the *Louvre* and the garden of the *Tuileries*. Opposite stood the majestic, spire-crowned cathedral of *Notre Dame*. Beyond were the wooded hills of *Montmartre* while, on the left, more spires pierced the sky.

Delia slowly paced out the great circle, stopping every few feet to take in another view. "I don't think I have ever been so high. Isn't it magnificent? Everything looks completely different."

Stephen had become accustomed to the way she worked, making many rapid drawings as well as notes on colour and light. As soon as possible, she would begin a larger work, combining the different aspects. Her memory for detail was superb, although sometimes she would appeal to him for assistance in determining an exact shade or nuance. He wondered what she might have achieved if her father had not died so prematurely. Would she have continued to work alongside him? There were some women artists, he knew, not least Angelica Kauffman, in the previous century.

"While *madame* is occupied, perhaps you might like to hear of the Battle of Paris, sir? It is easy to explain the dispositions from up here."

Strange to think that less than six months ago, the Allied armies had converged on the city now spread so peacefully below them, Stephen thought, as he heard how 'the Russians came from there, and the Prussians, there, *Monsieur*'. But *all they that take the sword shall perish with the sword*, and Paris could count herself lucky that Tsar Alexander, whose own city of Moscow had burned as Napoleon's troops entered it, had desisted from firing the city. He refrained from saying this to their helpful guide. Paris was at once a city defeated and a city liberated. While the royalists celebrated the restoration, not everyone in the city was of the same mind and, especially when one excluded the old nobility, there were many who regretted the loss of their Emperor.

Stephen said as much to Delia as they walked back to the apartment.

"Yes, there are undercurrents everywhere. While some welcome *les Anglais*, others see us as invaders, conquerors. I wonder was it a good idea to make Wellington ambassador here. And, of course, he had to acquire the palace occupied by Napoleon's sister, Pauline. Was that not adding insult to injury?"

"I suppose it was; although he did buy it—it was not requisitioned."

"That is true. Your aunt seems ready to leave."

"Yes. It was important to her to go to Court; seeing the Bourbons restored was a good omen for her. I hope she does not find her own home destroyed or vandalised."

"Or occupied by strangers. Has that occurred to her, do you think?"

"I don't know. We debated whether to send ahead, advising of her return, but it is difficult when we do not know who has survived or who remains loyal. England has been cut off from the Continent for so long."

"I love this theatre," Delia said as they took their seats in the *Opéra Comique* that evening, "it is so pretty, and how clever that carriages can enter below, especially on a wet night like tonight. It is a pity architects do not think of these things more often. What are we to see?"

"Three one-act operas, starting with *Le Caliph de Baghdad*," Stephen said. "I understand they are most entertaining."

Delia had to laugh at the story of the disguised potentate who won his lady's heart, only to be rejected as too shabby by her mother. As always, the quality of the singing was excellent, and she applauded vigorously at the end.

"I enjoyed that," she said, idly watching the general coming and goings as calls were made and latecomers admitted. Below, in the parterre, a group of men and lightly clad women were taking their seats. A black-haired man threw back his head and laughed. He looked familiar, but she had made so many new acquaintances in recent weeks that she could not place him. The orchestra struck up again, and she turned her attention to the stage. But something nagged at her, and in the next interval, she glanced down just as he scrutinised the tiers of boxes. Their eyes met. Her stomach clenched as she saw recognition dawn on Purdue's face. At once, she turned her head, refusing to acknowledge him. For the rest of the performance, she kept her gaze focussed on the stage, but if one of her companions had asked her to describe the plot of the last piece, she would have been found sadly wanting.

She might have expected it, Delia told herself. He had sold the house he had inherited in Suffolk; sold it to her husband, in fact, constrained to do so by the deed that had split the original estate. Had her husband not said something about Purdue planning to go abroad? She had been too upset that night to remember much of it. When she thought she might encounter some old acquaintances in Paris, she had never thought of gentlemen—it had always been ladies she imagined; some of those who attended the house party in May, for example. Was that only four months ago? It seemed an age, and another life away.

~~~

Gianluca presented himself the next morning, the shabby remnants of his uniform made as tidy as possible. Agreement was quickly reached. Learning that they planned to depart at the end of the month, he immediately took over the preparations for the journey.

"We cannot be sure that we will find everything as it should be along the way," he said. "Over ten years of war has left much destroyed. We must be prepared to cater for ourselves if necessary. Each carriage should have a basket equipped with glasses, plates, cutlery, and space for food that can be replenished every morning. We should also take foods that will not spoil easily: sausage, ham, and cheese. And wine, of course. Bread can usually be purchased. Two carriages with four horses each? That must also be arranged. Leave it with me, Milord."

~~~

"A gentleman to see you, Milady."

Delia lifted the card from the silver salver and dropped it as quickly. "I am not at home."

Stephen was alarmed by her sudden pallor and brittle tone. "Delia, what's wrong?"

She said nothing, just gestured towards the salver in Piero's hand.

"May I?" At her nod, he took the little card. "Purdue. What brings him here?"

"I don't know. I cut him at the Opéra last night."

"Last night? You said nothing."

"It wasn't worth mentioning. He was in the pit, looking up at the boxes, that was all. He found me through that dratted

113

paragraph in *The Morning Chronicle,* I suppose. It would be easy enough to find where Lady Mary was staying. It is the height of impertinence, to call here."

"It is indeed. It might be better to see him and be rid of him. Will you allow me to do so?"

She looked at him gratefully. "Would you, Stephen?"

"Of course. Show him into the book-room, Piero."

When Stephen went into the little room overlooking the inner courtyard of the house, he found a lean man of about his own age idly inspecting the titles of the books that lined the walls.

"Mr Purdue?"

"I am he. You have the advantage of me, sir."

"Lord Stephen FitzCharles."

Purdue bowed. "My lord." When Stephen showed no inclination to break the silence, he said, "I wished to enquire after Lady Loring. My uncle was a neighbour of hers in England; in fact, I sold the place to Sir Edward Loring after my uncle's death. I thought it would be a neighbourly thing to call on her here."

"Did you indeed?" Clearly the man never suspected that Delia had told him the whole story.

"In case there was any little service I might render her."

"There is none."

Purdue bowed again. "Then, my lord, I shall take my leave. Pray assure her ladyship of my good wishes."

Stephen looked at him closely. "I shall, sir. Will you take a glass of wine before you go?"

Purdue looked quite surprised at this olive branch, but gracefully accepted it and made polite conversation for fifteen minutes before leaving.

"And that was that. I thought it better to be civil," Stephen said to Delia. "There was no point in putting his back up. He meant it too, with his good wishes. You need not fear anything from him."

"Thank you for dealing with him. I'm glad we are leaving at the end of the month. I should hate to encounter him somewhere I could not ignore him."

"I do not think you need worry. From what he said, he spends most of his time in the *Palais Royale,* and was talking of going on to Italy. Naples, perhaps."

Some days later, the cavalcade set off for the south. Delia was not used to travelling in such style. Piero's brother Gianluca was a watchful guard on Lady Mary's box, a service that Piero did for Stephen. Weather and other circumstances, such as the availability of sufficient fresh horses at each station, permitting, they would reach the south coast in two to three weeks. A relay of couriers rode ahead to arrange for these changes, and to bespeak bed-chambers and dinners for each night. This had been Gianluca's suggestion, and he had recruited the three former cavalrymen who were more than happy to avail themselves of this opportunity to return home at Lord Stephen's expense.

"I'm surprised he didn't suggest a fife and drum to lead us," Stephen remarked.

"Or a running footman to go ahead and clear the road," Delia said. "Does anyone still do that?"

"Not since old Queensbury died, I think."

"You have to admit Gianluca did very well, down to arranging for their livery. Besides, with him in charge, no innkeeper would dare cheat us."

Interlude—Sir Edward Loring at Boyce Grange, Lincolnshire

Sir Edward Loring refilled his glass with his host's excellent port and passed the decanter to his left. They were a small group; the only other guest was Sir Jethro's cousin, the Venerable Archdeacon Barnaby Boyce. They had enjoyed a rewarding day with the guns and, after a good dinner, had reached that stage of imbibing when even the most tight-lipped of men may find himself spilling his inmost secrets. So it was with Sir Edward and before long he had told the story of his erring wife who, instead of remaining penitently in Harrogate as he had instructed, had departed for the flesh-pots of Paris where she was most likely living in sin with a duke's son.

"And the damnable thing is that, apparently, I can have no resource to the courts," he finished. "I do not have sufficient proof of infidelity, I am informed."

"Very likely not," said the archdeacon who had tut-tutted through Sir Edward's recital, "but you can put a stop to her gallop by suing for restitution of conjugal rights, in other words by demanding she return under your roof. If she refuses—why, under last year's Act, she can be imprisoned for six months."

Sir Edward shifted in his chair. "To be frank, I am not keen to wash my dirty linen in public. It would drag my daughter and daughter-in-law into it."

"Perfectly understandable," Sir Jethro said. "But would you have to? A letter requiring her to come home, and advising her of the consequences if she does not comply, should be enough to bring her to heel."

"How old is your lady?" the archdeacon asked. "Forty? Fifty? I take it she is no longer breeding?"

"Yes, no. I had bad luck there too—only one child, a girl, by her."

"Hysteria," the other man said firmly. "It gets worse when women reach a certain age. You would be surprised at the cases that come before the Ecclesiastical Courts. Some of them have to be confined for their own good. You should retrieve your lady before matters get completely out of hand. If she is staying with this Lady Mary, it should be quite easy to find her."

"I am not about to traipse to France at my time of life or attempt the journey home with a recalcitrant wife in tow!"

The archdeacon watched sadly as the last drops from the decanter dripped into his glass. "Supposing," he said to Sir Edward while his cousin rang for another, "there was an agent whom you could charge with fetching her and returning her to you; would you do so?"

"What do you mean?"

"My wife's nephew and his wife are at present in Paris. My wife has a fondness for him—he's the youngest son of her dead sister. A bit of a scapegrace, if I am to be honest, but he has a certain native ingenuity and mother-wit. I am sure he would undertake this commission for you. And as his wife is with him, there would be nothing improper about your lady travelling with them."

"How would he do it?"

"I would leave that to him—he is quite resourceful and good at getting his own way. He has never had any difficulty in charming the ladies. If you furnish him with a letter for your wife, and another one authorising him to act on your behalf, and the necessary funds, of course, that should suffice."

"It's worth trying, Ned," Sir Jethro said. "What have you to lose? And once you have her safe at home, keep her there. Your mistake was in letting her leave the house in the first place—you had no control over her then."

Kept awake by a surfeit of roast cheese that Sir Jethro had ordered up to 'close the stomach' before they retired, Sir Edward considered what to do about his wife. He had erred in leaving her in Harrogate for the winter, he concluded. Jethro had the right of it—better to have her under his roof. Thanks to Jethro's invitation, he had been spared the assemblies and other festivities of Bury Fair Week where he could have been expected to be the recipient of many comments about his wife's doings in France and enquiries as to her connection to Lady Mary Arkell. But he would not always be able to avoid such questions. Far better to be able to say he expected her return by Christmas. If she were properly repentant, he could even allow Chloe to return and summons his mother as well, so that the house would not be so damn empty.

He would make sure Delia was no longer able to come and go as she pleased by engaging a companion for her, one who knew which side her bread was buttered, and would apprise him of any suspicious behaviour on the part of his wife. He smiled grimly to himself. Some dragon like that finishing governess would do nicely. He would explain that his wife had not been well and must not be allowed to over-tax herself. And if she resisted, he would summon the doctor to treat her hysteria and keep her quiet.

Chapter Ten

They had been travelling for more than a week now; the landscape glimpsed through the carriage windows constantly changing in a living Book of Hours. Delia cherished little vignettes—a castle on a steep hill above a river, a small square occupied by a bustling market, an unmown meadow veiled in dew-spangled gossamer and sparkling in the early morning sun. The constant medley of sounds—hooves and wheels, the cries of postillions and shouts of ostlers—was punctuated by the blare of post and coach horns, a barking dog, or the squawks and cackles of an escaped flock of hens as they were pursued by an apron-flapping housewife.

Forests gave way to fields, fields yielded to rows of vines where peasants, men and women, stooped to cut the clusters of ripe grapes, filling baskets that in turn were emptied into huge vats on ox-drawn carts. Sometimes when the travellers wished to stretch their legs at a *Relais de Poste*, strolling away from the inn yard with its overwhelming reek of all things equine, they could smell the sweet, heavy scent of macerating grapes.

It was all so foreign, so different, so exhilarating.

From the day they arrived in France, Lady Mary had encouraged her party to eat as the French did, a light breakfast, dinner shortly after midday and a not so heavy supper in the evening. "It makes me angry when I see fat Englishmen demanding their steaks and roasts, and turning up their noses at anything unknown. And then they complain that their food is ill-prepared, but it is partly their own fault for insisting on everything being done their way. Or they suffer from indigestion or other stomach complaints. The diet that is suitable to England's cold, damp climate, is not appropriate for the south of France or Italy."

One experience of such a John Bull and his family at the communal dining table in an inn on the way to Paris had convinced Delia of the merits of this advice. Thanks to the advance notice provided by their couriers, landlords on their journey south had been happy to provide a separate table for their group of twelve rather than have them struggle to find places at the *table d'hôte.*

That first day, Delia had been interested to see the party sort itself without much ado. Lady Mary and Stephen sat opposite each other in the centre of the table. She sat on Stephen's right, her maid on her other side, while Piero took his left. Lady Mary was flanked by her maid and Gianluca, with the coachmen and three cavalrymen taking the remaining places. Delia enjoyed the convivial atmosphere of these communal meals, where their attendants neither lacked the respect due to their employers nor demonstrated an unworthy obsequiousness.

"I can't imagine a similar group of diners in England," she had said afterwards to Stephen. "I don't know who would have been more shocked by the idea, my husband or my maid. This harks back to feudal times, doesn't it, the household eating together?"

"I suppose it does. They will serve you in a private apartment if you insist, but you pay through the nose for the privilege, with long delays and an indifferent meal into the bargain. This is much better."

Today, Delia could no longer ignore the malaise that gripped her. Her head ached, there was a dull pain at the pit of her stomach, and the thought of food nauseated her. Pulling the brim of her bonnet lower to shade her eyes, she lay back against the squabs and tried to rest. She was on her own, thank heaven. This stretch of the highway ran parallel to the mighty Rhone River and Stephen, as was his custom in clement weather, had hired a riding horse for the last stage before they stopped to dine. Other days she had envied him this freedom, had even toyed with the idea of learning to ride, but not today. At the sound of hooves at the side of the carriage, she sat up. "Stephen?"

He came at once to the window. "What is wrong? Are you unwell?"

"Yes. A dreadful headache." She pressed her handkerchief to her lips.

Stephen turned away, calling, "Gianluca!"

She lay back, letting the sound of voices outside wash over her. Then he was there again.

"Can you hold on until the next village—about three miles? Gianluca will ride ahead and enquire about the best place for you to recover. I would prefer to avoid the *Relais de Poste* if possible. There will be no rest there, with all the comings and goings."

That was true. The idea of a night's peaceful rest was most enticing. Whether it was due to the jolting and swaying of more than a se'ennight on the road, or her recent, frequent indulgence in the pleasures of intimacy, Delia did not know, but a dragging sensation at the pit of her stomach warned her that her monthly courses might be heavier than usual, so much so that it would be impossible to manage while travelling.

"Stephen, see if he can find somewhere for a couple of nights; I don't think I shall be able to continue tomorrow."

Gianluca had been directed to this quiet house owned by a widow who was willing to let them have three bedrooms as well as a private salon, and accommodation for the ladies' maids and milord's factotum. The carriages, coachmen, and couriers must stay at the *Relais de Poste*, she added.

Soon Delia found herself reclining on a day-bed in the salon, sipping a cup of her hostess's *tisane de tilleul,* 'made from my own tree, Milady; later I shall send up another tisane, especially for *les problèmes menstruels.* It is my grandmother's recipe—very good.'

The salon was cool and airy. Tall windows stood wide; their openings shaded by louvred shutters that protected from the glare of the sun while permitting air to circulate. Gauzy curtains billowed lightly. Unlike at home in England, the shutters were fixed to the outside wall, Delia noticed. Here, evidently, it was more important to protect against the heat than the cold. It was so good not to be moving, she thought drowsily.

"Delia?"

She opened her eyes at Stephen's murmur.

"Your room is ready. Shall I help you upstairs?"

"Please. I'm so sorry…"

"There is no need to be sorry. I think we shall all be glad of a respite."

"I shall certainly be glad of a day in bed, but it will be very boring for you."

"I'll be able to occupy myself, don't worry. Here you are."

He stood back to let her enter another airy chamber where her maid waited beside a crisply made-up bed, her mistress's nightgown spread out, ready for her. Fresh towels hung on a rack beside the wash-stand and her toiletries had been set out on the dressing-table. A pretty arrangement of lavender and roses added a light, refreshing scent to the pleasant space.

"I'll look in later, see how you go on," he said. "Rest now, my dear."

~~~

Stephen felt a huge surge of relief the following evening when Delia entered the salon wrapped in a loose gown of rich, dark, pink cotton scattered with golden daisies. A pretty lace cap tied with matching pink ribbon and decorated with a little bunch of pink and gold flowers covered her hair. She had lost the pallor that had frightened him yesterday, and the dark circles under her eyes had vanished.

He came over to kiss her gently. "I am glad to see you look so much better, my love."

"I feel so well that I thought I would come down for a little while at least. You will excuse my morning gown, I know. I didn't feel like getting fully dressed."

"No, of course not." He lifted a decanter invitingly. "Will you take a glass of the local wine? They grow different grapes here than in Bordeaux or Burgundy, but very good."

"Why not?" She settled against the cushions of the day-bed, tucking her feet under her. "What you have been doing, apart from tasting wine, that is?"

"Exploring the village and the countryside, both of which are full of Roman and medieval remains. I must be grateful to you for forcing us to stop. It is a pity to rush through the way we have done."

"I think your aunt is anxious to reach her destination. Perhaps next year we could come back for a couple of weeks, especially if Madame Clément would be willing to let us stay again."

"An excellent suggestion." He handed her a glass of dark red wine. "See what you think of this."

"Mmm." She inhaled the rich aroma. "It's quite heady, isn't it?"

"Too heady?"

"I won't know until I have tried it. It will be a change from Madame Clément's tisanes, although they are—splendiferous."

Stephen smiled at the word even as he wondered what exactly was in Madame's brews. The important thing was that they had worked, he supposed, as he took the chair opposite Delia and stretched out his legs. This was so domestic, he thought, just sitting quietly together. He liked that she had not felt it necessary to change into afternoon dress. He had changed out of his riding clothes when he came in, so as not to bring the reek of the stables into the salon—he would stay as he was, he decided. His trousers, comfortable coat, and simple neckcloth would do very well. No need to put on a high, starched collar and elaborate cravat.

Her comment about staying longer another time pleased him. It was two months since she had come to him. Little by little, she was emerging from her shell; she was more carefree, quicker to laugh, or, unbidden, make a suggestion or express her opinion. She had been responsive in bed from the beginning, but at first with a sort of surprised hesitancy as if unsure what was permitted.

Now she smiled at him over the rim of the glass. "I must thank you for looking after me so well. Gentlemen generally do not want to be bothered by women's megrims."

He shook his head. "Not women in general, perhaps, but I must be concerned about the women I care about. But we men are very ignorant of the female mysteries."

"That is true. We are taught never to mention them to our fathers and our brothers. And to husbands, they are either an inconvenience or a sign of failure."

She did not often refer to her marriage, and he would prefer to forget it altogether. Almost as if he had guessed his thoughts, she said, "What we are now, beloved companions, is the best of all. To be with someone, not because you were born into the same family or tied together in matrimony—the connection can grow freely, unrestricted by the expectations of society and all the rules that are dinned into us even before we can repeat them." She raised her glass to the light. "Isn't this a beautiful colour?" she asked dreamily. "It matches my gown. Stephen, I am so glad we can never marry; it is perfect as we are."

It was a splash of cold water in his face. He would ask nothing better than to marry her; his sole regret was that it was not possible. In the depths of the night, when she slept peacefully by his side, he wondered if it were worth testing the waters to see if her husband would divorce her. But sometimes the church forbade the 'guilty' party to remarry, or at least not her partner in infidelity. And could he expect her to go through such an ordeal just to satisfy his wishes? Well, he had his answer. Very likely she would turn him down. 'Can't we go on as we are?' she would say.

She began to sing a jaunty tune, at first under her breath, but soon he could make out the words: "'For Jenny had vowed away to run with Jockey to the fair'." Her glass tilted as she repeated the line and, laughing, he went to take it from her.

"I don't think wine and Madame's brews go well together."

She did not protest, just slanted a look at him as she continued singing.

"Peace! I will stop your mouth." He kissed her lingeringly, tasting again the rich wine. "I like to see you happy, even a little tipsy."

"Only with you." She reached up to stroke his cheek. "Only with you."

Stephen tapped on Delia's bedroom door the next morning. "Delia?"

"Come in, Stephen. I'm over here, at the window."

"I came to see if you would like to go for a stroll, but I see you are occupied."

"I thought to take advantage of our free day here to catch up with my painting. The morning light is good and the paints will have a day to dry. If you can give me half an hour, I would love to accompany you."

He came over to see what she was working on. He had learned to see the world with different eyes through her sketches and drawings; fascinated how sometimes she would select a small detail rather than the larger aspect before her. She had a gift for capturing a likeness that, while not caricature, conveyed the essence of her subject in the way a formal portrait could not.

Now he admired a vivid depiction of their three cavalrymen, about to depart, greatcoats rolled and fixed on top of their knapsacks, and a haversack slung over the right shoulder. Alert, proud, despite the shabby remnants of their uniforms, they clearly enjoyed this non-military excursion. One had already mounted and held the reins of two other horses while his comrades hurried from the inn where their party had spent the night. The first brushed his moustaches into place with his forefinger while the other had turned back to salute the pretty maid who stood in the doorway.

"That is really excellent. I can hear the stamp of hooves and imagine what the maid has just said."

"Would you like me to do another for you once I have more time?"

He hesitated. "If I am to be honest, then I would like that one. I love the immediacy of it."

She looked up at him. "You have a very good eye, Stephen. Have you never drawn or painted yourself?"

"No," he answered, regretfully. "Boys are not taught such things or, at least, I was not."

"It is never too late to start." She rummaged in her satchel and retrieved a sketchbook, some pencils, and an India rubber. "Here, take these. See how you get on. There are some tricks, like perspective, but I can easily show them to you. Start with simple objects," she continued. "An apple or a glass or a candlestick. Concentrate on what you actually see rather than what you think the thing is; look at the play of light and shadow."

"Yes. Thank you, Delia."

"It's as if the seasons are rolling backwards," Delia said later as they strolled through the little village. "In Paris, it was definitely autumn—the leaves were starting to turn and there was that delightful crispness in the air, especially in the mornings. Then there was the wine harvest. But here it is still summer."

"English summer, at least. The real summer heat here is very different. Then it is best to do as the natives do. Rise early, eat your dinner around midday and afterwards take a long nap when the sun is hottest. The evenings are more pleasant. The sun sets earlier than in our northern regions, but the differences are not as extreme, so while we may not have the very long summer days, December days are not as short."

"Is there snow?"

"Rarely down at the coast, but in the mountains, certainly."

"Mountains!" To his amusement, she gave a little wriggle of excitement. "I have never seen really high mountains. It is all so wonderful and so different."

~~~

"The sky has changed again," Delia said some days later. "It is bigger somehow. We must be near the sea."

"Yes. Tomorrow we should reach Marseilles. Gianluca has sent one of the couriers on ahead to see if *La Sirena* is in port."

"The yacht? So soon?"

"It is two months since we disembarked at Calais," he pointed out. "Given fair winds, she should be here, and newly provisioned. We can avoid crossing the mountainous areas between here and Nice, and be there in two or three days."

"Two or three days! How far is it then to the *Villa Della Torre?*"

"Less than an hour. It is in the hills behind Villafranca, which is beside the town of Nice—just high enough to make the summer less uncomfortable."

"Today is Monday, so we can hope to arrive there on Thursday?"

"Or Friday morning. It is better not to arrive too late, as it will take some time to unload and arrange for carriages and mules to take us up to the Villa. We are fortunate that we can take the post road to Turin for most of the way."

When they arrived in Marseilles, they found *La Sirena* lying quietly at anchor in the sheltered harbour. There was something welcoming, Stephen felt, in the sight of the red ensign at the stern of the two-masted yacht. They had reached the last stage of their journey. He hoped it would not end in disappointment for his aunt, who in recent days oscillated between hectic bursts of chatter and long silences, but dismissed any enquiry as to her well-being with a firm 'I am quite well, thank you'.

While the horses were unharnessed and the carriages lifted on board, Stephen and his ladies strolled along the quays and the tree-lined *Canabière*.

"We should buy some Marseilles soap while we are here," Lady Mary said, suddenly.

"Anything else, ma'am?" Stephen asked, after she had arranged for two big blocks of soap to be brought at once to the yacht.

"I can't think of anything else, Stephen, not when I don't know what to expect at the Villa. It was just when I saw the sign for *Savon de Marseilles* that I remembered how good the soap is. Oh dear, I am glad you and Delia are with me. I do not think I would have had the courage to come on my own."

"Did you have the opportunity to make any arrangements for the Villa and the estate before you left?" Delia asked.

"After the revolution in France, we moved most of our capital to England. Then, when we decided I should leave with the girls, I took my jewellery and other small, valuable objects with us. Piero's and Gianluca's father, Luca, is—was our steward; we don't know, of course, if he is still alive—but all was arranged so that he could manage everything on our behalf. His father and grandfather had worked for the *Della Torres* for decades and we trusted him completely. I last heard from him during the peace of Amiens. All was well then, he wrote, but that was eleven years ago. Since the resumption of hostilities, I've been afraid that our property was confiscated by the French or had troops billeted there, or was occupied by some official for his own use. That would probably be the least harmful, I suppose. An army can cause terrible damage, even if it is only passing through. Everything that can be eaten or drunk is consumed, trees felled for firewood, what is moveable or removable is plundered."

"We'll hope it will not have come to that, but damages can be repaired, and usurpers ejected if they are still there," Stephen said. "The sacrifice made by your husband and son will not have been forgotten, I am sure."

"I hope not. They are very much in my mind these last days."

"It is only natural that old memories are revived as you near home," Delia said sympathetically.

"I have been dreaming that I arrive at the Villa and they are there to welcome me. I call out joyfully, but when I step down from the carriage to run to them, they are gone."

"Oh! My dear ma'am! How terrible."

Tears filled Lady Mary's eyes. "Although Luca told me where they are buried, I suppose in my heart of hearts, I thought they would still be here. Waiting."

131

Delia pressed a handkerchief into the older woman's hand. "That is heart-breaking."

"One would think after so many years, I had accepted it," Lady Mary said, drying her eyes.

"It is easier for the head to accept such things than the heart," Stephen said quietly. "One cannot force such things. But you are not alone, Aunt. Shall we see if they are ready for us?"

Jean, one of the cavalrymen, was waiting at the yacht to make his farewells. "If you don't need me anymore, Milord. My home is a day's walk from here. I wish to express my gratitude for aiding me to come so far."

"Thank you for your services. How many years have you been away?"

"Five, Milord."

"God speed you on the final stage of your journey." Stephen put his hand in his pocket and withdrew some gold coins. "To help you on your way."

"Thank you, Milord!" Jean saluted, then clasped his comrades' hands before turning on his heel and walking away.

They all watched silently until he disappeared from view. Gianluca made the sign of the cross. "May the Virgin protect him and us, and guide us all safely home."

"Amen," Lady Mary said quietly.

Interlude—Lieutenant and Mrs Crosbie in Paris

Lydia Crosbie watched her husband shave. She loved this private view of him; naked to the waist so that she could appreciate the musculature of his magnificent torso, which, in her opinion, rivalled those of the marble statues in the *Louvre*. He wielded the razor skilfully, concentrating on providing the smoothest of finishes and the sharpest of edges around the dark side-whiskers that framed his handsome face. Now he wiped the last of the lather away, took a little flask and poured some liquid into his palm. An aromatic scent filled the room as he carefully patted the *Eau d'Houbigant* into his cheeks. Napoleon's perfumier was expensive, but Lydia delighted in indulging her husband with such trifles. Her pin money of one thousand pounds a year came from a trust set up in accordance with her late father's will. George was at first miffed that he would not have control of the capital, but had acquiesced when it was pointed out to him that his debtors could never attach her settlement.

"We shall share it," she had promised him. She knew her George—an inveterate gamester; money seemed to run through his fingers, but so handsome and charming that she found him irresistible. They had met when the Militia was stationed in

Manchester and married the day after her twenty-first birthday. Some called him a scapegrace and a ne'er-do-well, but, 'he is my scapegrace', she had said. For all her proper upbringing, he called to some deep wildness in her and the prospect of marriage to him was much more appealing than the thought of being tied to any of the older, more staid, even titled fortune-hunters who approached her.

Three years later, she had not regretted her choice. As long as the war lasted, they were somewhat constrained by his military duties, but with the Peace, the Militia was disembodied and George need only serve the peacetime twenty-eight days each year. Now they were enjoying a belated honeymoon in Paris. Thanks to George's inventiveness in the marriage-bed as well as his use of cundoms to prevent him spilling his seed inside her, she had been spared pregnancy. 'Time for that later', he had said to her, explaining that there were many ways a man and woman might pleasure each other without any risk of conception. She had proved to be a willing and apt pupil. Now she left the bed and went to embrace him from behind, pressing her bare breasts against his naked back while her hands went around to the front of his pantaloons.

"Again? Greedy little thing," he said as his hands covered hers. "We must be quick."

"Just you, then. I'll take your vowels—her teeth nipped at his shoulder—you can pay me later, with interest."

"Damn it, Lydia! Where's that towel?" He hastily pushed his pantaloons down out of harm's way and pressed the towel into her busy hands.

~~~

After a pleasant day spent looking into the shops on the Boulevards and strolling in the garden of the *Tuileries*, they returned to their neat apartment on the second floor of a house in the *Rue Saint-Benoît*. Lydia grumbled as usual about the necessity of climbing so many flights of stairs but she agreed that to pay the equivalent of thirty pounds a month for the splendid first-floor apartment was an unnecessary extravagance, 'and even then, we must go up the grand staircase which is the longest'.

Arrived at their rooms, she went into the bedroom to remove her bonnet and tidy her hair while George flicked through the little pile of correspondence that had been delivered during their absence.

"Here is a little packet from the Venerable the Archdeacon," he called to his wife. "What will it have cost us to receive it, I wonder? What the devil does he want?" he added, breaking the seal carefully. "Good heavens!"

"What is it?"

"A letter of credit for seven hundred pounds as well as a sealed letter addressed to a Lady Loring and an unsealed one addressed *To Whom It May Concern*."

"Seven hundred pounds? He must have some commission for you; to purchase an old master of some virginal saint or martyrdom, perhaps."

"No, it's not that," he replied absently. "It's—well, see for yourself."

Cathedral Close, 2 October 1814

My dear George,

You will be surprised to receive this letter, I daresay, but the fact is that an opportunity has arisen for you to be of assistance to an old friend of my cousin Jethro.

Sir Edward Loring is most anxious to have his wife, who is at present in France in the company of Lady Mary Arkell, the Contessa Della Torre, returned to him and their marital home at Loring Place, near Bury St. Edmunds, Suffolk. It occurred to me that you and your good lady are perfectly placed to accomplish this, as Mrs Crosbie's presence will be essential for the long journey home.

We understand that Lady Mary intends to leave Paris shortly and travel to her late husband's ancestral home in the County of Nice, and it is more than likely that you will have to follow them there. Should the lady be unwilling to return, I remind you that a husband may determine where his wife lives and has the right to command her presence; indeed, he may resort to the Ecclesiastical and Civil Courts to ensure her compliance. We wish to avoid this, however, and I rely on your powers of persuasion and general resourcefulness to overcome any such difficulty and convey her safely and securely to her husband.

The enclosed bank draft is to cover your expenses to a maximum of six hundred pounds. Over and above this, in recognition of your efforts, Sir Edward offers you a gratuity of one hundred pounds now and another hundred when the lady is safely delivered to him.

Your aunt sends you her love, and her regards to Mrs Crosbie, as do I.

I remain your affect. uncle,
B. Boyce.

P.S. Sir E. struck me as being quite 'pernickety' and to avoid acrimony, I recommend that you keep a record of your outgoings. A Dutch reckoning will not suffice.

Lydia looked up from the letter. "It sounds as if they want you to kidnap this lady if necessary. What a lark!"

"Not kidnap," he protested. "Coax and cajole her, perhaps."

"Do you think we should do it?"

"We have seen everything to be seen in Paris. Why not let this Sir Edward pay our way south, and our journey home as well, with all our expenses, and two hundred pounds on top of it?"

"When you put it that way—what does the other letter say?"

"Very little: *I hereby authorise Lieutenant George Crosbie to make all necessary arrangements and act on my behalf in all matters regarding the return of my wife Delia, Lady Loring, to our marital home at Loring Place, Suffolk, England.* Signed *Sir Edward Loring, Bt.* It's enough, I suppose. I'll lock these away until tomorrow, when I take the letter of credit to *Peregaux Lafitte*. While I'm there, I'll make some enquiries about this Lady Mary; if anyone knows, Philips will know." He smiled at her. "Now, what shall we do this evening?"

Chapter Eleven

Confiding to the others appeared to have helped Lady Mary, or perhaps it was the more familiar surroundings of the yacht that had improved her serenity. A steady west wind enabled them to make good progress, and it was possible to sit, wrapped up, in a sheltered part of the deck, letting the dramatic landscape pass by.

Delia could not take her eyes off the rugged coastline, backed by mountains that ran down to the sea, creating bays where houses clung to the slopes above little harbours. They anchored in one of these each night, when a crew member would row a small boat to the shore and see what fresh provisions, perhaps fish or vegetables, might be obtained, as well as arranging for bread to be supplied in the morning. As usual, there was no milk to be found, and she had long since resigned herself to taking her tea without it.

"It doesn't keep in the heat," Lady Mary had explained. "They turn it all into cheese. In Provence, it is goat's milk anyway."

The third night on board, they anchored in the little fishing harbour of Cannes. Unusually, Friday morning found everyone on deck early, all looking very spruce. The men stood at attention while tears came to Lady Mary's eyes as a flag displaying a white cross on a red field edged with blue was run up the mast.

"The old flag of the Duchy of Savoy, to which the County of Nice belongs," Stephen murmured to Delia. "During the occupation, we would have had to fly the French tricolour if we were putting into Nice."

When the cook came forward with a tray of glasses and some dark green bottles, to Delia's surprise, it was Stephen who stepped forward to pour a generous measure of a clear liquid into each glass. He slanted a glance at the two ladies and their maids, and poured smaller measures for them.

"It is *Grappa*, a pomace brandy made from the residue of the grapes after wine-making," he said as the men helped themselves to the glasses. "Sip it slowly; it is very strong."

Lady Mary raised her glass. "Some of you have served me faithfully throughout our exile, others have also endured an unwanted absence from home. I thank you all and wish you all good fortune. *Al ritorno a casa!* To homecomings!"

There was a murmur of assent as everyone drank. Delia was grateful for Stephen's warning as otherwise she would have surely spluttered the burning liquid over the deck.

There was a little buzz of excitement as the men dispersed. The captain and crew had reached the end of their long voyage and could look forward to some days' leave ashore while, for the others, it was indeed a homecoming. What would it be for her, Delia wondered? What would their every-day life be like without the daily spur provided by travel? Would she and Stephen continue to deal as well together?

~~~

"Nice." Stephen nodded towards the little town and harbour huddled below a hill-top ruin, a sweep of mountains behind it.

The crew neatly took in the sails and cast anchor.

"Now we wait," Stephen said.

As usual, they could see people on shore looking and pointing towards the strange vessel. Then two men appeared and walked purposefully towards a shallop that was drawn up on the shore. Soon it was launched, with four rowers propelling it forward.

"Time for us to go inside," Stephen said, leading Delia into the day cabin. Here Lady Mary waited and, to Delia's surprise, Piero and Gianluca took up positions outside, as if on guard. She watched through the windows as the boat neared and then disappeared.

"Port officials. They'll climb on board."

Soon they heard voices outside, then the cabin door opened to admit Captain Arnold and another uniformed man.

"My lady, may I present Captain Martin of the Port Office?" Captain Arnold said formally. "Captain Martin, I have the honour to announce the Lady Mary Arkell, *Contessa Della Torre*, who returns from exile."

"*Contessa.*" The captain saluted, then bowed deeply. "May I be the first to welcome you home?"

"Thank you, Captain. It is good to be here after so many years."

If Delia had not been watching Lady Mary so closely, she would have missed the slight relaxation of the other's shoulders and her polite smile changing to a genuine one.

"We will do our best to make the process of disembarkation as easy as possible for you," the port officer said. "If you wish, while we complete the formalities, my gondola can take one of your servants ashore so that he can make arrangements for your transfer to your Villa."

So the Villa was immediately available, Delia thought as Lady Mary nodded graciously. "That is exceedingly kind of you, Captain Martin. My major-domo will be ready in ten minutes if that suits you."

"Gondola?" Delia said to Stephen as they watched the shallop pull away. "I thought a gondola looked completely different; more exotic like in my father's engraving of Venice. I am quite disappointed."

He laughed. "Here, they call these boats gondolas as well. I agree, they are not as picturesque."

"What happens now?"

"The officials will look at our papers and decide what we need to pay. Then we will be allocated a berth where we can disembark. I hope that by then Piero has arranged for mules for the carriages."

It was almost two hours before *La Sirena* had completed the tricky manoeuvre and reached her assigned berth. Her sails were furled for the last time on this voyage, but before the crew was dismissed, she would be scrubbed from top to bottom.

Again, the passengers retreated to the cabin, safely out of the way, while the travelling chariots and baggage were unloaded. Piero had returned with four stout labourers to assist with this operation while two grooms waited with five mules. Nearby, a cluster of curious onlookers gathered, all more than ready to comment on the foreign yacht.

Through the open window of the cabin, those waiting heard, *"La Sirena! Quello era lo yacht dei Della Torre."*

This was followed by an excited babble that increased when the two travelling chariots appeared and the mules were harnessed to it.

At last, Captain Arnold came to announce, "My lady, all is ready for you."

"Thank you, Captain."

Stephen offered his aunt his arm. "May I assist you, Aunt?"

Silence fell when the two appeared at the top of the gangway. Then an old man exclaimed, "La lady. La Lady Mary returns."

"I thought no one would know me," Delia heard her ladyship murmur to Stephen.

A little group of English tourists stood aloof from the excited Nissards, but were no less interested in the proceedings. Delia hoped they would be able to escape being accosted by someone claiming acquaintance. In Paris, she had learnt how the English loved to meet fellow-countrymen 'of the right sort' when abroad.

Lady Mary must have felt the same, for she said to Stephen, "Remind me to make it clear that I am not at home to callers for the first days, or not to English callers," she amended.

"Yes, ma'am," he said smartly.

They paused on the quayside to let the two remaining cavalrymen make their farewells. Lady Mary nodded graciously to the Nissards and entered her carriage, followed by her maid, who had been with her since they left so many years ago. Stephen handed Delia into their carriage; the other servants took their places, and they were off.

They threaded their way through narrow streets and small open spaces bright with flowers until they reached a magnificent square surrounded by imposing three-storied buildings all painted in the same reddish ochre, with the windows outlined in a lighter colour.

"I remember this. It's the *Piazza Vittoria*," Stephen said. "Once we cross it, we are on the post road." He indicated an ornate, monumental stone gate. "Through there."

"How impressive," Delia said.

"It is the beginning, or end, if you will, of the so-called Royal Road to Turin."

The road now ran alongside a stream that meandered through banks of pebbles where laundresses bent assiduously to their tasks, their heads protected from the sun by wide-brimmed, flat-crowned straw hats.

"I suppose on a hot day, it is better to paddle in cool water than toil over a steaming copper," Delia remarked. "Everything will dry quickly here as well. Oh, look!" She pointed to where two women stood at a big balance. "They must charge by weight rather than by item. I like their hats—they provide good shade without being close to the head like a bonnet—just what I'll need if I am painting or sketching."

"And here I thought you were offering to wash my shirts," he teased her. "We'll see if we can find you one."

"What is the river called?"

"The *Paglion*. The laundresses can work safely now, but when the winter snows melt in the Alps, it turns into a raging torrent, sweeping all before it."

"It is hard to imagine bad weather here, it is so idyllic. I don't think I'll ever tire of seeing orange and lemon orchards, or olive groves, especially old olive trees. And the flowers!"

After some miles, they turned into a side road that ascended through olive groves until they stopped at a pair of heavy, rusty iron gates. Judging by the weeds and grass growing beneath them, it was a considerable time since they had been opened, although the smaller gate to the side appeared to be in regular use.

Gianluca, who had ridden ahead, dismounted while Piero descended from his seat beside the coachman. He carried a big key, as well as a goose feather and a bottle of oil. Having liberally anointed the lock, he inserted the key. After a moment, it turned and the lock opened.

Lady Mary's maid appeared at the window of Stephen's and Delia's carriage. "Her ladyship's compliments and would you please join her in her carriage."

The brothers solemnly opened the gates and the coachman's horn blared as the carriages drove through. Where in England they would now have taken an avenue through parkland, this was more a lane through leafy citrus orchards, the trees hung with lemons and oranges.

"The orchards look in good heart, Aunt," Stephen said. "Better kept than this lane," he added as the carriage lurched.

"In the circumstances, that is sensible," Delia said. "If resources are limited, why waste them on a carriage drive that is rarely used? They have kept the growth in check, at least."

"True."

After about a quarter of a mile, they rounded a bend and could see the house ahead. It was built in a simple, classical style with a mansard roof, three stories high, in the centre block while, judging by the stone balustrades, the side blocks, one storey lower, had roof terraces. The now familiar shutters shaded the windows and the small flight of steps that led to the front door was sheltered by a portico supported by two plain columns.

"It is beautiful," Delia said. "I love how the dark green of the cypresses sets off that faded, golden stone in living marks of admiration."

"A delightful comparison," Lady Mary said. "You do see things differently, Delia. I must thank you for having opened my eyes to so much that is beautiful on our way here."

"And mine," Stephen said, to Delia's pleased embarrassment.

"I wonder is anyone here," Lady Mary said as they neared the Villa. Even as she spoke, the front door opened and a balding, elderly man clad in the formal dark suit of clothes of a steward in the previous century appeared. "Luca!" she gasped.

Almost before the carriage rolled to a stop, Piero was at the door, offering his hand. "My lady."

As she descended, the old man started forward. *"Contessa!* My lady? Is it you indeed?"

He broke off and said uncertainly, *"Piero?"*

"Si, Padre, e anche Gianluca," Piero answered. His voice shook as he announced the return of his brother.

Gianluca dismounted quickly, handed his reins to the groom who had come with the mules, and came to stand before his father, who looked from his two sons to his returning mistress and back again, as if unsure whom to greet first.

In the end, he dropped to his knees as if his legs could no longer support him, and looked up to the heavens. *"Lord, now lettest thou thy servant depart in peace, according to thy word.* You have heard my prayers and fulfilled your promise, as you once did to holy Simeon."

"And you have served as faithfully as he, Luca," Lady Mary said gently. "Rise and embrace your sons."

When she extended her hand, he bent over it in the bow of a faithful courtier. "But first, my lady, you will allow me to welcome you home."

~~~

"Sleeping Beauty's castle must have felt like this," Delia muttered to Stephen as they followed Lady Mary and her steward into the *Villa Della Torre,* the old man's expostulations alternating between delight at his mistress's return and dismay at the lack of any time to prepare for her.

"In what way?"

"Somnolent, torpid even, as if nothing has stirred here during your aunt's absence. Everything is shrouded in dust-sheets; the curtains are drawn, and the shutters closed. They have kept the dust at bay, but that is all. It is devoid of any life. There is not enough sustenance here for a bluebottle, let alone a mouse."

"For which we surely must be grateful. Or would you prefer it to be abuzz with life? I imagine Luca has done his best with the resources at his disposal."

"You are right. I did not mean to criticise—"

"No, you are right, too. There is something of the enchanted castle here."

"I could have wept when he sent his sons to find their mother. I have been afraid all along that there would be no one to receive them."

"I too. I am also glad that they can meet her privately. To witness such an encounter would be too much of an intrusion."

They had progressed down a hall to double doors that opened on a large drawing-room running across the width of the main house. The steward darted from chair to sofa to chair, removing dust-sheets, while Stephen went to the row of tall windows on the back wall. Some of the fittings appeared to have rusted fast, but he was able to open enough to admit the daylight and illuminate the pastel landscape paintings on the walls.

"How charming. As if they have brought the outdoors inside," Delia said.

"There!" Having wrenched open a pair of French doors, Stephen wrestled the shutters behind them back, flat against the wall. Light flooded into the room. "Come, Delia."

She followed him onto a wide, roofed terrace, set between the two side wings that extended some fifteen feet beyond the centre of the house. "It's like an outdoor room, just open on one side." She crossed the terrace to the low balustrade that was either side of a central flight of steps leading down to a terraced garden whose abandoned plantings sprawled down the hillside. Once they had been carefully tended, and the bones of the layout were still apparent. Below and to the sides was spread an expanse of verdant hillside planted with olives, figs, almonds, and other fruit trees, and lapped at its base by the bluest of seas that reached to the horizon. To their right lay Nice and the hills of Provence, while on the left was another bay and more mountains.

"You can see the Alps better from the upstairs terraces," Stephen said. "Here, the house is in the way."

Delia looked at him, dazed. "Dear God," she whispered. "I have never seen anything more beautiful."

"Yes," Lady Mary said behind them. "It is splendid, isn't it? But it is even more wonderful to find Luca and Marta still here and apparently well. We'll leave them to their reunion with their sons for now." She looked around. "There used be chairs here."

"I'll bring some out, Aunt," Stephen said. "There is no point in ringing for servants just yet."

"Luca will want to know about rooms," Lady Mary said after some time. "I have my own suite, of course, above the drawing-room but where would you like to be?"

Stephen and Delia looked at one another. Delia remained silent; she did not know the house and, as an insignificant guest, did not wish to be too forward in expressing her wishes.

"It is so long since I have been here, Aunt," Stephen said. "Perhaps you should also consult Luca in case some rooms are uninhabitable for some reason—a broken window, or leak in the roof, for example."

"Very true. May I ask what your plans are? Do you intend to continue on to Naples or Rome? You must know you would both be most welcome to stay here for the winter if you wish. I have come to value Delia's company as well as yours, Stephen," she added, "but you must do exactly as you like."

Again, Delia and Stephen exchanged glances.

"We haven't really thought about it, Aunt," Stephen said. "We shall certainly remain here for the time being."

"Why don't you show Delia the house and let her decide what rooms she would like? I shall sit here quietly for the moment."

She looked tired, yet content. "May we do anything for you, ma'am?" Delia asked as she rose.

"No, unless—do you have your flask in your pocket, Stephen?"

"Of course."

"Pour me a little brandy, if you will."

"Shall I find your maid and send her to you?" Delia asked as Stephen complied.

"No. They will come to find me soon enough. I shall be glad of a quarter of an hour to myself."

"I can understand her wishing to be on her own," Delia said as they crossed the drawing-room. "It must be an overwhelming experience to return here after so many years. I am sure she feels the absence of her husband and son. How did she learn of their deaths, do you know?"

"That of her husband was reported in the accounts of the Battle of Mondovi, in 1796. A fellow officer finished up some months later in Naples and was able to entrust a letter to the British Ambassador, Sir William Hamilton, who sent it on to England. It was only then that she learnt that her son was also dead."

"Poor lady. How old were her daughters?"

"Let me think. Alienora was twenty-three. She had married Qualter the previous year. Camilla is six years younger; she had not yet come out."

"She must have met Mr Lyndall in her first Season," Delia said, surprised. "Susan is sixteen, is she not?

Stephen laughed. "The families know each other forever; he was waiting for Camilla's come-out to propose. They married in June '97. My aunt did not have the heart to make them wait. She said, 'Life is fleeting and we should accept happiness when it is offered to us.'"

Interlude—Lieutenant and Mrs Crosbie in Nice

"You want to go where?" Lydia Crosbie straightened up from the trunk that held her gowns and turned to stare at her husband. She could not believe that George, of all people, was suggesting they go to church. "Have you suddenly turned papist?"

"Good heavens, no. My uncle would disinherit me on the spot."

"But there is no Protestant church here, is there?"

"No, but my uncle informed me that they are allowed to practise their faith privately, provided they do not attempt to proselytise. The English, therefore, meet for Divine Service each Sunday at one or another of their homes. I have already learnt that this coming Sunday it is at Lady Woodburgh's."

"And you think we should join them?"

"Only consider, Lyd. This gives us the *entrée* to the highest circles here. Perhaps Lady Mary Arkell will be there with Lady Loring in tow. If not, where better to enquire about them?"

"I suppose you are right."

"Therefore, you should call on Lady Woodburgh and beg permission to come on Sunday."

"Oh no, George Crosbie. You are not throwing me to the lions—or lionesses—like that. We shall call together. A handsome young man is far more likely to appeal to her."

So it was. Her ladyship graciously assented and Sunday found the Crosbies climbing the stairs to the magnificent apartment she had rented for the Season. Some thirty persons had assembled, among them an elderly clergyman who took it upon himself to preach a lengthy sermon. Afterwards, refreshments that were more valedictory than welcoming were offered, but George had sufficient time to enquire about Lady Mary.

"I should be surprised to see her here," one lady sniffed. "I believed she turned Catholic when she married."

"No," another put in. "The Arkells are one of the old, recusant families."

"Ah, I see. I have an introduction…" He broke off, leaving his interlocutor to assume that the introduction was to Lady Mary herself.

"Indeed? Then, I fear, you shall have to make your way to the *Villa Della Torre*. It is off the road to Turin, on the other side of the Paglion, on the slopes of *Mont Gros*. You can safely take a carriage."

"Excellent. Thank you, ma'am."

Chapter Twelve

Within the space of a week, the Villa had come alive again. Windows were opened, rooms aired, and furniture uncovered. Only the largest items had been left in place; everything else had been packed safely away in the attics, out of the way of casual looters or those seeking a night's billet. Lady Mary had taken the most valuable small *objets d'art* with her to England and these were also now restored to their old places.

Lady Mary had returned to her former suite above the grand drawing-room, while Delia and Stephen had laid claim to the top floor of the centre block of the Villa.

"Provided the stairs are not too much for you," Stephen had said. "We shall be more secluded, can enjoy the roof terraces, and the old schoolroom looks north and would be ideal as a studio."

"That would be wonderful, if your aunt will not consider it too much of an imposition."

"Nonsense. She is delighted that we have decided to spend the winter with her. Are you sure you don't object, Delia?"

"No. Why would I? I have grown very fond of her, and I would not like to think of her here by herself. What will the servants make of it?"

"It is not their place to make anything of it," he said shortly. "However, I think they just assume that we are married. On the road, everyone started calling you Lady Delia, and it is simpler for them than Lady Loring, which they tended to make into Lady Laura, but Italian women don't take their husbands' names anyway, so it wouldn't matter."

"And I still wear my wedding ring." She spread her left hand. "I don't like to take it off in case I meet someone from home."

"Would you replace it with one I give you?"

"Not replace it, Stephen. It would seem like living a lie. But if you wish to give me a token of our love and commitment to one another, I'll wear it gladly."

~~~

Delia's painting materials had arrived from Paris. Leaving her happily arranging her studio, Stephen decided to walk down into Nice. If they were staying for some months, they would need horses or mules. He didn't care which. And he must consider what to do about the horses he had left at Arkell House. There was no point in leaving them idle indefinitely.

When, if ever, would he return to England? Had he committed himself and Delia to a perpetual exile? Unless she was willing to act the penitent, she must stay abroad as long as her husband was alive. Stephen did not regret the impulse that had led him to carry her off to the Continent, but he must admit to himself at least that he had not properly considered the consequences for both of them.

Pausing to select a stout walking stick from the selection in the hall, one that would support him on the steep incline and be useful for repelling snakes and stray dogs, if necessary, he set off down the mountain path that led to Nice.

The morning was crisp and sunny—soon it would get hot, but for now, it was pleasant to stride along, releasing the scent of dried herbs and grasses that grew between the stones. To be alone with his thoughts—he hadn't realised how much he needed it. Delia was used to living with others. He wasn't. It was five months since he had come to stay with his aunt in Yorkshire, since he had met Delia again.

He had enjoyed various liaisons and affaires before, but had never had a mistress in keeping. Nor had he ever been tempted to marry. Why was that? Had Delia imprinted herself on him to such an extent that no other woman could satisfy him? The only answer he could give was that with her he felt at ease, could be completely himself. There was no deceit, no pretence between them.

He was not normally given to spontaneous, impulsive decisions—he had become quite set in his ways, he realised, but as soon as Delia re-entered his life, he was twenty again. What had he expected when he asked her to come with him? He had asked her to be his wife in all things but name. He had imagined some rustic idyll, ultimately setting up house somewhere there was no English 'colony' as in Nice; where no one would enquire too closely into the affairs of the foreigners. Now that he had seen how quickly English tourists were swarming over the Continent, he realised that might have been easier said than done.

Aunt Mary's timely intervention had certainly had made things easier for them. Delia's reputation was not ruined, as it would have been if they lived together publicly. At the *Villa Della Torre*, there was space enough on their floor for them to have their own sitting-room as well as two bedrooms and her studio. Of course, they would take their meals with his aunt and keep her company some of the time; even accompany her when she went into society. She had not yet begun to do so, although the first callers had found their way to the Villa; old friends of the Nissard nobility who were delighted to see her returned to them. She had insisted on presenting 'her nephew' and her 'dear friend who is spending the winter with me' to them. He had wanted to protest, "She is mine," especially when he had recognised the speculative glance of the matchmaking mamma. But in public, he and Delia must pretend to be no more than the coincidental guests of the *Contessa Della Torre*. If only they did not have to conceal the true connection between them.

He would find a ring for her, he resolved, a ring that would secretly bind her to him. He would also write to Henderson in York, instructing him to arrange for the sale of his horses and curricle, and to dismiss the groom he had retained to look after them. A friend had been happy to take his set in Albany, so there was no need to worry about that. He supposed he should write to his nephew, the Duke of Gracechurch, and advise him that he would remain abroad for the foreseeable future. He could be reached care of his London man of business.

"Lord Stephen FitzCharles, is it not?"

Jerked out his reverie, Stephen stared at the plump, older man bowing to him. He was strangely familiar, but he could not place him. Clerical or donnish black was supplemented by a modest white cravat instead of linen bands, and the doffed hat revealed a balding pate. Benign grey eyes peered through round steel spectacles. Stephen mentally superimposed a neat grey wig on the scant locks. "Dr Costain," he said triumphantly, pleased to have recognised his former tutor. "How do you do, sir?"

"Tolerably, my lord, tolerably."

"What brings you to Nice?" Stephen asked, surprised that the other man had left the protective walls of his Oxford college.

"My wife has not been well. Yes, I see you are surprised, my lord. I married some fifteen years ago and have a living near London. But my wife has such a persistent cough that we thought we would try the change of air now that travel is possible again. We are here for the winter. And you, my lord?"

"I escorted my aunt, the *Contessa Della Torre,* to her family home."

"Ah, so you will be joining our little colony here in 'Newborough'?"

"No, although I am, of course, pleased to meet an old acquaintance," Stephen said politely.

"Ladies." Dr Costain bowed to two passing females in fashionable bonnets and before Stephen knew it, he had been presented, invited to call, and pressed to attend Sunday Divine Service, "read so beautifully by our friend here, at dear Lady Markham's."

He managed to extricate himself without making any definite commitment and decided he had had enough of Nice for the moment.

"I fear our presence is now known," he said ruefully to Lady Mary and Delia that evening and, sure enough, a steady trickle of English callers found their way to the Villa.

"We must return these calls," Lady Mary said some days later. "I think we should purchase a small carriage for paying visits; I am too old to walk down into town and up again, as many of the ladies do. Will you look into it, Stephen?"

"Certainly, Aunt. I'll look for a pair, so that we can take one of the travelling chariots if we wish to make a longer journey. I might look for a riding horse or mule as well. What about you, Delia? We could go into the mountains a little."

"I have never learnt to ride, but the local women seem perfectly happy perched on their mules. They, the mules I mean, seem more solid and more placid than the horses ladies ride at home. I should like to try."

"*Brava!* Between your mule and your Nissard straw hat, you will be taken for a native."

"All the better. Then no one will bother me… I spoke too soon," she muttered to Stephen when Luca came in, presenting visiting cards on a silver tray.

"Mr and Mrs Crosbie have called, my lady."

"Crosbie, Crosbie?" Lady Mary frowned. "Do we know them from before?"

"No, my lady. They are quite young, younger than milord."

"Hmm. I don't like the idea that I have become a sort of raree show for tourists in my old age. I am not at home, Luca."

The steward disappeared only to return some minutes later. "Mr Crosbie asked if Lady Loring is at home. He is the bearer of a letter for her."

"Then request him to give it to you."

"I did, my lady, but he said he was required to present it personally."

Delia felt sick, immediately transported back to Loring Place and another insistent but unexpected caller, Mr Chidlow. She looked at the others. "I have no idea who he is, but I had better see him, I suppose. You say his wife is with him, Luca?"

"Yes, Milady."

"You can see them in the library," Lady Mary said. "Take Stephen with you."

Delia paused at the door to the library, transfixed by the classical features of the man lounging at the window. An exquisite profile, artfully tousled curls, broad shoulders, and narrow hips reminiscent of Apollo Belvedere, seen just recently at the *Louvre*. His companion was pretty, but hers was the prettiness of youth rather than lasting beauty. She was frowning and twisting her fingers together. "I told you so." She broke off when she saw Delia and Stephen.

"Lady Loring, Lord Stephen FitzCharles," Luca announced.

Crosbie straightened to his full height. "Lady Loring." He bowed. "George Crosbie at your service. May I present my wife?"

"Mrs Crosbie." Delia nodded acknowledgement of the young woman's curtsy.

Crosbie glanced at Stephen, who hovered protectively near the door. "May we speak in private, my lady?"

Delia was tempted to say that he could speak freely in front of Stephen, but thought there was no point in revealing their hand at this stage in the game. For a game it was, she was sure of it, and not a pleasant one.

"Lord Stephen, would you mind?"

Stephen bowed and stepped outside, but left the door open. He would not go far, she knew.

She looked pointedly at Mrs Crosbie, who flushed and, in turn, looked pleadingly at her husband. He cleared his throat.

"My wife and I are here as emissaries of Sir Edward Loring. I have a letter for you from him."

She took it and slipped it into her pocket. "Thank you." She would wait to read it until she was alone. The visitors waited expectantly, but she did not invite them to sit.

Mr Crosbie cleared his throat again. "In fact, one could say that we, that is I, represent Sir Edward here in an important matter."

Delia raised her eyebrows. "Oh?"

"Yes. I am charged with escorting you back to England, to your marital home."

"Indeed? I am surprised that Sir Edward thinks I would I agree to travel in the company of two complete strangers."

"We can take time to get to know one another," Mrs Crosbie put in.

"That will not be necessary," Delia said icily.

"One way or another, you must comply, ma'am." Crosbie's face hardened. "I need hardly remind you that it is your husband, not you, who decides where you live. The law supports him in this." He showed her a sheet of paper. "Here is my authorisation to act on his behalf."

She snatched it from him. "*To Whom it May Concern*," she read aloud, and continued to read silently. "What arrant nonsense!" She folded the sheet and tucked it into her pocket.

"That is not yours to keep," he said sharply.

She shrugged. "I am the only person concerned by it."

"It is not addressed to you."

"I think it is."

"Lady Loring, you will return that paper at once." He advanced on her, then stopped, clearly frustrated by the fact that her pocket was under her dress, reached through a slit in a side seam.

Thank heavens she preferred a pocket to a reticule when at home, Delia thought.

"Lydia! Come here!"

What? Was he going to have his wife take the document from her by force? She picked up a little bell and rang it vigorously. "I'll have no more of this nonsense."

Stephen appeared in a flash, Luca a couple of moments later.

"Mr and Mrs Crosbie are leaving, Luca. I am not at home, should they call again."

"Very good, my lady."

"I'll see them out," Stephen said abruptly.

As soon as the trio had disappeared from view, Delia collapsed into a chair. She was shaking.

Tight-lipped, and more briskly than politeness demanded, Stephen ushered the unwelcome couple out of the house and down the steps.

"You may find your own way from here. I would remind you that, between us, my aunt and I have considerable influence both here and in England. It would be most ill-advised of you to discuss Lady Loring's private affairs, to attempt to discredit her in any way, or to force yourself on her notice again. You will not like the consequences. Good day to you."

When Crosbie began to expostulate, "My lord, I fear you misapprehend—", Stephen raised his hand. "No more."

As soon as they walked away, he went back inside. "Luca, is Gianluca here? Tell him to follow that pair and see if he can find out where they are staying."

Delia was huddled in a chair in the library, her face white. Her lips trembled when she tried to speak. He knelt beside her and took her in his arms.

"Oh, Stephen!" She began to sob.

"Shush now, they're gone. Shssh." He rocked her gently, murmuring nonsense until she calmed. He pressed a handkerchief into her hand and she sat up and dried her eyes.

"I never thought he would do such a thing—send someone to retrieve me, like an escaped convict, or a parcel he had mislaid."

She fished in her pocket and handed him a sheet of paper. "Just look at that!... *make all necessary arrangements and act on my behalf in all matters regarding the return of my wife Delia, Lady Loring, to our marital home.* Crosbie seems to think it gives him authority over me! He did not like my taking it from him at all."

"You were magnificent," Stephen said, rubbing his cheek gently against her hair.

"I was so furious." She showed him a sealed letter addressed to her. "I have not had the courage to open this. I'll do it now, while you are with me." She cracked open the seal and unfolded the sheet of paper, then held it so that they could read it together.

Loring Place, 1 October 1814

To Lady Loring

Madam,

I was appalled to learn from a public newssheet that you have taken leave of your senses and left England for the Continent without my knowledge and consent.

"That is a lie," Delia said. "I gave my maid a letter for him, advising him of my intention."

"He could claim that he only knew you had done so when he read the report, but that is splitting hairs, or even say he had not received your letter."

"Hmmm."

You are hereby instructed to return immediately to England and to resume residence at our marital home, Loring Place. Mr Crosbie, by whose hand you receive this letter, and his wife will escort you and you are to obey their directions in all things. Fail to comply at your peril as the full rigour of the law, including imprisonment, may otherwise be visited upon you.

Your injured husband,
Sir Edward Loring

Delia cast her eyes to Heaven. "What nonsense! Who does he think will imprison me? The authorities here?"

Stephen flicked the letter contemptuously. "This is an empty threat. It is impossible that his cases could have been heard both in the Ecclesiastical and Civil Courts in less than two months and during the long vacation at that. You'll note he says 'may be visited', not 'will be visited'. He is trying to frighten you into compliance."

"Supposing Edward did sue for… what did you call it, restitution of marital rights? Could he then apply to the courts here to have any verdict fulfilled?"

"I seriously doubt it. It is a civil matter, after all, and a protestant marriage if it comes to that."

"I wonder how this Crosbie comes into it. I have neither heard of nor seen him before today."

"That is also strange." Stephen shook his head. "If your husband were not so old, I would say it is some foolish scheme dreamt up by a couple of jug-bitten friends late at night."

She sighed. "You may well be right. Sadly, Edward is the sort that, once committed, would see it through, too."

"I hope we have put an end to it now. Do you intend to reply to this?"

"My instinct is to have no more to do with him. But I should like to consult your aunt first."

Lady Mary peered distastefully at Sir Edward's letter. "The man must be deranged to write such a thing. Common sense would suggest that he take a more conciliatory tone; tell you your daughter asked for you, say he was prepared to forgive and forget, and to start afresh."

Delia inhaled sharply. "Such an appeal would be very difficult to resist but, if he were capable of issuing it, it is quite likely that it would never have been necessary. To be fair, while he might insinuate that he has already had recourse to the law even if that cannot be the case, he would not attempt to lure me with false forgiveness—and it would be false, unless he had had a huge change of heart."

"In such a case, one could expect him to come and fetch you himself," Lady Mary said. "He is not too old or infirm to travel, is he?"

"No. he was sixty in May and is accustomed to spending days in the saddle." Delia looked again at the letter. "I don't know whether to reply or not."

"What would you say?"

"That I am surprised that he would even suggest that I travel in the company of complete strangers and, given the lack of a conciliatory tone in his letter, I see no point in our attempting to live together. I shall therefore not return to England."

"Returning slap for slap is not going to improve matters," Lady Mary said.

"Presumably Crosbie will have to report on the failure of his enterprise," Stephen put in.

"Yes. Let that be my reply." Delia handed him the letter and the authorisation. "Burn these, if you please."

He nodded and went over to drop them in the hearth. A tinder box stood ready on the mantlepiece, and the sheets soon blazed brightly. When the flames died down, he used the poker to ensure that nothing was left but fine ash.

"And let that be the end of Mr and Mrs Crosbie," Delia said. "I hope we do not run into them in town. They will hardly have the effrontery to come here again."

~~~

"Gianluca. What have you to report?"

Gianluca shook his head. "That is not a happy couple, Milord. He set off at too fast a pace for her, and she started scolding as soon as she thought they were unobserved. I could not understand what she was saying—my English is not so good and she spoke very fast, but there was no mistaking her tone. Then, when it got steeper, she began to slip and slide. He stopped when she called to him and came back and gave her his arm. Now he started to complain, but more about the reception they got here, I think;

again, it was hard to understand, but he mentioned la Lady Mary and Lady Loring. That is Lady Delia, I think?"

"Yes. Go on."

"Her tone changed then, and she seemed to be soothing him; at any rate, his humour improved. She was limping by the time they reached the town—her shoes were too light and she may have got a blister. They have taken lodgings at the edge of the English quarter, west of the Paglion—one of the smaller houses. I had a drink at the tavern opposite. They are not the usual English sort— they are too young, and neither appears to suffer from the chest like so many of the visitors do. They were looking for rooms for two weeks only, and he became irate when he was told they were let only by the month. They arrived with the *diligence* from Paris, but he has been enquiring about hiring a felucca."

"He has, has he? Keep your ears open, Gianluca. There is something havey-cavey there. Now, what's the best place to buy mules and a small carriage?"

~~~

After the shock of the Crosbie's visit, Delia was happy to remain for the most part on the *Della Torre* estate. While Stephen and Gianluca continued their search for 'handsome mules, not the downtrodden beasts you see at the liveries', she took her easel and materials to particular viewpoints where she could indulge in painting larger scenes.

"I must work up my sketches," she said to Stephen, "but we will have some wet and windy days, I am told, so I must enjoy the end of summer while I can."

Having first protested that it was not suitable for *una signora*, Luca's wife, Marta, had bought her one of the washerwomen's broad-brimmed hats, which she wore on these excursions together with a loose, long-sleeved gown that was soon spattered with colour. After the first day, she had dashed off a quick self-portrait for Chloe, writing under it *I wonder would you recognise your mother in this costume.*

Generally, she painted in the mornings. They took their main meal around midday and rested afterwards. She would see the need for this *riposo* when the weather was warmer, Lady Mary said. "I have become accustomed to it, and as everyone does it here, one might as well do it too."

Delia soon discovered there were many advantages to the *riposo*. At first, it seemed very daring to lie down with Stephen in the early afternoon, but she very quickly came to enjoy these languorous hours in a dim, half-shuttered room.

"Sometimes I think I was only half-alive before," she said once, as she lay with her head on his shoulder. "Everything seems so much more vivid here. At first, I thought it was the light, but now I think it is because I am happy in a way I never was before."

"I feel it too," he said. "Before, the most one could hope for was a sort of contented boredom."

"Or bored contentment," she said with a smile. "If nothing bad had happened, it was a good day."

"Did bad things happen that frequently?"

"Oh, there might have been a household disaster of some sort or another. Looking back, I was lonely, and always a little on edge. If Edward was unhappy about something, he spoke to me, then I had to ensure it didn't happen again. But I don't want to talk about him. This is a happy house. You can feel the respect and affection go in all directions."

"That is Aunt Mary. Her houses always feel like home, not just somewhere to sleep and eat, but here is something special."

Chapter Thirteen

Five sets of hooves clattered cheerfully on the stony lane that was the rear entrance to the *Villa Della Torre*. Stephen rode his new saddle mule and led the white female he had selected for Delia. Gianluca, who had also bought a saddle mule, followed with the two new carriage mules.

"A good morning's work," Stephen called as they neared where the lane veered right towards the stables. A narrower path continued towards the left for a couple of hundred yards, ending at a cliff above a picturesque ravine.

"What the devil!" Stephen frowned at the horse and carriage blocking the way and shouted to the coachman dozing on the block. "Hey! This is private property, not the place for your *riposo*! Take yourself off at once."

The driver stirred and called back, "I'm not sleeping, *signore*, or at least only until the *inglese* returns."

"Englishman? What Englishman?"

"A crazy one. This is the third day he has had me drive up this way and wait. A different place each time. He is collecting plants, he said."

"I don't care what he is doing. He won't do it here."

"Help! *Aiuto! Aiuto!*"

Delia! Stephen threw the leading rein of the white mule to Gianluca, clapped his heels to his mount's sides and headed in the direction of her cries. Beneath them, he could hear a male voice swearing in English. He exploded onto the cliff top to see Delia struggling frantically with George Crosbie, who had seized her by the waist. Her back was to him and she must have realised that her half-boots would do little damage to his hessians, but she fiercely jabbed her elbows into his midriff while jerking her head back so that the stiff brim of her straw hat caught him in the throat or face.

"Stop, you doxy!"

Stephen turned the mule so that it stood crossways, blocking the narrow path. "Put her down this instant!"

Crosbie's grip slackened as he turned to confront his challenger. Delia slipped from his grasp, swung around, and slapped him across the face. "How dare you! What the devil do you think you are at, laying hands on me like that? I shall have you arrested for assault, sir."

"Assault? It is no such thing. I'm merely fulfilling my obligation to your husband. If you had obeyed and come willingly…"

"Obligation! Faugh! You should be ashamed of yourself. And he too." With every word, she took a step nearer, causing him to back unsteadily away from her.

He must have realised he was getting uncomfortably close to the edge of the cliff, for he suddenly exclaimed, "Oh, the hell with it! Why should I saddle myself with a harpy? If your husband is fool enough to want you back, let him collect you himself."

He swept up the hat that must have fallen off in the initial confrontation, and barged past Stephen, whose mule bridled and brayed loudly. The others joined in the wild cacophony, kicking out in a flurry that sent Crosbie crashing to the ground, where he tried frantically to protect himself from their sharp hooves.

At last, he sat up and looked around warily, only to face Gianluca, who sat impassively on his mount, a pistol in his hand.

"Up! Slowly. Hands in the air. Come to me."

When Crosbie did not respond, Gianluca raised his pistol. "Now! Do not make me ask again."

Crosbie rose stiffly. As the man made his way to Gianluca, Stephen edged past him so that he was between him and Delia. She came to him at once.

He touched her cheek. "Did he hurt you?"

"I don't think so. I'm more shaken. And furious."

"We'll get you back to the Villa. I daren't let go of these reins. Can you walk beside me, or would you prefer to sit in the saddle while I lead you?"

She smiled sheepishly. "I don't think this is the time to experiment, do you? I'll walk."

"Gianluca! Take him to the stables. We'll decide there what to do with him," Stephen called.

Gianluca nodded agreement without taking his eyes off his captive. "You, sir. Move."

Crosbie cast Gianluca a resentful glance, but began to walk in the direction indicated. As they neared the waiting carriage, the coachman opened the door and Crosbie dived into it, calling 'drive on'. But Gianluca was at the horse's head before the man could climb onto the box, and Stephen had closed up behind. There was no way out.

"Forward." Gianluca pointed ahead, and the coachman complied.

"In here." Stephen led the way to the harness room that also served as a sort of common room for the stable workers.

Gianluca, who had a firm grip on Crosbie's arm, steered him to a bench. "Sit."

"Go to the devil! I'm not your dog." Crosbie swung around to glare at Stephen. "You'll regret this, FitzCharles."

"On the contrary, you will regret your attempted abduction of a lady."

"It's not an abduction. I have her husband's permission."

"But not her consent. I doubt very much that the senators here would support you. Once you appeared before them, that is. There is no *habeas corpus*, and, of course, they are still dealing with the after-effects of the French occupation. You would probably be imprisoned for several months before the trial," Stephen added helpfully.

He had no idea how much of this was true, but best to make the situation appear as dire as possible. The important thing now was to remove the Crosbies from Nice as discreetly and quickly as possible. He looked at Gianluca. "Do they still sentence criminals to the galleys? Have you read Smollett's *Travels Through France and Italy*, Crosbie? He gives a graphic description of the conditions on them. Or you might be sentenced to the *strappado*. A man is never the same afterwards, I'm told."

Crosbie had grown pale and beads of sweat stood on his forehead. "They would not dare condemn an Englishman to such punishments."

"Shall we put it to the test? Lady Loring only has to lay a charge against you. There are two witnesses in addition to your driver, who can attest that you have been lying in wait for the last couple of days. That makes it intentional and with malice aforethought, does it not? That should add to the sentence."

"Think of my wife!" Crosbie said desperately. "What would become of her if I am torn from her?"

"If you pen the authorisation, I am sure we can find someone to escort her back to England," Stephen said carelessly. "It won't matter that she does not know them, after all, or how roughly they treat her. Your permission will excuse it."

"Perhaps that is simplest," Gianluca said. "If he does not return, I mean. No need to bother the senators. There are still many brigands in the mountains. And deep ravines. After so many years of war, what is one more dead man?"

"You wouldn't do it!" Crosbie said desperately. "Lord Stephen!"

"No," Delia said. "I could not have that on my conscience. He said he had a yacht waiting; we could be away as soon as I liked. Why don't we put him and his wife on it and get them out of Nice and into France? They can go wherever they like from there. Let them go, provided they swear never to return here."

"An excellent suggestion. I'll go with them," Gianluca said, "just to ensure that they do not turn back."

"Well, Crosbie?" Stephen asked. "Will you leave quietly or take your chances with the senators?"

"You leave me no choice," Crosbie said sullenly. "Damn all old fogies. That is the last time I do a favour for one."

"Why? How did you get involved in this?" Delia asked curiously.

"Sir Edward and my uncle met at his cousin's home. My uncle knew we were in France…"

"Who is this cousin? No, don't tell me. Sir Jethro Boyce?"

When he nodded, she raised her eyes to Heaven. "You had the right of it," she said to Stephen. "A scheme dreamt up when they were in their cups."

"Where is your wife, Crosbie?" Stephen asked.

"Waiting, at our lodgings."

"We'll go there first. Gianluca, if you go in the carriage with him, I'll see my lady into the house and ride down after you."

"Very good, Milord. Would you be good enough to ask Piero to bring my saddle-bag and bed-roll down to the harbour? He will know what I need."

~~~

"What a farce," Delia said as she and Stephen strolled back to the Villa, her hand tucked safely into his arm. "And all because three inebriated men got a bee in their bonnet. What on earth made Crosbie agree to it?"

"Money? He strikes me as being a bit of an adventurer."

"Perhaps. Well, if Edward sent him funds, his money was spent in vain."

Stephen laughed. "How satisfying that they will both receive their just deserts."

She yawned hugely. "I suddenly feel very tired."

"Fighting does that. You should lie down for a while."

She shook her head. "First, I must send someone to fetch my materials. The easel is probably safe, but what of my paper and sketch book, not to mention my paintbox? The watercolour I was working on is probably ruined by now."

"Leave it to me. I'll have Luca arrange it. You must rest."

~~~

It was several hours before Stephen returned. He smiled at Delia when he came into their sitting-room. "Between the dust from the ride with the mules, and now up and down to the harbour, I'm not fit to be near you. Let me wash and change, and then we can talk."

"Have you eaten?"

"Not since breakfast."

She went to the door. "I'll have something brought up. What would you like?"

"Whatever is quick, but some coffee as well as wine. Thank you, my love."

He hurried into his bedroom, where he quickly stripped. The water in the big ewer on the wash-stand was cool and refreshing. He filled the basin and plunged his head into it, sluicing off the combined dust and sweat, then washed his torso and legs. Revived, he dressed quickly in drawers, shirt, and trousers, throwing a light silk banyan over all. A swipe at his hair with the towel, followed by a quick comb with his fingers, and he was ready. He thrust his feet into slippers and returned to Delia.

A plate of bread, olives, and thinly sliced ham awaited him on a small table drawn up to his favourite chair, together with a beaded jug of the local pale pink wine. "They will bring up an omelette and the coffee in a few minutes."

"Thank you." He sat and stretched his legs gratefully.

She poured him a glass of wine. "What took you so long?"

He began to laugh. "A more ill-conceived abduction you cannot imagine. Did he seriously think you would wait submissively in the carriage while he collected his wife, her maid, and his valet, not to mention the last of their baggage? And then, at the port, we had to waken the captain from his post-prandial rest and he had to send someone to look for the rest of his crew. And during all of this, you would have sat there as meek as a monk's mouse, with nary a tweak nor a squeak to you?"

She laughed too. "I don't think he intended to abduct me, but more to convince me. I imagine he is well used to wheedling women into doing what he wants. His whole plan was frustrated when your aunt would not receive him. He had thought to insinuate himself into her good graces, and mine, and only then raise the subject of my return to England. But I wanted nothing to do with him and told him, in Luca's presence, not to call again. After your warnings, he did not dare approach me openly."

She paused at the tap on the door, called, "Come in," and waited while Stephen was served coffee and a plump, green-flecked omelette. Then she helped herself to wine and came to sit beside him.

"What happened this morning?" Stephen asked.

"He suddenly appeared on the cliff path. When I asked him what he was doing there, first he said his wife was interested in the plants of the area and he wanted to collect some for her. I pointed out that he was trespassing and said he must have known this because there are gates across the lane. He hemmed and hawed, then said he wanted to talk to me in private. He had heard I spent the mornings painting and had ventured to seek me out. He hoped that, as a right-thinking Englishwoman, I would defer to my husband's wishes, even if I had been misled into assuming I could lawfully accompany Lady Mary. He would make it as easy as possible for me; we could slip away—he had a yacht waiting—and I could send her ladyship a letter from the harbour. When I told him, point blank, that I had no intention of accompanying him and that I would call for help if he did not leave instanter, he suddenly looked like thunder and said, 'We'll see about that.' And then he seized me."

She put her hand on Stephen's. "I did call for help, and would have fought until the end, but I was never so happy as when you burst onto the scene, mules and all. It was a magnificent entrance."

His hand twisted and caught hers. "I was afraid you had fallen, at best, on the path, at worst, over the cliff. You fought splendidly, my love."

"I did my best. He tried to take my hat off, but it was tied too tightly. I couldn't see, of course, but going by his yelps and oaths, it was quite effective."

"Indeed, it was; his face is quite cut up. The mules did not leave him unscathed either."

"I cannot say that I am sorry for it. Edward must be paying him, for I cannot imagine him doing it for nothing, even to oblige a relative. To be honest, it debases all of them. And me."

"Never you," Stephen said quickly. "Remember, it was not your choice to leave your home, and you were forbidden to return there. You would have gone otherwise in September."

"That is true. For Chloe's sake. I still would, Stephen. If he arrived at the door tomorrow with her, and they offered forgiveness and asked me to come home. It would break my heart to leave you, but I could not refuse." She shook her head. "It won't happen. He would have to suffer a Damascene conversion, like Saint Paul, before he would do such a thing."

It hurt that she could speak so easily of leaving him. Then he saw the pain in her eyes. She pays for her happiness every day, he thought. The more she loved him, and he had no doubt that she loved him dearly, the greater her fear of being forced to make an impossible choice. He could not blame her for putting her daughter first, but he despised her scheming swine of a husband who seemed determined to keep her on the rack.

Chapter Fourteen

Lady Mary began to pay a judiciously selected round of calls in her new carriage. More visitors from England arrived, electrifying the English colony with the news that the Princess of Wales, who had left England, perhaps for ever, in August and had been steadily been making her way south from her native Brunswick, had now arrived in Rome and proposed to spend the winter at Naples. This was not so far from Nice that a visit could not be expected, perhaps after Christmas.

Although sympathetic towards the Princess, who was even more unfortunate in her husband than she was, Delia was not among those who hoped for such an event. Lady Mary's small circle of intimates provided as much company as she needed. Stephen had presented Dr and Mrs Costain to his ladies, and Lady Mary and Delia had taken a liking to the former don and his frail wife, Lady Mary going so far as to send the carriage for them as Mrs Costain would be unable to manage the uphill walk to the Villa. The fresher air at the higher altitude proved invigorating to her; she breathed easier and found it possible to walk on the flat ridge. She accepted gratefully when Lady Mary offered to send the carriage once a week, saying she would welcome her company.

At Marta's suggestion, instead of an English ladies' saddle, Delia had opted for a padded saddle of the type that the peasant women used, with saddle-bags for her painting paraphernalia. "It must look quite rustic, and I am sure would cause a lot of hilarity at home, but I feel comfortable and secure in it," she said. "And who is going to see me, after all?"

Seated side-saddle on the sure-footed mule, she explored the surrounding countryside with Stephen, meandering up and down the mountain paths and through plantations of citrus and olive trees. As the days grew shorter and less hot, they frequently took a pick-nick with them rather than returning for the midday meal, tethering the mules and spreading a rug in a secluded, picturesque spot to enjoy some cheese and ham, olives and dried figs or other fruit and a glass of wine. Sometimes a passer-by, usually a local, stopped to chat and to suggest a particular aspect the visitors might like to see, but generally they were alone.

~~~

Gianluca returned from Marseilles, bringing goods, including a generous selection of English newssheets and periodicals. He had assisted the Crosbies to obtain at a reasonable price *une chaise de renvoi*, a carriage hired in Boulogne for the journey to Marseilles that now needed to be returned to its home inn, explaining that this would provide them with much more flexibility and comfort than relying on the public *diligences*, as they had when travelling south.

"We parted the best of friends," he reported to Stephen. "He is quite easily led, that one. If his wife does not take him in hand, he will run aground sooner or later. Not every man would have dealt with him as mildly as you did."

"I suppose you think I should have called him out."

"A Frenchman or an Italian would have."

"I was very tempted to, or at least take a horsewhip to him, but thought it more important to avert a scandal. The English colony is a hotbed of gossip; most of them have little to do except write and receive letters. Word would have quickly reached England, where in all likelihood it would have been blown up out of all proportion. And there would be no one there to defend Lady Delia."

"Will he keep his mouth shut, do you think?"

"If he opens it, he will make a laughing-stock of himself; first for having accepted such a commission and then for failing to execute it."

Lady Mary was thrilled by the bounty of reading material. The weather had changed; it was a dull, wet day, and she had had a fire lit in the library, "More for comfort than for heat. No one will call on such a day. We'll have tea and read together. I must start a list of new books—I always did that so that if someone was coming from England, I knew what to ask for. I'll start with *The Morning Chronicle.*"

Stephen chose *The Times* and Delia, the latest issue of *La Belle Assemblée.* Apart from the sound of pages turning, all was quiet. Although each was focussed on their own journal, there was a sense of joint enterprise, of togetherness, that was emphasised when someone read out a snippet of news, a description of a play, or a few lines of verse. They set their papers aside while Luca supervised the setting out of the tea equipage, adding a plate of little cakes flavoured with candied orange peel and another of macaroons.

"The macaroons are too sweet for me, but these are delicious." Stephen passed his cup for more tea and helped himself to another orange cake. "There is something very reviving about freshly made tea. How much did you bring with you, Aunt?"

"Enough for a year, at least. Another cup, Delia?"

"If you please. I never thought I should be glad of a wet day, but it is cosy to sit around the hearth, enjoying the scent of wood smoke and the faint crackle and hiss of the fire.

"It reminds one of England," Stephen said, "especially with the newssheets." He put down his cup, wiped his fingers and picked up *The Gentleman's Magazine*. "Let us see what Urban has to offer. He is generally a prosy sort of fellow."

"Look at the births, marriages, and deaths," Lady Mary suggested. "They are concise, at least."

He obediently flicked to the back and began to read aloud. Apart from the announcement of the heir to an earldom, the births were of little interest. "Marriages," he proclaimed, then, in a completely different voice, "Delia! Listen to this. *At Swanmere church, Sir Julian Swann-Loring, grandson and heir of Lord Swanmere, and son and heir of Sir Edward Loring, to Rosa, only daughter of the late Capt. Charles Fancourt R.N.*"

"What? Let me see." She took the periodical from him, tilting it towards the candles to see better. "Miss Fancourt." She closed her eyes as an immense wave of gratitude and relief washed over her. "She was Chloe's governess for ten years and is sincerely attached to her. Oh, thank God!"

She hastily put down the magazine and accepted the handkerchief Stephen pressed into her hand. Smiling through her tears, she said, "I know she will be good to Chloe. If she has married Julian, he will speak for his sister too. Who knows, they may even take her to live with them; they will certainly bring her out when the time comes."

"That is certainly good news," Lady Mary said. "Although I am surprised at Swanmere approving a match between his heir and his sister's governess."

"He, Swanmere, I mean, got to know her when he stayed with us in May for Sir Edward's birthday celebrations. He admired her singing, and I know Julian asked her to keep an eye on his grandfather during the ball. Swanmere is also great friends with the dowager Lady Loring and she may have had something to say. However it came about, I can only be pleased."

"Do you think I might write to Miss Fancourt; send my good wishes on her marriage?" Delia asked Stephen when they were on their own.

"Why not?"

"Even if she does not reply, she will know how to reach me. And it will be a little connection with Chloe." She bit her lip. "It's not only that, Stephen. I am so relieved to know that she took no lasting harm from May's events. Julian was very concerned about her; it was he who chased down Purdue and got the full story from him. Of course, that finished me, but I could not blame him."

He took her in his arms. "You have paid dearly for your slip. Endeavour to put it behind you now, my love. Write your letter if it will help you, and let go of the rest."

~~~

"Captain Arnold called to see me earlier," Lady Mary said to her nephew.

"Oh? What did he want?" Stephen asked.

"After some beating about the bush, it emerged that he wanted to know my intentions for the yacht. It must have new sails and some other work done, especially if I want to take it back home next year."

"Do you intend to go back to England for the summer?"

"I don't know, Stephen. I am getting too old to go back and forth the way we used to. I must decide where I wish to end my days. My daughters and grandchildren are in England, but they may be happy to visit me here…"

"As I always will be."

She sat looking at him for some moments, then said, "Do you think you could make a permanent home here, you and Delia? We have made a very pleasant company these past months, have we not?"

"Yes, indeed."

"Think about it, Stephen. The *Villa Della Torre* is mine outright, and my daughters are very well provided for. You are like a son to me and I should be happy to know that you would live here after me. If you were agreeable, we could draw up a deed of gift. I would retain the right to live here, of course, but that should not be a problem."

Stephen had never been so taken aback. After a moment, he kissed his aunt's cheek. "You are very generous, Aunt, and I shall think about it, I promise you." He smiled ruefully at her. "As long as Loring is alive, Delia cannot return to England, I know. I have been considering where we might make a home. Perhaps Nice is too—English."

And Loring knew they were there. Would he be foolhardy enough to make another abduction attempt? Crosbie had been sent home with his tail between his legs. It was unlikely Loring could make any new arrangements before the spring. But what then?

He and Delia made no secret of the fact that they shared a bed. Servants talked. How would Lady Mary's daughters feel about coming to stay if Delia and Stephen were so blatantly in residence? All in all, it might be better if they moved further south in the spring—to Rome or Naples. As for the yacht…

"I own I would much rather travel by land than by sea," he said to his aunt. "The roads have improved considerably since the last century, have they not?"

"Yes. The journey here was quite comfortable." She sighed. "I held on to her, I think, because as long as I had her, I could tell myself I would return here one day. And I felt an obligation to those of the crew who had come with me."

"Did you use her much?"

"Once or twice a year, perhaps. Otherwise, she could be hired through my agent at Bridlington. She paid for herself, which was all I cared about. But now… Arnold said there was someone interested in buying her. I'll have my agent here look into it, but I think I'll accept."

Chapter Fifteen

Loring Place, Suffolk, end December 1814

The servants were on the lookout. As soon as the first carriage halted, Meadows, the butler, opened the door. Sir Julian Swann-Loring jumped down and turned to offer his hand to his wife. His eyes narrowed when he saw Mapps, his father's land steward, waiting on the gravelled carriage sweep.

"How is he?"

Mapps raised a hand and let it fall. "The fever is still very high, Sir Julian."

"Who is looking after him?"

"Mrs Walton and his valet, together with a nurse the doctor sent."

"I'll go up to him." Julian looked at his wife. "I'll join you, grandmother, and Chloe in the drawing-room shortly."

"Go ahead, don't worry about us," Rosa said. "Meadows, what rooms have been prepared for Sir Julian and me?"

"The blue suite, my lady. Here is Mrs Walton to take you up."

The housekeeper looked tired and drawn, but she came forward with a smile. "Welcome back, my ladies, Miss Loring. It is only a pity that you have come on such an occasion."

"Indeed, Walton," the dowager Lady Loring said. "Let us go up."

Rosa couldn't remember ever having been in the blue suite before. It consisted of two large bed-chambers linked by a sitting-room. The furnishings were of good quality but old-fashioned. Fires were burning in all three rooms, and pots of forced pink tulips provided a vibrant contrast to the faded draperies. The surroundings don't matter as long as the beds are comfortable, she thought, as she took off her gloves, bonnet, and pelisse.

She drew out a chair at the round table in the centre of the sitting-room and sat. "You must be exhausted, Mrs Walton," she said sympathetically. "Pray sit down and tell me what has been happening here. We knew nothing until the groom arrived yesterday. We set out at first light."

Mrs Walton subsided with a grateful sigh. "Thank you, my lady. May I first wish you and Sir Julian happy? I think that was the last good news we had here. This is not how we had hoped to receive you."

"Thank you."

"When Sir Edward came back from Swanmere after the wedding, he was not in the best of humours, but I can't say what set him off. He spent some days in Ipswich, as was his custom." The housekeeper flushed. "I'm sorry, my lady; did Sir Julian mention…?"

"The establishment there? Yes, he did. But say nothing of it to Miss Loring or her ladyship."

"No, my lady. Well, after that he went to stay with Sir Jethro Boyce for some shooting. I don't know if you remember him—he stayed with us for Sir Edward's birthday in May?" At Rosa's nod, she continued. "The master was in a strange mood when he came back. In the middle of November, he told me to make sure that Lady Loring's rooms were ready for her—he wasn't sure when she would return, but before Christmas, he said. And then he said she was to have a companion, and what room would be suitable for her? I suggested your room, I mean the one you used to have on the third floor..." She stopped, clearly embarrassed.

"Yes?" Rosa said encouragingly. The governess returning as wife of the heir was something they all must adjust to.

"But neither her ladyship nor the companion came. About two weeks ago, a strange gentleman and his wife, a Mr and Mrs Crosbie, called to see the master. I don't know what it was about; they were with him for about an hour, and then he rang for Meadows to show them out. He was quite snappish afterwards. They both had bad head colds, and the lady was coughing to such an extent that Meadows had me make tea for her, saying the master would not think to order it.

"Well, he must have caught it from them, mustn't he? Within two or three days, he was sneezing, but he paid no attention to it, and continued to ride out as usual. Then it went to his chest—first a cough, then it hurt him to breathe, and his valet thought he was feverish. He didn't want the doctor, but when it got worse, we took it on ourselves to send for Dr Hastings, who said it was an inflammation of the lungs. He bled Sir Edward, and prescribed draughts for the fever and to purge him—said we should try to give him tea and broth and the nurse should bathe his limbs in an attempt to reduce the fever. We did all that, but he did not improve, only got worse. The evening before yesterday, the doctor said all we could do now was wait for the crisis. Either the fever would break soon or, if it continued so high, it would be too much of a strain on the heart. We should send for Sir Julian, he said, which we did first thing yesterday morning."

"I see," Rosa said quietly. "Thank you, Mrs Walton. I'm sure you have done everything you could. It is in the hands of God, now."

She said the same to Julian when he came in ten minutes later.

He nodded. "He was quite restless during the night, the nurse said, but now he seems more in a stupor than asleep. He did not respond to my voice or my touch. It is strange to see him so still. Hastings will call again later, she said." He sighed. "Let us join Grandmother and Chloe. They will be wondering, too."

"Yes, but first—did you know your father was expecting his wife home before Christmas?"

"What?"

"So Mrs Walton said. That must be why he refused our invitation. But she never came, nor did a companion who was to come too."

"A companion?"

"Mrs Walton did not say anything more. Perhaps he thought Delia would be lonely. It sounds as if he had a change of heart. But there was nothing of that in her letter. If anything, it read as if she expects to be abroad indefinitely."

"Yes. Have you replied yet?"

"No. I was waiting until after Christmas. I would not say anything to Chloe until we know more."

"No, definitely not. She has had so much to deal with this year."

"How is Papa? May I go to him?" Chloe asked as soon as Julian and Rosa came into the drawing-room.

"He is sleeping now," Julian said. "Perhaps later, after the doctor has been here."

"It is strange being back here, especially without Mamma. The house feels empty—unlived in. I should not have left him alone for so long."

Poor Chloe. He could hardly explain to her that her father had kept a mistress for over twenty years, and would have regarded his daughter's presence at the Place a hindrance to his enjoyment of that woman's company.

While Julian racked his brains for a soothing response, his grandmother snorted. "If you had been here these past months, you would have been mostly on your own, child. Have you forgotten that, between shooting and hunting, your father rarely ate at home at this time of the year?"

Chloe smiled reluctantly. "That is true. Most evenings we were an all-female company at dinner."

"And it was his choice not to come to Swanmere for Christmas," Lady Loring continued. "You have no reason to reproach yourself, Chloe. None of us could have foreseen this."

"I suppose not."

They were interrupted by the arrival of the tea-tray. The room looked more cheerful once the curtains were drawn, shutting out the grey December twilight, and the candles lit, but the conversation remained slow and sombre, the participants always alert to the sound of steps or the opening of a door.

They separated again to change for dinner, a quiet meal that was interrupted by the arrival of the doctor. Julian went to meet him. He returned half an hour later, looking very grave. "There is no hope. We are talking hours rather than days, Hastings says. If you wish to say a last goodbye, you should come now, but you must be aware that it is unlikely he will respond."

Lady Loring got up heavily from the table. "He is my son," she said simply.

"Come, ma'am, I'll take you up." Julian offered his grandmother his arm.

Chloe's lips trembled.

"Would you like me to go with you?" Rosa asked her sister-in-law quietly. "You can decide upstairs whether you wish to go in. Perhaps you would prefer to remember him as you knew him."

"I must go in," Chloe said resolutely. "I shall always regret it if I don't."

Sir Edward lay propped against pillows in the big four-poster bed. A small fire glowed in the hearth and, apart from the shaded bedside candle, a candelabrum on the mantelpiece provided the only other light in the big room.

When Julian led his grandmother in, the nurse and valet withdrew from the bedside. The old woman stood, her mouth working, as she looked down at her only son. "I brought you into the world, and now I must see you out of it," she whispered. She bent and kissed his sunken cheek. "Go with God, my son. Until we meet again."

"Do you think we will?" Chloe muttered to Rosa from the door. "Meet again, I mean?"

"I don't know in what way, but yes."

"It is strange to see him in nightshirt and nightcap. He is not a fussy dresser, but precise. You never saw him in a banyan, like Lord Ransford sometimes, or Lord Swanmere."

"He is considerably younger than Swanmere, and was always in good health up to now. He liked to be out and about."

"That makes it harder." The girl squared her shoulders. "Let us go in."

Lady Loring held out a hand to her granddaughter and Chloe went forward hesitantly until she stood beside her.

"Poor Papa." She took his hand and stooped to press a kiss on his forehead. "That is how you used kiss me 'good night'. Good night, Papa, and, and…" She could say no more, nor stop the tears rolling down her cheeks.

"Come and sit down, my love." Lady Loring led her over to the fireplace. "Julian," she said to her grandson, "have Dover bring my prayerbook. We shall say the prayers for the sick together."

~~~

Sir Edward died peacefully just after dawn. His dazed family gathered, numb, and pre-occupied by all that must be done within a week. Letters must be written, the parson notified, solicitors summoned, the funeral arranged. Bed-chambers must be made ready for possible visitors and meals planned when there was no real idea of how many must be catered for.

"It is fortunate that the larder and pantry are well-stocked," Mrs Walton observed to Rosa. "We did not know what to do for Christmas, and then, with the master so ill, there was no proper celebration. Cook roasted a turkey, and we had mince pies and plum pudding, but our hearts weren't in it, you might say."

"Do you still have the bills of fare from the house party in May?" Rosa asked. "We could take them as a guide, bearing in mind that not everything will be in season."

"That's a good idea, my lady. There's over a week's worth there, and Cook is familiar with all the dishes."

Mourning was another problem. Neither Chloe nor Rosa had any blacks, while the dowager's mourning garb was so outmoded that she could no longer wear it. Bury's best dressmaker came with her assistants, laden with bolts of black crape, silk, velvet, and the appropriate trimmings, ready to stay until the ladies' immediate needs were met. A milliner called with black bonnets and gloves while black shoes and half-boots were hastily commissioned from the shoemaker, who fortunately had lasts of the ladies' feet.

Then the servants had to be suitably arrayed, and provision made for the mourners at the funeral who would expect to receive gloves and weepers at the least, and a rich armozeen scarf, hat band, and black silk gloves must be ordered for the officiating clergyman.

Amidst all this bustle, Sir Edward's family grieved and his servants wondered what would become of the Place.

"I do not see her old ladyship returning to live here on her own, or with Miss Chloe," Mrs Walton said to the select group that took dessert in the housekeeper's room. "Nor is Sir Julian likely to be here more than once or twice a year."

"What about the mistress?" the butler asked. "Was she not to return? She might still do so. Perhaps they were delayed by the weather."

"Even if she does, Lady Swann-Loring has the say now," Sir Julian's valet pointed out.

"Miss Dover, from what you say, your lady and Miss Chloe are well-settled at Swanmere?" Mrs Walton asked the dowager Lady Loring's maid.

"I would have thought so. And they are better off there too, than on their own here," Dover said.

~~~

Although she had lived in his home for over ten years, to Rosa, Sir Edward had never been anything other than her ultimate employer; captain to Lady Loring's first lieutenant, if she were to think in navy parlance.

He had taught her to ride when she first came to the Place, at the same time as he taught Chloe, saying that if she was to be in charge of his daughter, she must be able to ride well. He had been a gruff, demanding instructor, but he treated her no differently than he treated Chloe, and had purchased a good horse for her. Apart from that, until Chloe had been deemed old enough to dine downstairs, her only interaction with him had been the hour before dinner when she brought her pupil to the drawing-room, although frequently he had not been there. He was very much the master of the house; his orders were to be obeyed, and his final say brought any discussion to an end.

So far as she knew, he had not objected to Julian's marriage to his daughter's former governess, but he had also not gone out of his way to make Rosa particularly welcome, his attitude in striking contrast to that of Julian's maternal grandfather, Lord Swanmere and paternal grandmother, Lady Loring.

While shocked at Sir Edward's sudden death, she did not mourn him; her concern was for those who did, especially his mother. Once over the initial distress, Julian's and Chloe's heartache was tempered by the fact that he had been a distant parent, of Julian because of his father's resentment of the

Swanmere inheritance, and of Chloe because he did not really know how to talk to a child. Their connection in the past year had grown stronger and, had circumstances not led to Chloe making her home with Julian and Rosa, father and daughter might well have drawn closer now that Chloe was adult. But Chloe also felt lost; Rosa could well remember that feeling of having been cast adrift in the world, your anchor gone, when her own mother died, two years after her father. She had not been much older than Chloe was now.

Chloe had been most distressed by the paragraph in *The Morning Chronicle*, the dowager had said. Something else to lay at the younger Lady Loring's door. What did that lady think now of her illicit tryst with Purdue? Had it been worth it?

Two days later, all the plans were made, but no relatives had yet arrived to attend the funeral. "The calm before the storm," Julian said at breakfast as he passed his coffee cup to Rosa.

"Probably because it is New Year's Eve," Chloe said suddenly. "Last year, when Mamma and Papa went to the Harbisons' Ball, they said I would be able to come with them this year. And now—" She burst into tears. "Who would have thought it?"

Julian put his arm around his sister. "Who would have thought it, indeed? It has been an eventful, even tumultuous year, has it not?"

"It's all Mamma's fault. If she had not misbehaved, Papa would not have been here on his own. He might never have taken ill."

"You cannot be sure of that," her grandmother said. "Do not tease yourself with pointless ifs and ans. Our days are numbered, but it is not given to us to know when we shall be called. Indeed, it seems very strange to me that Edward should be gone and I still here."

"It is best that we cannot see the future," Rosa said. "When I was at school, some girls talked about having their hands read by a fortune-teller, but I never wanted it. Better to be surprised when fortune smiles on us—and when she frowns, *sufficient unto the day the evil thereof.*"

"Talking of fortune smiling, this day last year, none of us thought that you and Julian would be married by today," Chloe said. "That was the best thing that happened this year."

"I agree." Julian's eyes met Rosa's in a mutual smile.

"Papa wasn't very kind to Mamma, was he?" Chloe asked suddenly.

"Why do you say that?" Julian asked.

"I never saw him smile at her, the way you just smiled at Rosa, or heard him say something nice to her. Lord Ransford does it too, and Mr Glazebrook; I noticed it when we were staying with them while you were on your honeymoon. They don't do it as often, but they have been married much longer," the girl continued, as if she were trying to work something out, "but you could see there was a, a tenderness between each couple. But not between Papa and Mamma; at least I don't remember it. Maybe I was too young to notice it. Why do you look at one another like that?" she demanded of the other three.

Lady Loring sighed. "I fear you are right, child."

"Was it like that between them from the beginning?"

"I don't remember. We were taken by surprise—he had gone to visit his great-uncle in Harrogate and returned with a bride. He had written to us of his intention to wed, but it all happened very quickly. And I think she was surprised to find that your grandfather was still alive, and that she would not be mistress of her own household. But all that changed within six months, of course, when he died. Well, you have seen the turmoil caused by such a death. Edward inherited, and I stepped down."

"And now Julian inherits and Mamma would have to step down. But we are not going to live here, are we, Julian?" Chloe asked. "We can't leave Lord Swanmere and the castle."

Lady Loring put down her tea-cup. "Yes, what had you thought to do about this house, Julian?"

"In the first instance, it must depend on you, Grandmother. Under Grandfather's will, you have a lifelong right of residence here. That still stands."

"You won't want to stay here on your own, will you, Grandmother?" Chloe cried.

"You need not answer that now, Grandmother," Julian intervened. "If you wish to remain here, then that will be arranged. However, I speak for Swanmere as well as for Rosa and myself when I say that we should be delighted if you were to make your permanent home at Swanmere."

Lady Loring brushed at her eyes. "You are very kind, all of you," she said huskily. "I had been thinking I should return here in the New Year so that Edward was not alone, but now… it does a house no good to be left vacant."

"What about my mother?" Chloe asked. "Is there a similar provision in Papa's will?"

"Not in the new will he made in August," Julian replied. "But of course he might have changed that. We shall know more when his solicitor calls on Monday."

~~~

"Chloe is taking this hard," Julian said to Rosa that evening as they enjoyed the solitude of their own sitting-room.

"It is compounded by her mother's absence which, you will admit, makes everything more complicated. She feels orphaned but, knowing that her mother still lives, she is torn between longing to see her and anger at being abandoned. She is still only sixteen, and quite mercurial, as is normal in girls of that age—one minute up in alt and the next in the dumps."

"She is growing up fast. That comment about my father not being kind to Delia…"

"Yes. I had never put it into so many words, but I never noticed any rapport between them, the way there was between my own parents."

"It leaves me with a problem. I spent the day going through my father's recent correspondence. He kept several letter books, mostly to do with the estate, but two were personal. One had copies of the letters he wrote, and another where he pasted in letters he received. I do something similar." Julian put down his glass. "The thing is, he wrote to Delia at the end of July."

"Did she get it before she left?"

"She must have. It was a cold letter. He reprimanded her for keeping the carriage, instructed her to send it back here, and said she was to remain in Harrogate for the winter, after which he would judge whether and on what terms she might be permitted to resume her marital duties. He signed himself, 'your injured spouse'."

"That does not sound very forgiving. I wonder did she feel that he was bamboozling her; holding out the hope that he would eventually relent, but determined to oppress her as much as

197

possible? I know Chloe hoped he would forgive her mother and allow her to come home in September."

"I think that was the original idea."

"Presumably that was what Delia told Mrs Eubank too. So she would have had to explain why she needed to remain over the winter, which is the dead season in Harrogate, I believe. Poor woman. She must have decided it was not possible."

"There was also a letter from Sir Jethro, drawing my father's attention to the article in *The Morning Chronicle*. That may have incensed him further, but he did accept an invitation to visit Sir Jethro. After that, there was a letter to a Lieutenant Crosbie authorising him to act on my father's behalf in arranging for the return of Lady Loring to her marital home, and another, very formal one to her, instructing her to return home at once with this lieutenant and his wife—"

"Crosbie," Rosa interrupted. "That was the name of the couple that called on Sir Edward a little over two weeks ago. Mrs Watson swears he caught his illness from them."

"They don't appear to have succeeded in their mission," Julian said dryly. "But, Rosa, in this last letter to Delia, my father quoted some recent Act and threatened her with imprisonment if she did not comply."

"What! I cannot believe it of him."

"He may not have intended to follow through, for it would have meant going to court, and he assured me he would not do so. But the threat was made."

Rosa shook her head. "It certainly makes me better disposed towards Delia."

"What will you say when I tell you that there was also correspondence with a Mrs Hayes, engaging her as a companion to Sir Edward's sickly wife? Part of her duties would be to ensure Lady Loring did not over-exert herself, as she must lead a very quiet life. She was to take up her position today, but he wrote to her on the eighteenth, telling her she would not be needed."

Rosa looked appalled. "He did plan to imprison her, but here."

"I fear so." Julian picked up the decanter. "What am I to say to Chloe about this? Does my grandmother need to know any of it, and should I write to Delia and tell her that her husband is dead? It is likely that she will see a notice in one of the newspapers or journals, but I cannot be sure."

"Of course you should write to her," Rosa said. "She was his wife, and mistress of his household for twenty years. Does that count for nothing? And she is entitled to know the provisions of his will. Chloe has to know that you are her guardian, not her mother, but I think you should also reassure her that you would not prevent her from seeing Delia privately at least, if she returns to England."

"What about writing to her? Should I allow it?"

"She is both sensible and tender-hearted, and already feels sympathetic towards her mother. If you forbid any contact, she may come to resent you and go behind your back. It is more important that she feels she can discuss the whole situation with you, now and in the future."

Chapter Sixteen

Stephen had to smile when he came into Delia's studio. Wrapped in a big apron and her hair covered in a make-shift turban, she was completely engrossed in painting a large landscape based on sketches taken from the yacht, with ranges of hills climbing from a little port to snow-dusted peaks against a blue sky. As he watched, she dabbed red roofs on the white houses of the little town, then changed brushes and colours to add an arched brick bridge over a river.

When she stood back from her easel, he said, "There is a letter for you, Delia. It has a black seal."

"No!" She dropped the brushes into a jar. "Open it. Quickly, Stephen! Tell me it is not, not…"

"No," he said as urgently. "Edward. It's Edward. Your husband."

"Edward." She looked at him pleadingly. "You are sure?"

"Certain. See for yourself."

She put out a wavering hand, then suddenly gave at the knees. Stephen jumped to catch her and carried her to the old settee against the wall.

"Have you nothing to drink here? No?" He took his flask from his pocket and held it to her lips.

She sipped, coughed, and pushed the flask away from her. "I'm sorry. I'm better now. I was terrified…"

"I know." He retrieved the letter from where it had fallen and spread it out for her.

She shook her head. "You read it to me, please."

He slipped his arm around her and she leaned against him, listening.

"Loring Place, 4 January 1815

"My dear Lady Loring,

"It is my sad duty to inform you that Sir Edward Loring, my esteemed father and your husband, departed this life at eight o'clock in the morning of the 29th of December 1814 following a short illness. He had recently contracted a heavy cold; this developed into an inflammation of the lungs from which he could not recover. He was laid to rest here yesterday."

"Three weeks dead already," she murmured. "Is there more?"

"As circumstances prevent your attendance here, I further wish to inform you of the provisions of Sir Edward's last will and testament that concern you:

"Firstly, my sister Chloe is entrusted to my sole guardianship and will make her home at Swanmere Castle. I hope I need not assure you that I regard this as a sacred responsibility and will strive always to do what is best for her. In this I will be supported by my wife who, as you know, is bound to Chloe by ties of deep affection, as is my grandmother, Lady Loring, who will also remove permanently to Swanmere."

"It is best for her, I suppose." Delia's voice was flat, as if she tried to hide her feelings. Stephen pressed a kiss to her hair and continued, *"I should also add that her father made generous provision for Chloe, including a future dowry.*

"Secondly, in accordance with the terms of your marriage settlement, you will receive a jointure of four hundred and eighty pound per annum, to be paid quarterly. Please be so good as to advise me where these payments should be made.

"Finally, you do not have a right of residence at Loring Place or any other property owned by my father. Although no final decision has been made as yet, it is likely that the Place will be let for the next years."

She took a deep breath. "So I am formally cast out. How disappointed he must have been that he could not alter the settlement." She touched Stephen's hand. "He would have been really galled if he knew of your generosity."

"Had he previously arranged a residence for you?"

"I assumed so. I have never seen his will, but I would have expected some arrangement to be made for an establishment for Chloe and me. He recently bought another house adjoining our estate. Perhaps he intended it to be a dower house. There is none—his mother lived with us."

"The letter goes on: *Any personal belongings of yours that are at the Place will be packed and sent to the address of your choosing."*

"That is Julian's doing, or Miss Fancourt's, I imagine. Edward would have had them tossed out of the window."

"Is there much?"

"Enough. I took the most important things with me in May. But there remain clothing and fripperies, books and ornaments. They are all in my bedroom and sitting-room."

"He adds, *Lady Swann-Loring joins me in thanking you for your good wishes on our recent marriage. I am happy to tell you that, apart from the natural shock and grief caused by the sudden loss of her father, Chloe is in good health and good spirits, although she misses her mother and asks me to send you her dearest love.*"

"Oh, Stephen! Let me see." She took the paper and pressed her lips to the precious words. "How kind! He must not be completely opposed to the idea of my maintaining a connection with her."

Stephen hugged her. "That is excellent news, indeed. Sir Julian closes by saying, *We shall not remain long at Loring Place, so all future correspondence should be addressed to Swanmere Castle.* He remains your obedient servant, Sir Julian Swann-Loring."

Delia was silent for a couple of minutes, then she said hesitantly, "Do you think that means I might write to Chloe? That they would give her my letter?"

"I think it is worth a shot. Although this letter is quite business-like, there is no hint of animosity; in fact, I would describe the tone as conciliatory. He goes out of his way to reassure you about Chloe, he passes on her message, and there is also the offer to send you your belongings. All in all, it is very heartening. Delia? Delia?"

He felt a tremor run through her. When she turned her head, he saw her lips tremble and tears fill her eyes and silently flow down her cheeks. He had never experienced anything as heart-rending as this silent weeping. Taking out a handkerchief, he began to blot her tears, all the time cradling her and crooning a nonsensical litany of comfort. At last, she stopped crying, and, still silent, rested her head on his shoulder.

~~~

Why had she cried so, Delia asked herself afterwards? It was not grief; she could not mourn the man who for twenty years had so effortlessly imposed his will on her, little by little clipping her wings until she perched voiceless within the cage he had erected around her. To him, she was a possession—his wife, who, together with his horses and his dogs, bore mute witness to his position in society. No, her tears had been tears of relief that she was free; that she need no longer fear another attempt to force her to return to him. And the even greater relief at the tone of her step-son's letter; it had been perfectly civil; he had assured her of Chloe's well-being and conveyed her 'dearest love'. 'Future correspondence' could certainly include a letter to Chloe.

~~~

She would not go into mourning for her husband, Delia announced at breakfast the following morning. "No one else here is aware of his death and even if it should appear in one of the journals that reach here, that will be several weeks hence and it is quite likely that nobody will make the connection."

"An unnecessary fuss would only encourage the ill-bred to look for explanations to which they are not entitled," Lady Mary agreed. "I suggest you remain secluded for these last few weeks before the beginning of Lent, after which everything will be quieter."

"It is strange to be so completely independent." She looked at Stephen. "Do you think I could ask Mr Henderson to act for me? Could my jointure be paid to the same account as your settlement is?"

"I'm sure it could. I found Henderson most understanding, and it would have the advantage that he is already aware of your circumstances. You would not have to explain everything again."

"As for my belongings…"

"Why not have them sent to Arkell House," Lady Mary said. "There is room enough to store them there. You have plenty of time to make decisions now."

"Yes. I need not be afraid of returning to England for one." She smiled at Lady Mary. "Thanks to your kindness and foresight, it seems that we have avoided being the subject of ill-natured gossip. I am deeply grateful to you, ma'am. Without you, my boats would have been burnt to a cinder."

~~~

"I'm worried about Delia," Stephen said a couple of weeks later to his aunt. "She has dealt with the more pressing matters— written to Henderson, who is happy to act for her, and now to Swann-Loring, and also to her daughter. But she is still very unsettled. She does not sleep well, or eat properly, and I don't know when she last picked up a pencil or paintbrush. She is—not blue-devilled, but—melancholy. Sometimes she is so deep in thought that she jumps if I say something, but when I ask what is she thinking about, or what is worrying her, she says, 'nothing'. She doesn't smile as much, and rarely laughs. If I say, 'come for a walk', she comes along, but there is none of the old enthusiasm, and if I did not suggest it, she would sit inside all day."

Lady Mary patted his hand. "When you consider all she has gone through these past eight months, it is no wonder that she feels overwhelmed. Very likely she is relieved at Sir Edward's death—who could blame her—but also feels guilty about this. Either she is grieving—they were married for twenty years, after all, and he is the father of her child—or she feels guilty that she cannot grieve. It is probably a mixture of both. Then, her daughter has been taken from her and access to her is dependent on another's goodwill. This Sir Julian may seem more kindly disposed to her than his father was, but if that changes, there is nothing Delia can do about it. That sort of helpless, hopeful waiting for a reply to a letter, is extremely enervating. And, I imagine, she feels rootless."

"Rootless?"

"She no longer has a home, not even in name," Lady Mary pointed out. "Perhaps I am splitting hairs here, but there is a difference between not wishing to return and being forbidden to return. Crosbie was tasked with returning her to the marital home, remember? She chose not to go. But now she has been told she no longer has any entitlement to it. Deep in her heart, she probably wonders where she belongs now."

"With me," he said promptly. "As soon as a reasonable time has passed, say six months, I'll ask her to marry me. But I don't want to hurry her into it; in fact, I think she has acquired such an aversion to marriage that it will be difficult to convince her."

"It would make her return to England very easy. But I agree, it is too soon to say anything. You must give her time. Be patient, and continue to try and distract her. Instead of asking her what she is thinking about, share your own thoughts. After Easter we might plan a little excursion—to Genoa, say. And I should put in an appearance at Court in Turin before I leave Nice."

Interlude—Miss Chloe Loring at Swanmere Castle

Chloe Loring sat at the writing-desk in her sitting-room at Swanmere Castle. When she had come here for the summer last year, she had shared this suite with Rosa. When the castle became her permanent home, after Julian and Rosa had returned from their honeymoon, her new sister-in-law had suggested that Chloe remain in the suite. "That way, if you have another young lady to visit, the two of can be private here whenever you wish." Chloe hoped that her friend Ann Overton would come later in the year. They had corresponded regularly since last summer's visit by the Overton family, and Ann had written a most touching letter after Papa died.

But today she must devote her attention to another letter, one she had never expected to have to write. In the schoolroom, she had practised writing letters appropriate to all sorts of circumstances, but the situation of a sixteen-year-old daughter writing to her errant mother was one Rosa had never imagined. But Chloe had now had two letters from Mamma, the one last August and the one that came three days ago. It was up to her to decide whether she would reply, Julian and Rosa had said. They would not forbid it.

When she had privately sought Rosa's advice, Rosa had said, "I do not think anyone should be punished indefinitely for one error of judgement. We are taught to forgive, are we not? Too often, one hears of a death-bed reconciliation. Think how much regret the survivor must suffer if their hard-heartedness was the cause of an unnecessarily long estrangement. Think of all the missed years."

And sometimes a reconciliation was not possible. Had Papa regretted his treatment of Mamma at the end?

Chloe shivered. But enough dawdling. She had prepared her pen and her paper lay ready.

Swanmere Castle, 7 February 1815

To Lady Loring at the Villa Della Torre, Nizza

Dearest Mamma,

Thank you for yours of 19ᵗʰ January and for your condolences on the recent death of dear Papa. As you rightly point out, he was always a good and kind father to me and that is how I shall remember him. My grandmother 'strives to bear her loss with Christian fortitude', but her grief runs very deep, I think, especially as she and I have not lived at the Place since July when we first came to Swanmere.

(The finishing governess you engaged did not suit at all and was removed from the Place within a day of her arrival. Someday, I hope to be able to tell you the story of those eventful twenty-four hours.)

Julian then kindly invited Grandmamma and me to stay at Swanmere for several weeks, together with Miss Fancourt and Julian's widowed cousin, Mrs Overton, and her son and daughter, Hal and Ann. Hal's schoolfriend Robert came with him and we formed a merry company, taking it in turns each evening to entertain the others. While we were there, Julian and Rosa, as I now call her, drew nearer to one another. As you know, they were married last September and Papa agreed that I should live with them permanently. Grandmamma and I went to stay with the Ransfords while Julian and Rosa were on their honeymoon and we returned to Swanmere mid-November. Papa came to the wedding but declined a later invitation to spend Christmas here with us. I last saw him the day after the wedding, apart from going in to bid him a final farewell the night before he died.

You may imagine how happy I am that Rosa is now my sister. Apart from the closeness between us—I feel I can discuss anything with her—I feel privileged to live with her and Julian and to observe, daily, such a happy marriage. Julian is quite a different person—where before he was inclined to be aloof, now he is so involved in our every-day lives. This change had started even before their betrothal. Rosa no longer feels she has to guard her feelings. It is only now that I realise how much she hid behind her governess mask.

You too, I think, hid considerable unhappiness from me. I am sure this was to protect my childish innocence. I do not wish to pry into your secrets, but must acknowledge this sacrifice.

Rosa and I have discussed the events of <u>that</u> day last May, and have agreed to forget them; to let bygones be bygones. Dear Mamma, I hope that we can meet when you return to England. Grandmamma says this should be possible, privately at least, *without my endangering my prospects. I don't think that I want any prospects that would require me not to know you. However, that is all moot at present as we are all agreed that I shall not come out this year. In fact, I am not sure that I want to appear on the marriage market at all. It strikes me as a singularly poor way of finding a good husband.*

Julian and Rosa will go to London for some weeks after Easter, when Lady Ransford will present Rosa to the Queen. We are all (except Rosa) agreed that she should have her own presentation, and not be presented together with me next year. And when you consider the life that she has led up to now, I think she should enjoy being Lady Swann-Loring without having to chaperon a younger sister-in-law. I think many newly married ladies would not relish such a prospect only a year later. But she will have a wonderful husband at her side, and I am sure will be the envy of many ladies who cast their eyes on Julian in recent years.

I have reached the end of my sheet, Mamma, and must stop. I send you my fondest love,

Your loving daughter,
Chloe Loring

Having signed her letter, Chloe turned it and wrote along the margin.

P.S. I forgot to say that when they were packing your personal belongings at Loring Place, I took the Dresden Harlequin and Columbine from your sitting-room. They now dance on my mantelpiece and remind me of how you used to put them on the table when I was small, so that I could look at them more closely. I thought you wouldn't mind, but wish to tell you they are here. I shall take great care of them, I promise you.

She folded the sheet neatly, addressed and sealed it. Julian would know how to send a letter abroad, she thought, and went downstairs and across into the old part of the house. Her brother sat at his desk in the library reading some long document.

"May I disturb you?"

"Gladly." He put down the parchment and rose.

She showed him the letter. "I've written to Mamma and don't know what to do with the letter. Shall I leave it with the post as usual? Should Lord Swanmere frank it first?"

"Yes and no. A peer may only frank letters sent to addresses within the United Kingdom. The Post Office will send it to the Continent via the packet boat, and the other postal services will send it on."

"It sounds so simple, but must take a lot of organising, especially when several different countries are involved. I wonder how they work out who is paid how much by whom."

Julian shuddered. "Some clerk, who is not paid nearly enough, is tasked with it, I imagine. I should hate to be responsible for it."

Chapter Seventeen

Chloe's letter came on the last day of February. When Stephen returned from an errand, he found Delia dozing on the day-bed, the letter pressed to her heart. She looked more at ease than she had for some weeks, her lips curved in a tender smile.

She opened her eyes at the sound of his boots on the wooden floor. "She wrote to me, a sweet, kind letter. She and Miss Fancourt are willing to let bygones be bygones. She even speaks of meeting me privately."

He stooped to kiss her. "That is good news, indeed."

"Yes." Her eyelids fluttered closed and her breathing slowed and deepened.

Stephen glanced around then tiptoed into his room, returning in his stockinged feet with the quilted coverlet from his bed. He spread it gently over her, tucking it around her shoulders. "Sleep well, my love."

She didn't stir, and he left her to her dreams, hoping that Chloe's letter would prove a turning point for her.

~~~

"The first of March and already the middle of spring," Delia said. "Isn't it glorious? We would hardly see a leaf yet in England and whatever flowers dare open risk a severe battering by wind and rain. While here—" She spread out her arms and twirled around, her face raised to the sun.

She resembled a spring flower in her billowing, yellow skirts and green spencer, Stephen thought. Although she had said she would not wear mourning, until today there had been touches of black in her dress—a ribbon, or gloves, or some lace in her hair.

She spun around again, laughing joyously, then put one hand to her head and clutched his arm with the other. "Oh! My head is spinning. I'm too old for such antics, or at least to sit plump on the ground as Chloe used do when she made herself dizzy."

"Here." He steered her to a larger stone at the side of the mountain path. "Sit for a moment. Look out at the horizon."

"I love it when the sea sparkles like this, and the contrast of the white sails against the blue. There are more ships out today. Look there, to the west, a little flotilla. The captains must no longer fear the winter storms."

"That reminds me; my aunt spoke of undertaking an excursion, to Genoa, perhaps, or to Turin. She should put in an appearance at Court, she said." When Delia did not immediately respond, he added, "Or perhaps you would prefer not to be jolted about in a carriage or brave the waves? Do you still feel out of sorts?"

"Now that my mind is at ease, I feel much more the thing. But would it not be better to wait until after Easter? They take Lent very seriously here, do they not?"

"You are right. My aunt must have forgotten that."

"How far is Harrogate from Peterborough?" she asked suddenly.

"I don't know exactly, but more than one hundred miles. Why?"

"Peterborough is about ten miles from Swanmere. I don't have to be afraid of being in England anymore, and Chloe hopes that we can meet privately, at least. I was trying to think where I could stay within a day's travel from Swanmere. I could hardly expect them to put me up, could I?"

"I suppose not. Were you thinking of staying with your mother?"

She made a face. "I could not bear all the explanations. I hoped Lady Mary might allow me to stay at Arkell House, but it is too far away."

"Not allow you, allow us," he said firmly. "Or are you planning to cast me off once you are back in England?"

"I should, and retire to a quiet cottage where I can live on my jointure; see if I can regain some respectability. I don't want to, Stephen, but you will agree that I cannot take you to Swanmere. It would be the outside of enough for me to arrive there with my lover."

"Do you think they would immediately assume that we were lovers?"

She looked at him, amused. "They know. I told Chloe I was abandoning my marriage and placing my trust in you. Remember, I thought we would be travelling alone. It was only after I joined you that you told me Lady Mary would accompany us. That story is probably good enough for the wide world, but not for Swanmere."

"I had forgotten." He broke off at the sound of English voices. "We had better walk on."

Within minutes, he was raising his hat to several members of the English colony, including Dr and Mrs Costain. "A beautiful morning, is it not?"

Having paid due English respect to the weather, the conversation moved to more interesting topics. The Princess of Wales was expected daily, they were informed, and much discussion was devoted to the propriety of calling upon her and the appropriate etiquette should one be summoned by her. Appealed to, as one more familiar with court matters, Stephen merely said, "One should not be lacking in courtesy towards Her Royal Highness."

"We shall do our best to keep our distance," Lady Mary declared the following evening. "You never know what she might do. In Geneva, last October, she insisted on having a ball got up at short notice and the unfortunate hostess charged with this task had great difficulty in drumming up enough personages to attend it. The Princess then arrived dressed *en Venus* or, as my correspondent put it, 'rather not dressed, further than the waist'. Nobody knew where to look."

Stephen covered his eyes with his hand. "What a vision! We shall definitely not seek her out."

Rapid footsteps announced the arrival of Gianluca onto the terrace. "My ladies, Milord, *l'Empereur…*"

"The Emperor? Napoleon? What about him?" Stephen asked, when Gianluca stopped short. "He's not dead, is he?"

"*Non*, Milord. He landed at Saint-Juan yesterday with one thousand men and now marches towards Grasse."

Stephen felt his jaw drop. The two women were equally stunned. At last, Delia said, "The little flotilla we saw yesterday, Stephen. A thousand men."

"Did he meet no resistance?" Lady Mary asked.

"No, Milady. They spent last night on the beach at Saint-Juan and marched through Cannes this morning, then turned north.

"Towards Paris, then?" Stephen asked.

Gianluca shrugged. "Who can say, Milord. But he said he would return with the violets."

"You sound pleased, Gianluca. I thought you were glad to be home."

"I am torn, Milord. I am a proud Nizzard and deplore the occupation of my country. If the French were to invade again, I would fight with the last drop of my blood. But he is *l'Empereur*. All who fought under him must revere him. To see him caged on that small island was intolerable. If he remains within the present borders of France, I would rather see him on the throne than fat Louis or another Bourbon."

"It is unlikely that will happen. And I doubt if he will simply be returned to Elba, either. I imagine they will find somewhere more distant to cage him."

~~~

"There was mounting 'mong Graemes of the Netherby clan;
Forsters, Fenwicks, and Musgraves, they rode and they ran:
There was racing and chasing on Cannobie Lee,
But the lost bride of Netherby ne'er did they see."

Stephen looked up from his newspaper at Delia's dramatic recitation. "Why do you quote *Young Lochinvar*?"

"Because of the racing and chasing after Bonaparte. There must be a thousand rumours; Massena has left Marseilles and Ney is on the march, but he still seems to elude them. And the English here are all atwitter, wondering should they go or should they stay. And if they decide to leave, in which direction should they go?"

He folded his paper and set it aside, then patted the sofa beside him. "Come and sit down; tell me what you think of it all. Are you worried?"

"Not hugely."

"There are several questions to be considered." He marked each one on his fingers:

"One: can he remain at large?

"Two: if so, will he succeed in ousting the Bourbons again?

"Three: if he does, will the Allies tolerate it?

"And four: if not, when and where will it come to a confrontation between them?

"Every day that takes him further away from the south coast makes it less likely any encounter will be here, especially when you consider that the armies have, to a large extent, been sent home, some disbanded. The one thing we can be sure of is that his present course is towards Paris and, by extension, towards England. Therefore, the wisest thing is to stay put until we know more."

"That is very logical."

"Don't you agree?"

"I do. We are safest here for the moment."

"There is something else I want to talk to you about." He turned slightly on the sofa so that he faced her.

"What is it? You look very serious."

"Do you remember the day I asked you to come to the Continent with me?"

"Yes."

"I asked you to be my wife in everything but name. It was not possible for us to marry then."

"No."

He felt rather than heard her soft reply. Was she agreeing with him, or already rejecting him? He pressed on. "You are now free to marry. I would rather have waited some months to discuss matrimony, but these are uncertain times and I don't want to risk our being separated if it can be avoided. Delia, sweetheart, I love you dearly. You have already entrusted yourself to me in every way but one. Will you take that final step and do me the great honour of becoming my wife?"

She took a deep breath, then another and another, quicker and quicker, pressing her hand to her breast as it rapidly rose and fell. Beads of perspiration stood on her brow as she stared into nothingness, the only sound the agitated see-sawing of her breath.

"Delia?" When she didn't react, he snapped his fingers in front of her face. "Delia!" He felt a wretch using such a sharp tone with her. Her gaze met his fleetingly, then darted away. "Come," he said more gently, taking her hands in a firm clasp. "Breath with me, in and out, in and out. Slower with each one. Come, my love. In and out, in and out. Even slower. That's the way."

Little by little, her breathing eased. After a while, her hands stirred in his and returned his clasp. "That's it, my darling," he whispered. "Almost there."

A couple of breaths more and she managed to smile weakly at him. "Thank you. I don't know what happened to me."

He lifted her hand to his lips. "Better now?"

"Yes."

"Should I ring for tea?"

"Please."

When the equipage came, he refused to let her officiate but made the tea with brisk efficiency. "What? Do you think I am incapable of it? I am no Lord Henry Danlow, but I can make a perfectly good cup of tea."

"Indeed, you can." She raised her cup in a little toast to him. "Who is this Lord Henry?"

"The worst sort of dandified idiot; he refuses to drink any tea that does not meet his impossibly high standards, no matter how exalted the occasion. I have seen him push a cup away at Carlton House because it was not to his taste."

"What a nincompoop!" She put down her cup. "These past months have been all holiday, a long honeymoon. We have no duties or responsibilities, no customs or habits to distract us from one another. I know very little about your other, your bachelor life, for want of a better word."

"Is that why you were suddenly so panic-stricken?"

"I think so. Suddenly it seemed as if history repeated itself." She put her hand on his arm. "Don't look like that. You are not another Edward; I know you cherish me as he never did. What reminded me of the past is that I know very little of your everyday life in England. Look how you speak so casually of Carlton House. I had to remember that it is the home of the Prince Regent. I have never set foot in London or moved in *ton* circles, let alone royal ones. How would I fit into your life?"

"You wouldn't have to." He smiled. "Now it is my turn to say, 'don't look like that'. I mean, my life would change completely if we were married. I have not waited all these years for you to come back into it just to continue as a tonnish bachelor, lounging between my clubs, Angelo's, the Park, and my choice of evening parties. It gets very boring, let me tell you.

"This is what I imagine. We would decide where we wanted to live; buy or even build a house. There would be a studio for you. We could decide to what extent we wished to go into society—you might enjoy a London Season, visit the British Museum and the Summer Exhibition at the Academy. I would like you to meet my friends, and my nephew, the duke, and his wife. We could also travel. Or, this house could be our permanent home—my aunt has offered it to me—and we would visit England from time to time. But these would be our decisions, Delia, not mine alone."

"Good heavens!"

"Also, depending on Bonaparte, who knows when we will be able to return to England? I should be very surprised if by then there were any hint of scandal attached to our marriage. While it might not be tactful for me to accompany you on your first call at Swanmere, I hope that afterwards your daughter and her family will not refuse to meet me. It would be too much to hope that Swann-Loring would permit her to live with us, but you should be recognised and accepted as her mother."

"Stephen! What dazzling prospects you tempt me with. Pray don't think I do not appreciate them when I ask for time to reflect."

"Supposing we leave it to fate," he suggested. "If Bonaparte is recaptured and safely returned to Elba or elsewhere, you may have all the time in the world. But if he succeeds in taking Paris and the Allies continue to support Louis, war will be inevitable. Then I may press you for a quicker decision."

"Very well. Thank you, Stephen." Her colour had come back, and she smiled tremulously. "You are very good."

He shook his head and put his arm around her. When she rested her head on his shoulder, he gently laid his cheek against her hair. They fit together perfectly, he thought. That would do for now.

Chapter Eighteen

Dazzling prospects indeed. Delia tried to think soberly and sensibly about Stephen's offer, but no matter how hard she tried, she drifted into impossible daydreams of a home, a loving husband, Chloe calling, if not staying with her; later, perhaps, a grandchild to indulge. She tried to imagine Stephen dandling a chubby infant that pulled at his cravat and hair, and had to smile. While she must be happy that he had not married, and so was now free to marry her, she was sorry that he had missed the experience of fatherhood.

Or—she froze and began mentally to count the weeks. Giving up, she hurried to the writing-desk where she kept her private journal and frantically turned back the pages. The week before Christmas. It couldn't be. She paged forward again but did not see the little star she used to mark the day her courses started. She had felt out of sorts towards the end of January, she remembered, but had put that down to the shock of Edward's death, and in February there had been her worry about Chloe. Although it had improved, the queasiness that she had ascribed to nervous strain had not vanished. Her breasts were tender to the touch. She had winced the other evening, and Stephen had been most apologetic, although he had done nothing unusual.

Now she slipped her hand over the curve of her belly. There, at the base, was it fuller and firmer? It was so long since she had carried Chloe that she could not remember those first changes in her body. Hughes, her old maid, would probably have noticed them, and also commented on the absence of her courses, but a new maid would not be so familiar. If she herself had thought of it, she would have put it down to her advancing years. She would be forty-five in August.

She had thought she was unable to bear another child, but apparently not. It would be three months on the fifteenth. If her courses did not come, she would have to tell Stephen. And marry him. She would have no choice.

She shivered. Supposing Edward were still alive. Any child she bore would be legally his. There was some Latin tag to that effect; she remembered him quoting it last year when there had been some talk about the father of the child a recently widowed titled lady was expecting. If a boy, it would succeed to the title, ousting the elderly heir presumptive, a cousin of the deceased peer.

But that was irrelevant now, thank heavens. And Stephen had already said he wanted to marry her; she need not be afraid he agreed only because of the baby. Would he be pleased? It would make the carefree life he had envisaged more difficult.

Was she pleased? She loved the idea of carrying Stephen's babe, but was not so happy at the thought of marrying again. Once bitten, twice shy. But she could not bear a child out of wedlock, allow it to suffer the opprobrium Society reserved for such innocent unfortunates, just to placate her fears. And it would be unfair to make Stephen pay for Edward's sins, especially when he had shown himself to be completely his opposite. Look how he had provided for her from the very beginning. And he had gone into exile with her, without a word of complaint. He would be a good, loving husband and father, she was sure. Now it was for her to change her life for him.

~~~

"He has reached Lyon, with eight thousand men and thirty cannons," Stephen said two days later. "When you consider he landed with only one thousand, it shows how many have gone over to him. It all depends on Ney, now."

Dr Costain, who, with his wife, had called at the *Villa Della Torre*, said, "The town is full of English who have come here from Marseilles and talk of going on to Genoa if they can find a boat to take them."

"What do you propose to do?" Delia asked.

"We shall leave with the majority," Mrs Costain said. "And you?"

Delia looked at Stephen. "As long as Bonaparte heads north, we remain here."

"Yes," Stephen said. "Don't forget his brother-in-law still sits on the throne of Naples."

"I had forgotten about Murat," Delia said to Stephen when their callers had gone.

"Hmmm."

"You seem distracted. What's wrong?"

"If all the Anglican clergymen leave, who will marry us? I'm not sure I could convince a Catholic priest to officiate, especially when you are so recently widowed. Costain would do it, I am sure."

"Would such a marriage be legal?"

"Perhaps not here, but certainly in England. But you could say that of all Protestant marriages. We are of age, and have lived here for several months now. Technically we would need a licence to marry without calling the banns, but in the circumstances, I doubt if it would matter. I could appeal to the archdeacon, I suppose, as the senior cleric here."

"It might be better," she said slowly.

"What do you mean? Delia, was that 'yes'?"

At her nod, he caught her to him. She did not struggle within his embracing arms, but held him off, her hands flat against his chest. "I have something to tell you. You may think me very foolish not to have realised, and I still am not quite sure, but I think, no, I am almost certain that I am with child."

"Delia!" Without letting her go, he retreated until the back of his legs hit the seat of a chair, collapsing onto it like a marionette whose strings had been cut. He drew her close so that she stood between his thighs. "A child! Our child." As he spoke, he gently caressed her belly, shaping it with his hands.

Delia quivered at his tender touch. "You can never be completely certain until the quickening, but everything speaks for it."

He rested his head against her breasts, then jumped up. "What am I thinking? You must lie down at once. Are you well? Should we fetch a doctor? What do you need?"

Laughing, she let him lead her over to the day-bed. "I am quite well, especially now I know why I was so often queasy, especially in the mornings. I only realised the other day, but when you said that about the clergymen leaving, I thought I should tell you now."

"Good God, yes. It is vital that we are married before the child is born, especially if it's a boy."

"Why a boy, specially?" she asked. "Are girls so inferior?"

"No, but they cannot inherit a dukedom. I do not want to have my line cut off just because we could not find someone to marry us."

"Your line?"

"Yes. My nephew has two sons, so it is not an issue at present, but if, God forbid, something happened to them, or the sons only had daughters, my descendants would be next. I can't help but consider it, Delia. The importance of securing the succession is engrained in us from a very early age. That is why my father married again; he had one heir, but wanted a second string to be sure."

"In that case, why did you not marry years ago?"

"My father was dead by the time I was old enough to marry, so he could not pressure me into it and neither my brother nor my nephew, to give them their due, tried. I did not want a marriage of state and you are the only woman I have ever imagined spending my life with."

"Oh, Stephen! That is the nicest thing anyone has ever said to me." She turned in his arms and kissed him.

After some time, he lifted his head. "Are you sure this is safe; it won't harm you or the babe?"

"Certain. But could we not go into the bedroom? It is more private."

~~~

Stephen's daily reports on the progress of the marriage arrangements were punctuated by details of Napoleon's inexorable onward march.

"Ney has gone over to Bonaparte with his six thousand men," he announced five minutes before he said, "The archdeacon has agreed to issue a licence. He has offered to conduct the ceremony and the Costains will be the witnesses."

"Not your aunt?"

"He does not think it wise. Anglicans are allowed practise their religion in Nice, but in private, and she is Catholic. He could be accused of attempting to proselytise if she were there."

"That is a pity. She is so kind. I would like to have her there."

"The archdeacon will leave on Monday." He kissed her hand. "Will you marry me on Saturday, Delia?"

"With all my heart."

~~~

What did a widow of not quite three months wear to her very quiet, private, second wedding? Not black, Delia decided, but nothing too bright either. In the end, she decided on a gown of evening primrose trimmed with blonde lace, and a spencer to match. Pale yellow gloves and shoes and a neat bonnet—Stephen detested the modish, deep-brimmed, Oldenburgh bonnets—tied with evening primrose ribbons and decorated with a small bunch of flowers, completed her ensemble.

Although not permitted to appear in Protestant clerical garb in public, within his own rooms the archdeacon was properly garbed in cassock and surplice, with linen bands at his throat. It brought a welcome sense of familiarity to the proceedings. The furniture had been rearranged, with a small table serving as an altar; instead of prie-dieux for the bride and groom, two cushions were placed on the floor before two high-backed chairs.

"Dearly beloved, we are gathered together in the sight of God, and in the face of this Congregation, to join together this Man and this Woman in holy Matrimony."

Although the congregation numbered only three persons, including his wife, the archdeacon continued reading the full service, even enquiring if any of those present knew of any impediment to the proposed marriage.

"Who giveth this Woman to be married to this Man?"

After a pause during which they all looked at each other, Dr Costain moved from Stephen's right, where he had been standing as best man, to Delia's left. "I would be honoured to stand your friend, ma'am."

Delia placed her right hand on his and was so transferred via the archdeacon to her bridegroom. Stephen raised her hand to his lips. It was a real kiss, his lips cool on her bare skin, and his eyes met hers with that intimate little smile that had become so familiar over the past months. She found herself smiling back, the two of them encased in their private world, until the archdeacon cleared his throat.

"Ahem. Repeat after me. I, Stephen Richard Aylwin, take thee, Cordelia Elizabeth, to my wedded wife…"

Stephen's eyes never left hers, nor hers his as they made their vows.

Then the gold ring slid onto her finger and was held there as he said, his voice deepening, *"With this Ring I thee wed, with my body I thee worship, and with all my worldly goods I thee endow."*

He meant it, every word of it, she realised; to him, it was no empty formula but solemn promises. He would keep his word, as she would keep hers.

~~~

"So, Lady Stephen," Stephen said as the carriage made its way through the narrow streets.

Delia looked dismayed. "I don't have to be called that now, do I? At the Villa, I mean. I have just got used to Lady Delia, and it will be too confusing for the servants. I imagine most of them assume we are married."

He considered her thoughtfully. "You may continue as Lady Delia," he said after a few minutes, "as long as you don't forget to whom you are now married."

"I feel much more married than I did after my first wedding," she admitted. "When we made our vows, it was as if we were creating something new, just for us. I wanted to give you a ring too, to say—" She looked away, flustered.

He seized her hands. "Say it to me now, Delia. Please," he urged. Was he finally to hear the declaration he longed for?

She turned to face him and took a deep breath. Her grip tightened. He barely heard the first words; then her voice grew stronger. "I love you, Stephen, and am your wife until my dying day. I shall cradle your children in my body and, in my heart, make a home for you and them."

"My darling. Yes. No longer two, but one. At last, I have come home." He reached over and pulled down the blinds that shaded the carriage windows, fastening them securely before he took his wife in his arms and kissed her ardently.

~~~

"Welcome home, my dears, and congratulations." Lady Mary came to embrace them when they arrived back on the terrace at the *Villa Della Torre*. "I thought you would have been back long before this."

"The archdeacon insisting on reading the full form for the Solemnization of Marriage from the prayerbook," Stephen said, "including the final homily."

"All went well, I trust."

"The only hitch was when he asked who gave the bride away," Stephen said with a grin. "We stood and looked at one another like fools."

Delia raised her eyes to Heaven. "It is ridiculous that an adult woman has to be given in marriage, as if she cannot decide for herself."

"It never occurred to me that you would need someone, especially as there was no grand bridal entrance."

"What did you do?" Lady Mary asked.

"I was tempted to say I gave myself, but before I could, Dr Costain volunteered," Delia replied.

"Then, afterwards, the archdeacon had to write out three sets of marriage lines," Stephen continued.

"Three?"

"I asked for them as there is no parish register or similar where our marriage is permanently recorded. Now we each have one, and I shall send one to my man of business by one of our naval ships if possible, as there is no post via Paris. Even if it takes six months to get back to England, it will be on the way."

Lady Mary nodded. "That was wise."

Delia untied her bonnet and put it to one side. "Then his wife insisted we drink a glass of wine and have a little nuncheon. So, between one thing and another, we were there for more than three hours."

Lady Mary went to a side table where a bottle of champagne stood in a wine cooler. "I hope you will allow me to drink your health as well."

"But of course. Shall I open that for you?" Stephen asked.

"Please do."

He cut the twine that held the cork down in the bottle with his penknife and began to ease the cork out. It exploded with a loud plop, the effervescent wine rushing after it. Stephen skilfully filled the glasses and took them to his aunt and his new wife.

Lady Mary raised hers. "My dear Stephen and Delia, congratulations on your wedding and my very best wishes to you both for many years of happiness together. Delia, welcome to our family. I am now your aunt, too, and should be pleased if you would address me accordingly, with no more 'Lady Marys'."

Delia found it impossible to express how moved she was and simply kissed the older woman's cheek. "Thank you, Aunt Mary. I shall be more than happy to."

~~~

In these unsettled times, there could be no wedding journey to ease the transition from one life to another and, indeed, life at the *Villa Della Torre* continued as it had heretofore. But there was a new ease between Stephen and Delia; the wedding and their subsequent conversation in the carriage had freed them on a deeper, personal level. They talked more about themselves, their inmost feelings, described past hurts that had long lingered but now were healed.

"I did not realise how rootless I felt until you said you would make me a home in your heart," he said one evening as they lay in one another's arms. "I was essential to nobody's happiness."

"You are essential to mine," she assured him with a soft kiss.

"I know what you mean. After my father died, there was no one to whom I really mattered, who was interested in my thoughts and ideas, who cared whether I was happy or not. I mattered to Chloe, of course, but in a different way; our relationship was still very much mother and child. I hope, when we meet again, that it will be different, more equal. I wonder when she will get my letter."

"Try not to worry. You know she is safe."

"That is true. Think of all the families of soldiers—what they must be suffering now, after they had thought it was all over."

~~~

While little changed at the Villa, much happened outside its walls. As Napoleon continued his march north, news came that, at the Congress of Vienna, the assembled envoys had declared him an outlaw, his former enemies forming a seventh coalition and mobilising their armies. All this notwithstanding, on the twenty-first of March, the official organ, *Le Moniteur,* reported from Paris:

The King and the princes departed during the night.

His Majesty the Emperor arrived this evening at 8 p.m. at his

Tuileries Palace. He entered Paris at the head of the same troops

which were sent this morning to prevent his passage.

233

Details of new ministerial appointments came next, followed by a series of proclamations. *L'Empereur* had retaken his throne.

"That's that," Stephen said. "All the Allies, and we, can do is wait and see which way the cat jumps. Will he squat in Paris and let them invade, or will he take the fight to them?"

"It is a pity they would not just let him be, within his own borders," Delia said. "I doubt if he has much appetite for war now. I imagine he would be a better ruler than Louis."

"Every crowned head in Europe would feel threatened," Lady Mary said. "Remember, he started his climb to fame during the revolution and laid waste to much of Europe in his craving for power. It would seem most unfair if he were allowed to reign in France as if nothing had happened."

"And so they risk their crowns, if not their heads," Stephen said drily. "He is a clever general, and prides himself on being a lucky one. Now it will all depend on a toss of a coin."

"And on the lives of tens of thousands more men," Delia said. "Rulers never seem to think of the true cost of their wars."

Interlude at Swanmere Castle

Villa Della Torre, Nizza, 15th March 1815

Miss Chloe Loring, Swanmere Castle, Swanmere,

Dearest Chloe,

I scribble this note in haste to give it to one who departs later this day for Genoa, and she will ensure that it is posted there, *although I do not know what round-about-route it will take to reach you. From what we hear, no letters are passing through Paris at present and so I take advantage of this opportunity to write to you.*

Briefly, I must tell you that I and all of our party are well. We are determined to remain here for as long as possible. Napoleon has announced that his eagles will fly from steeple to steeple and will soon perch on those of Notre Dame. *We must assume that he intends to accompany them to Paris—all the indications point that way, and all the more reason for us to remain here at the south coast. However this develops, it will be far from here.*

So there is no need for you to be worried, Chloe, even if you do not hear from me for some months. It will be because the posts are disrupted, not because I am not well or simply have not thought to write. You are always in my thoughts.

You will, I hope, have received my reply to your last, which I posted on the second of March. My caller is anxious to be off, and so I will close by sending you my dearest love, and my compliments to all at Swanmere Castle.

Your loving mother,
Delia Loring

Six weeks. It had taken Mamma's letter six weeks to reach her. In the meantime, the Duke of Wellington had travelled to Brussels from Vienna and taken charge of the Allied armies already gathering there. That certainly suggested Mamma had been right to remain in Nice.

Chloe had tried to work out the distance from Brussels to Nice in the big atlas—it must be several hundred miles. But one could not be sure where the battle would take place, Julian had said. Perhaps Boney would lure his enemies deep into France, or he would prefer to engage the Russians, Austrians, and Germans who were advancing on the Rhine, which was the border with Germany. That would be nearer Switzerland and the Alps. Nice was south of the Alps.

Before, she had been too young for war and battles to concern her. But now she knew people like her cousin, Major Frederick Raven, who, his niece Cynthia Glazebrook had written, was with his regiment in Brussels. She had met other officers too last autumn when she and Grandmamma had stayed with the major's parents, Lord and Lady Ransford, and had danced with some of them at the assemblies. Weather-beaten, lithe, entertaining men, still flushed with the victory over Boney and delighted to be at home in England again, able to dance with an English Rose, as one put it. It was dreadful to think of them pierced by a bullet or a sword.

Grandmamma said the Prayer in Time of War every night, but Chloe imagined that people on both sides prayed for victory. Perhaps it was selfish, but she could at least pray that those she knew remained unharmed.

Chapter Nineteen

By the end of May, Delia was noticeably *enceinte*, and feeling the heat of the Nice summer. "I am so glad that we live up here," she said one day to Stephen. "I think that will be my last visit to town until after the baby is born. By the time the temperature has cooled to a more bearable heat, I shall be so large that I won't fit into the carriage. At least these *empire* style gowns accommodate a pregnancy easily, as the waistline is up under your bosom, anyway."

"And are very becoming." He patted her belly, smiling when he felt a little kick. "The beginning of October, you think?"

"That is what the nurse said."

He laughed. "It is a pity we cannot predict Bonaparte's movements and the outcome of all this as easily."

"This waiting is terrible. Worst of all, is not being able to write to Chloe. I have not yet told her of our marriage. I don't know how she will take it, or the news that she will soon have a sister or brother. I have caused her a lot of heartache already—I hope this will not add to it."

"Why don't you write to her, anyway? I'll check daily if an English naval ship has put in to the bay below; I'll be able to see it from here with the telescope. We can then ask the captain to take a letter."

"That's a splendid idea, Stephen. I'll write today."

"Address it to Lord Swanmere, with the letter to Chloe inside," Stephen advised. "Of course, it could take months for such a letter to reach her, depending on the course the captain must take."

"That doesn't matter. I'll write again by post as soon as the circumstances change. This cannot continue indefinitely." She smiled at him. "Thank you, Stephen. I feel better when I can do something. I think we all do."

~~~

She handed Stephen the letter that evening. "I have said nothing about the baby. I am not so young, after all, and I don't want to tempt fate. Better to tell her when the child is here, safe and well."

"But all is going well, is it not?" he asked, alarmed.

"Yes. I feel well and the nurse is happy with me. And I do not have to worry that it will not be a boy. You really don't mind."

"I shall be happy with whatever comes." He slipped his arm around her. "It surprises me how much I am looking forward to being a father; I had never before thought of it. I suppose I was waiting for you all the time."

"Oh, Stephen!" She turned in his arm and reached up to kiss him. "I never expected to be so happy, either."

~~~

"Delia! Aunt!" Stephen hurried out onto the shaded terrace, waving the latest copy of the Gazzetta. "It has happened. Listen. 'His Majesty the King has been advised by a special envoy from His Imperial Majesty, the Emperor of Russia that the Allied armies led by the Duke of Wellington and Prince Blücher have secured a complete victory over a French army, commanded by Bonaparte at Mont-Saint-Jean on the eighteenth and nineteenth of June.'"

"Thank God," Lady Mary whispered. "The eighteenth, you say, Stephen? That is ten days ago."

"*Mont-Saint Jean?* Where is that?" Delia asked.

"It can hardly be far from Brussels. There was no report of Wellington leaving there." Stephen leafed through the newssheet. "Ah, here is a report sent from Heidelberg that puts Wellington at Mont-Saint-Jean near Waterloo and Blücher at Vavres. Where's the atlas?"

The three headed to the library, where they were able to satisfy themselves that the battle must have taken place near Brussels. The following day, they pored over Lord Stewart's letter to the English Minister in Switzerland, describing Wellington's most glorious victory and the ensuing rout of the French, who abandoned artillery, ammunition waggons, caissons, and baggage. Five hundred cannons were taken as well as the personal belongings of Bonaparte, who was said to have left the army.

"Twelve thousand dead on our side alone," Lady Mary said. "It doesn't bear thinking about."

Subsequent reports confirmed the abdication of Napoleon in favour of his four-year-old son.

"He never gives up completely, does he," Stephen said on reading this. "What is the poor brat to be emperor of? Cockaigne? Cloud Cuckoo Land?"

"What is more to the point, what is to become of his father? They will hardly send him back to Elba."

"He should be put in front of a firing squad," Stephen said.

"I agree," his aunt said. "When I think of all the suffering his overweening ambition has cost the world—the lives lost, the families bereft, the wounded who still suffer from their injuries, not to mention the towns destroyed and countrysides ravaged, I do not think he should be given another chance. This last escapade alone has resulted in tens of thousands dead and wounded. Where could one send him where one could be sure he would not try to escape again?"

"Some remote, desolate island, little more than a rock," Delia said. "He deserves neither comfort nor consideration."

Book 2

Chloe

Chapter Twenty

Weymouth, July 1815

Chloe followed Cynthia Glazebrook up the short ladder into the bathing machine and latched the door firmly. Cynthia had already started to undress and Chloe joined her as the little hut on wheels lurched into motion, backed by a horse from the smooth sands into the sparkling waves.

It was not easy to strip off their loose morning gowns and undergarments, then pull their shapeless flannel bathing dresses over their heads in the swaying machine, but they managed, steadying one another as necessary. Soon they heard the slap of water against the wooden wall.

"Hurry." Chloe tugged down the turban-style cap. It wouldn't keep her hair completely dry, but would protect it unless she yielded to the tempting buoyancy and lay flat on the watery surface.

The movement stopped, and they heard the horseman's knuckle-rap before he moved away with his mount. Nan, their dipper, immediately turned the hour-glass that would tell her when their allotted time was up. "Ready, ladies?"

"You're first, today," Cynthia said, as Nan opened the door and released the canvas hood that should protect them from prying eyes. Nan knew the girls enjoyed their dip in the ocean and that there was no need for her to plunge them in willy-nilly. She offered a supporting hand as, one after the other, they slid into the water, and then kept a minatory watch against any male who dare approach too near her charges.

Chloe gasped and spluttered at the first cool shock and then ducked down so that her shoulders were completely covered. When she stood, the water came to just above her breast. She did not know how to swim, but Cynthia, who had learnt in the big pond at Hooke Manor, had shown her how to float on her back and even manage a couple of strokes before her feet were drawn irresistibly to the sandy bottom beneath the sea. It felt different, as if permanently rippled by the incessant waves and was strewn with shells. Chloe would have loved to retrieve one, but was too nervous to dive down for it. She had to content herself with the ones she found on their regular strolls along the beach.

Her flannel bathing dress was loose, with wide sleeves, permitting a full immersion in the salt water; she moved languorously, enjoying the refreshing caress on her bare skin, along her limbs and around her torso. This was so much better than a bath at home, where a damp chemise clung everywhere, making it hard to wash properly. After sea-bathing, her skin felt like silk, scrubbed by the finest particles of salt and sand.

Chloe looked along the line of bathing machines, each with its occupant bobbing in the water in front of it. They were well enough spaced that they did not intrude upon one another apart from the shrieks of a neophyte as the dippers dunked her vigorously. A mouthful of salt water soon silenced her, however.

Cynthia drifted towards her. "This is wonderful, is it not? I am so glad Mamma thought of inviting you to join us this summer. It would not be half as much fun on my own."

Chloe had to agree. She had been surprised by Cousin Amelia's invitation to spend the summer with them. Cynthia had been so opposed to any suggestion of a come-out this year and this, combined with the uncertainty caused by Bonaparte's escape from Elba, had led her mother to agree to defer it for another year. She hoped that if Cynthia and Chloe could cement their friendship this year, they would be able to support one another next Season.

Chloe had hastened to agree. She had first met Cynthia when the Glazebrooks had come to Loring Place last year for her father's birthday celebrations and, again, when they had met at the home of Lord and Lady Ransford, Cynthia's grandparents, on her way to Swanmere the following July. A summer with Cynthia, first at the Glazebrook's home in Cambridgeshire and then here in Weymouth for July and August, seemed much more appealing than one spent alone in Swanmere. It would not be like last year when she had had Ann, her brother Hal, his friend Robert, and the boys' summer tutor for company. She would be the fifth wheel on the coach, with Julian and Rosa married and her grandmother and Julian's grandfather, now firm friends.

"Time's up, ladies," Nan called, and the girls obediently scrambled back into the bathing machine. There was just time for a brisk rub down before they dragged their chemises and petticoats over half-damp skin, donned loose wrappers, tied their bonnets, and enveloped themselves in shawls. The damp flannels and towels were bundled together to be handed to the servant who waited patiently for them on the beach and would follow as they hurried back to their lodgings on The Esplanade, eager for breakfast and to make plans for the rest of the day.

There was so much to do in Weymouth—walks, rides, visits to the libraries and, of course, the balls. Some days they undertook outings in the surrounding countryside and even, once or twice, a boat trip along the coast. They practised their music; a harp for Cynthia and a pianoforte for Chloe had been hired, as had a French lady who came twice a week to speak to them in her native language and a dancing master to give them a final polish.

Mr Glazebrook joined them when Parliament rose, accompanied by Cynthia's brother Martin, whom Chloe also remembered from last year's house party. He was twenty-two, of age, but not so old that his acquaintances could be considered old fogies.

"I don't know what it is," Cynthia explained, "but gentlemen of one's own age are really still boys."

"Perhaps it is because most of them are at Oxford or Cambridge," Chloe replied. "Before that, they were at school, so they are not accustomed to the company of ladies."

"That is so true. It is different with officers, especially those who purchase their colours when still quite young. I have met several through my uncle, although he is very old; thirty-five, if he is a day."

"Julian was thirty-five when he married; of course, Rosa was also quite old, almost twenty-eight."

Cynthia pounced on this statement. "A difference of seven years. You prove my point. But I think that is enough."

"Do you really want to marry so soon?" Chloe asked.

"No, but it pays to think about these things; then one is prepared."

"Prepared for what?"

"For meeting single gentlemen. The Season is not called the marriage market for nothing. I intend to make a list of what I will look for in a husband, and what will absolutely not do."

"That seems eminently sensible," Mr Glazebrook said. His face was solemn, but Chloe noticed the little twinkle in his eye. "Shall you subject them to a *viva voce?*"

"A what, sir?"

"An oral examination—or shall you put your questions to them in writing?"

"How absurd! I shall have more—"

"Finesse," Chloe supplied when her friend hesitated.

"Exactly. Once one has decided what one wants to know, there are ways of discovering it. Some things are immediately apparent, like if he is slovenly or over-dandified, but it will take longer to learn whether he is generous or mean-spirited, for example."

"Or a fortune-hunter," Chloe put in.

"Ah! Do you have your own list, Chloe?" Mr Glazebrook enquired.

"Not a list as such, sir, but, yes, there are qualities I would look for in my husband. The most important is kindness."

There was a little pause. Mr Glazebrook folded his newspaper and set it aside. "That is essential, I agree. But how do you propose to discover in advance whether he is kind? Many a man has dissimulated to promote his courtship."

"That is the problem with the Season," Chloe said. "From what I hear, it is quite artificial, as indeed is the life one leads here."

"In what way?"

"It is all pleasure, with very little duty. And while one meets many people, it is almost impossible for a young lady to have a private conversation with a gentleman before they are engaged."

"Agreed."

"The best thing is if the two families are on visiting terms so that one has the opportunity of observing the other in their familiar surroundings and can see how they treat their parents, brothers and sisters, the servants even."

"That is an excellent point," Mr Glazebrook said. "I suppose house parties are a good solution, apart from being on good terms with one's neighbours, that is." He smiled across the table at his wife.

She laughed and said, "It worked for us, at any rate. While I am glad that you girls are giving some thought as to what makes a good husband, there is no need for you to take it too seriously yet. My mother insisted I had at least two Seasons before I accepted any offer."

"I remember," Mr Glazebrook said wryly. "She also told me that I must allow other men to court you; only so, could I be sure that I was truly your choice of husband."

"She what?" Cynthia said. "I cannot imagine it of Grandmamma."

"You must remember that when I first met your mother, I was twelve and she seven," her father said. "She wanted her daughter to see something of the world before she married a nabob's son."

"Why is that?"

"Nabob comes from a Hindi honorific but became a derogatory term for a man who made his fortune in India, as my father did. He was the younger son of a younger son and had little or no prospects here. There are always those who begrudge another his good fortune, no matter how hard-earned it is."

"That is sadly true," his wife said, getting up. "We must leave you, gentlemen, if we are to be ready for Monsieur Bouvier. Are you sure you do not want to join us, Martin?"

"Yes, do come, Martin," Cynthia said. "It helps to have someone else to dance the gentleman's steps."

"Very well, Sis. I'll look in later."

"Kindness," Mr Glazebrook said ruminatively when he and his son had sat down again. "An undervalued virtue, I agree."

"Indeed. What I particularly liked was the implication that she expected it of herself as well. She spoke of observing how *they* treat their relatives, etc."

"True. A taking little thing, isn't she? A year younger than Cynthia, which makes her five years younger than you, i.e., within the tolerated age difference."

Martin began to laugh. "You go too fast, sir. I'm not hanging out for a wife yet. I must decide what I want to do with my life first."

~~~

The London mail arrived in Weymouth mid-afternoon and it had become the custom for the Glazebrooks and Chloe to gather around the tea-tray, open their letters and share items of interest with the others. Rosa wrote faithfully to Chloe each week, as did her grandmother and Ann Overton, but so far there had been no further correspondence from Nice. Julian would have sent it on, Chloe knew.

251

"At last!" Cousin Amelia said. "My mother writes that she has heard from Frederick. He is well, in Paris with his regiment and expects to be there until the end of September at least."

"Paris," Cynthia sighed. "How I wish we could go there."

Her father looked at her, amused. "For someone who refused point blank to go to London this year, you have become quite adventurous, Miss."

"I didn't refuse to go to London; I refused to come out," Cynthia said indignantly. "I should love to see the sights of London, too."

"Are you still so opposed to coming out?" Cousin Amelia asked. "It will not be so different to here—on a larger scale, of course."

"And no morning sea-bathing," Martin put in with a grin.

"She can ride in the Park," his mother said. She turned again to her daughter. "You have got used to going to the balls and assemblies here, and the calls and all the rest of it."

Cynthia sighed audibly and closed her eyes, her features set in the resentful patience of one resigned to suffering yet another disquisition on a familiar yet distasteful topic. Mrs Glazebrook's expression changed, too; she looked both anxious and apprehensive, Chloe thought. The uneasy silence was broken by Mr Glazebrook.

"I'll make a bargain with you, Cynthia. If you agree to come out next year, we'll go to Paris in September and visit Frederick. But you must promise that after Easter you will come with us to London; you will be presented to Her Majesty at the first drawing-room thereafter and otherwise participate in the Season cheerfully—with no more moping or days spent in the sulks."

"Papa!" Cynthia's eyes had popped open in astonished pleasure, but now she looked accusingly at her sire. "How can you say such a thing to me?"

"Very easily. You have shown during our stay here that you know how to go on in society, so I must assume that your behaviour earlier this year was a deliberate attempt to coerce your mother into yielding to your will. There will be no more of that. Either you behave like a well-bred adult woman or you will return to the schoolroom at Hooke Manor and follow a schoolroom regime."

Chloe was embarrassed for her friend. How mortifying it must be to be dressed down so, and before others. Martin must have felt the same, for he caught her eye and nodded towards the door. Together, they rose as quietly as possible and left the room.

"Whew! It isn't often my father gets the bit between his teeth, but when he does—"

"Is he being unfair, do you think? A year can make such a difference to one's self-confidence."

"Perhaps. But she made my mother very unhappy in the spring, with her indifference to everything that was suggested. You saw her about to fall into her old habits. I think it is good that she knows that such behaviour will no longer be tolerated. It is very hard to counter, you know, unless you are prepared to thrash it out of her, and my mother would never permit a hand be raised to Cynthia although I got my share of whippings, at home and at school." He grinned at her. "They did me no harm. Put on your bonnet and we'll go for a stroll—better not be caught here in the hall if she comes out in a huff."

When Chloe returned to their shared bedroom an hour later, she found Cynthia more subdued than usual. She made no reference to the little scene in the drawing-room or to her friend's reddened eyes, but went to her clothes-press to inspect her ball gowns. "I hope my new gowns will be ready soon. With two balls a week, people must be very used to seeing these. I wonder if I can vary the trimming on this for tomorrow night."

"Let me see." Cynthia got up from the day-bed where she had been reclining and came over to look. "It's not as simple as it looks," she said finally. "You could do a lot of damage to the gauze unpicking the ribbon, and I doubt if you will find anything as good as the little clusters of flowers to match the bodice. Maybe something different for your hair, or a new fan? We could go to the shops before breakfast. We won't be bathing as our hair was washed this morning in preparation for the ball tomorrow."

Chapter Twenty-One

Clad in the best that Paris had to offer, from the tilt of his hat to the sheen of his cane, George Crosbie strolled along The Esplanade, conscious of the appreciative eyes that followed him but deliberately paying no attention to his admirers. From time to time, he raised his hat and bowed to an elderly lady or exchanged nods with another gentleman. Once he gallantly retrieved a runaway hoop, returning it to its owner with a bow for the harassed nursemaid, and he also ducked into the stationers to purchase a stick of black sealing wax.

Mr Crosbie lost no time in presenting himself to Mr Rodber, Master of Ceremonies at the Assembly Rooms, and was soon to be seen in both card and ball rooms where he distinguished himself equally well. Each morning, he exercised a handsome bay gelding, to the envy of those who had restricted themselves to hired riding hacks during their stay in Weymouth and now had to admire horse and rider moving as one. Gentlemen, and those forward females who happened to pass by the place where males bathed as nature had intended, attested to his prowess in the water and his splendid physique.

Soon, the murmurs began. 'No, not a soldier, but served in the Militia for at least ten years.' 'A lieutenant, I believe.' 'Connected to the Crosbies of Wiltshire, I understand.' 'A widower, they tell me.' 'Last December.' 'That explains why he dresses in shades of black and grey. Such delicacy.' 'Inconsolable, I am told.'

No one thought to ask for the source of this information, but within a week everyone knew all there was to be known about Mr Crosbie. 'A welcome addition to our little society,' was the verdict and 'we must see if we can turn his thoughts to happier things'.

Just as this information was disseminated to the inquisitive, little snippets about other visitors reached Crosbie's ears. He was an adept navigator of the shoals of gossip, knowing when to appear interested, when to feign deafness, and when to prompt with a judicious 'Indeed?' or 'You don't say, ma'am'. When among his own sex, he knew when to comment on 'A pretty little filly' or 'A cosy armful'. He was no stranger to those useful little pamphlets listing heiresses and their fortunes, and had also learnt how to look up the fine details of a will at the various Ecclesiastical Courts. You could never be too careful about these things.

'A nabob's granddaughter'—promising. 'Devoted companion left a fortune by her dead mistress'—worth investigating. Fortunes could be small or large; on the other hand, the mistress is unlikely to have tied the bequest up in strings the way a father would. 'Successful fortune-hunter, now widow'—could she be beguiled? 'The Loring heiress'.

"Not Sir Edward Loring's daughter? I am shocked, ma'am, to learn of his death. My late wife and I called on him just before Christmas. Before the end of the year, you say? Dear me."

The old man must have caught the nasty infection that had carried Lydia away, George Crosbie thought with cold satisfaction. Lydia's death had robbed him of half of her trust fund; the half that would have gone to their children, had they had any, and now returned to her family. It was true that he had inherited the other half of the capital free and clear, and ten thousand pounds was nothing to be sneezed at, but he had liked Lydia, damn it! He had devoted two years to snaring her, and another year to training her in the ways of a wife. But she had tamed him, too. He would never again let a female hold the purse-strings.

He had no intention of marrying again, or not for some years at any rate, but old habits died hard, and he did not intend to do without female company. Just be careful not to be trapped into matrimony, he admonished himself. Some of these wenches are quite cunning.

~~~

"My goodness, Chloe, if it were not for her dark hair, this Flora would be the image of you."

"Let me see." Chloe joined Cynthia to examine the engraving of a classically draped young woman with flowers in her hair and spilling from her kirtled overskirt as she walked along a river bank, leaving a trail of blossom behind her. She lifted it out and tilted it so that she could read the name of the artist. "'Alex. Eubank delt'. What does 'delt' mean?"

"It is short for the Latin 'drew', Miss," the shopkeeper said. "Alexander Eubank drew this, it says, referring to the original work, from which this engraving was made." He pointed to the other side of the engraving. "This is the name of the engraver."

"Eubank," Cynthia said, excitedly. "Don't you have an uncle Eubank?"

"Yes. But I think this may have been my grandfather. He did paint, I know. And she," she pointed to the laughing, flower-wreathed girl, "must be my mother when she was younger. How did you come by it, sir?"

"His son approached me some twenty years ago. He was clearing out his father's studio over in Brighton. I bought this and some others that I thought would make good prints. I had the engravings done bit by bit. That's the last one."

Chloe hesitated. She had no picture of her mother. If there had been a portrait at the Place, she would have asked Julian for it. None must have been made, although there were ones of her father and his first wife, Julian's mother. That was strange, she thought. Julian was already talking about having an artist come to Swanmere to paint Rosa. Her mother's father had died long before her marriage, she knew. Chloe had never met her other grandmother.

"How much is this?"

The shopkeeper looked at her. "It is the last one, and that style has gone out of fashion. I can let you have it, framed, for a guinea."

She had spent very little of the money she had brought with her. Apart from her allowance, Julian had given her an additional ten pounds and both her grandmother and Lord Swanmere had tucked some guineas into her hand, 'so that you may treat yourself, my dear.'

"Very well. How soon will it be ready?"

"Tomorrow evening. To be kept for Miss?" He raised his pen expectantly.

"Loring." Chloe handed him a guinea and waited for him to write out a receipt. "Thank you." Followed by Cynthia, she walked to the door, not sparing a glance for the man who stood back to let them pass.

She had not felt so happy for a long time. She could not wait to pore over the framed engraving, scrutinising every small detail. That her mother was the model, she was sure. She remembered a painting her mother had once shown her; a much younger Mamma stood at her easel while her father leaned forward to comment on some aspect of her work. That had disappeared; she had not been able to find it. She hoped Mamma had taken it with her, that Papa had not destroyed it.

As the two young ladies left the printshop, Crosbie eased forward to the counter where the print still lay. He coolly turned it with one finger so that it faced him. Yes. That was a much younger Lady Loring. So Eubank was her maiden name. And from Brighton. An artist's daughter—surprising that Sir Edward considered her to be a fit wife for him.

"May I help you, sir?"

"Do you have anything more of this Eubank's work?"

"I'm not sure, sir. If you would care to look in again tomorrow?"

"Certainly." With a bit of luck, he could contrive to be here at the same time as Miss Loring collected her print.

Mr Crosbie strolling at his heels, Mr Rodber cleaved his way through the crowd in the Assembly Rooms Ballroom, "like a tug with a ship of the line," Martin Glazebrook muttered to Chloe. His mother had prevailed upon him to escort them this evening, promising that his father, who was dining elsewhere, would join them later. The master of ceremonies was clearly bent on fulfilling a request to present the gentleman to a particular lady; sidelong glances were accompanied by a susurration of comment as he made his way past the little groups of hopeful ladies, all of whom would have been willing to oblige a personable gentleman desirous of dancing.

The Glazebrooks, with Chloe, stood at the far end of the room. Soon it became apparent they were either to be favoured or publicly spurned. Cynthia and Chloe exchanged uneasy glances. Mr Crosbie's chiselled features and slight air of melancholy had not escaped their notice, but neither of them had considered herself worthy of being singled out by him. They were too young and had not yet come out in London. Their fans opened and fluttered to conceal their faces as the two gentlemen neared.

Mr Rodber stopped and bowed. "Ma'am, young ladies. May I have the honour of presenting Mr Crosbie to you as a dancing partner? Mr Crosbie, may I introduce Mrs Glazebrook, Miss Loring, Miss Glazebrook, and Mr Glazebrook."

Even as her mother inclined her head, Martin nodded and the two girls sketched their curtsies, Cynthia fumed inwardly. Once again, she had to yield precedence to Chloe. Is this how it would be if they came out together? Would she always have to take second place to the baronet's daughter? The fact that she was granddaughter of a viscount and daughter of a member of Parliament meant nothing, apparently. The most she could claim was to be the daughter of an esquire, one rank above the daughter of a gentleman.

Tonight, however, things were to be different. Having completed the formalities, Mr Crosbie invited her to stand up with him for the next dance. Doing her utmost to suppress a pleased smile, Cynthia placed her hand in his and allowed him to escort her to the middle of the floor, where a new set was forming. There was just one couple before them. The lady would call the first dance but, as dances were usually danced in pairs, Cynthia and her partner would lead the second, which she would call.

Mentally thanking Chloe's former governess, Miss Fancourt, who had made them practise just this event last year, Cynthia smiled at her partner, determined to enjoy this little victory over her friend. Perhaps it was petty of her, but most evenings, Chloe was invited to dance first and Cynthia was left wondering was she to be a wall-flower.

Her cousin did not seem perturbed, however, and chatted happily to Cynthia's mother and brother. Of course, Chloe always had Martin in reserve; Martin, who was Cynthia's brother. There was something particularly dreary about dancing with one's brother, Cynthia thought. Even as she watched, the master of ceremonies returned with another gentleman and within a couple of minutes, he and Chloe had taken the bottom of the set.

"You look very serious."

Cynthia started. "It's nothing. Just a wayward thought."

"Wayward? I like that in a woman."

The glint in Mr Crosbie's eye suggested only one meaning of 'wayward'. Cynthia felt herself flush and was glad when the leading gentleman, having spoken to his partner, called out the figure to be danced. Very easy to follow, thank goodness.

She had recovered her composure by the time they were halfway down the dance. His innuendo just showed that he regarded her as a woman and not a green girl. There something thrilling about dancing with him; the touch of his gloved hand on hers seemed more personal; she loved the way that his eyes met hers as they turned around each other, the little smile with which he welcomed her after the dance had separated them.

"Do you stay long in Weymouth?" he asked as they waited for the second dance to begin.

"Until the end of August."

"Do you enjoy it here?"

"Yes. So far, anyway. There is so much to do."

"Such as?"

"Oh, sea-bathing, walking, riding—" She broke off at the arrival of Mr Rodber to request her to call the dance.

"Hands across, back again, down the middle, up again and poussette," she murmured to her partner and had the felicity of hearing him repeat it loudly for the benefit of the couples below them.

When they joined both hands and turned in the poussette, she could have danced forever with him. But finally, the music stopped. He offered his arm again and escorted her back to where her mother stood.

"Most enjoyable, Miss Glazebrook. Thank you," he said as he bowed.

She inclined her head with a smile, and their dance was over. But not the ball. Whether it was because she had been so singled out by Mr Crosbie, or because her resulting happiness was infectious, Cynthia danced every dance thereafter so that when eleven o'clock struck, she was almost relieved that no more could be required of her that evening.

"That was a most successful ball," her mother said when they had gathered in their drawing-room for their usual review of the evening. "You both did very well, girls. It is not always easy to remain attentive when confronted with a dead bore, or to keep smiling when partnered with a bad dancer, but it is all a matter of practice. You will find that girls who appear dull or lacking in interest will attract fewer partners."

"That is only reasonable," Martin said. "A fellow is much more likely to invite a lady to stand up with him if he knows he will be accepted with a smile and some conversation. For every 'catch', as you girls describe them, who knows he only has to throw the handkerchief, there is a young cub making his first appearance and hoping that he won't make a complete ass of himself."

"I never thought of that," Chloe said. "How do you decide whom to ask to dance?"

"When you have just come on the town, usually your host or hostess will present you to some partners so in the beginning, you have no choice. As the Season goes on, you also look out for the ones you have already enjoyed dancing with but, if they are unmarried, you must be careful, too, that you don't have them thinking you have fallen in love with them. Never dance with a lady twice in one evening is my motto. At a public ball, you have to rely on the master of ceremonies if there is no common acquaintance who will introduce you. I like a lady who looks lively and not as if she would have preferred to stay at home with a book, which is not to say that I disapprove if she enjoys reading."

"But if she is at a ball, she should appear to enjoy the ball?" Chloe asked.

"Exactly. And I tend to avoid the belles of the ball, generally they are not worth the effort."

"Why ever not?" Cynthia asked.

"They think that dancing with them is reward enough—they need not make any additional effort to engage your interest. But then I am not a prize on the marriage market. You should see how the wealthy and titled are lionised, really pursued by both mothers and daughters."

"Well, you have opened my eyes this evening, Martin," Chloe said. "I shall pay more attention to these interactions in future."

She enjoyed talking so freely to Martin, who behaved as if she were another sister rather than a rather remote cousin. Julian was so much older, more like a father really, and he had never encouraged her to see the world through a gentleman's eyes, as Martin did. During the following days, she found herself fascinated by the little scenes and dramas that were played out, almost unnoticed, whenever men and women came together. She began to distinguish the aloofness that came from shyness from that which was grounded in arrogance, and genuine from false friendship. Little by little, she established her own circle of young ladies where the tone was one of helpful amity. Smiled on by the older ladies, who were delighted to see their daughters so at ease, gentlemen also gravitated towards it, sure that they would be included in the conversation and always able to find a partner without having to make a public matter of it.

Cynthia tended to hover on the edge of the group, depending on who else was there on any given occasion. She was inclined to be moody, Chloe found, especially if she did not have a partner for the first dances. Mr Crosbie had stood up with her twice since that first evening and on each occasion, Cynthia had beamed. Was she developing a *tendre* for him, Chloe wondered? She herself did not like him; there was something sly about him, she thought, almost calculating, as if he was always assessing those about him.

Strictly speaking, an introduction as a dancing partner in the ballroom did not entitle a gentleman to presume any further acquaintance, but when they encountered him one morning riding on the Downs about Osmington Mills, Cousin Amelia nodded to him, whereupon he lifted his hat and bowed.

"A wonderful morning, is it not?"

"Yes," Cynthia said eagerly. "We bathed this morning, but could not bear to stay in Weymouth afterwards."

"Intrepid," he remarked. "Have you seen the chalk image of the King riding, cut into the hillside? No? You must go back inland, towards Osmington. May I escort you?" Without waiting for an answer, he fell in beside Martin, who led the little group; the two girls rode in the middle and Mr and Mrs Glazebrook brought up the rear.

Glancing back, Chloe saw Mr Glazebrook raise his eyebrows at his wife, who shrugged but said nothing. After some time, the huge figure came into sight.

"What do you think, ladies?" Mr Crosbie asked.

"Quite impressive," Cynthia said, "but it could be any rider in an old-fashioned hat, could it not?"

"I cannot but wonder why someone went to all that trouble," Chloe remarked. "It's not as if the poor King could see it. How long will it be before it is grown over?"

"A couple of years, I expect," Martin said. "When was it done, Crosbie?"

"Six years ago, I am told."

"That suggests that someone is going to the trouble of clearing it. It may survive a little longer."

"Let's ride on," Cynthia said impatiently.

"Lead on, then," Martin said.

She tapped her heel to her horse's side. "Such a slug. I wish I had my own Bess. Next time we go away like this, we must take our own horses with us."

"I agree," Martin said, as he turned to follow. "What's the point of having them eating their heads off at home?"

"You are right," his father agreed. "What the—? Cynthia!"

"Something must have startled her horse," Martin called as he set off in pursuit of his sister, who clung to the reins as her mount raced headlong along the path. Mr Crosbie was ahead of him and soon caught up with the bolting horse.

"Sit up and loosen your reins," he called to Cynthia, as he approached on her left side. "Try to turn him to the right in a big circle. That's the way. Slow down, Glazebrook," he shouted back to Martin. "We don't want him to think this is a race. That's excellent, Miss Glazebrook, he's responding already. Keep it up. You're doing well. Keep circling. We're fortunate that we have plenty of room here. Slow again, into a trot. Well done!" He kept pace with her on the outside of the circle. "Now see if he will walk for you."

She complied, patting her mount's neck. "Good boy," she murmured as he obeyed. Finally, he halted and stood head down.

"Well-ridden, Miss Glazebrook," Mr Crosbie said.

"Thank you, Mr Crosbie. I was concentrating on keeping my seat, and could not think what to do." She patted the gelding again. "And to think I had just called him a slug."

"Impugning his honour? That would have done it," Mr Crosbie said with a smile.

"What happened, Sis?" Martin asked.

"A bird. It exploded from the undergrowth, just under his feet. He threw up his head, I cried out, and he was off."

Cynthia's parents had ridden up by now. "Thank you for your assistance, sir," her father called. "I dread to think what might have happened."

"It was nothing," Mr Crosbie answered modestly. "I suggest you walk him a little more, Miss Glazebrook; let him catch his breath."

"I think we all need to," Cousin Amelia said.

Indeed, it could have ended differently, Chloe thought. Life can change in an instant; be snuffed out like a candle. If Cynthia had fallen and got her foot caught in the stirrup, she would have been dragged behind the bolting horse. Martin looked very serious. She smiled over at him. "We must be grateful Cynthia is such a good rider."

"Yes. It could have gone so wrong." He shivered. "It doesn't bear thinking about."

Mr Crosbie escorted them to their lodgings and begged leave to call the next day to enquire how Miss Glazebrook went on after her adventure.

"Of course, Mr Crosbie, you must always be welcome," Cousin Amelia said.

Chloe dismounted and handed her reins to Martin. He and his father would return the horses to the livery stables.

"And I'll have a word with Jones," Mr Glazebrook said. "That horse is not suitable for a lady."

Chloe slipped her arm into Cynthia's, who had turned very pale and was shaking slightly. "Let us go in. We will all be glad of a cup of tea."

Interlude at Swanmere Castle

Weymouth, 24 July 1815

To Sir Julian and Lady Swann-Loring

Dearest Rosa and Julian,

I *hope you have been missing me, for you will see me sooner than you think. The Glazebrooks have decided to cut short their stay in Weymouth, as they have now decided to go to France in September. Major Raven is stationed in Paris with his regiment and they wish to take advantage of this. We leave Weymouth therefore on Monday the thirty-first. Would it be possible for you to send the carriage to collect me at Hooke Manor on the following Saturday?*

I look forward to seeing you both again, and also my grandparents. I say grandparents, for I have quite come to think of Lord Swanmere as the grandfather I never knew. Pray tell him and Grandmamma that I missed our newspaper readings and shall be happy to resume them.

Later. Cousin Amelia came in while I was writing this to invite me to go to France with them. They enjoyed having me as their guest, they said, and they think I am a good influence on Cynthia.

It is quite a flattering thing to have said of one, I suppose, but I hope they do not say it to her, for it must make her hate me. I know I would hate anyone who was supposed to be a good influence on me.

It is a wonderful opportunity, of course, but I am not sure I like the idea of being away from home for some more months. My cousin could not say how long they will remain abroad. She will write to you separately. It is fortunate that as an MP, Mr Glazebrook can frank it so that you will not have to pay for two sheets.

Please let me know what you think. I will be guided by you. If you decide I may go, I do hope that I can see you both before we leave England. Rosa, please also give some consideration to what warmer clothing I should take with me, and if there is anything else I'll need. Or would it be best to buy anything necessary in Paris?

Pray give my dearest love to Grandmamma and Lord Swanmere.

Do let me hear from you by return.

> *Your loving sister,*
> *Chloe Loring*

P.S. If any letters should have arrived for me, please send them with the carriage to Hooke Manor. C.L.

Lady Swann-Loring looked up from her sister-in-law's letter. "She is so excited. What do you think, Julian?"

"It is an excellent opportunity, I suppose."

"You sound reluctant."

"Yes. I don't know. What if she runs into her mother?"

"It's unlikely they would be in Paris at the same time," Rosa said. "But would it be so dreadful if they were? It is over a year since Delia left England, and more than that since she went to Harrogate. There has been no talk at all, and anything that arose now could be dismissed as ill-natured gossip. To my mind, the worst thing of all would be for Chloe to give her mother the cut direct. It would be most unbecoming in a girl of her age."

Julian bent and kissed her. "You are quite right, as always, my love. Let us see what my cousin says."

Apart from assuring them that Chloe would be as carefully chaperoned as their own daughter, Amelia Glazebrook's letter contained nothing new, apart from setting the twenty-seventh of August as the day they wished to leave for France.

"Even if it is only for two weeks, Chloe should come home first," Rosa said firmly. "We would like to see her again, as would her grandparents. We must also see to her laundry and her wardrobe. You must collect her, Julian. She shouldn't travel on her own."

Chapter Twenty-Two

Mr Crosbie called as promised the following day. Cousin Amelia had decreed that Cynthia rest that morning, but by the time he came, she was up and dressed in her most becoming morning gown of muslin sprigged with pink carnations and trimmed with pink ribbons. Her dark hair was caught back with matching ribbons in a deceptively simple style.

"I see you well, I trust, Miss Glazebrook."

"Yes indeed, sir. I was a little shaky yesterday, but a good night's sleep set me right."

"Shall I see you at the ball this evening?"

"I hope so, for it will be our last one. We leave here on Monday."

He looked surprised. "Monday? I thought you were fixed here for August."

"That was our original intention, but we have decided to go to Paris in September and will need some time to prepare," Cousin Amelia said. "My brother is there with the army of occupation."

"A fascinating city, indeed. We were there last autumn, my late wife and I. Poor Lydia." He sighed. "Do you know, Miss Glazebrook, sometimes you remind me of her."

Cynthia looked as if she did not know how to reply to this remark. Mr Crosbie did not wait for an answer, but turned to

Chloe. "Do you accompany your cousins to France, Miss Loring?"

"They have been kind enough to invite me to do so," she replied calmly. What business of his was it?

"You have a relative there already, do you not? There was a Lady Loring in Paris last autumn. We met her later in Nice."

Chloe's heart thumped in her breast and for a moment, she felt sick. Who was he to mention Mamma? She pinned a smile of polite interest to her lips. "Indeed, sir?"

Martin smoothly turned the conversation. "Nice was occupied by the French under Napoleon, was it not? Had it already been restored to the King of Sardinia then?"

"Yes."

"It is strange to imagine a land border," Cynthia said. "Just imagine the other side of the road being in a different country."

"We are an island people," Mr Glazebrook said. "It is what makes us different from others."

"Indeed." Mr Crosbie rose. "I'll take my leave of you, until this evening."

"It is such a pity we are leaving so soon," Cynthia said to Chloe as they dressed for the ball. "I would have liked to know Mr Crosbie better."

"He seems interested in you. How does he measure up to your husband criteria?"

"Let me see." Cynthia began to count off on her fingers. "He is exceedingly good looking, perhaps too handsome. He was quick to respond yesterday, and his intervention was helpful. He is an excellent dancer, and a passable conversationalist. That is all in his favour. But he reveals very little of himself. I have no idea of his family circumstances, other than that his wife is dead."

"Does he have children?"

Cynthia stared at her. "He never said, one way or another. I could not tolerate a man who denied his children, or left them to another to bring up."

"They may not have had any," Chloe said. "How long were they married?"

"I don't know."

Chloe shrugged. "There is no point in trying to find out now, is there? We shall probably never see him again. But we should add 'openness about his family' to the husband list." She laughed. "I daresay he would be incensed to learn that he had fallen short in so many areas."

Cynthia sighed. "He is very attractive. But, as my old nurse says, 'there's more to marriage than four bare legs in a bed'."

"Cynthia!" Chloe didn't know where to look. But later, when she thought about it, she had to admit the sense of the old saying. But there has to be some attraction, some spark, she thought. She had never really experienced it, but she could see it between Rosa and Julian. When Chloe and her grandmother had returned from their stay with the Ransfords after Rosa's and Julian's wedding, the newly-weds had politely but firmly explained that they were not to be disturbed in the two hours before dinner.

"They are wise to establish some time for themselves," Grandmother had said. "A marriage must be cultivated if it is to bear fruit."

Chloe had wondered uneasily if Grandmother had meant babies, but then thought the old lady would not have been so direct. This was part of the 'more to marriage', she thought now, grateful to have the opportunity to learn these things before embarking on her Season.

~~~

The ballroom was fuller than usual tonight. The Glazebrooks were not the only guests leaving on Monday and all seemed to have taken this last opportunity of meeting their new friends and acquaintances. In Chloe's circle, there was a flurry of invitations to dance amid much laughter as the gentleman sorted out which lady was available for which set.

"It is such a pity that Mr Rodber insists on stopping on the first stroke of eleven o'clock," one young lady complained. "We might have danced until midnight or even one o'clock."

"Let us sit together for tea," a gentleman proposed. "The first into the tea-room should reserve places for the others."

"An excellent suggestion," another approved, and so it was decided.

The first sets were beginning to form and everyone hurried to take their places. Tonight, the master of ceremonies need not strive to fill a set or to find partners for neglected ladies. The floor was so full that the older ladies and chaperons had to push their chairs as far back against the wall as possible. The musicians struck up with a new vivacity and the dancers, too, had a new vigour. Smiling eyes met as hands touched and separated. 'Shall we two ever meet again?' some seemed to say while others, who would remain for another month, murmured, 'Let us not waste the time that is left to us.'

When Mr Crosbie arrived just before nine o'clock, the tea-room was abuzz with conversation. He stood in the doorway for a couple of minutes, making no attempt to join one of the tables. He was soon captured by Mr Rodber, who introduced him to a mother and daughter who had arrived only that week, and he later led the daughter out for the first dance after tea. By the time he made his way around the ballroom to the Glazebrooks, it was after ten.

He bowed. "May I have the pleasure of dancing this next with you, Miss Glazebrook?"

Cynthia smiled regretfully. "I am afraid I am already engaged, Mr Crosbie, and for the next set too, which is the finishing dance."

"Thank you." He turned to Chloe, although he had never so far invited her to dance with him. "Miss Loring, dare I hope?"

She shook her head. "I regret, Mr Crosbie."

"You come far too late, Crosbie," one of the other men interrupted. "*Carpe diem* and all that."

"Yes," another said. "The early bird…"

"Careful, Mathers. Can't go calling the ladies worms, you know."

Mr Mathers reddened. "Didn't mean to give offence. But it's not the thing to come after tea and try to snaffle our ladies." He offered his arm to Cynthia. "Miss Glazebrook, this next is ours."

With a ripple of laughter, the couples began to pair off for the next dance.

An icy Mr Crosbie bowed stiffly. "Goodbye, Miss Glazebrook, Miss Loring. Miss Loring, pray give my compliments to Lady Loring, or"—he smiled coolly—"Lady Stephen FitzCharles, I should say. I have it on the very best of authority—archidiaconal, no less, that she has recently changed her name."

Chloe froze, her hand tense on her partner's arm. She raised her eyes to look deliberately at her tormentor, then turned away and walked onto the dance floor without saying another word. Fortunately, Cynthia and Martin had already left the group, and the comment had meant nothing to those remaining. 'Forget it for now,' she said furiously to herself, then smiled brightly at the young man standing opposite her. "How this evening has flown."

Somehow, she managed to forget her distress and get through the last sets, but when they made their final farewells and were walking back to their lodgings, it all came flooding back. Mamma remarried! And she did not tell me. She fought to stifle a sob as she bade the others, 'Good night'. No, she would not join them for a glass of wine. She preferred to go directly to bed; she could feel a headache starting—probably because the rooms had been so crowded tonight.

"Of course, my dear. Go on up," Cousin Amelia said sympathetically. "Do you have lavender water? A little on your temples will help. Send your maid down if there is anything you need."

"Thank you. Good night, ma'am."

Parker was waiting for her. A former laundry maid at Swanmere, whom the housekeeper, Mrs Godin, had described as a hard worker with plenty of common sense, Parker had become her maid last year when she and Grandmother had gone to the Ransfords. Now, properly trained by Grandmother's Dover and befriended by Rosa's maid, Lambton, she had become a stalwart ally. After a glance at Chloe, she set about getting her into bed as quickly as possible.

"Good night, Miss," she said as she drew the bed curtains. "Should I put out the candle?"

"No, leave it for Miss Glazebrook. Good night, Parker."

Chloe listened to the maid's soft footsteps, then the click of the closing door. Her throat ached with unshed tears. She had wanted nothing more than to set them free but, now that she was alone, she remained dry-eyed in the dark, once again the girl to whom Mamma's maid had brought a letter last August, the girl Mamma did not love enough to stay for.

What should she do? She would have to tell Julian and Rosa, of course, but need she mention Mr Crosbie's comment to the Glazebrooks? If he were going to cause talk, it would be better if they were prepared. They had not discussed her mother at all; they knew from that horrid *on-dit* that she was abroad with Lady Mary Arkell and, just after Christmas, there had been no question of summoning her home for Papa's funeral. At that time of the year, it could take weeks for her to make the journey.

There's no point now in trying to seek her out in France, Chloe thought. She had hardly admitted this secret wish to herself; how she had pictured Mamma's face lighting up when she heard Miss Loring announced; how she would open her arms, overjoyed that her daughter had forgiven everything and come to her.

But when Chloe tried to imagine their meeting now, she was back in the gamekeeper's cottage near the Place, her mother furious as she hissed, "What are you doing here? How dare you sneak up and spy on me?"

Suddenly, she sat up in bed. Supposing Mr Crosbie called again before they left? She must warn Cousin Amelia. Surely, she would agree not to receive him? The others were still downstairs. Chloe pulled back the bed curtain and slipped out of bed. She slid her feet into slippers and pulled a dressing-gown on over her nightdress, picked up the candlestick and made her way to the parlour. They knew Mamma was abroad—she need not explain anything more about that.

Chapter Twenty-three

Chloe peered impatiently through the window of the front parlour of Hooke Manor. Julian had written that he would spend the previous night at the Ransfords and call to the manor this morning at ten o'clock. She hurried out as soon as his curricle turned onto the carriage sweep, followed by the carriage for Parker and the trunks.

"Julian! Oh, I am so pleased to see you. How good of you to come yourself."

"How could I resist the opportunity of two long drives?" he teased her as he caught her in his arms. "You look well, Pet. The sea air seems to have agreed with you."

"I had the most wonderful time. But come in here." She tugged him into the parlour. "We'll go in to the morning room in a bit. There is something I must tell you first."

"If it is that you have received an offer of marriage, you are far too young," he said firmly.

"No. Not I but—one of the other visitors to Weymouth, a Mr Crosbie, said that he had it from an archdeacon that Mamma had married Lord Stephen FitzCharles." She had meant to introduce the subject more calmly, but it all came out in a rush.

"What?" Julian said, frowning, then "Crosbie—where have I heard that name before?"

"I don't know. But do you think it is true? And she never told me?"

"As to that," he said, and took a letter from his pocket. "This came for you two days ago. It was enclosed in one addressed to my grandfather and posted here, not abroad."

She snatched it from him. "That's Mamma's hand and seal. Do you think she is back in England?"

"There is only one way to find out."

Biting her lip, Chloe carefully broke the seal and opened the letter. "She cannot have written it recently—only see how deep the folds are. Oh, it is dated the first of June. Weeks before Waterloo. Shall I read it to you?"

"If you wish."

Villa Della Torre, 1 June 1815

Miss Chloe Loring

Dearest Chloe,

I write this letter in the hope that an English naval ship will put in here and I can send a letter via the captain. Even should this happen, I have no guarantee that you would receive it within a reasonable (or even unreasonable) length of time, but I can at least hope you will one day read these lines. It is several weeks since we have seen an English ship in the bay below us; everyone has been told to keep an eye out and as soon as one is spied, the letter will be taken down at once.

The most important thing I must tell you is that Lord Stephen and I were married at the end of March by Archdeacon Burton, two days before he and other visiting Anglican clergymen left for Genoa. Although we would have preferred to wait for at least six months after your father's death, given the present uncertainties, we felt it wiser to take advantage of the Archdeacon's presence here and marry sooner rather than later.

Please be assured, Chloe, that this second marriage does not change my love for you or your importance to me. I am aware that your brother is your guardian and that, until you are of age, I have no say as to where you live. Once you are of age, you can, of course, make your own decisions. I am sure you are happy to be at Swanmere with Julian and his wife, but you should know that Stephen welcomes you as a daughter, and our home will always be open to you. We have not yet decided where we shall live permanently, but you will be one of the first to know once we have reached a decision.

Although my formal name, according to English usage, is now Lady Stephen FitzCharles, the servants here continue to refer to me as la Lady Delia. *They were used to saying* la Lady Mary *and cannot be expected to understand the intricacies of the English forms of address. I admit that I am happy to hear my real name—the name I think of as my real self—on their lips. Why, do you think, do the English obliterate a lady's name when she marries? It is not so everywhere.*

Do you find it difficult to get information about what is happening in Europe? We no longer receive English newspapers here. We get the occasional Moniteur *from Paris and the Sardinian/Savoy* Gazzetta Piemontese *continues to print reports from all the capital cities, although sometimes with a delay of some weeks. It is strange to read of the Queen receiving someone at Buckingham House in the midst of all the worry about war, but it reminds us that most people are able to continue their lives as usual. I hope that that is the case for you.*

It is interesting that Louis XVIII did not flee to England this time, but has set up a court in exile in Ghent. Let us hope this is a good omen. Wellington has taken command in Brussels, we hear, which is some comfort. Did you know that Napoleon's brother-in-law, Murat, who contrived to remain as King of Naples even after Bonaparte's first defeat, seized the opportunity to rise against Austria and was roundly defeated? As a result, King Ferdinand was restored to the throne of Naples.

It has become very hot here, and everyone takes a long rest in the afternoon. We ladies are now wearing our lightest cottons and muslins, and the gentlemen also have donned lighter garb, in particular exchanging their tight cravats and stiff, high collars for softer collars worn turned down and open at the neck. Unlike in England, where summer alternates between sunny and rainy days and weeks, here it will remain sunny and hot until September, when it will start to get cooler. It is hard to believe, I know, but the winter here is more like spring in England.

Dearest Chloe, I wish you sunny days and a pleasant summer. I shall enclose this letter in one addressed to Lord Swanmere as Stephen thinks this is more likely to encourage the captain to take it for us, and shall include my compliments to him and the other residents of Swanmere there.

Farewell, my darling girl. Remember, you are always in my thoughts and prayers. God bless you and keep you until we meet again,

Mamma

Chloe had tears in her eyes by the time she was finished reading the letter. "She did not forget me," she whispered. "What did she say in the letter to his lordship?"

"Nothing, except the usual courtesies. She reserved the news of her marriage for you, so that you were the first to hear it. Did you say anything to Amelia?"

"Yes. I thought I should in case Mr Crosbie called again, so that she would know not to receive him." She looked at Julian. "He said it in the Assembly Rooms, just as a dance was starting. Quite maliciously, I thought, so as to overset me."

"What? Was he your partner? I hope you left him standing."

She smiled faintly. "I did, but he wasn't my partner. He came late and neither Cynthia nor I had a dance free. Some of the other men began to twit him about early birds and I think he got annoyed."

"What did Amelia say?"

"She was most kind; they all were. Mr Glazebrook insisted on giving me a small glass of Madeira, as a composer. He said we should not be too surprised, that Elba was not far from Nice and Bonaparte's escape may have caused Lord Stephen to offer Mamma the protection of his name. And he said, too, that the post was very likely disrupted for a long time. And Cousin Amelia said we certainly would not be at home to him, Mr Crosbie, I mean, if he should call again."

"Did he?"

"No. But what should we do now, Julian?"

"Nothing. It is up to them to announce the marriage if they wish. Should word of it spread via this archdeacon, and we are asked about it, we simply say that we wish them happy. If you wish, you can divert the inquisitive by telling them how your mother had to wait for the navy to put in so that she could send you a letter, but you do not owe anybody any information."

Chloe nodded. "That makes it easier."

"Come, let us join the others. I should like to be gone within the hour. We shall have the whole journey to talk."

~~~

Rosa must have been looking out for them, for she came out from the Great Hall as Julian pulled his team up.

"Welcome home," she cried, hugging Chloe. "You look positively splendid."

"It was wonderful. We must go all together next year. I'm sure you would love the sea-bathing."

Rosa laughed. "I'm not sure about that, but we'll see. Are you hungry? Did you stop for a nuncheon?"

"Yes, and no." Julian bent to kiss his wife. "Let us wash off the dust of the road, and we'll be with you."

"I suppose I should write to my mother," Chloe said as she helped herself to another cheese tartlet.

Rosa looked serious. "Think carefully about what you want to say to her. The marriage cannot be undone and, indeed, it is the best possible solution for her."

"In what way?"

"Any talk from last year, and that will only have been local, must have died down by now, and, thanks to Lord Stephen's aunt, a further scandal has been averted. Don't begrudge your mother this new happiness, Chloe, or resent it. I resented my mother's remarriage, and it soured our relationship for the time she had left."

"But you were sent away to school," Chloe said. "I still think that was very unfair. Lord Stephen, Mamma says, welcomes me as a daughter and I shall always have a home with them. I think that is very good-natured of him."

"That is something you can say in your letter. You need not accept him as a father, especially as you have never met him, but you can show that you are well-disposed towards him. And wish them happy."

"Yes," Julian said. "I was never more than polite to your mother, and I regret that now. When I was eighteen, she offered friendship, saying I should call her Delia, but I declined." He shook his head. "What a stiff-rumped pup I was!"

"Have you heard from Robert, Rosa? His stepmother was not kind to him."

"Yes. His father is taking more of an interest in him, and has taken him and Hal to London to see the sights."

"That's wonderful. Ann is in Lyme Regis with her uncle and his family. I had hoped we might be able to meet, but it was too far to ride there and back in a day, and enjoy a comfortable visit, and neither the Glazebrooks nor the Overtons wanted to stay overnight." She sighed. "I wish Mrs Overton would marry again. I am sure she would leave Ann and Hal in their uncle's care—he is their guardian—and then we could arrange for them all to come here again next summer."

"Do you think it is likely?" Rosa asked.

"She is away a lot, paying long visits to her friends, Ann says. Ann spends most of her time at the big house. Her grandmother talks of bringing her out next year, but Ann is afraid it would turn into her mother's Season. She could hardly be excluded, after all, and, well, you know how she is." Chloe started to laugh. "Remember when she called you a staid old bachelor and threatened to take you in hand this last Season, Julian? You gave her such a set-down, told her she would turn into a meddling tabby everyone tried to avoid."

"Did you really?" Rosa asked her husband. "How brave of you."

He laughed. "It didn't stop her suggesting Chloe and Ann have a joint come-out at Swanmere House, did it? And I might leave all the arrangements to her, what's more."

"The sad thing is that I would love to come out with Ann, provided we could keep Mrs Overton at bay," Chloe said. "I wonder does she ever realise that she spoils things for herself by being too forward?"

"You sound just like Grandmother," Julian said with a grin.

Chloe looked slightly appalled at Julian's remark, but stood to her guns. "I'm right, am I not, Rosa?"

"Yes," her sister-in-law said. "She is not very clever, I think."

"She has not changed since she was a child," Julian said. "She was a pretty girl, adept at getting what she wanted. If a direct appeal did not succeed, she batted her eyelashes or touched a little handkerchief to them, as if she were crying. She could usually conjure up a tear or two, what's more. But what was appealing at six and even sixteen is not as charming at thirty-six."

"Ann is not at all like that," Chloe said.

"I imagine she learnt very soon that she could not compete with her mother," Rosa said. "I think Ann is right to be worried about her come-out. Mrs Overton would not enjoy being relegated to the matrons and chaperons."

"She would not have much choice," Julian said. "Her daughter will not be the only one coming out and the other ladies will not stand for her nonsense."

~~~

"What do you think, Grandmamma?" Chloe asked sometime later. "Will this marriage have restored Mamma's good name?"

"The fact is, she never lost it, not publicly at least," Lady Loring said. "Your father put it about that she had gone to Harrogate for her health—he was too proud to admit what had happened. I don't know how Lady Mary Arkell's intervention came about, but it was inspired, as it was to present her at the French court. I have no doubt that Lord Stephen will arrange to have her presented here and all will be well."

"Julian and Rosa have said she may come here. Shall you object to receiving her?"

Lady Loring paused. "No. Everyone should be given a second chance. You may send her and Lord Stephen my compliments when you write. I knew his mother slightly. A pleasant woman, if not over-endowed with intelligence. But that was probably better if she was to spend much time in waiting. A very tedious occupation, I believe."

Chapter Twenty-four

~~My dear Mother,~~

~~Please accept my felicitations on your recent marriage to Lord~~
~~Stephen FitzCharles~~.

No. That was too stiff and formal. Chloe dipped her quill into the ink-pot and tried again. She would write her letter and then make a fair copy to send to Mamma.

Swanmere Castle, 6 August 1815

To Lady Stephen FitzCharles
Villa Della Torre, near Nice

Dearest Mamma,

Thank you for your recent letter. How clever of you to lie in wait for a naval ship and send your letter that way. It reached Swanmere just over a week ago, and Julian brought it with him when he collected me from the Glazebrooks at Hooke Manor. They had invited me to spend some weeks with them this summer, including the month of July at Weymouth, where we enjoyed sea-

bathing, riding, and attending the balls in the Assembly Rooms. I
had a truly splendid time.

Chloe paused. Should she mention Mr Crosbie? No. Best to forget
him.

*Please accept my felicitations and good wishes on your
marriage to Lord Stephen FitzCharles. I wish you both very
happy. It is kind of him to offer me a home, but I am happily settled
at Swanmere. I hope that one day it will be possible to meet him.
Do you plan to return to England before winter?*

*The Glazebrooks have invited me to accompany them to Paris
in September, where Major Frederick Raven is at present with his
regiment. It is very exciting. I suppose it is too much to hope that
you might be there at the same time. Cousin Frederick is to
procure accommodation for us, so if you applied to him, he would
be able to give you our direction.*

Chloe lifted her pen. Was that too much to ask? Perhaps. How
long would it take this letter to reach Mamma?

*I don't know how long it will take this letter to reach you, so
you may not be able to get to Paris in time. The Glazebrooks are
inclined to change their plans at very short notice; initially we
were to spend August in Weymouth as well, then they suddenly
fixed on Paris and off we went home so that we could prepare. I
am at Swanmere for a couple of weeks, and then Julian will bring
me back to Hooke Manor. It is fortunate that he enjoys driving his
curricle, as otherwise I would be confined to the carriage. I shall
have enough of that with the Glazebrooks, but at least we shall
not all be squeezed into one carriage with the youngest sitting*

bodkin. They take three carriages, one for Cousin Amelia and her husband, one for Cynthia, Martin, and me, and one for the servants (three maids and two valets) and extra baggage. Cousin Amelia doesn't approve of making indoor servants take outside seats on such journeys. They only catch cold and are inclined to be grumpy, she says, especially if they have spent the day shivering in the rain. One can hardly blame them.

My maid, Parker, is quite nervous about going to Paris and I have been teaching her a little French. We practise in the evening when I am dressing for dinner. How glad I am that you insisted on Madame Lebrun coming every week to practise conversation. I wonder how I shall manage when everyone around me is speaking French, even the little children.

All are well here at Swanmere. Rosa and Julian send their best wishes to you and Lord Stephen and my grandmother and Lord Swanmere send their compliments.

Please keep me informed of any plans you have to return to England so that I can be sure that we will meet. Julian and Rosa say that you and Lord Stephen would be welcome to call at Swanmere and even stay here. It is most handsome and conciliatory of them, and I hope that you can meet them in a similar spirit.

With fondest love,
Your daughter, Chloe

Chloe folded and sealed her letter. Now she must consider her wardrobe and select what gowns she wished to take to Paris. She hoped there would be time to have some made there.

~~~

Paris, 21 September 1815

Dearest Rosa and Julian,

We leave Paris tomorrow. On reading this, you will be as surprised as I was when Cousin Amelia broke the news at breakfast this morning. I cannot say that I overly regret her decision.
Can you imagine London with French troops encamped in Hyde Park, and Russian and Prussian military in all the squares and open spaces, their tents pitched and their campfires burning? Soldiers of rank are billeted willy-nilly on the populace, so that an officer might appear at a gentleman's door and demand the use of the best rooms in the house. Foreign military promenade in their exotic uniforms, dragging their clattering sabres across the pavements and cobblestones, swarming into the inns, ale-houses and coffee-shops, loudly demanding service in their own language. They are everywhere; in the theatres and the shops, and at all the sights.
Every so often, one or more of these occupying armies holds a parade, as if to demonstrate their strength and superiority. At the same time, our own defeated, wounded army is making its way home. And the English themselves are divided in loyalty—some holding to the recently deposed monarch while others welcome the return of an exiled king. So it is in Paris today.
This all combines in a hectic, febrile atmosphere that is anything but pleasant, especially for females who are subjected to constant, inquisitive, scrutiny by the moustachioed soldiery—

Hussars, Chasseurs, Cossacks—all of whom vie with one another in the splendour of their elaborately decorated coats and strange head-gear. Our kilted Highlanders also attract their share of feminine admirations, though for myself I do not find the male knee particularly attractive.

After our first exploratory walk, Mr Glazebrook decreed that we three ladies, including Cousin Amelia, were not to go out without him and Martin. Cousin Frederick agreed. In fact, he wrote to dissuade his sister from coming, but his letter did not arrive in time. He good-naturedly made himself available as an additional escort and cicerone, as he put it, and we could move about safely while in his company. He is due furlough, Cousin Amelia said, and has agreed to accompany us on our journey south.

Yes, south. Your eyes do not deceive you. I would have considered it more sensible to retreat rather than advance, but, having come this far, Cousin Amelia is determined to go on. We may reach the coast in two weeks, she says, and is talking of spending the winter there—if she does not go home for Christmas, of course. Everything is possible. I am torn between dread of the journey and hope that we might pause for some time in Nice. I do not know if Cousin Amelia remembers that that is where Mamma is, and I shall not draw her attention to it. I would like to call at the Villa Della Torre, but not with a retinue of Glazebrooks. That first meeting must be as private as possible.

Chloe put down her pen. I have changed, she thought. I am no longer the girl who surprised Mamma in the cottage that day. Supposing that had never happened? Mamma wanted to bring me out this year, and Julian offered to give a ball for me. Papa was agreeable. Would I have enjoyed a Season, especially if we had gone to London directly from the Place? I don't know. Would they have expected me to marry the first eligible man who proposed? I had never discussed it with Mamma. Thank heavens it didn't happen. I cannot imagine being betrothed or even already married.

It is all very exciting and at times I have to pinch myself and say, is this really Chloe Loring who hardly left Loring Place for the first sixteen years of her life? I am glad I had the opportunity to experience so much this past year. Dear Rosa and Julian, I don't think I ever thanked you for everything you have done for me these past twelve months and more. You have given me a home, but have also encouraged me to spread my wings, safe in the knowledge that I can return to you at any time. I am most fortunate to have you as my brother and sister.

I shall continue to make the most of these new experiences and look forward to telling you all about them when I return. I am keeping a journal, as you suggested, Rosa, so that I do not forget anything.

I must finish, as Cousin Frederick said he would call for any letters we may have. I have no address to give you for the next weeks but shall write again as soon as we reach our as yet unknown destination.

I send you my fondest love, also to Grandmother and Grandfather,

Your loving sister,
Chloe Loring

~~~

Newborough, Nice, 10 October 1815

Dearest Rosa and Julian,

Not only have we arrived in Nice, we have taken a house here to the end of the month, with the option of renewing it by the month. I cannot say yet how likely it is that we stay on here. I imagine that it will depend on the arrival of more 'hivernants', as they call the English who come to stay for the winter. At present, there are very few here. In other years, many would have reserved their accommodation for the coming Season before they left in the spring, but most failed to do so this year due to the uncertainty around Bonaparte. As a result, the Glazebrooks had an excellent choice of houses and apartments.

The journey here was arduous, but also fascinating. Ideally, one would take several weeks to make it, allowing for sufficient time to stop and explore the different regions and view the antiquities that we had to pass with, at best, a brief glance from the carriage window. When we had to wait for fresh horses, we always took the opportunity to stroll around the area near the posting inn. Even the smallest village has something of interest.

The latter part of the journey, from Lyon, was along the banks of the mighty river Rhone. If we had been travelling by diligence, and not with our own carriages, we would have been able to take the 'coche d'eau' or water-coach for some of the time, which would have provided a pleasant diversion.

We are all well, although tired and stiff from the constant jolting and confined space of the carriages. We varied our company regularly. In the mornings, we separated by age, and after dinner, which was taken around noon, by sex, as we ladies agreed that was more conducive to an afternoon rest. In the evenings, after supper, we gathered in the largest bed-chamber to talk, play cards, or take turns to read aloud. Cousin Frederick brought a copy of Mr Smollett's Travels *and it was entertaining to compare his (Smollett's) comments with our own experiences. Sometimes we sang—I taught them* Il es Bel et Bon, *although not as well as Ann did it last year. We sang the main air as a round, with only the natural harmony this brings, but it still sounded well and everyone was amused. It reminded me of those happy weeks at Swanmere last August.*

I intend to call at the Villa Della Torre *as soon as I can manage to do so discreetly, and will let you know how I get on.*

In the meantime, I send you my fondest love, also to Grandmother and Grandfather.

Your loving sister,
Chloe Loring

Chapter Twenty-Five

"Martin, will you ride with me today? Cynthia is indisposed and stays in bed this morning."

"Of course, Coz."

"Can you arrange it before the others come back? I have a particular place in mind I'd like to go to. I'll explain on the way."

Martin drained his coffee cup. "Better go around to the livery at once, then. Are you ready?"

"I must change my slippers for boots and fetch my hat, gloves, and whip," Chloe said. "Just give me five minutes."

Half an hour later, they were mounted on two mules and following a local muleteer through the gate onto the Royal Road to Turin.

"What is this *Villa Della Torre*?" Martin asked.

"It is the home of Lady Mary Arkell, *Contessa Della Torre*. She is Lord Stephen FitzCharles' aunt and, as far as I know, he and my mother are at present her guests."

Martin whistled. "You wish to call on your mother? Is she expecting you?"

"No. I thought about sending a note, but I wanted to keep it as quiet as possible." She glanced sideways at Martin. "I haven't seen her for over a year. We have exchanged letters, but it has been difficult with the interruption to the post during the Hundred Days."

The road climbed steadily and already they could see the mountains. Ahead of them, the muleteer moved to the side, motioning to them to do the same as a coach and four came around a corner at speed.

"Shall we stay long on the post road?" Martin asked when the dust had settled.

"We turn off after another mile or so. It's a strange method of progression, isn't it? We are not actively riding—our beasts simply follow the one in front. Mules are best for the mountain paths, they say. They are more sure-footed than horses."

"I'm sure you would be glad of that if you had to cross those high passes."

She laughed. "I was just imagining what my father would say if he could see me now. He was always so particular about horseflesh."

"I remember visiting his stables while we were at Loring Place last year. He had some magnificent animals."

"I think he must have spent half his life on horseback. But he wasn't sentimental about them. He enjoyed horse-trading; after the first time he sold my pony, I made him promise he would never do so without consulting me. My father could not see that it mattered, as long as I had a pony."

Martin laughed. "I can just imagine you at—what were you, nine or ten?—laying down the law to him."

Chloe shook her head. "I didn't throw a tantrum. I was inconsolable, and, in the end, it was my tears that did the trick. My governess tried to explain that as I grew, I needed a bigger mount and that Molly was more suited to smaller children, but it was the shock, you see. I went out one morning and she was gone, and the new pony there in her place. He even tried to buy Molly back, but she had been sold on."

"I understand. As the elder, I never suffered such a shock, for my ponies were passed on to Cynthia and I didn't have a mount of my own while I was at school—it was not worth it for the few weeks a year I was at home."

"That must have been terrible."

"Not having a horse or not being at home?"

"Both, I suppose, but really being sent away for so long."

He shrugged. "You get used to it."

Maybe that was why gentlemen tended to lack sensibility, Chloe thought, remembering how, last year, Robert and Hal used laugh everything off. They must learn it at school. She looked up at the muleteer's shout. He had stopped and was pointing to the right.

"It looks as if this is where we turn off. What time is it?"

Martin tugged out his watch and flicked it open. "Just past noon."

Just after noon. Was it too early to pay a call? Should she have waited until later? But then she might not have been able to slip away. Would Lady Mary find it strange that her callers arrived on muleback? Perhaps she should have taken a carriage? Then she could have worn something other than a riding habit. Mamma had had this habit made for her last year, as part of the clothes for the house party. She had felt so grown up in it. It had still seemed quite *à la mode* in Weymouth. Would Mamma be at home? Would she be happy to see her?

As the Villa came into view, Chloe felt a cold weight settle in her stomach. She swallowed and pressed the back of her gloved hand to her cheek. Was she too warm? Was her hair still tidy?

"Ecco la Villa Della Torre," the muleteer said.

Martin dismounted and came to assist Chloe slide to the ground, then handed the reins of their mounts to their escort. The front door remained closed and Martin rapped firmly on it. After some minutes, he raised his riding crop to knock again, but then they heard rapid footsteps approaching. A harassed-looking footman pulled the door open. Further back in the hall, Chloe saw an elderly man—a butler?—stop and listen.

"Signore, Signorina?" The footman's tone stopped just short of 'what do you want?'

"Mr Glazebrook and Miss Loring to see Lady Stephen FitzCharles," Martin said briskly.

"I regret—it is not possible—"

Chloe interrupted before he could shut the door. "Pray tell Lady Delia that her daughter has called."

"Her daughter—*sua figlia*?"

When his voice rose in surprise, the other man was suddenly beside him. "You are Lady Delia's daughter? Miss Loring? *Grazie a Dio*. This way." He quickly led them down the hall and through a drawing-room onto a shady terrace. "Pray wait here. Please be seated," he added hastily, gesturing to an array of chairs and sofas, and hurried out.

"What a magnificent view," Martin said. "The sweep of the bay below, and the hills behind."

Chloe was looking at the door through which the man had vanished. "Something's wrong, Martin."

"Wrong? In what way?"

"The servants move too fast. Butlers, especially, always proceed at a more stately pace. And look there." She pointed to a table where insects buzzed around the remnants of a meal. "He didn't even notice it, or send the footman to clear it away. What's more, the house and gardens are too quiet. It's as if someone is ill, very ill."

"You may be right. Someone's coming."

A middle-aged, shirt-sleeved man strode onto the terrace. He was unshaven and looked drawn and haggard. "Miss Loring?"

"Yes?"

"Thank God. Some good angel must have sent you. Please come with me. I am Stephen FitzCharles." He looked over to Martin. "Please wait here, sir. My aunt will be with you shortly."

Chloe caught up the train of her habit and hurried after Lord Stephen, who was taking the broad staircase two steps at a time. "Is it Mamma?" she gasped when they reached a landing. "Is she ill?"

He looked back. "Not ill, no. She gave birth last night, to a baby boy." He ignored Chloe's gasp and continued, "It was a long labour, and she was very weak by the end. Afterwards, she fell asleep, as we thought, but we have not been able to rouse her this morning. The nurse is afraid that she has slipped into a stupor. Miss Loring, if anyone is able to penetrate the mists that surround her, it will be you. Are you willing to try?"

Chloe's heart stopped. "Courage, Chloe," she said to herself, then she took a deep breath. "Chloe," she said resolutely. "My name is Chloe. I doubt if Mamma will respond to Miss Loring. Where is she?"

"In here." He opened a door and stood back to let her enter a large bed-chamber. Mamma lay propped up against pillows in a big four-poster bed, her arms resting on top of the coverlet, down by her sides, like a doll a child had tucked into its little cot. A mixture of perspiration, blood, and a variety of herbal and medicinal aromas—she recognised lavender and the pungency of hartshorn assailed Chloe's senses. A neat, middle-aged woman, probably the monthly nurse, stood at the other side of the big bed, beside a table littered with bottles, glasses, and cups.

Chloe's memory darted back to her last sight of her father on his death-bed. Was history so cruelly to repeat itself? She tiptoed towards the bed. Mamma's hair was combed back from her forehead and tucked under a nightcap that framed her face, a face as white as the cap and lace-trimmed bed-gown she wore; the only colour came from her winged eyebrows and the fringe of lashes lying on her cheeks. Then she saw that Mamma's bosom lifted slightly with each faint breath and, compared with Papa, she breathed easily and steadily.

"Mamma," she sighed with relief and then, louder, more insistingly, "Mamma!"

The nurse looked intently at her patient and snapped something. One word. It was followed by a quick murmur in a language Chloe did not understand.

"Louder," Lord Stephen translated. "Speak louder and more insistently. She thinks she saw a response."

"Mamma!" Chloe peeled off her gloves and dropped them on the floor. Perching on the side of the bed, she cradled her mother's limp, cold hand in her warm ones. "Mamma! It's Chloe. Wake up!"

Mamma's eyelids fluttered and closed again. Her mouth opened slightly, and she touched her tongue to her pale lips.

"Have you something to moisten her lips?"

The nurse tilted a spouted cup so that a couple of drops fell on the dry mouth. Mamma's lips moved. The woman spoke to Lord Stephen, gesturing, and he slipped his arm beneath Mamma's shoulders and raised her to rest against him.

"Tell her she must drink," he said to Chloe. "It is a cordial that will strengthen her."

"Mamma! Sit up and take your medicine," Chloe ordered. She laughed suddenly, a short, shrill sound. "How often did you say that to me when I was a little girl? Come now, sleepyhead." Her voice cracked, and she brushed away a tear. "Mamma. Wake up for your Chloe. Mamma!" She shook her mother's hand. "Must I get angry with you?"

"Chloe?" It was the faintest whisper.

"Yes. Open your eyes and take this draught. It will help you." The heavy eyelids lifted. "Chloe. Don't be angry. Please."

Chloe blinked tears away. "Oh, Mamma. I'm not angry, I promise you. Now drink this." She took the cup and held it to her mother's lips.

Mamma swallowed obediently. "Ugh."

"Is it nasty? Shall I make you some tea to take the taste away? There is nothing like it when you have been poorly."

"Tea, please." Mamma raised a wavering hand and touched Chloe's cheek. "Is it really you?"

"Yes. I'm staying in Nice with the Glazebrooks."

"No. Stay here."

Chloe looked at Lord Stephen. "If I may."

He smiled wearily. "Of course, Chloe. There could not be a more welcome guest."

Her mother turned her head from side to side. "My baby?"

"He is in the nursery," Lord Stephen said. "Shall I fetch him?"

"Show Chloe her brother."

"Yes, my love." Lord Stephen laid his wife down gently and kissed her brow. "I'll just be a minute, Chloe. I'll order the tea as well."

"Lord Stephen, could someone bring up a tea equipage? I would like to make Mamma's tea myself."

"I'll see to it."

"He's nice," Chloe said when he had left the room.

"Yes."

The nurse had refilled the little cup and gave it to Chloe. She held up three fingers.

"You must take three more of these, Mamma."

Her mother made a face but drank obediently. When Lord Stephen came in carrying a little bundle swaddled in white, she struggled to sit up against her pillows. Chloe helped her. Mamma held out her arms, and he carefully placed the baby in them, before supporting his wife again.

Mamma carefully opened the topmost shawl to reveal a tiny face with eyes squeezed tightly shut. "This is Alexander Stephen FitzCharles. Alexander, this is your big sister, Chloe Loring."

The baby turned his head and opened dark blue eyes. His little mouth worked as if sucking at something invisible.

"Oh, he is beautiful," Chloe said. She gently touched his cheek. "Welcome, Alexander Stephen."

The nurse came over. Mamma nodded in response to her question and opened her bed-gown. The woman helped her put the baby to her breast. Mamma gave a little yelp—the strangest sound Chloe had ever heard her make.

"What's wrong?" she asked.

"Nothing," Lord Stephen said. "He's got the knack of it now. He took your mother by surprise, that's all."

"Should she be doing that when she is so weak?"

"Signora Marta says it is good both for her and the baby. But if it gets too much for her, we'll find a wet nurse."

A footman and maid brought in the tea equipage and some plates of biscuits. Chloe slid off the bed. "I'll bring her tea when she is ready. We don't want to scald the baby."

"He has finished."

The nurse took the baby. Lord Stephen settled his wife against her pillows and took the infant, then came over and sat in the chair next to Chloe's. "Ten minutes, Signora Marta said," he murmured.

The tender look on Lord Stephen's face brought tears to Chloe's eyes. She looked away and busied herself with the tea-tray. It was soothing to carry out the familiar task; to hear the varied sounds of the ritual—the clink of the caddy spoon against the glass bowl as she mixed the leaves, the hissing of the tea-urn, the chink of china cups and saucers. Then there was the dry, astringent smell of the tea-leaves and the glorious, aromatic explosion when boiling water was poured onto them. How often had she watched Mamma make tea, and begged to be allowed make it herself? Mamma, too, seemed to enjoy watching her, for she kept smiling over at Chloe.

There was no milk, of course. Chloe had already learned not to expect that here. "Would you like more sugar than usual, Mamma, as there is neither milk nor cream?"

"About half as much again, please."

She stirred the tea until the sugar had dissolved, laid two long, oblong biscuits studded with almonds on the saucer and carried it over to Mamma.

"Thank you, my love."

"Can you manage?"

"Draw the table a little nearer. Excellent. Now, have your own tea. Or, Signora Marta?" Mamma spoke to the nurse, who nodded.

"Prepare a cup for the signora just like mine," Mamma said. "Stephen will have to wait until he gives Alexander back."

It was the strangest tea-drinking ever, and the nicest. When the nurse had drunk her tea, she retrieved the baby and withdrew.

Mamma held out her hand. "Come and sit here, my love. I want to hear about everything since we last saw each other. Start with Miss Dismore."

"Miss Dismore? Oh, the finishing governess." Chloe began to laugh. "To begin with, we forgot all about her—"

By the time she had finished the story, Mamma and Lord Stephen were helpless with laughter. "Oh," Mamma said, pressing a hand to her stomach.

"Are you uncomfortable, Mamma?"

"A little. I need—pray ask Signora Marta to come in. She will help me." Mamma looked at Lord Stephen. "You must rest, but first, please arrange for Chloe to stay here." She looked at Chloe anxiously. "You will, won't you?"

"Yes, of course," Chloe said quickly. She didn't know what the Glazebrooks would say; she hoped they wouldn't be in a pet about it, but if Mamma wanted her, she would stay. She leaned over to kiss her mother's cheek. "Rest well, Mamma. I'll come up again as soon as I may; you just need to send for me."

Tears filled her mother's eyes. "I can't believe that you are really here. How did that happen?"

"It's a long story," Chloe said. "I'll tell you later. Now, here's Signora Marta to look after you."

~~~

Martin shot to his feet with a look of relief when Chloe and Lord Stephen appeared on the terrace. His companion, an elderly lady, stood more slowly. She looked at Lord Stephen.

"Well?"

"All's well, Aunt, very well. She sat up and drank tea with us. Signora Marta says there is no more cause for concern."

"Thank God. And this is Chloe? You are very welcome, my dear. You must have got quite a fright."

Chloe curtsied. "Indeed, ma'am. But all's well that ends well."

"I beg your pardon, Aunt, Chloe. I don't know where my manners are," Lord Stephen interjected. He looked at his aunt. "Ma'am, may I present Miss Chloe Loring? Chloe, my aunt, Lady Mary Arkell, *Contessa Della Torre*."

Chloe curtsied again.

"Come, sit down," her ladyship said. "You must be exhausted. Will you take a glass of wine?"

Chloe remained on her feet. "No, thank you, my lady." If truth be told, she longed for the necessary and dared not drink any more until she had availed herself of that useful institution.

"Aunt, Delia would like her daughter to stay with us, and Chloe has kindly agreed to do so."

Martin looked up at Lord Stephen's statement, but said nothing.

"I'll write a note to your parents, explaining, Martin," Chloe said hastily. "Lord Stephen, would it be possible to collect my maid and baggage?"

"Certainly. I'll send the carriage down for her." He looked at Martin. "Perhaps Mr?"

"Oh, I'm sorry," Chloe said. "In all the confusion, I forgot to present my cousin, Mr Glazebrook. Martin, this is Lord Stephen FitzCharles."

Martin bowed stiffly. "My lord."

"Mr Glazebrook." Stephen held out his hand. "I'm afraid we were all at sixes and sevens earlier."

"It is of no matter, sir. May I congratulate you on the birth of your son and heir?"

A huge smile lit his lordship's face. "You may indeed. Thank you."

"If you write your note, Chloe, then I'll be off," Martin said. "They will be wondering what has happened to us."

"There is a writing table in here," Lord Stephen went to the drawing-room door.

"Chloe," Lady Mary said, "I may say Chloe, may I not, for you are now one of the family, pray convey my compliments to Mr and Mrs Glazebrook and invite them to call in a couple of days, when your mother is more recovered."

Chapter Twenty-Six

Chloe handed the note to Martin.

"Thank you, Coz. I shall see you again in a couple of days, I have no doubt. But if there is anything I can do—"

"I know, Martin. Thank you. Pray make my apologies to Cousin Amelia for leaving so abruptly."

He nodded and turned to Lady Mary. "I shall take my leave of you, ma'am."

"I'll walk out with you," Lord Stephen said. "Arrange for the carriage to be sent. Where are you staying?"

Chloe watched the two men go into the house. She suddenly felt very weary, light-headed even.

"Come, sit down, child."

"Thank you, ma'am, but—if I might first—the necessary?" Chloe felt her cheeks grow hot as she stammered her request.

"Of course. How remiss of me." Lady Mary picked up a little hand-bell and shook it. "My maid will look after you, my dear. When you are refreshed, return here for some sort of a late nuncheon." When the butler appeared, she said, "Luca, send Elena to me, and have hot water brought up to the rose bed-chamber. Then arrange for a quick repast to be served here, say, in fifteen minutes."

Some minutes later, a trim, older woman arrived. She reminded Chloe of Grandmother's maid, Dover.

"Elena, this is Miss Loring, Lady Delia's daughter, who will be staying with us. Show her to the rose bed-chamber—Luca will send up hot water—and assist her for now. Her own maid will join her later."

Elena curtsied. "Very good, Milady. Please come with me, Miss Loring."

To Chloe's relief, the maid spoke fluent English, although with a foreign accent. She led Chloe to a pleasant airy room near that of her mother and directed her immediately to the screen, behind which she found a close stool where she could ease her aching bladder. When she emerged, Elena was pouring warm water into a marble basin. She gestured to a chair in front of a dressing-table.

"If you will sit here, Miss, we'll take off your hat, the ruff, and chemisette. When you have washed, I'll tidy your hair and put you to rights again." She tsked. "We cannot do much else apart from a quick brushing of your skirts."

Chloe complied, feeling thirteen again. But she was not thirteen; she was almost eighteen and a young lady, not a child. She squared her shoulders and met the maid's eyes in the mirror. "The riding habit will do for now. Lord Stephen has sent for my maid and to have my trunks fetched."

"Yes, Miss."

Chloe washed her face, neck, and hands, then sat again for Elena to tidy her hair and replace the chemisette and ruff. She shook her head when Elena picked up her hat. Lady Mary had worn neither hat nor gloves—the shaded terrace obviously counted as part of the house rather than the garden.

"That will do. Thank you, Elena."

When she returned to the terrace, Lord Stephen half-sat, half-lay sprawled in a chair, his head back and his eyes closed.

"There you are, my dear," Lady Mary said. "Stephen, come and eat. Then you must lie down for a couple of hours."

A round table was set for three and her ladyship invited Chloe to sit on her right. She took the lid off a large cream and gold tureen and began to ladle the contents into bowls.

"That smells heavenly, Aunt," Lord Stephen said as he took his place.

"Chicken broth. Just the thing for Delia, but we can all do with something nourishing and soothing today."

The aromatic broth contained succulent vegetables, herbs, and delicate little dumplings of chicken forcemeat that dissolved on the tongue. Chloe spooned it up eagerly; she had not eaten much at breakfast and it was now past three o'clock in the afternoon.

"Will you be comfortable in the rose bed-chamber, Chloe?" Lady Mary asked. "It is beside the one your mother is using at present."

"Yes, thank you, my lady."

Her hostess frowned. "Not 'my lady'. Call me Aunt Mary, if you please. Your mother is now my niece and your new brother is my great-nephew. That makes you one of the family."

"Thank you, Aunt Mary. You are very kind."

"Not at all, my dear."

Chloe observed her new stepfather, who was filling their glasses with a light-red wine. How should she address him? He seemed perfectly amiable, but she could not imagine saying anything other than the formal 'Lord Stephen'. She hoped he would not expect her to call him 'father'. She was too old for that.

The tureen was replaced by a platter of cheese, grapes, and walnuts, little bowls of jewel-coloured preserves and an oblong board with a golden, flat bread glistening with oil and decorated with rosemary.

"La Fougasse," Lady Mary said as she cut it into broad fingers. "It is a speciality of the region, but must be eaten fresh. Try it with this fresh cheese and the quince preserve."

The cheese was little more than solid curds, tangy and creamy that melted into the warm bread and was delicious with the amber jelly.

"It tastes of summer," Chloe said. "Indeed, is hard to imagine that it is almost November when we can sit outside like this. How long can you do so?"

"Most of the year," Lady Mary said. "There are, of course, rainy and wintry or windy days when it is not possible, and at the height of summer, one must stay indoors during the heat of the day, but I never tire of this panorama. It is different every day."

"And so beautiful."

Lord Stephen drained his glass and got to his feet. "Pray excuse me, Aunt. I'll just look in on Delia—"

"And then you must lie down on your own bed," his aunt said firmly. "I am sure Chloe will be happy to sit with her mother while you rest."

"Of course," Chloe said eagerly. "You must be exhausted, Lord Stephen."

He smiled at her. "Thank you, my dear."

"Please ask Delia if I may look in for five minutes as well," Lady Mary said. "I will not tire her; just to see the baby."

~~~

Mamma looked a lot better than she had earlier. She wore a fresh bed-gown of muslin sprigged with roses. Her hair was no longer plastered to her head under the night cap but had been combed and arranged in a long, loose plait that lay over one shoulder. The room had been tidied and the litter of cups and glasses removed from the side table. Lady Mary (Chloe must get used to thinking of her as Aunt Mary) admired the baby, congratulated his parents, and impressed on his mother that she must continue to rest and recover her strength, then firmly conducted her nephew from the room.

"Poor Stephen," Mamma said with a smile. "But he must rest. I don't think he slept more than an hour last night."

Chloe laughed. "I thought she would nip at his heels next, like a sheep-dog."

"She is very persistent, but also very good-hearted. It is thanks to her that I have managed to avoid a great scandal and shall be able to take my place in society when we return to England. She has never made me feel inferior, or obliged to her in any way; on the contrary, she has welcomed me into her family without any reservations or hesitation."

"Unlike the Lorings?"

Mamma looked at her sharply. "What makes you say that?"

"Grandmamma as good as admitted it, and Julian, too, said he was not kind to you when Papa brought you home."

"He was not unkind—"

"Not actively, perhaps, but he recognises now that passive unkindness or disrespect can be more difficult to combat than outright incivility, which could be more easily challenged."

"That is true. When did he say that?"

"While we were at the Place, after Papa's death. We talked a lot then and, well, since you left, I have had the opportunity to observe other married couples and see how they deal with one another."

"I see. You have grown up a lot this past year, Chloe. I am only sorry it had to be this way."

"Yes. I don't know." Chloe shuddered. "When I think that you might have brought me out this year, and I might even be married by now—"

"I would never have forced you into marriage, never!"

"But I might have drifted into it, thoughtlessly. Now I am much more aware of what to look for in a husband. Cynthia Glazebrook and I are creating a list of Husband Criteria by which we shall assess our suitors when we come out."

Mamma sat up. "That seems eminently sensible to me. I remember Cynthia from last year. Do you and she get on well together?"

"Well enough. She is not my friend the way Ann Overton is."

"Ann Overton?"

"She is a cousin of Julian's. She stayed at Swanmere last summer with her mother and brother."

"You were at Swanmere last summer? Tell me all about it."

Mamma listened intently to Chloe's description of the previous summer, then asked abruptly, "Did you hate me?"

Chloe looked back on those weeks. "I don't know what I felt," she said in the end. "I was confused and angry and upset, but I also knew it was Papa who had sent you away. Then, when I got that first letter, that you were going abroad with Lord Stephen, I felt you had chosen him, Lord Stephen, I mean, over me."

"It was not like that," Mamma cried. "Your father refused to allow me to come home that September; I should remain in Harrogate for the winter, he said. When it was over, he would judge whether and on what terms I might resume my marital duties. He said nothing about you, not one word. I did not know if he would ever permit me to see you again. As far as I knew, you were still at the Place and under his influence. I am surprised he gave you my letter."

"He didn't. Julian gave it to me. Hughes came first to Swanmere, you see."

"If I had only known you were there, I would have risked writing to you much sooner."

"I could have written to you," Chloe said remorsefully. "I didn't have my grandmother's exact address, but I imagine a letter sent c/o Mrs Eubank, Harrogate, would have reached you. I just didn't think of it. I am sorry."

"Don't blame yourself," Mamma said quickly. "As I said, you have grown up since then. You have learnt to make your own decisions. I am glad."

Interlude at Swanmere Castle

Rosa was resting on the day-bed in the solar. Julian bent and kissed her, patting her slightly rounded belly. "How are you both today?"

"Much better now that the sickness has stopped. Did the post come?"

"Three letters from Nice, or Savoy, I should say. One is from Chloe but I don't recognise the other hands."

"Let me see." She took the letters, inspected the handwriting, and shook her head. "Nor I. Well, there is a simple way to find out. We'll open Chloe's first."

He sat beside her, lifting her feet onto his lap as she broke the seal. "Well? What has Miss to say?"

Rosa gasped. "I don't believe it."

"What?"

"She has a new brother. Delia has a son."

"A son? Good God!" Julian began to laugh. "That would have my father singing small, if he only knew."

"What do you mean?"

"When he was in his cups, a favourite complaint was that she had not borne him a son. The blame was laid squarely at her door, of course."

"Of course." Rosa went back to her letter. "Delia was quite poorly when Chloe called, all unknowing, the day after the birth, and was insistent that she move to the *Villa Della Torre*. Lord Stephen and his aunt supported this wish, and Chloe and Parker are now ensconced there. She began to read aloud;

"*Martin Glazebrook had accompanied me when I first went to the Villa. He took a note back to his parents, and Lord Stephen sent the carriage for Parker and my baggage. The Glazebrooks were quite put out, I think, but they could not remove me and so had no choice but to comply with Lord S's request. Lady Mary Arkell had invited them to call some days later when my mother would be somewhat recovered, but Mr Glazebrook rode up the next day asking to see Lord Stephen. I'm not sure exactly what passed between them; to me he said that he considered himself in* loco parentis *to me and I should have sought his permission before leaving his roof. I said that while I appreciated his sentiments, my duty to my mother must be paramount, especially at such a critical time for her, and that I had felt it incumbent on me to accede immediately to her wishes. He asked how long I intended to stay there. I really had not thought about it but, when so pressed, replied that at least as long as she was confined to her room. She was still very weak, and anything I could do for her, I would. He then handed me the money he was keeping in his strongbox for me—I had forgotten all about it, but he said I should have some independence—and said that I should not hesitate to return to them when I felt able to. So, we parted quite amicably.*"

Julian grinned. "For not yet eighteen, you must admit she handled it superbly. She is a credit to you, Miss Fancourt."

"Say rather to all the ladies who influenced her—her mother and grandmother as well as me. I admit she could hardly refuse to stay at the Villa in such circumstances. She goes on to say,

"I did not tell him, but may tell you that my mother endured a very long labour and must take things very easily for the next weeks. She hopes to be able to feed the baby herself, for the monthly nurse assures us that that is best for mother and child, and therefore must conserve her strength.

"The baby—my brother; is it not strange, Julian, that he is as much younger than I as I am than you?—is tiny, but Lady Mary says all new-born babies are so small, and he will grow quickly. His name is Alexander Stephen, with probably two more names for his godfathers. Alexander is for Mamma's father, who died before I was born.

"Both Lady Mary, or Aunt Mary as I am to call her, and Lord Stephen are very kind. His lordship is besotted with his new son, and also very attached to Mamma, I think. There is an ease between them that I do not remember noticing between her and my father. She talks sometimes of when I was born, and how happy she was in those years before she had to give me to you, Rosa. Sometimes she sings to the baby, little nonsense rhymes and tunes that sound familiar, as if she sang them also to me."

Rosa stopped reading. "Do you think we'll remember the songs our mothers sang to us? It is such a pity our baby will have no grandparents."

"Strictly speaking, Delia will be a step-grandmother," Julian pointed out. "We'll have two great-grandparents, and a very devoted aunt. And don't forget Robert. How do you think he will react to being an uncle?"

"Very well, provided we make it clear that he is still important to us. He will be wary after the way his step-mother treated him. I must make sure that he and Hal come next summer." Rosa sighed. "What a strange mixture of a family we are. Chloe's new brother is not related to you at all, but it does not feel like that."

"We'll work something out," Julian said comfortingly. "I would like our children to have a large family circle; it does not have to be strictly according to blood."

"No. Ties of affection can be as strong as those of kinship. Just think of the Chidlows."

"Exactly. Now, what odds will you give me that these two letters, both of which are addressed to me, not to us, are from Glazebrook and Lord Stephen?" He opened one as he spoke and glanced over it. His tone changed. "FitzCharles writes, '*It must have been some good angel that led your sister to our door that day. My wife, who had suffered through a long and painful labour, had fallen into a sort of stupor from which we could not rouse her. The voice of the daughter whom she had missed so sorely this past year succeeded where all else had failed. Although still very weak, she delights in Chloe's presence and I am inexpressibly grateful that she immediately consented to remove here to be with her mother. Rest assured that we shall take the greatest care of her.'*"

"Good heavens." Rosa had turned quite pale. "Chloe did not say how serious it was."

"She may not have realised, when Delia responded to her. We can be proud of her, I think."

"Yes."

"The third letter is indeed from Glazebrook. He is put out that Chloe did not consult him or his wife before going to visit her mother but accepts that, in the circumstances, she made the right decision to remain at the Villa. They will continue to keep a parental eye on her as long as they are in Nice, but will not be able to adapt their own plans to suit Chloe's wishes."

"I suppose that is too much to expect."

"It may be that they must leave her behind when they quit Nice, he says."

"But that means that Chloe most likely will not return for months and months." Tears filled Rosa's eyes. "It is most fortunate that she was there to help Delia, but otherwise I regret we allowed her to go to France. I do miss her." She sniffed. "I thought we would make the baby's clothes together."

"Rosa." Julian lifted her feet from his lap and slid along the day-bed until he could take her into his arms. "I cannot help you there, apart from keeping you company or reading to you while you sew."

She laid her head on his shoulder. "The last child to be born here was your mother, and that is more than fifty years ago. Apart from your grandfather, nobody here has any idea how things were done."

"At least you will not be hidebound by tradition," he pointed out. "What about the vicarage sewing circle? Could you not enlist them? Would they not be happy to help prepare for your baby?"

"I am sure they would. I would not ask them to give up their charitable work on my account, but I could invite them to meet here once or twice as well. I must consult Mrs Musgrave—I do not want to usurp her authority. And I must speak to Mrs Godin as well. Lambton knows, of course—a maid knows everything—but you are the only other person to know, so far. But I soon shan't be able to hide it."

"Why do you want to hide it? It is a perfectly normal event, is it not?"

"I suppose so. But it's very personal, very intimate." She sighed. "If truth be told, I miss my mother. It seems foolish when she is gone more than ten years, but I would give anything to be able to talk to her. And I cannot help remembering that she died in childbed."

"Rosa!" A chill ran down Julian's spine. "You are not to talk like that! I will not allow it. You will be perfectly well, and our child will be well too. Understood?"

"Yes, Sir Julian." Her tone was meek, but there was a wicked glint in her eye. "Are you about to turn into a dictatorial husband? Shall I start calling you, 'Sir Canute'? Must we go to the coast to see if the tide obeys you?"

"Minx!" he said and kissed her.

"Tyrant," she retorted when she was able.

He laughed, but then said seriously, "If I could be, I would, but only in this, Rosa. I would do anything to ensure your safety. Promise me, at least, that you won't hide your concerns from me, and will ask me if there is anything you need from me or others."

She looked at him for a long moment. "Yes. I promise. I'm sorry, I was trying to do it all by myself, again. I'll go and see Mrs Musgrave tomorrow. Then we can tell the great-grandparents-to-be, and start thinking about setting up a nursery here and at Swanmere House."

He kissed her again. "Excellent. Will you write to Chloe?"

"Yes, but not to tell her about our baby. I can understand why Delia did not tell her either. There is nothing she can do from such a distance, and she cannot travel on her own. Better to wait until the child is safely here to tell her she is an aunt."

Chapter Twenty-Seven

Chloe sat, unseeing, in her bedroom, Mamma's letter open in her lap. Mamma had given it to her together with a handsome sketchbook bound in red leather just before she took her afternoon rest.

"These are for you. I wrote the letter and started the book in June of last year, when I feared I might never see you again. Even if I were not able to give them to you, I hoped that one day they would come into your hands. Read them, look at them now. Start with the letter. That was too private to put into the book."

Harrogate, 21 June 1814

My dearest Chloe,

I cannot know if you will ever see these lines. I have been forbidden to write to you and, even were I to disobey and risk posting this letter, I doubt that it would ever reach you. I have therefore resolved to write frankly to you, and to keep this letter safe until a happier and more opportune time permits me to put it into your hands. But it may also be that you receive it only after my death. I cannot bear the thought that your last memories of me should be tied to those final, dreadful days at Loring Place.

Please, I beg you, look beyond them to the happy times we spent together.

Chloe, I first must tell you how sorry I am for everything. If only I could turn back the clock and resist the temptation to stroll down the primrose path, how much agony and suffering we would both have been spared. Looking back now, I cannot understand how I came to commit such a folly, but stray I did and now must do penance for it. But grievous as that sin was, what sickens me most are its consequences. I will never forgive myself for raising my hand to you. Taken by surprise, I allowed my temper to control me. But, believe me, Chloe, I never wished nor intended to injure you. Nightly, I see you stumble and fall, hear the crack of your head against the hearth, relive those long minutes when you lay senseless. All I could think of was you. And in my distress, I again trusted one—P—who was unworthy of that trust and, unthinking, let him decide what to do next. By the time I came to my senses, I was trapped in a web of deceit and saw no way out.

I have paid the price but, what is worse, you must pay too, in that you are deprived of a mother's care. But not of her love, Chloe. I will love you until I draw my last breath. You have been my joy and my delight since the day you were born. I beg for your forgiveness and shall pray constantly for your happiness.

Mamma

A big tear splashed onto her hand and she hastily put the letter aside and fished for her handkerchief. Poor Mamma. What agonies she had gone through. And how presumptuous of Papa, to separate them just to soothe his own hurt pride. Had he once thought of the pain he caused? He had not told her that he had forbidden Mamma to write to her, but she had suffered under Mamma's silence. Christ had forgiven the woman taken in adultery, but Papa had set himself up as Mamma's inquisitor and torturer, racking her with false promises and desperate hope.

She sighed and opened the book. Smiling, she read the inscription and turned the page to find a portrait of herself in the gown she had worn at Papa's birthday ball. Opposite was a self-portrait of her mother. *So that you do not forget what I look like* was written under it. Mamma was smiling, but her eyes looked haunted. What had she been thinking as she sketched her own features, mixed the colours to depict herself?

She had not thought Mamma so talented. She must have learnt from her father, Chloe thought as she slowly turned the pages. She had a unique style, not precisely caricature, but more personal than a classical painting. Her figures brought life onto the page. And the accompanying descriptions were clever, too. She paused for a long time over the painting of a happy party at Lady Mary's Yorkshire home. They all seemed to be enjoying themselves. Mamma sat to one side, painting. Had she seen herself as an observer, not quite one of the company?

"Excuse me, Miss Loring. Mr and Mrs Glazebrook, Mr Martin, and Miss Glazebrook have called. Lady Mary and Lord and Lady Stephen are resting, but I said to Luca that I would see if you were awake."

"I'll come down, Parker. Ask Luca to show them into the drawing-room."

"Should I order the tea equipage?"

"Yes, do." Chloe tucked the letter into her jewel-box and turned the key in the lock. Later she would suggest to Mamma that they burn it. It was for no one's eyes but theirs.

She could hear the murmur of voices as she came into the hall—a family conversation, a complaining tone, and Mr Glazebrook's snapped, "That's enough, Cynthia."

Chloe regretted that her soft slippers made no sound on the marble hall floor. When he saw her, the footman walked purposefully to the drawing door, silencing the visitors as he opened it.

The Glazebrooks sat at right angles to each other on two sofas, ladies on one and gentlemen on the other. Cynthia looked flushed and angry while her father's frown and thinned lips suggested a man clinging to the last vestiges of his patience.

"Good day, Cousins. I trust I see you all well."

"Good day, Chloe. I am glad to see you have not succumbed to this infernal habit of an afternoon rest," Mr Glazebrook said as he and Martin rose to their feet.

"Not yet. I think it is because of the heat in summer," Chloe said as she sat and they took their seats again. "My mother says they tend to sit up later then. I imagine it is all a question of what you are used to."

"Indeed, indeed."

"How does your mother, Chloe?"

"Much better, thank you, Cousin Amelia. She itches to be allowed downstairs, but the monthly nurse is quite insistent that she lies in for at least another week."

"Better to be safe, I suppose, but too long in the bed is weakening, too."

"Mamma moves around her room and takes her meals at the table now. She hates eating in bed, she says."

"Does the baby still look like a tadpole?" Cynthia asked.

"Cynthia!"

"Well, he did, Mamma," Cynthia defended herself.

Chloe just smiled. She knew what her cousin meant, even if she was not about to admit it. "He changes day by day. His eyes are open a lot more now and he looks around, as if taking an interest in everything."

"Excellent." Mr Glazebrook cleared his throat and looked at his wife.

"Yes, that is indeed splendid news, Chloe," she said. "Especially as the purpose for our call is to tell you that we have decided to quit our apartment at the end of the month."

"Have you found a nicer one?"

"No. You misunderstand me. We leave Nice on the thirty-first. We have decided to return to Paris."

"In three days' time?"

"Yes."

"It is so dreary here, with very few English visitors. I had thought there would be more happening," Cynthia said.

"And I prefer to have my brother's escort on the journey," Cousin Amelia said. "The presence of an English officer in our party must afford us better treatment."

Chloe wondered what Mr Glazebrook thought of this, but perhaps he welcomed the masculine company.

Cousin Amelia continued, "Three days must be sufficient time for your maid to prepare and pack your things. After all, you were able to remove here with no notice at all."

Chloe closed her eyes against a sudden dizziness. After a moment, she was able to say, "I had not thought of leaving here so soon."

"Surely you do not expect us to wait on your convenience?" Cynthia said.

"That is enough, Cynthia," Mr Glazebrook said. "Chloe, the fact is that your brother entrusted you to our care. I expect you to respect his wishes and return with us."

Would Julian really expect her to comply with the Glazebrooks' demand? Chloe wished she could have heard from him, but they had not been long enough in Nice for her to receive a reply to her letter advising him and Rosa of Alexander's birth. Surely her first duty was to Mamma? She would like to see her completely recovered before leaving. But if she did not go with the Glazebrooks, when could she expect to return to England?

The arrival of the tea equipage offered some respite. She moved to the table and concentrated on the little task. As soon as she began to fill the cups, Martin came to take them from her and hand them round. When he returned to claim his own cup, he took a seat near her, with a friendly smile. Unlike his father who wore clinging pantaloons with an immaculately tailored coat of dark blue English superfine and a carefully tied neckcloth, Martin was less-formally dressed in pale Cossack trousers strapped under the soles of his boots, a chestnut coat worn over a wide-collared shirt and yellow-and-green handkerchief knotted loosely at this throat.

"I like your attire," she said. "It looks very comfortable."

He shrugged. "There is little point in dressing here as if for Rotten Row."

"You should see the straw hat he bought for riding in the mountains," Cynthia said. "He looks like a peasant."

"It is cool and the wide brim helps reduce the glare from the sun," Martin said.

"That seems sensible," Chloe said.

"But no good to him when we go home," Cynthia pointed out.

Had she always been so mean-spirited, Chloe wondered? Why should Martin not enjoy a change of costume. She lifted the teapot invitingly. "More tea, Cousin Amelia? And you, sir?"

Martin obligingly collected the cups and redistributed them, then passed a plate of finger biscuits studded with almonds and raisins. "Try one of these, Mamma."

Amelia shook her head, but Cynthia took one and dipped it into her tea.

"Well, Chloe?" Mr Glazebrook said. "You have not answered us."

"I regret I cannot do so at present, sir. I must consider how my mother does, and what her plans are. We have not yet discussed anything beyond the every-day. I shall let you know tomorrow what I decide."

Mr and Mrs Glazebrook fixed her with disapproving stares. They treated her like a child, she thought. Here, at the Villa, she was regarded as an adult. She had crossed an invisible frontier in the not quite three weeks she had spent here and could not go back.

"Decide?" Mr Glazebrook said. "The decision is not yours to make."

"I am sorry to contradict you, sir, but it is. I have a higher obligation here and am old enough to make up my own mind."

"Make up your mind about what?" Lord Stephen asked as he strolled into the room.

"Whether to return to Paris with my cousins in three days' time," Chloe said calmly. "A cup of tea, sir?"

"Thank you. I certainly hope you will not leave us so quickly."

"I am *in loco parentis* to Chloe," Mr Glazebrook began.

"Surely not, when she is under the same roof as her mother," Lord Stephen replied. "What is your preference, Chloe?"

"I should prefer to stay longer with Mamma, but I cannot remain here indefinitely, sir. I have loved ones in England too."

"Would you be happy to remain here over the winter and return with us next year? I should prefer not to travel during the worst of the bad weather, especially with an infant."

A weight tumbled from Chloe's shoulders. "That would be ideal, sir. Thank you."

"I don't see any problem with that, do you, Glazebrook?" Lord Stephen said. "We'll engage to see Chloe safely to Swanmere in the spring."

"But will it be in time for her to come out with me next year?" Cynthia demanded.

"I doubt if that will be possible," her mother said. "It is most unlikely that she will reach Swanmere before Easter, and then she would have to have her court gown and all her other dresses made. It would be too late."

Cynthia pouted. "I was relying on your company, Chloe. For the journey home, as well. It will be a dead bore without you."

"Thank you, Sis," Martin said. "Now I know what you think of my company. Chloe, for my part, although I shall miss you, you are doing the right thing." He turned to his mother. "If the circumstances were reversed, would you not expect Cynthia to remain with you?"

"That's diff—" Cousin Amelia caught Lord Stephen's eye and stopped. She put down her cup. "If that's your decision, Chloe, we shall take our leave of you. Lord Stephen, pray give our compliments and good wishes for a continued recovery to Lady Stephen. And our compliments to your aunt, of course."

"Thank you. Perhaps you would dine with us before you depart?" Lord Stephen said. "The day after tomorrow? Is Major Raven still with you? Then we should be delighted to see him too."

"Thank you; much obliged," Mr Glazebrook said. "Chloe, if you have any letters you wish to send with us, you may give them to me then."

~~~

"I don't see why we have to dine with them," Cynthia complained as the Glazebrook carriage left the *Villa Della Torre*.

"Really, Cynthia, at times I despair of you ever acquiring some common sense," her father said. "Firstly, it is good manners to accept the invitation; like it or not, there is a family connection between us. Secondly, I am fond of Chloe and do not want to part on bad terms. Thirdly, Lord Stephen is the son of one duke and uncle of another. The connection can only be to our advantage, and especially to yours when you come out, if not in your first Season, then in later ones."

"And fourthly, we'll be sick enough of our own company by the time we reach Paris," Martin said. "This will be a welcome diversion."

"You will dress properly, Martin," his mother said. "While that—garb may be tolerated for a morning call, it will not do for a formal dinner invitation."

"Yes, Mamma," he said meekly. Some battles were not worth fighting.

Epilogue

Chloe and Delia

Part One Swanmere Castle

May, 1816

Chloe sighed with relief as the carriage drew away from *The Duke's Head* in Lynn Regis. Today was her very last day of travel. It was almost five weeks since they had left Nice, travelling first by felucca to Marseilles, from there by carriage to Antwerp via Brussels, and then by yacht from Antwerp to Lynn Regis, where they had arrived yesterday. Leaving at the end of March, they had travelled northwards with the spring, but had not been spared April's blustery showers. In deference to Delia and Alexander, who had not yet been weaned, they had travelled at a relatively slow pace, stopping for a longer break at dinner-time and not driving into the night. They had rested for a couple of days in Dijon and again in Brussels, but today she felt she never wanted to see a carriage again.

It was wonderful to be back in England. While she had loved the adventure of being abroad, the excitement of new sights and experiences, strange customs and different languages, a constant, underlying tension in trying to understand and be understood was always present. There, she could take nothing for granted while here, she knew the underlying, unspoken assumptions that shaped society.

Parker had felt the same. "I could have kissed that chap when he said, "Ere, love, let me give you a 'and,' although, of course, I did no such thing but let our men help me off the boat. There's no place like home, is there, Miss?"

"No," Chloe had agreed. It was like the relief when you took off tight stays, but of the mind rather than the body.

They should reach Swanmere by mid-afternoon and all were to spend at least one night there before the others continued on their travels. They had occupied the carriages as had become usual on the long journey; Chloe together with Lady Mary, and Mamma and Lord Stephen with Alexander. Lord Stephen's travelling chariot was commodious enough that they had been able to fit it with a cradle where the baby could sleep, although once awake, he sat either on a lap or on the seat between the passengers. Sometimes, he even tried his legs on the floor of the carriage. Each day, Chloe had travelled for a couple of stages with him, allowing one of his parents a respite either in Lady Mary's carriage or on horseback, as was frequently Lord Stephen's choice.

The group was more harmonious than the Glazebrooks had been; everyone listened to everyone else, decisions were made jointly, and there were no sudden changes of plan unless someone was indisposed, when arrangements were swiftly changed without rancour or reproach of any kind. It was a continuation of life at the Villa where every effort had been made to make Chloe feel at home. She had been afraid she might feel excluded by Lord Stephen and her mother who, strange as it seemed, were still newly-weds, but she had been included to such an extent that she had found herself telling her mother she did not need continuous entertainment but was quite happy to spend some hours on her own each day. "I am used to it at home; Julian and Rosa may not be disturbed in the two hours before dinner, and we all enjoy the quiet time."

"A sort of *riposo,*" her mother had said with a little smile. "It is a good idea."

~~~

Chloe had not travelled this road before, skirting the fens and crossing innumerable little streams and rivulets, many of which were artificial constructs to keep the ever present water at bay. Mamma was fascinated by subtle colours of the flat, watery lands punctuated now and then by a church tower or a windmill assiduously pumping water into a stream or little canal.

"Such immense skies, and such cloudscapes," she said when Chloe joined her in Lord Stephen's carriage. "How I should love to paint here."

"Rosa has done some wonderful watercolours at Swanmere. You must ask her to show them to you."

Alexander began to cry and Mamma lifted him from the cradle and sat him on her lap so that he could look out the window. "There's Papa," she said, pointing to Lord Stephen, who had decided to ride this stage. "Pa-pa," she repeated, with exaggerated lip movements. "Pa-pa."

She pushed down the glass and Lord Stephen came nearer. "Is all well?"

"Pa!" Alexander said, with a huge, gummy smile. "Pa!"

Lord Stephen could not have looked prouder if he had just been dubbed knight. "Yes, Pa-pa. What a clever boy!"

"We must see about getting him an English nurse," Mamma said after she had closed the window again. "We cannot have Italian only spoken in the nursery."

"I suppose not. Will you keep Maria on?"

"It depends. I promised I would pay the cost of her journey home if she wished. But—I think Piero is quite *épris* there. If she returns his interest, I hope that they will remain here. Stephen would hate to lose him. We'll have to see."

"Give him to me." Chloe held out her arms to the baby, who was reaching towards her. She touched her cheek to his silky, dark curls. "I'll miss you, little brother. I have so enjoyed watching you grow to be such a big boy."

"You don't suppose Julian would agree to your continuing on with us?" Mamma asked hopefully.

"He might, but—pray don't be offended, Mamma, but I would prefer not to suggest it. He and Rosa would be hurt, I think, although they might not say anything; they were so kind to me last year, when I felt so lost. I have missed them, and my grandparents, too. I read to them every day, when I am at home."

"At home," Mamma repeated. "Yes, Swanmere is your home now. But you will visit Stephen and me once we have found our own home, will you not?"

"Of course. Have you decided where it is to be?"

"Not yet, but I think not more than a day's drive from Swanmere, so as to make visiting easier."

Chloe leaned over to kiss her mother's cheek. "That would be splendid. And we shall write frequently."

Soon they could see the spires and towers of Peterborough Cathedral pricking the sky. They would break their journey here to allow Delia to nurse Alexander undisturbed and to refresh themselves before embarking on the final stage to Swanmere. Piero had ridden ahead to bespeak a bed-chamber where Delia could nurse her son in private as well as a nuncheon to be served in a private parlour. Stephen stayed with the little procession of carriages and was at the door of the travelling chariot to take a fretful Alexander from his mother.

Maria came up. "I'll take him, my lord, get him changed and comfortable."

Delia shook out her skirts and took her husband's arm. "Almost there. Come, let us stroll a little before we go in. I need to stretch my legs."

He put his hand over hers. "Nervous?"

"A little. It is almost two years since I left Loring Place." Her hand tightened on his. "That morning—he ordered the carriage for seven o'clock. Hughes brought me a cup of tea and a slice of toast at half-past six; he had told everyone that I was unwell, so I was only given plain food and not a lot of it in the days before I left. At seven, he came to my door. All he said was, 'It is time to go, madam. See that you use this time wisely.'"

"He led the way downstairs, into the empty hall, as far as the front door where the carriage waited. He said no more. There was no ceremony, no farewells. A footman waited at the open carriage door and the coachman was on the box. Hughes and I got in, the door closed, and we drove off.

"Chloe and her grandmother had already been sent to Edward's sister, Lady Undrell. Julian and his grandfather were at the Place, but I did not see them again after it all came out. My meals were brought to me. He made me promise to remain within the grounds that last week. If I refused, he would instruct the servants to disregard any orders I sent to the stables. And, of course, I was not at home to anyone who might have called." She shivered. "I know I was grievously at fault, Stephen, but it is a terrible thing to be shunned in one's own home. I felt erased from the family, from society even."

"It is sickening how self-righteous he was. I wish it had been possible to call him to account for his behaviour."

She had to smile. "I would have loved to see his face if you had turned up at the Place and challenged him."

"It is unfortunate that the Code of the Duello does not allow for a lover to call out a husband, no matter how appallingly his treatment of his wife. Well, he's dead now. And you are no longer isolated, with nobody to stand up for you. Swann-Loring has been quite conciliatory in his letters, and you are completely reconciled with Chloe. As to your former mother-in-law; I think we can rely upon my aunt to deal with her if necessary."

"Yes. That does make it easier to face them. We had better go in. Alexander will be hungry."

~~~

Both Chloe and Delia had bought new bonnets and pelisses in Brussels for this final stage of the journey.

"It does help to know that you are well turned out," Delia said when Stephen admired her plum-coloured redingote and bonnet of pink *gros de Naples* trimmed with plum ribbons and flowers. "I just hope Alexander does not ruin it for me," she added with a glance at the baby.

"With luck, he'll sleep for this stage."

Stephen took his sleeping son from Maria and laid him in the cradle, tucking the soft woollen blankets around him. Ahead of them, Chloe stepped into his aunt's carriage. Maria went to take her seat with the servants, and Stephen nodded to Piero. *"Avanti!"*

~~~

"Not long, now," Chloe said to Aunt Mary. She could not sit back against the squabs, but leaned forward to peer out the window, looking for familiar landmarks. At Swanmere, they would also be on the lookout. Jenkins, the gatehouse keeper, would have deployed his children, some to keep watch for the approaching carriages from the upper floor of the half-timbered gate house, others to run to the castle and alert the family and servants.

There was the forge; the great horseshoe-shaped doors wide open and the fire glowing in its depths. A groom holding the reins of two horses stood outside, chatting to a couple of villagers. They looked up at the sound of the carriages and doffed their caps as Chloe and Lady Mary swept past. The horses slowed to pass through the village where Mrs and Miss Musgrave, the vicar's wife and daughter, stopped at the churchyard gate to see if they recognised any travellers. Chloe opened the window of the carriage and leaned out, waving. The ladies smiled and waved back. She must call at the vicarage as soon as possible.

Now they were crossing the bridge into the castle park. One more turn and, "There," Chloe said, pointing to encircling walls, above which a wide, steep roof with a tower at each end could be seen. "It is more impressive from the other side, from the mere."

"Are there swans on the mere?"

"Of course."

They passed under the gatehouse arch into the walled courtyard. The rose bushes were in full, glossy leaf, but this was the only hint of the masses of colour and scent that would greet visitors later in the year. Julian stood waiting at the castle while, to the right, servants emerged from the door at the base of the north tower and took up their positions.

The carriage had barely rolled to a halt when Julian had the door open. He caught his sister around the waist and hugged her before lifting her down. "Welcome home, Pet."

Chloe returned the hug. "It's wonderful to be here."

He released her and went to offer his hand to Lady Mary, who stepped down a little stiffly.

Chloe took a breath. "Aunt Mary, may I present my brother, Sir Julian Swann-Loring? Julian, my kind hostess for the past months, Lady Mary Arkell, *Contessa Della Torre*."

Julian bowed. "Welcome to Swanmere, my lady."

"Thank you, Sir Julian."

A footman shut the carriage door and motioned to the coachman to move on, to make way for the next carriage. Lord Stephen alighted first, took the baby, and clamped him against his shoulder as he offered his free hand to his wife to help her down.

Mamma looked tense, Chloe thought, and took a step towards her. Was she supposed to introduce her too? That would be ridiculous. After all, she had been Julian's stepmother for twenty years.

"Lady Stephen, Lord Stephen, welcome to Swanmere," Julian said, adding with a smile, "And this young man must be Alexander."

"He is indeed. Thank you, Sir Julian," Lord Stephen said. Alexander was looking around with interest; spying Chloe, he stretched out his arms with an urgent babble.

"Do you want Chloe? Come then." She took the baby, who patted her cheek with his soft palm, then began picking at the forget-me-nots that trimmed her new bonnet.

Julian offered Lady Mary his arm. "Pray come this way, my ladies, my lord. My wife and grandparents are waiting to greet you."

To Chloe's surprise, he led them not to the Great Hall, but to the entrance to the new wing, and from there to the drawing-room where Lady Loring, Lord Swanmere, and Rosa had gathered. Chloe had supposed that this change was in deference to the two old people, but then she saw that Rosa cradled...

"A baby?" Chloe cried. "Rosa! You have a baby, and never told me." She hurried towards her sister-in-law, hardly noticing when her mother took Alexander from her, and subsided onto the sofa beside Rosa. "What is it? When was it born? Why didn't you tell me?"

"You might have worried." Rosa kissed Chloe's cheek and placed the swaddled bundle in her arms. "Meet your niece and goddaughter, Katharine Martha Chloe Swann-Loring. We call her Kate. She is one month old; it would have been impossible for you to be here on time."

Chloe peered at the little face. "A little girl. She is beautiful. And so tiny." She looked over at Alexander. "It is hard to remember that he was so small too, isn't it, Mamma?"

"You were as tiny," her mother said with a smile. "Remember," there was an infinitesimal pause before she finished, "Sir Julian?"

"How could I forget it? Chloe was the first baby I ever saw, or heard," he added with a teasing smile for his sister.

"I remember her too," Grandmother said. "But with all this excitement, we have forgotten our manners." She drew herself up and said formally, "I am happy to see you well, Lady Stephen."

"Thank you, Lady Loring, and I, you." Mamma inclined her head to Julian's grandfather. "Good day, Lord Swanmere."

He bowed in return. "Welcome to Swanmere, Lady Stephen."

Reminded of his duties, Julian hastened to make the final introductions.

"Pray do sit down," Rosa said. "Or would you rather go first to your rooms?"

"No, I thank you," Lady Mary said. "We had a longer stop in Peterborough so that this young man," she nodded towards Alexander, "would be comfortable when we arrived."

"He is already very active. How did you manage with him on such a long journey?" Rosa asked.

"We had a cradle fitted in the carriage, so he did not have to be held while he was asleep," Lord Stephen said. "Otherwise, we shared the burden, you might say, although my wife bore the brunt of it, as he is still nursing."

"Not for much longer," Mamma said wryly. "He already has two teeth. But there can be no doubt that it was most convenient for the journey."

"Where do you go from here?" Julian asked.

"To London," Lord Stephen said. "I wish to present my wife and son to Gracechurch and I imagine he is there for the Season. In addition, two of my young cousins, my aunt's granddaughters, have come out this year, so they and their families are in town as well."

"One of my great-nieces has also just come out," Lady Loring said.

"Oh, have you heard from the Glazebrooks, Grandmamma?" Chloe asked. "Is Cynthia enjoying herself?"

"I think she is, now that the presentation is over. She does not want for partners at any rate, her mother says. It will be your turn next year, Miss. No more jaunts to the Continent until you have done your duty."

"I could not have come out this year anyway, with Rosa increasing," Chloe pointed out.

"Hmph. I suppose not."

"Lord Stephen, did you see the recent notice that the Bishop of London has set up a book in his registry where foreign marriages and births of British subjects might be recorded?" Julian enquired.

"No. When was this?"

"Several weeks ago now. I asked my secretary to keep it, as I thought it would be of interest to you."

"That was most kind of you, Sir Julian. I was wondering what I should do," Lord Stephen said to the room at large. "I shall have them added to the family records at Stanton, of course, but I didn't know if there was some formality to be observed, too."

"The surprising thing is that until now, apparently not," Julian said. "It simply wasn't possible to record such events, burials too."

"That is strange. The army and navy would keep their own records, I suppose, but not everyone who dies abroad is a soldier or a sailor."

Lord Stephen seemed both surprised and pleased by Julian's thoughtfulness, Chloe thought. It boded well for their future relationship. Now if only Mamma were less wary. She sat very erect, with her shoulders squared, her eyes flicking from one person to another. Impulsively, Chloe handed Kate back to Rosa and stood. "Mamma, come and sit here with Alexander, see what he makes of Kate. I," she added proudly, "am the only person who is related to both babies. I am Kate's aunt and Alexander's sister. And you both," she added to Lady Loring and Lord Swanmere, as she took a seat near them, "are great-grandparents. Aren't babies wonderful?"

"Yes, although I have been a great-grandmother these many years," Grandmamma said. "Have you forgotten the Undrell children?"

"I had," Chloe admitted.

Kate opened her eyes and emitted a snuffling little squeak, much to Alexander's surprise. He leaned closer to inspect this strange bundle that had suddenly sprouted waving arms and spread fingers. He reached out his own hand. Mamma caught it and touched it softly to Kate's. "Gently, now. She is so much smaller than you."

Kate squeaked and burbled and Alexander babbled in response. Rosa and Mamma smiled at each other and then at their babies.

"One could swear they understand each other," Mamma remarked. "Enjoy her while she is so tiny. It is such a beautiful stage and ends so quickly."

"Yes, even this first month has made such a difference. In the beginning, I was almost afraid to touch her and Julian was terrified, but he soon got the knack of it."

"I don't remember very much of that first day after he was born. Nothing really, until I heard Chloe's voice. Her coming was like a miracle, Stephen said."

"I'm so sorry you had such a bad time."

Chloe and Lord Stephen exchanged satisfied smiles as the two new mothers' voices lowered to a confidential murmur punctuated by their babies' chirrups. After some time, Kate began to sound more fretful. When Rosa excused herself, the party broke up for the moment.

"That was quite strange," Delia said to Stephen in the privacy of their bed-chamber. Alexander was in the adjoining nursery with Maria; their bags had been unpacked, and the servants had left. She had removed her bonnet and pelisse and sat at the dressing-table, looking at her reflection in the looking-glass.

"In what way?"

"As if Lady Stephen is a completely different person to Lady Loring. Apart from Chloe, they all treat me the same way as they treat you."

"It is one way of dealing with what could be an awkward situation, I suppose. Would you prefer it if they threw your failings in your face or made it clear that you were admitted only out of tolerance or magnanimity?"

"No—but I lived with the dowager for twenty years. Julian was my stepson—perhaps, technically, he still is; I was Miss Fancourt's employer...."

"But you have not been any of that for two years. And you have changed considerably."

"In what way?"

"You look ten years younger, for a start. When we met again, you looked drawn, on edge. You seemed to live in apprehension of a blow."

"He never raised his hand to me," she said quickly.

"But he could have, with impunity, and he let you know it. There are blows that harm the body and those that harm the spirit."

"That is true."

"You no longer fear them," Stephen said quietly. "You are happy, you are loved, you are able to explore your talents in a way that was forbidden to you for so long. Lady Stephen is a different person to the Lady Loring they knew." He came and stood behind her, pulling her back against him. The face in the looking-glass softened and smiled up at him. "That is Lady Stephen—or Delia, as she should be."

"Yes." She got up from the stool and turned into his arms. "I love, and my love is valued and returned, oh, a thousand-fold. Without the giving and receiving of love, our lives are hollow."

~~~

In the end, they stayed three nights at Swanmere, to forge new alliances, as Stephen put it. Chloe was the linchpin that held everyone together. Her remark about being so closely related to both babies had resonated with everyone; through her, Alexander and Kate would grow up as friends, almost cousins, and it was therefore essential that the older generations were on good terms. The fact that Julian, Rosa, and Delia had all changed their names since they had last met at Loring Place made it easier to make a new start. By the end of the first day, it was agreed that the Swann-Lorings and the Stephen FitzCharleses would be titular uncles and aunts to each other's children, and the adults were to use one another's Christian names.

"What about you, Chloe?" Stephen had said later, when they sat together with Mamma. "Must you still 'Lord Stephen' me?"

"I could say 'Step-papa', I suppose," she said doubtfully, "but it does not seem very respectful."

They had developed a very comfortable relationship in the six months at the *Villa Della Torre* and while he had never assumed any authority over her, or treated her as less than an adult, there was an affectionate benevolence in his attitude that assured her of his protection.

"Why not just 'Papa', then?" Delia asked. "It would be simpler for Alexander when he is older. You call me Mamma and refer to Stephen as Papa when talking to Alexander as it is."

"I should be most honoured," Stephen said, "but if you prefer not, I shall understand. You can just say, 'Stephen', if you wish."

It was good that everything had been smoothed over, Chloe thought, but she did not want to erase Papa's memory. He may have been more distant as a parent and, in hindsight, she could see that life at Loring Place had not always been easy for her mother, but she did not want to behave as though he had never existed. Julian had later regretted that he had refused Mamma's offer to call her Delia when he was eighteen.

She took a breath. "If I were younger, it might be different but, I'm eighteen now. If you truly do not object, I shall call you Stephen—and refer to you as my stepfather. I am most appreciative of your kindness to me, and to Mamma, and wish to acknowledge that."

"What a splendid girl you are," he said, and offered her his hand. "It's a bargain."

Part Two London

London, May 1816

At the house in South Audley Street that the Qualters and Lyndalls had taken for the Season, Delia and Stephen bade a fond farewell to Lady Mary amid promises to meet again in a day or so. They then continued on to Gracechurch House. Delia was much less nervous at the prospect of staying with a duke and duchess than she had been at confronting her former governess and family-in-law at Swanmere Castle, but when the carriage drew up, she swallowed and smoothed her skirts as best she could. The duke's and duchess's recognition was essential for her acceptance into the best circles, and while she had no particular ambition to move there, she also did not want to be excluded from them, if only for Chloe's sake.

By the time Stephen had a curious Alexander safe in his arm and could extend his free hand to Delia, a taller gentleman had come down the imposing stone steps and stepped between them. "Permit me, Lady Stephen."

Delia took the proffered hand and stepped down from the carriage. He must be the duke, she thought; there was a distinct resemblance to Stephen. They looked more like brothers than uncle and nephew, but Stephen was only ten years the elder, she remembered, as she gathered her skirts prior to climbing the steps to the house. The large hall was floored with squares of black and white marble. Apart from an elaborate, round, marble-topped table, the only ornaments were two magnificent, life-size, classically draped statues that faced one another from scallop-shell-topped alcoves. She longed to inspect them more closely, but a dark-haired lady stood waiting, flanked by a boy and a girl.

"Welcome," she cried. When she stood on tiptoe to kiss Stephen's cheek, Alexander reached out to her and she took him as naturally as if she had known him all his life.

Stephen took Delia's hand. "Duke, Duchess, my forward son has already introduced himself, but I have the honour to present my wife, Delia. Delia, my nephew, the Duke of Gracechurch, the Duchess of Gracechurch, my great-nephew, Lord Jasper FitzCharles, and my great-niece Lady Tabitha FitzCharles."

Delia curtsied deeply. "Your graces, Lord Jasper, Lady Tabitha."

Once the children had made their bow and curtsey, the duchess said, "Come into the parlour. I am sure this young man is keen to get onto the floor after being cooped up in a carriage all day. Is he crawling yet?"

"No, but I think it will be soon," Delia said. "He pushes himself up on all fours and rocks back and forth, but then collapses again."

"And looks puzzled?" the duchess said.

"More pleased with himself. Let me take him until he becomes accustomed to a new room. Then, I'm sure, he will want to be set down."

"We'll play with him," Tabitha said. "We found a ball and rattles, didn't we, Mamma?"

"That was kind of you," Delia said. "How old are you?"

"I'm nine and Jasper is twelve. Stanton is seventeen, but he isn't here; he's at Oxford."

"Oxford?" Stephen said. "Good heavens. It seems like only yesterday that he went to Harrow."

"Yes," the duchess said. "They grow up so fast."

As if agreeing with her, Alexander struggled to be set down on the carpet. Tabitha and Jasper plumped themselves down beside him and he smiled delightedly, reaching out to touch their faces.

"Did you come up after Mayday as usual, Duchess?" Stephen asked.

"No, a week later. We had to be here for the drawing-room the Queen held on the sixteenth to mark Princess Charlotte's wedding. And a dreadful crush it was, too." The duchess looked from him to Delia. "What are your plans?"

"We have none as yet," Stephen said. "I have any amount of business to attend to, including registering our marriage and Alexander's birth with the Bishop of London's new registry. Then we must find somewhere to live. We're looking for a place within a day's drive of Swanmere to make it easier for Delia's daughter, who lives there with her brother, to visit."

"And not too far from Stanton either, I hope," the duke said.

"Why don't you stay here for the remainder of the Season?" the duchess asked. "We can introduce Lady Stephen to the *ton* and, should there be another drawing-room this year, I would be very happy to present her." She added to Delia, "Lady Stephen, even if you have been presented before, you must endure it again following your marriage."

"That is very good of you, Duchess," Delia said, her head spinning at the thought of being launched willy-nilly into society. She would need gowns and a nursemaid; she must start weaning

Alexander, who now sat, a familiar, pensive look on his face. Time to go. She scooped him up.

"If I could perhaps be shown to our room, Duchess," she said apologetically.

"Yes, of course. It is not your usual room, Stephen," the duchess added as she pulled the bell-cord, "but a suite that is better suited to a family. Lady Stephen, just ring if there is anything you need."

~~~

Preparations had already begun for the duchess's annual rout party and all that needed to be done was for them to add any names they wished to the invitation list. The white satin gown Delia had worn to be presented at the French court would do perfectly, minus the train and augmented by a flounced, lace overdress with a little colour added to the bodice and sleeves; alterations the duchess's maid could do in a trice.

A week later, Stephen came into Delia's dressing room just as her maid was setting a turban of white and rose satin, ornamented with an ostrich plume, on her head.

"Very elegant, but it just needs one thing." He handed her a box. "To mark your formal appearance as my wife."

She looked at him in the mirror, then down at the box. "Thank you."

"You must open it," he said patiently.

She flicked the little catch and lifted the lid. "Oh! How beautiful. Thank you, Stephen. Will you put it on for me?"

Neither noticed the maid slip out as he lifted the necklace of garnets and pearls and carefully put it around her neck.

"It sits just right," Delia said.

He took out the pair of earrings and handed them to her. "You must do these yourself; I should be afraid to try."

Smiling, she slipped the hooks through the holes in her earlobes and stood to face him. "They are perfect. Thank you so much." She reached up to kiss him. "That is on account. I must be careful not to crush my gown. Later, I'll thank you properly. What time is it?"

"A quarter to nine."

"We should go down, I suppose. Where are my gloves and fan?" She drew on the long gloves. "Can you tie the strings, or should I call the maid back?"

"Allow me." He tied the little bows and offered her his arm. "Shall we go?"

Fifteen minutes later, they stood with the duke and duchess at the entrance to the great drawing-room in Gracechurch House. The hall door below was open and they could hear carriages draw up; voices echoed in the stair hall, and the first guests emerged onto the landing, a tall, handsome couple who were announced as Mr and Mrs Fitzmaurice.

"Olivia and Luke," the duchess exclaimed. "How good of you to be punctual and not leave us standing here like Patience on a monument."

Mrs Fitzmaurice smiled. "I am so used to being early at your parties, but did not expect to be the very first."

"And all the more welcome. You know Lord Stephen, of course. Lady Stephen, may I introduce our very good friends, Mrs Fitzmaurice and Mr Fitzmaurice."

After a brief exchange of compliments, the Fitzmaurices had to make way for the next couple. Guests were soon arriving steadily and Delia's head buzzed with murmured names, many of which were familiar from the newssheets and society reports. Her face ached from smiling and she was grateful that the precedence accorded her as the wife of the younger son of a duke limited the number of persons to whom she owed a curtsey. With so many new faces, it was a particular pleasure to greet Lady Mary, her daughters, and their families; she hoped there would be time to talk to them later.

The clamour of voices grew louder and louder until she could no longer hear the string quartet playing in the music room at the far end of the long room. Beyond it was the small drawing-room, although small was relative—it was larger than the drawing-room at Loring Place. Tonight, card tables had been set up there, although most of the guests would not linger but simply traverse the rooms and make their way downstairs again via the wide corridor, on the other side of which were supper and dining rooms. Delia had been awe-struck by the idea of having a whole floor purely for entertaining, so that several hundred people could be accommodated without any disruption of the day-to-day routine of the great house.

She stiffened when she saw Lord and Lady Ransford approach with the Glazebrooks. She had not seen Edward's cousin and his wife since the house party two years ago. Did they know the true story about her banishment to Harrogate, she wondered uneasily, then reassured herself that they would not have accepted the duchess's invitation if they proposed to cut the connection. But they were perfectly polite, if not as affable as the Glazebrooks, who were quick to claim their previous acquaintance in Nice and enquired kindly after Chloe.

At last, the flow of guests trickled to a halt and their hosts were freed to circulate in turn through the crowded rooms. Delia's and Stephen's progress was slow due to the number of people who waylaid Stephen, either to congratulate or twit him on his unexpected marriage. He bore it all with good humour, and a certain pride, especially when he had the opportunity to mention Alexander. Their experiences in Nice just at the time of Napoleon's escape attracted much interest, especially when it emerged that they had not joined the other English visitors in their headlong departures.

"The worst was the lack of news," Delia told one group. "The post to England had stopped, of course, and we had to depend on the Paris and Turin newspapers to discover what was happening. As long as Napoleon was in Paris, we were safe, but there would always have been ample time to depart if matters had gone the other way. It takes time to move an army, after all."

"How intrepid," a gentleman said. "Where would you have gone?"

"It would have depended on where Boney was going," Stephen said. "We had a yacht ready to depart, and could have made for Naples, or Malta at short notice. Fortunately, it was not necessary."

He nodded farewell and moved on to Lady Qualter, who had beckoned to them with her fan from the sofa she occupied with her daughter, Anna.

Anna rose immediately, saying to Delia, "Pray sit, Cousin. You have been standing so long."

"Thank you." Delia subsided gratefully. "I have never been at such a large party."

"At least here there is room enough for so many," Lady Qualter said. "Other hostesses with far less space invite the same number and it is much less pleasant."

Anna shuddered. "Such dreadful crushes—you cannot imagine it. You are carried along, pressed between the same couples, until you are finally spat out onto the pavement again. This is thinning out nicely now."

A young man appeared at her elbow and bowed. "Miss Qualter, there is to be dancing in the music room. May I have the honour?"

Lady Qualter smiled benevolently as the young couple walked away. "Now, tell me, what are your plans? Where do you go from here?"

"We don't know, as yet," Delia answered. "Our most pressing need is to find somewhere to live. We hope to purchase a property that is within an easy day's drive of Swanmere and Stanton, but have not yet had the time to investigate properly."

"Would you consider somewhere fully furnished?"

"To rent, you mean? I suppose we could take it for a year. What do you think, Stephen? It would give us more time."

"No, this is for sale," Lady Qualter said. "Qualter's sister was talking about it only the other day. The Old Hall near Wellingborough, a pleasant little town on the river Nen in Northamptonshire. Its previous occupant, an elderly lady who was the last remaining member of her family, directed in her will that it be sold with all furnishings and fittings and the proceeds used for charitable purposes. She could not bear to think of her family home being dissolved after so many generations, but of course most people have their own belongings and do not want to have to deal with other people's impedimenta. Personal items, such as her clothes, have been removed, of course, but otherwise the house is fully equipped and it occurred to me that it might suit you better than one that had to be fitted out before you could move in. This way you can make changes *peu-à-peu*, instead of doing it all at once."

"Provided there was nothing in the deed of sale that prevented us from disposing of anything we did not want," Stephen said.

Lady Qualter frowned. "My sister-in-law did not mention anything like that, but it might be the reason why it is taking so long to sell it."

"It is certainly worth investigating. Can you find out anything more; who is dealing with the estate, for example?"

"My sister-in-law will know," Lady Qualter said.

"Excellent. Thank you."

Part Three Wellingborough, Northamptonshire

Old Hall, May 1816

Delia immediately fell in love with the Old Hall. "It fits into its surroundings like a jewel in a ring. You can feel the care that has been lavished on it."

Inside, it was warm and welcoming; furniture and wood panelling gleamed with decades of polishing and glass and porcelain sparkled. Family portraits and other paintings hung on the walls, gilded ornaments stood on the mantelpieces, and one room held a display of Meissen china that made Delia gasp. "Is that really included in the sale?" she asked Mr Underwood, the executor.

"Yes, my lady. Miss Dixon hoped that whoever bought the house would appreciate her treasures."

"Thank you, Mr Underwood," Stephen said when they had completed their rounds of the house. "We should like to confer in private."

"Certainly, my lord. I shall leave you to your deliberations. I shall be across the hall in the book-room when you need me. Shall I have them bring in some refreshments? A glass of Madeira, perhaps?"

"That would be most welcome."

"Well?" Stephen said to Delia over Madeira and a plate of excellent little drop cakes.

"It's perfect for us, is it not? The bones are good—I mean the way the rooms are laid out and while the furnishings may not be the latest, they are still pleasing to the eye, and comfortable. Indeed, there are some very good pieces, like the cabinet of Meissen."

"I agree, but I think Underwood has factored in too high a value for the contents. He cannot expect to achieve the same return as if he were to sell each separately at auction."

"I suppose not. It is almost six months since Miss Dixon died, so perhaps he will be prepared to compromise."

"It is just the right distance from Swanmere and Stanton, and we could move in at midsummer. I'll be glad to be under our own roof. We've done enough travelling for now."

"The offices are surprisingly modern; there is a new Rumford stove in the kitchen, and everything is spotless, which speaks well of the servants." The testatrix had directed that those of her servants who chose should continue to be paid by her estate for six months following her death so that the property would be kept in good order and in the hope that the new owners of the Hall would be willing to take them on.

"Will we have a use for all of them, do you think?" Stephen asked.

"I'm inclined to keep them all on for a quarter and see how things work out. It will depend on how well-disposed they are to such a change. If we come to terms with Mr Underwood, I'll talk to them before we leave."

Mr Underwood was prepared to listen to reason and an hour later, the housekeeper, cook, three maids, a footman, a groom/coachman, a gardener, and two boys were assembled before Delia.

"I must commend you on your faithfulness to your late mistress's last wishes," she said. "Lord Stephen and I have agreed to acquire this property and we are willing to offer each of you a quarter's trial. But you must be aware that there will be changes. We have an infant son, so the house will not be as quiet as you are used to"—there were smiles at this—"and our own servants will accompany us. We expect them to be made welcome and that together you will form a harmonious household. If any of you prefer not to remain here, please advise Mr Underwood. You will receive an additional quarter's wages in lieu of notice and must leave on the twenty-third of June."

The servants shuffled and exchanged glances. Finally, the housekeeper asked, "Please, my lady, what servants will be coming with you?"

"Our major-domo who will be steward here, my maid, a nurse, and a coachman," Delia said.

"I won't stay if another man comes in over my head," the Old Hall coachman said truculently.

"Very well," Delia answered. "Mr Underwood, will you make the arrangements, please?"

"Certainly, my lady."

"Thank you. Does anyone else want to say something? No? That will be all."

"You gave the coachman short shrift, didn't you?" Stephen said after the servants had filed out.

She shrugged. "If he was not even prepared to try, there was no point in keeping him on. It is foolish of him, for we shall need a groom once we have our own horses, but better to employ someone who is not bearing a grudge. And it stopped the others trying to bargain with me."

"Indeed," Mr Underwood said. "I shall take my leave of you, my lord, my lady."

"Thank you," Stephen said. "My man of business will be in touch with you."

~~~

Midsummer, Old Hall

Delia bent and kissed her sleeping son's brow. "Sleep well, my dearest," she whispered. "Good night, Maria."

"*Buona notte*, Lady Delia."

Delia tiptoed out of the new nursery and crossed the landing to her own room. Alexander had been restless, not wanting to settle, and had had to be soothed with an extra feed tonight. It was no wonder, she supposed, with all the upsets of the day. They had arrived at the Old Hall at midday, but it had taken hours before inventories were checked, rooms arranged, trunks unpacked, and initial attempts made at combining the two sets of servants. Cook had served a cold collation at noon, but had made more of an effort with dinner, including a dish of trout, some lamb cutlets, asparagus, and a light, sweet gooseberry fool.

Stephen was waiting for her. Clad in a light banyan, he stood at the window, looking west to where the last reds and oranges streaked a dark blue sky. He held out his hand. "So here we are, just over two years since we met again. They have been quite adventurous, have they not?"

She sighed and rested her head on his shoulder. "Yes. But we are home now. At last."

Background Notes

This is a work of fiction but set in a real time and place. While it would not be possible to list all the sources consulted, I wish to mention the following:

- Stephen's freeing of the enslaved people on the estate he inherited in the West Indies and his arrangements for them to be brought to Philadelphia as free men and women is based on the action taken by the Quaker David Barclay in 1795. Stephen tells his aunt about this in Chapter Two

- In Chapter Five, Stephen quotes the solicitor, Mr Henderson as saying that *'no woman of delicacy'* would apply to the courts to have her conjugal rights restored. This is the phrase used by Lord Brougham in a debate on the Custody of Infants in the House of Lords on 30 July 1838

- For information about the English in Paris in 1814 and in Nice in 1815, until the escape of Napoleon from Elba, I am indebted to the anonymous author of the *Diary Illustrative of the Times of George the Fourth*, first published in 1838.

- In 1814, the *Opéra Comique* was based in the *Salle Féydeau*. It had merged with the *Théâtre Feydeau* in 1801

- The Apollo Belvedere was among the works of art looted by Napoleon and displayed in the Louvre. It was returned to the Vatican in 1815, after Napoleon's final defeat at Waterloo

- Where available, I have used contemporary spellings e.g., Peregaux for the modern Pérregaux and Paglion for the modern Paillon
- The town of Lynn Regis in Norfolk is today called King's Lynn
- The extracts from the marriage ceremony are from the 1803 edition of the Book of Common Prayer
- On 23 March 1816, the Deputy Registrar of the Bishop of London, who was responsible for foreign chaplaincies, inserted in *The London Gazette, The Times and The Morning Chronicle: **FOREIGN MARRIAGES, &c. &c. Bishop of London's Registry, No. 3", Godliman Street, Doctor's-Commons.** THE Lord Bishop of London having been applied to, in numerous instances, to permit foreign marriages, births, and burials of British subjects to be recorded in his Registry, has permitted a book to be kept therein, in which the memorials of the same may be entered and preserved, at the request of such persons as are desirous thereof. JOHN SHEPHARD, Dep. Reg.*

If you enjoyed reading Lady Loring's Dilemma, you will love the first book in The Lorings saga.

A Suggestion of Scandal

If only he could find a lady who was tall enough to meet his eyes, intelligent enough not to bore him and had that certain something that meant he could imagine spending the rest of his life with her.

As Sir Julian Loring returns to his father's home, he never dreams that 'that lady' could be Rosa Fancourt, his half-sister Chloe's governess. They first met ten years ago but Rosa is no longer a gawky girl fresh from a Bath Academy. Today, she intrigues him. Just as they begin to draw closer, she disappears—in very dubious circumstances. Julian cannot bring himself to believe the worst, but if Rosa is innocent, the real truth is even more shocking and not without repercussions for his own family, especially for Chloe.

Driven by her concern for Chloe, Rosa accepts an invitation to spend some weeks at Castle Swanmere, home of Julian's maternal grandfather. The widowed Meg Overton has also been invited and she is determined not to let such an eligible match as Julian slip through her fingers again.

When a ghost from Rosa's past rises to haunt her, and Meg discredits Rosa publicly, Julian must decide where his loyalties lie.

"A smooth read; providing laughs and gasps in turns. Readers will enjoy the cool-headed Miss Fancourt, while hoping that Sir

Julian puts the pieces of the puzzle together quickly! A host of other loveable and detestable characters keep the entertainment moving through the trials, tribulations, and victories of love."
Historical Novels Review

http://mybook.to/suggestionofscandal

About the Author

Catherine Kullmann was born and educated in Dublin. Following a three-year courtship conducted mostly by letter, she moved to Germany where she lived for twenty-five years before returning to Ireland. She has worked in the Irish and New Zealand public services and in the private sector. Widowed, she has three adult sons and two grandchildren.

Catherine has always been interested in the extended Regency period, a time when the foundations of our modern world were laid. She loves writing and is particularly interested in what happens after the first happy end—how life goes on for the protagonists and sometimes catches up with them. Her books are set against a background of the offstage, Napoleonic wars and consider in particular the situation of women trapped in a patriarchal society.

She is the author of _The Murmur of Masks_, _Perception & Illusion_, _A Suggestion of Scandal_, _The Duke's Regret_, _The Potential for Love_ and _A Comfortable Alliance_

Catherine also blogs about historical facts and trivia related to this era. You can find out more about her books and read her blog (My Scrap Album) at her website You can contact her via her Facebook page or on Twitter